AN ITALIAN ISLAND SUMMER

Sue Moorcroft writes award-winning contemporary fiction of life and love. *A Summer to Remember* won the Goldsboro Books Contemporary Romantic Novel award, *The Little Village Christmas* and *A Christmas Gift* were *Sunday Times* bestsellers and *The Christmas Promise* went to #1 in the Kindle chart. She also writes short stories, serials, articles, columns, courses and writing 'how to'.

An army child, Sue was born in Germany then lived in Cyprus, Malta and the UK and still loves to travel. Her other loves include writing (the best job in the world), reading, watching Formula 1 on TV, hanging out with friends, dancing, yoga, wine and chocolate.

If you're interested in being part of #TeamSueMoorcroft you can find more information at www.suemoorcroft.com by clicking on 'Street Team'. If you prefer to sign up to receive news of Sue and her books, go to www.suemoorcroft.com and click on 'Newsletter'. You can follow @SueMoorcroft on Twitter, @suemoorcroftauthor on Instagram, or Facebook.com/sue.moorcroft.3 and Facebook.com/SueMoorcroftAuthor.

Also by Sue Moorcroft:

The Christmas Promise
Just for the Holidays
The Little Village Christmas
One Summer in Italy
A Christmas Gift
A Summer to Remember
Let It Snow
Summer on a Sunny Island
Christmas Wishes
Under the Italian Sun
A Home in the Sun
Under the Mistletoe
Summer at the French Café
A White Christmas on Winter Street

Sue Moorcroft

An Italian Island Summer

avon.

Published by AVON
A division of HarperCollins*Publishers* Ltd
1 London Bridge Street
London SE1 9GF

www.harpercollins.co.uk

HarperCollins*Publishers*
Macken House, 39/40 Mayor Street Upper,
Dublin 1, D01 C9W8
Ireland

A Paperback Original 2023

2

First published in Great Britain by HarperCollins*Publishers* 2023

A catalogue copy of this book is available from the British Library.

ISBN: 978-0-00-852570-5

This novel is entirely a work of fiction. The names, characters and incidents portrayed in it are the work of the author's imagination. Any resemblance to actual persons, living or dead, events or localities is entirely coincidental.

Typeset in Sabon LT Std by
Palimpsest Book Production Limited, Falkirk, Stirlingshire
Printed and bound in UK using 100% Renewable Electricity
at CPI Group (UK) Ltd

MIX
Paper | Supporting
responsible forestry
FSC™ C007454

This book is produced from independently certified FSC™ paper
to ensure responsible forest management.

For more information visit: www.harpercollins.co.uk/green

Acknowledgements

If ever I run away with the idea that I write my novels alone, preparing the acknowledgements sets me straight. To everyone who helped in the creation of *An Italian Island Summer* – my thanks!

My brother Trevor Moorcroft, who compiled research on, amongst other things, reluctant fathers, drug assault, teaching English abroad and public transport in Sicily. Isabella Tartaruga, who answered so many questions about Italy and Italian people and their language – and then read an early draft of *An Italian Island Summer*. My brother Kevan Moorcroft for also reading an early draft and then advising on the head-hunting of Alfio. Author Adrienne Vaughan for information on the Dublin area; Vivienne Helm on overdose; Michelle Gialanze on hysterectomy and recovery. Especial thanks to cabin crew member Chloe Robinson who was so generous with her advice on airline protocol during a medical emergency; and to Domenica of Ceramiche Artigianali DoLù for answering my numerous questions about artisan ceramics. Any mistakes are mine, not theirs.

Thanks also to Mark West for being my ever-patient

beta reader and all the long authorly chats at the Trading Post, even though he has his own novels to write. Team Sue Moorcroft for their never-ending support, friendship and suggestions for character or place names. Social media friends for the fun and lovely messages. Pia Fenton and Myra Kersner for the writing retreats, Sunday evening WhatsApp calls and always being on the end of an email.

My books wouldn't reach readers if not for wonder-agent Juliet Pickering and the fabulous Blake Friedmann team; and everyone at Avon, HarperCollins, who publish my books with such skill and enthusiasm. Thanks also to my editors of foreign editions. It's a joy to work with you all.

And, most importantly, readers, for reading my books and following me on social media, subscribing to my newsletter or joining my street team; thanks for the lovely reviews and fabulous messages. And extra-special gratitude to those readers and reviewers who met Ursula as the best friend of Zia in an earlier book and asked me to write her story. I had no idea it would be so interesting until I began. I hope you enjoy Ursula's adventures in *An Italian Island Summer*. (If you missed Zia's story and would like to read it, grab a copy of *Under the Italian Sun*.)

For Hollie Clark Matthews
Thank you for making Paul happy

Prologue

Heart thundering, Alfio clawed his way out of a nightmare about a thrashing, furious sea and an angry father, '*Merda, Papà. No!*' still on his lips.

He hauled himself to a sitting position and let his breathing slow. Alfio had been eighteen when Domenico Tringali was lost to a boating accident in the bay across from the beautiful old family hotel in Sicily. Now Alfio was thirty-eight. For some reason, his dream father had been furious with him. The once-loving gaze had flashed, the brow furrowed, the jaw rigid, yet Alfio's real-life memories were of a laughing man who'd loved his family with all his big heart.

In the bed beside him, Hettie slept on, blonde hair tumbling about her peaceful face, her blue eyes closed. Her own apartment wasn't too far away, but at least half the week they shared a bed – an Englishwoman and an Italian man both living in Spain. Trying not to disturb her, Alfio slid from beneath the sheets and stole across the room to draw back the curtain and gaze at night-time urban Barcelona, its lights scattered like beads on black

1

velvet. Barcelona's contemporary apartment blocks weren't much like the Sicilian home he'd just dreamed of: Ortigia, where the squatter, beautifully ornate buildings had stood for centuries. Both cities lay beside the sea, but while Barcelona sprawled over hundreds of square kilometres, Ortigia – the island that formed the old city of Siracusa, connected to the rest of Sicily by two bridges – was a scant kilometre long.

In his nightmare, Papà had been begging Alfio to return. The actual words had evaporated from the dream on waking, but their urgency still raced through Alfio's veins. He wiped sweat from his face.

It wasn't hard to know why Ortigia was on his mind. His mother Agata and sister Nanda were struggling to run the family hotel, Residenza dei Tringali. Agata was recovering from a hysterectomy and had been let down by the first man she'd loved since Domenico's death; Nanda's baby, Marilù, also needed surgery and Nanda's British husband had left before the baby was born. Alfio spoke to them every few days and they insisted they were managing but the last two years had been hard on hoteliers. Additional staff were difficult to afford.

All his doubts and anxieties about his family welled queasily inside him as he acknowledged that he held down a good job in communications, making use of his fluent Italian, English and Spanish, and had financial reserves. Residenza dei Tringali had been in the family for four generations and family members had always pulled together to keep it going, so he'd offered to put money into the business. He'd been refused. But maybe it wasn't about money. Perhaps they needed more tangible help . . . ?

'Alfio?' Hettie interrupted his thoughts, her drowsy voice drifting from the bed. 'Are you OK?'

Alfio turned from the window. The sheet slipped from Hettie's white, naked shoulders. She was beautiful. They'd been together over a year, since a party at the home of one of his colleagues who attended the language school where she taught her native English. Impulsively, he crossed the room to land on the bed beside his free-spirited lover. 'If I went back to Sicily to help my family through their problems, would you come with me? There must be language schools in Siracusa. It is smaller than Barcelona, but still a city.'

Hettie drew back, her eyes enormous. 'Are you dreaming? Or am I?' She rubbed her face, as if still trying to emerge from slumber.

Softly, he laughed, slipping his arms around her warm body. As she was speaking of dreams in such a pleasant context, he didn't mention that his sudden compulsion to go home had arisen from a nightmare. 'It is nice to think that moving to Sicily with me feels like a dream, but we are both awake. You know that Mamma and Nanda are struggling. They need me there for a while.'

Hettie gave an un-dream like recoil. 'I don't know your family. I'm happy in Barcelona. My friends are here. My whole life. My apartment.'

Disappointed, he let her edge from his embrace. 'I often suggested we visit but you always put it off. You will make new friends. We could get an apartment together.'

She gazed at him with no sign of her usual ready smile. 'Like, *moving in* together? I'm not going to give up the life I've created because you find it convenient. We've never discussed moving in. We never really agreed to become exclusive.'

Her final word rattled around his head like a coin falling down a drain. 'We are not exclusive?'

Her gaze slid away from his. 'I didn't say we weren't,' she hedged. 'I'm just illustrating how big a step you're suggesting.'

Slowly, Alfio lay back against his pillow, shock melting his bones. 'But . . . are we committed or are we not committed?'

Hettie's shrug was irritable, and she gathered the sheet up about her breasts like a shield. 'Not *moving in* committed. Not *give up your life, Hettie*, committed.'

His thoughts whirled. He'd acted on impulse, being the emotional Italian Hettie teased him about being, but still . . . 'I apologise. I have been presumptuous,' he said stiffly. 'You are right. I asked you to give up a lot, with no warning.' For a minute, neither of them spoke. Mentally, he reran her comment about exclusivity and halted, as if it was an enormous wall his thoughts couldn't climb over. He summoned the phrase Hettie used about any awkward, loud kind of silence. 'The elephant in the room,' he murmured sadly, 'is that I must go, Hettie.'

She glanced at him, and her gaze softened, but she didn't give her answer even a moment's thought. 'I'm afraid I can't go with you.'

Chapter One

In the 1930s detached house in Swords, near Dublin, where she'd grown up, Ursula lounged comfortably on her parents' enormous grey sofa. The size of the furniture reflected the size of the Quinn family – four children, their partners, and two grandchildren – which frequently gathered in the pleasant, homey house. For much of the past year, Ursula's mother Colleen had been living here alone, but now, here were both parents not only together in the house but sharing a piece of furniture: a vibrant turquoise two-seater sofa with legs that reminded Ursula of giant cocktail sticks.

Her parents' relationship had always been volatile. In Ursula's childhood, love and laughter had outweighed shouts and sulks. But in her teens, the balance had shifted in favour of quarrels and wary distance, then separate rooms until, about ten months ago, Colleen and Stanley had progressed to separate homes. Colleen had tried to get Ursula and her siblings, Finola, Sorcha and Caden, to take sides. Stanley had refused to do any such thing but his withdrawal to a rented house in Malahide had held something of the outcast about it. It had been unpleasant, but Ursula had also felt some measure of relief that the worst had finally happened.

Now, however, she was catching meaningful looks from her mum that solicited answering smiles from her dad. Colleen and Stanley's arms touched. Their smiles matched. 'So, how's everything going?' she asked cautiously. When her parents had said they wished to talk to her alone, she'd anticipated regretful expressions and phrases like 'divorce' and 'selling up'.

'Grand,' rumbled Stanley, his ruddy cheeks becoming ruddier under his middle daughter's scrutiny, even as his eyes twinkled. His dead straight, salt-and-pepper hair and beard haloed his head – hair mainly pepper, and beard mainly salt.

Colleen flushed too. Her faded blonde hair was cut in a new, flattering style. 'It's great you came home for Easter, Ursula. We've told your sisters and brother and now we can tell you before they arrive for dinner tonight.' She paused impressively, her eyes shining, the same blue as Ursula's. 'Dad and I are putting our marriage back on track. We've been having counselling and want to be together to enjoy the grandkids.' Her lips curled in a fond smile as she mentioned the grandchildren that she invariably called 'little Kira' and 'baby Eoin'. 'Little Kira will start school this year and we're to fetch her at home time and keep her each day until Finola and Declan finish work. It'll save enormously on childcare fees. And when Bree's maternity leave ends, we'll help Caden and Bree with baby Eoin too.' When Ursula only stared, bemused, she clarified gently, 'Your dad's moved back in, darlin'.'

Ursula tried to absorb it. Her parents together again? She hadn't bothered even harbouring secret hopes for such

6

a thing. Sure, they'd once loved each other, but Stanley moving out amid Colleen's dark mutterings about 'his roving eye' had felt as final as Ursula's own divorce. 'Wow,' she breathed. 'Really?' Then hearing how tepid she sounded, beamed, and added, 'That's so great! But you took me completely by surprise.' She jumped up to give each of them a hard hug to cover her apprehension that the family would now be destined to see the relationship implode again, with a repeat of the heartache it had brought last summer.

She didn't envy her siblings who lived locally – Finola, Caden and Sorcha. They'd been more impacted by the split than Ursula, whose home was in England. At least, Finola, the eldest, and Sorcha, the youngest, had. Caden, like Stanley, didn't wear his heart on his sleeve.

'Truly?' Colleen queried, tilting her head and gazing keenly at Ursula like a bird listening for the tell-tale sound of a worm turning. 'We wouldn't blame you if you were sceptical. Our falling-out last year was . . . noisy. We know we upset the family.' Her fists tightened in her lap.

Stanley closed a big, comforting hand over his wife's. 'We're sorry it happened. But we've dealt with all the shite, hopefully.'

Shakily, Ursula laughed. Unlike Colleen, Stanley never exploded his emotions over others like the neighbourhood firework display, which you were obliged to witness if you liked pyrotechnics or to endure the racket from beneath the table with your eyes closed. She said, 'My own marriage ended ugly, so I'm not likely to judge.' Unexpectedly, she found she had to wipe tears from beneath her eyes. 'When you said you needed to talk, I thought you were going to ask me for tips, seeing as I've been through divorce.'

Concern flickered over Colleen's face. 'And are you

coping, darlin'? We don't want you getting into a state again.'

Ursula smothered a sigh. 'The only state I'm in is being completely over Stephan and the divorce. You know I am.' But she also knew that her family treated her differently since, in the horror of her lovely marriage turning into something dark and painful, she'd overdosed. It had been an aberration, and not even life-threatening because she'd called the ambulance herself, for feck's sake – didn't that tell everyone that she'd come to her senses? OK, she'd also suffered a few periods of mild depression as a teen, but none of that meant she needed shielding from life's realities now. She hadn't been medicated since she left Ireland for uni.

And yet, here it came. The look in her mother's eyes that Ursula had known her whole life long – the one that went with anxiety for one of her children. 'I'm sure we can't be blamed for worrying,' she began.

To avoid going over old ground, Ursula fell back on redirection – giving her mother something real to stress about. 'Actually, I want to tell you something.'

Two pairs of eyes settled on her, Colleen's searching blue and Stanley's faded hazel. Colleen and Stanley, despite problems between themselves, had always been concerned and supportive parents.

Ursula drew up her knees and looped her arms around them as she settled down to recount the latest bumps in her road. 'My life in Brighton's been changing for the last couple of years, not just because of divorcing Stephan, but also Zia moving to Italy and marrying Piero. She's been my best friend since we were students, and the place isn't the same without her. On top of that, my boss Lou's retiring to Greece with his boyfriend, so the tattoo parlour where I work is closing.' Her gaze fell on her own sleeve of ink, the elegant flowers and leaves lightly interspersed with geometric Celtic symbols of her Irishness. '*And* the tenancy on my flat's not being renewed. I have four weeks left at work and five in the flat.'

Stanley's brow creased with concern. 'Ah, Urs. All at once? That's not good.'

'Not good at all,' Colleen echoed. 'But, darlin', Brighton's a busy place and half the population wears body art. You'll get more work, surely?'

'Do you need money to tide you over?' Stanley put in. He'd worked in the Bank of Ireland until retirement and his mind always flew to financial logistics before any other.

She grinned. 'I'm fine for money, Dad, thanks. I've been earning around fifty K for the past few years—' she knew her parents had trouble believing a tattoo artist could be well paid '—and I haven't touched what I got from the house.' The quirky terrace by the racecourse she'd owned with Stephan, like most Brighton property, had been worth a tidy sum. 'I could get another job and another flat but I'm thinking of changing direction. I'm sick and tired of inking skulls and roses, of hairy men wanting a tattoo on their arse or worse, and idiotic students getting tattoos of each other's names when I know they won't be together by next week.'

Quickly, trying not to give them a chance to break in, she added, 'You remember I did that short course on painting ceramics in Italy? The one Zia's great-aunt Lucia ran? I loved it, and I'd like to study the subject more deeply. I might go on to supply shops in arty areas, or I might see what qualification I'd need to teach at a uni.' She felt mean about mentioning teaching because there was little chance of her doing anything so mainstream, as she knew she'd hate it. Her mother, however, would love the idea, judging from the years she'd spent bemoaning Ursula 'wasting' her fine arts degree on being a tattoo artist. Everyone in the family knew it was better not to provoke strong objections from Colleen, unless you wanted to be still defending your decision two hours later.

And, indeed, Colleen's lines of concern vanished like magic. 'Teaching! That would be a great job.'

Her father, who'd listened with narrowed eyes, didn't let himself be sidetracked by Ursula possibly changing her job title. 'Will you stay in Brighton?'

Ursula shook her head. 'Not in the short term, at least. That's not where I'll find the kind of training I want.' And she no longer wanted to live in the same small city as Stephan, who she barely recognised as the loving man she'd married. Getting away from Brighton felt like escaping from a dark room, but to admit that he was the reason would give him too much power, even if he didn't know she jumped each time she saw a man with fair hair like his.

Colleen sat bolt upright. 'Had you thought of coming home?' Then, perhaps reading apprehension on Ursula's face: 'Not here to this house, I don't mean, but to Ireland?'

Inside, Ursula softened at the hope in her mum's voice that the one bird who'd flown the nest might return. 'Sorry, but I didn't mean that, Mum,' she said gently. 'I'm looking at a course in Italy, where there's a traditional ceramics industry. Real artisan stuff.'

'Oh.' The brightness faded from Colleen's eyes, but she managed a smile. 'Zia and her aunt Lucia could put you in the way of the right opportunity in Italy, then?'

Ursula hesitated. 'It's tempting,' she admitted. 'But Lucia's factory mass-produces kitchenware for tourists to buy and take home with them. If I'm aiming for artisan – posher and artier, if you like – then finding the right teacher's important, and I need to choose her or him myself. But I have great news about Zia. She's pregnant! She called me a couple of days ago full of excitement about nest-building and morning sickness. Piero's over the moon, apparently.'

After giving Colleen time to exclaim mistily over the information that Zia and Piero were to become parents, Ursula went on. 'There's a course focusing on glazing, design and decoration in Salerno, which is on the coast and south of Rome. I'd do some work on my own and then go in for instruction and mentoring. It looks great, and I've sent off an email enquiry while I continue looking around.' Excitement stirred inside Ursula. 'I'd rent somewhere to live. It wouldn't have to be huge; just comfortable.'

Colleen did the head-tilting, penetrating-gaze thing again. 'Maybe you'll meet a new man, Ursula.'

Stomach shrinking, Ursula managed a laugh. 'That's not in the plan.' Singledom was her plan.

After the way things had turned out with Steph, she couldn't trust men.

In the evening came the promised dinner, allowing Ursula to sink deeper into the bosom of her family. She adored these gatherings, her Irish accent thickening as she laughed with her loved ones. Finola – eldest, kindest and bossiest sibling – arrived first. Her brown hair was showing signs of turning to the brindle of their dad's, unlike Ursula's blonde locks. Husband Declan and daughter 'little Kira' followed in Finola's train.

Dec just smiled, happiest when with his wife and

daughter while leaving the spotlight entirely to them, but Kira held up yards of blue satin with a transparent layer over them and shouted, 'I'm a princess! Do you like my dress, Auntie Ursula? It's like Elsa's from *Frozen*.' An overenthusiastic wave of her wand meant she had to make a sudden grab for her tiara.

Ursula clutched her cheeks to pantomime how impressed she was. 'Wow, wish I had a princess dress to help me look that beautiful.'

Next sibling down, Caden, arrived with pretty wife Bree in an SUV that looked designed for driving a rugby team around, rather than a couple with one six-month-old baby.

'Hiya, Ursula,' Caden murmured, dropping a kiss on Ursula's temple en route to the coffee pod machine and then clapping his dad on the shoulder with a remark about Rory McIlroy's progress in a golf tournament.

'How are ya?' demanded Bree, shoving baby Eoin into Auntie Ursula's arms, looking as if she needed a glass of wine more than an answer.

Sorcha, the only sibling below Ursula in the family tree, arrived in a brand-new Toyota. With a pat of her intricate plaits, she announced smugly, 'I'm making a bomb on Instagram and YouTube with my channels on hair, even if Mum doesn't think it's a proper job.' She hugged Ursula, and then studied her hair. 'I like the asymmetric bob. Suits you.' Ursula had been gently alternative since she'd been old enough to choose her own style. She eschewed blue plumes these days, though.

Before long, the meal was being carried to the huge refectory table in the kitchen extension that ran the width of the house, with doors that opened onto the garden. Everybody found seats, exchanging news sprinkled with

12

friendly insults, delighted and exasperated by each other as only family could be.

No present onlooker would have had an inkling of the moment last year when Colleen had screamed at Stanley to piss off and Stanley had answered, 'Right, I will.'

No one said, *Can you believe Mum and Dad getting together again? If it works out, it'll be easier on the rest of us.*

Voices were only raised to be heard over gales of laughter, or to cry, 'Stop hogging the chips, Cade,' and, 'Sorcha, how can you go vegan when Mum cooks chicken like this?' Caden explained why he was changing his golf instructor while Declan communicated to Kira that even princesses must have their hair tied back at mealtimes.

Ursula enjoyed the hubbub, one eye on her parents, who were seated together in the middle of one long side of the table. Colleen appeared unusually relaxed, only giving Stanley a good-natured shove when he teasingly declared that Kira got her princess tendencies from her grandma.

That set Kira off. 'So, Grandma knows that princesses wear their hair any way they want because they're *princesses*. Princesses can do *anything*.'

Princess Kira was looking flushed and mutinous, and perhaps to take the heat off her beloved granddaughter, Colleen said, 'Ursula, you haven't told everyone your news.'

The family turned its collective attention on Ursula. She said, 'The tattoo parlour's closing and I'm thinking about going to Italy to learn more about being a ceramics artist – a *ceramista*. I'll have to improve my Italian, though. At the moment, I can ask for beer, water or granita. That won't get me far.'

13

'She says she'll be all right for money,' said Stanley, in such a way that it sounded as if he had his doubts.

Sorcha looked thoughtful. 'You could start your own social media channels, get loads of followers and sell advertising. I'd support you, sis. I'm quite the influencer.'

Ursula shook her head. 'You know I'm off social media because it's too intrusive.' It hadn't taken her long to realise that Stephan was using her channels to keep tabs on her through mutual friends after she cut direct connections between them.

Her dad, who was impressed by Sorcha's ability to conjure money out of online advertising, said, 'Don't be too quick to discount things, Ursula. You don't want to go spending your capital. What you got out of your Brighton house will be devaluing already, just sitting in the bank.'

'I know you wanted me to buy another place straight away, Dad, but that would mean me grabbing the first job that comes along to pay the mortgage. Going freestyle for a while will leave me flexible and able to take time deciding what to do next.' Ursula patted her dad's weathered hand. 'The Irish can work in EU countries so I'm sure to pick up bar work or something to keep me going while I study. Or I could look into whether I'd need a licence to do freelance work in a tattoo parlour, if I had to,' she added, not particularly relishing the idea. It hadn't been until Lou had given her the news about the tattoo parlour closing that she'd realised how ready she was to leave that life.

'True enough,' Stanley rumbled.

After the meal was over, Colleen and Stanley cleared up – Colleen being notoriously exasperated by having things put away in the wrong places or the dishwasher

14

stacked 'badly', i.e. any way that wasn't her way. Sorcha got busy on her phone with some mysterious influencer task, while Caden and Bree said goodnight and carried baby Eoin off to settle to his last feed at home.

Declan and Princess Kira went out into the dusky garden to the swing at the far end, which stood beside the sandpit and the goalpost, all of which Colleen had bought and Stanley installed so the grandchildren didn't have to be bored on visits.

Ursula felt a tug on her arm and turned to find Finola beside her. At a significant look from her sister, she allowed herself to be guided outside to a spot by the mock orange bush. There, their conversation was covered by the creaking of the swing, Kira's excited chatter about playing outside when it was nearly night-time and Dec's absent-minded responses as he loomed behind, pushing her with one hand and checking his phone with the other.

Finola smiled and waved at Princess Kira, at the same time quietly asking Ursula, 'How do you feel about Mum and Dad getting back together?'

Ursula puffed out her cheeks. 'Taken by surprise. Mum says they've had counselling. Can you imagine Mum seeking help?'

Finola pursed her lips. 'It's taken a bit of getting used to. It would be great if they stuck together, though. Christmas was odd.'

Compunction speared through Ursula. Guiltily, she said, 'Sorry I didn't come over, but Zia and Piero had asked to stay with me, and I didn't have much time off – you wouldn't believe the number of young adults who spend their Christmas money on a new tattoo, sighing endlessly over the design and complaining that I'm hurting them when I start with the ink. It would have been hard to come to Swords, anyway, because I'd have to have chosen to stay with either Mum or with Dad and it would have felt like picking a side.'

'You could have stayed with me.' Finola shifted restlessly, the light from the house shining on one side of her face. After a moment's reflection she added honestly, 'No. Mum would have gone apeshit if you had. Unfortunately, she's always been possessive, even when we were kids and got too close to an aunt or spoke too enthusiastically about a friend's mum. Now she's a possessive gran. If she thinks Dec's parents are seeing more of Kira than she is, she gets in a huff and says, "What in the world have I done wrong, then?"'

Wrapping her arms around herself against the dropping temperature, Ursula snorted a laugh. 'I've been sent on many a guilt trip with those very words, but it always felt disloyal to admit it.' She'd dropped her voice, though she knew no one inside the brightly lit home could hear.

Finola sighed. 'It was that kind of thing that caused the trouble with Dad, of course. We all let her tantrums ride because we didn't know how to deal with them. We should have challenged her more often.'

'But she's so great when she's not being tricky.' Ursula felt she had to point that out, to balance out the criticism of the very mother who bustled around only on the other side of a wall, having made all her family welcome and cooked a gorgeous meal. 'All that stuff Mum said about Dad having a roving eye ... was he ever actually unfaithful, do you think? He's always acted as if it was just in Mum's head.' Finola wasn't just a couple of years older than Ursula, she'd also stayed here in Ireland, in Swords, and had much more opportunity to learn how things stood between her parents.

16

Finola quirked one eyebrow in response.

Shock shivered through Ursula. 'He *was?*'

'I don't *know*.' Finola looked torn. 'But Dad's been in no tearing hurry to go back to Mum, you know. I think he might have made the counselling a condition of him even thinking about giving the marriage another go. Like you, I'm amazed Mum agreed to it. Other folks' opinions aren't always popular with her.' Finola broke off to call across to her giggling daughter. 'Just five more minutes, Kira, then we need to get you home to bed.'

'But there's no nursery, tomorrow,' Kira protested, thrusting her feet energetically to encourage the swing to soar higher, craning back at her father as if hoping he'd enter the discussion on her side.

'If there were, you wouldn't be up even this late,' Finola answered, with motherly resolution. Then she lowered her voice again as she turned back to Ursula. 'I think Dad met someone else, while he and Mum were separated. Maybe he even holidayed with her, because he seemed to vanish a couple of times.'

Ursula tried to picture her dad with a woman who wasn't her mother. 'What would you think, if it was true?'

Finola shrugged. 'I couldn't hold it against him. He thought his marriage was over. And I don't know any of this for a fact,' she hastened to clarify. 'It's just how things add up to me.'

Ursula breathed the moist, chill evening air and thought how complicated families could be in comparison with life in her small flat in a Brighton terrace, with the sound of gulls and the sea for company and only herself to worry about. 'I couldn't hold it against him either,' she admitted fairly. 'Especially if he's now given up the other woman for Mum.'

17

'He's done it for us all, I think, or at least for family harmony,' Finola remarked sombrely.

Ursula was impressed by the quiet certainty of Finola's insight. 'If they're trying that hard to make another go of it for us all, they get full support from me.'

In the light from the kitchen window, Finola peeped at Ursula. 'You're coping with it all OK, right? It is shitty when your parents break up.'

'Of course.' Ursula let a snap creep into her voice. 'Don't you go all overprotective on me like Mum does. Jeez, Fin.'

'Sorry.' Finola folded her into a big hug. 'You just scared us that time—'

'That *one* time, when I felt desperate. *Desperate*, Fin! Real, terrified, gut-wrenching desperation. I promised you all I'd never take pills again, and I meant it, so please stop with this crap.' Annoyingly, Ursula heard her voice quaver.

Finola must have heard it too, because she assumed a bracing tone. 'Of course. I'm being stupid.'

'Yes, you are,' Ursula said with sisterly candour. Though they both laughed, Ursula still felt she had to explain herself, even if it was for about the twentieth time. 'You must remember that I'd believed our marriage to be as strong as titanium. I adored our little house, furnished and decorated with so much love. I thought I'd always have all that and was rocked by Stephan turning against me.'

Tentatively, Finola observed, 'Stephan's reaction to pain or grief was always anger.'

Ursula sighed. 'Yes,' she admitted. 'Being held up by a traffic accident set off a rant against the police, and news of a strike made him irritable with the government. That was how he processed things. But *my* Steph was lovely, loving, funny and caring. His anger was never directed at me.'

'Until it was,' Finola said simply.

'Until then,' Ursula agreed reluctantly. 'And of course mental illness shouldn't be glossed over or ignored, but I hate the feeling that the family still thinks I need cosseting and protecting.'

Finola threw her arms around Ursula. 'We don't mean to be overprotective. We just love you.'

Ursula hugged her back. 'I love you all, too. But I renounced the name of Shuttleworth and returned to being a Quinn. I'm over it. You're over it. We're all over it. The family doesn't need to treat me with kid gloves.'

Chapter Two

When visiting her parents, Ursula always occupied the sunny room she'd once shared with Finola, overlooking the street. It had been redecorated since the days of My Chemical Romance posters and a mini stereo bracketed with towers of CDs, but it remained the space where Ursula had stared at a ceiling full of glow-in-the-dark stars while her parents argued, apparently considering their furious whispers inaudible.

She'd been glad to move out to the UK and student houses shared with Zia and others.

This morning, thrusting those memories aside, she dressed and wandered downstairs, finding her mother at the kitchen table. 'Morning.' She dropped a kiss on Colleen's cheek on her way to the dark coffee gleaming appetisingly in the filter jug. 'Where's Dad?'

Colleen smiled over the remains of her breakfast. 'He's gone out for a bit. I wanted you to myself.'

Ursula glanced at her mum, whose hair had faded to a pretty ash blonde that went well with her new crop. 'Oh? For a shopping trip or something?'

'If you want,' Colleen began. Then she sighed and back-tracked. 'Actually . . . I was thinking more of a talk. I've been plucking up the courage to have conversations with all of you children, and as you're just here for the week I thought I'd start with you.' She gave a shaky laugh. 'You're the guinea pig.'

Worried by the tremor in her mother's voice, Ursula abandoned her quest for coffee and sank into a chair, trying to read Colleen's blue-eyed gaze. 'You're not sick, you or Dad?'

Colleen reached out to grasp Ursula's hand. 'Nothing like that, darlin'. We're talking emotional, not physical.'

'Oh.' To give herself a second to recover from the anxious moment, Ursula rose and got coffee for them both. 'Fire away, then,' She placed the cups on the table as she sat back down.

Despite the encouragement, Colleen stared into her coffee, apparently having to pay close attention to the stirring in of a spoon of sugar. Finally, her eyes still on her task, she asked, 'What do you think about me and Dad?'

Ursula frowned. 'You being back together? If you're happy, I'm thrilled.'

Her mother's smile flickered into life. 'Good, good.' She sipped the coffee, but still wore a pensive, cautious expression.

Ursula waited a beat. '*Are* you happy?' Her stomach shifted. Maybe they'd decided it wasn't working after all and her mum had been appointed to explain. She was surprised how much her heart sank at that idea.

But Colleen flushed, looking as near coy as Ursula had ever seen her. 'I believe we're getting there.' She hesitated, fiddling with her hair, before saying in a rush, 'What I

21

really want to tell you is that I didn't realise before how much I was to blame for the trouble between me and Dad. The counsellor, she made me examine my behaviour. It seems I have a need for reassurance and if I don't get it, I try and provoke it.'

'Oh?' Ursula said, carefully not saying, *Tell me something I don't know.* The counsellor was nothing short of brilliant if she'd got her mum to see her behaviour for what it was.

Colleen's brow puckered. 'Whenever I claimed Dad was playing away or watching other women, I was really trying to force him to deny it. Maybe even say something nice, like, "Colleen, you're the only one for me."'

'He did say that sometimes,' Ursula felt she had to remind her.

'I know.' Fresh lines seemed to bracket Colleen's eyes. 'But it was never enough. I'd refuse to believe him in a quest for yet more reassurance. He'd feel wounded and disappointed. There would be a row.' Colleen scrubbed at her forehead as if trying to rub away uncomfortable memories. 'It's so obvious once it's pointed out to you.' She swallowed, her throat working. 'The counsellor has also encouraged me to discuss with my nearest and dearest how my behaviour might have impacted on them.' Her voice cracked. 'Did I drive you away, love? You left home so young.'

Ursula's habit of non-confrontation with her mother kicked in. 'Loads of people leave to go to uni at eighteen, Mum. I liked Brighton and stayed, that's all. Then I met Steph and that was that.'

Rather than accepting this diplomatic reply at face value, her mother looked unconvinced. 'The counsellor said I should encourage you to be transparent and reassure you that I'm now able to have a difficult conversation without losing my rag or flinging accusations – my particular defence mechanism, it seems.' Her eyes turned down at the corners as if she was ready to flinch at Ursula's reaction.

Ursula sipped her coffee while she pondered her reply. At last, she said, 'As you've asked me to be honest . . . well, then, I hated the rows between you and Dad. The wonderful times outweighed the tricky ones,' she added hastily, at Colleen's suddenly woebegone expression. 'But the rows made me feel sad. Trouble is that you're so lovely most of the time that it's a double whammy when you explode.' She waited, half-suspecting that such an explosion was about to occur now.

Colleen took several gulps of coffee. At last, in a low voice she said, 'I acknowledge that behaviour. My counsellor thinks it stems from my childhood. My parents both died, as you know, and Auntie Bridie got stuck with me till I was sixteen, and then she expected me to leave. So now I have *abandonment issues* and *attachment issues*.' Her tone suggested the phrases tasted sour on her tongue.

Ursula's eyes burned. She dumped her coffee mug on the table so she could grasp her mother's hands. 'I didn't know it was as bad as that. I never met Auntie Bridie, and you never said she'd been . . . well, cold.'

A tear glistened at one corner of Colleen's eye. 'Who wants to admit they weren't wanted? When Finola was born, I did write to Auntie Bridie, asking if she wanted to see the baby. Eventually, she sent a postcard. I still remember her exact words: "I wish you well, but I've never been a social person."'

Ursula winced.

Colleen smiled mistily. 'So, I invested all my love in Dad

and you kids, and I suppose I felt entitled to a good return on that investment.' It was her turn to rise and refill the coffee cups. With her back to Ursula, she added, 'I was so scared Dad would meet someone easier to love. It made me clingy.'

Remembering Finola's words in the garden yesterday evening, Ursula felt she had to ask, 'Did he ever? Meet someone, I mean.'

Colleen returned to the table, the coffee mugs trembling in her hands. 'Not that I know of,' she admitted quietly. 'But he always had . . . women friends.' Her lips thinned in the displeased expression Ursula had seen a thousand times, often as a precursor to her – what was the expression her mum had used? – 'provoking reassurance'. Ursula had been put in the position of providing that reassurance so often that this time she let a silence elapse, her gaze settling absently on a new window blind with a posy of silk roses on the ledge beneath, both the same cheery yellow.

Colleen had made all the correct noises about inviting transparency – but how much did she mean it? Perhaps Ursula should put it to the test. Gently, she prodded. 'The phrase "woman friend" completely changes its meaning according to context, doesn't it? It can be a woman who's just a friend . . . or a woman who's more than a friend. Remember when you and your buddies Frank and Ella took up Latin dancing? You and Frank got fed up, so Dad and Ella carried on going to the classes. But after a week or two you got very upset and accused Dad of fancying Ella. Which kind of "woman friend" do you feel she was?'

Discomfort flashed across Colleen's face. She gave a pained smile. 'Ah. I suppose she was a woman who was just a friend.'

24

'Suppose? Or know?' Ursula pressed gently.

Colleen passed a hand across her face. 'I know,' she admitted wearily.

She looked so forlorn that Ursula softened. 'I understand possessiveness comes from insecurity, Mum. If you genuinely want transparency from someone who's been on the other end of unfounded accusations, I suggest that you believe in Dad. Consider him innocent until you have proof that he's guilty. Otherwise, you might as well save yourself the bother trying at this second chance on your marriage because your endless hints and digs will kill it.' Then, brought up short by the suffering on Colleen's face, she ended more gently, 'I didn't mean to be rough on you, but we all love you. Can you not just relax and accept that?'

Fresh tears sprang to Colleen's eyes, falling onto cheeks softened by middle age. 'I will try,' she whispered. Blundering to her feet, she got up to rip several sheets off the kitchen roll and blow her nose.

Finally, she turned back, composed and wearing a smile that looked as artificial as the silk roses on the windowsill. 'Now. Will we go on that shopping trip?'

Ursula smiled back and accepted the complete change of subject with a murmured, 'That sounds great.'

They spent the rest of the day in Dublin in the giant greenhouse that was Stephen's Green Shopping Centre as it was 'a nice soft day', i.e. drizzling and misty. After buying a few additions to their wardrobes, mother and daughter drove home to Swords in apparently perfect amity, neither of them referring to their earlier heart-to-heart.

Ursula ate dinner with her parents and then, gazing restlessly at the rays of evening sun piercing the clouds like enormous spotlights, proposed a fresh outing. 'It's dried up outside. How about we stroll round to see Uncle Gerry and Auntie Josie?'

Stanley laid down his newspaper, smiling, as he always did, at the idea of meeting up with his scamp of a brother. 'Sounds great.'

Colleen cast a covetous glance at the TV, the purveyor of the quiz shows she loved. 'My feet are still aching from traipsing around all those shops.' Then, to Stanley: 'I'd thought we'd spend the evening together, love. Ursula can go. Uncle Gerry and Auntie Josie will love to see her.' Colleen had never made a secret of the fact she thought Stanley's youngest brother a mischievous influence, much too keen on male-bonding drinking sessions for her taste.

'I'm sure they'd be happy to see us all,' Ursula pointed out, wishing that her parents weren't already falling into the old pattern of Colleen generally getting her own way. A few minutes later, though, she stepped into the dusk alone, pulling up her collar and zipping her jacket. She strode down the street towards the park where she and her siblings had played as children, nodding to neighbours, some who'd lived in the Seatown Road area for all of Ursula's thirty-two years. A briny tang in the air reminded her that the Broad Meadow River estuary was only a mile away, but she turned in the opposite direction to cover the few streets towards Gerry and Josie's house – freshly painted deep blue instead of its former white, she discovered upon arrival. Several neighbours had joined in the revolution by going for pink, yellow or grey, making a pleasing, chocolate-box splash of colour.

Josie, she soon discovered, was at church helping with the flowers for Easter, but Gerry greeted her as if he hadn't seen her for years, rather than in February, when she'd been home for a long weekend. His beard was bushier than Stanley's and split wide open as he boomed, 'Ursula! How are ya? Come here for a hug, darlin'.'

Warmed by her welcome and the volume of his very Irish, 'How ayya?' she allowed herself to be enveloped into the hug. Soon, she'd shrugged out of her jacket and was seated on his sofa, sucking the froth from a can of Guinness and listening to news of her cousins in Dublin and Kerry as well as Gerry's garden and his and Josie's holiday plans.

'You've painted your house a very cheery blue,' she observed, not mentioning the wobbliness of the lines she'd noted around the front door.

Gerry gave a great guffaw. 'Your Auntie Josie wanted it boring white again, but I bought the paint and started it while she was away at a spa weekend. You should have seen her face when she got back.' He beamed at the memory. 'Anyway, what's new with you?'

Once again, Ursula recounted her thinking-of-going-to-Italy plans, taking out her phone to show him the website of the teacher in Salerno.

Gerry scrolled through the pages, exhibiting great interest and asking questions. As he returned her phone he said, 'Would Sicily do for you, to study your ceramics, instead of Italy mainland?'

Ursula stowed her phone in her pocket. 'Being on the mainland would make it simpler to visit my friend Zia, and I haven't investigated teaching studios in Sicily. Though I'm sure it's a wonderful place,' she added politely.

Gerry, however, proved to have all the enthusiasm she lacked. 'But if I could give you a good reason to choose Sicily? Sort of fit you up with a situation?'

Ursula gazed at him, bemused. 'What kind of situation?'

Gerry leaned forward confidingly, his chair creaking.

'Our church and one in Sicily used to do youth exchanges. There's a woman, Agata Greco, who's kept in touch with someone at our church ever since. She owns a B&B in Sicily.' He screwed up his eyes in thought. 'Well, small hotel, it looks to me, but they don't do lunch and dinner. It's a grand old place, facing the sea in a place called Ortigia, joined to the rest of Siracusa with bridges.' He grinned. 'Kind of an island off the island, you might say.'

'Sounds lovely,' Ursula replied cautiously.

Gerry pulled the ring on another Guinness, though Ursula had barely begun hers. 'This Agata has had to have surgery. The person from our church, they were going to go over and help her this summer on a working holiday. They've had to back out for personal reasons, and Agata needs an extra pair of hands for the season. She can't lift, y'see, and needs rest.' Confidingly, Gerry went on, 'Her adult daughter's gone back to live with her, but she has a baby and the dad's buggered off and left. The baby's none too well either. Apparently, the hotel's suffered in the economic downturn, and Agata could have used the help.'

'That's a shame,' Ursula murmured, eyeing him suspiciously. 'You're not usually interested in people's family dramas.' Gerry was more about poker games and watching sport down the pub.

His guileless hazel eyes smiled. 'Well, Josie's involved with our church's helping-hands scheme.' He leaned over and gave Ursula's arm an excited little shake. 'The point is, you could take the place of this person who's had to back out. I believe you get room and board in exchange for working mornings, doing the guests' breakfasts and the like. You could find a ceramics course in Siracusa, because Sicily's a fine place for ceramics. I went once. They're in every shop – all yellow, blue and green.'

28

'Yellow for lemons, blue for the sea and green for the land,' Ursula added absently. 'I don't know, Uncle Gerry. Having an easy part-time job with accommodation drop in my lap is attractive, but what if I don't like this Agata or she doesn't like me?'

'But it could be perfect,' Gerry insisted. 'You'd be helping someone as well doing yourself a big favour and living for next to nothing. Tell you what.' He spread his hands like a magician reassuring an audience that he had nothing up his sleeves. 'Why don't I get a video chat set up with you and this Agata Greco while you research teaching studios in Siracusa? If you can't find a teacher or don't fancy it after that, then fair enough.'

'Well . . .' Ursula searched Gerry's face, trying to see pitfalls in his scheme. It would be great to benefit from the local church's helping-hands scheme, but Gerry was frequently full of enthusiasm for things that subsequently went wrong. Her mother would probably sniff and declare it one of Gerry's mad ideas, too good to be true. 'Surely she can get help from her own community?' she suggested.

Gerry shrugged. 'Not so far.' Then he let the conversation move on to his and Josie's retirement plans a year hence, opening a third can of Guinness as he waxed lyrical about the holidays they were going to take: '. . . so Josie doesn't have the opportunity to find too many DIY jobs for me about the house.'

When she finally rose to leave, Gerry got up to give her a hug. 'That gig in Sicily will be perfect for you, you know. Don't miss the chance. Auntie Josie would be pleased to set the video call up if there's any chance of helping this poor woman and at the same time help yourself.'

This time, Ursula didn't dismiss the idea out of hand. 'It does sound worth thinking about,' she acknowledged.

'Ask Auntie Josie to arrange the video call, then. Thank you.'

Soon, she was marching back through the dark evening beneath haloed streetlamps, crossing the main road and turning left on the route that would take her home, remembering her dad on these broad pavements, surrounded by the Quinn children on bikes or roller skates or scooters. She heard long-ago laughter and Stanley's good-humoured voice, while she waited for a string of cars to pass, headlights blazing, before she skirted the park and, finally, entered Seatown Road again.

She found her parents before the TV exactly as she'd left them, but for empty cocoa cups at their elbows. Her father looked up. 'How was that brother of mine?'

Ursula discarded her jacket and flopped onto the sofa, intending to keep her parents company for an hour or so. She quite liked quiz shows, too. 'Much as usual.' Conscious of her mother's rapt attention on a man who was on the brink of winning a car, she waited until the next ad break before enlarging on her evening. 'Uncle Gerry says he might know of an opportunity in Sicily, through your church.' She sketched in the details he'd given her. 'Gerry thinks I should talk to the woman – Agata. It's worth considering if I got room and board and was free in the afternoons to learn to paint ceramics.'

'Pish,' said Colleen comfortably. 'You know what they say – if something sounds too good to be true, it probably is, especially if Gerry Quinn's involved. You'd end up slaving in a kitchen for twenty hours a day.' Then she lost interest as the ad break ended.

It was Stanley who asked, 'Are you really interested in this Sicily scheme?' He sounded almost shocked.

Ursula shrugged. 'I'd only thought of the mainland, but

it could be good. I need to research Siracusa. If there's no good teaching studio, then there's no point me taking the idea any further.'

Colleen took her eyes off the screen for a second. 'If Josie's involved, I'd have more confidence in avoiding disaster than if it's just Gerry.'

Ursula laughed. 'Uncle Gerry's a bit mad; that's for sure.'

She found she couldn't be bothered to work out the convoluted rounds of the quiz show, so took out her phone to search the internet for *Siracusa ceramics teaching studio*, and was instantly bombarded by starry reviews of somewhere called Fabio Ceramiche. Itching to see more than the cramped screen allowed, she went to get herself a drink of water, intending to go upstairs and fire up her laptop. Turning away from the tap, she saw that her father had followed her into the enormous kitchen.

He came over to her with one of his ready hugs. 'Don't let Gerry talk you into anything you don't want to do.' He spoke softly, though the TV show blared loudly from the next room.

'I've stopped letting men persuade me against my instincts, since Stephan,' she joked. Half-joked. 'But I think it's an opportunity worth checking out.'

'Maybe.' But Stanley didn't turn away to return to the quiz. Instead, he took her hand and patted it. 'Darlin', I'm trying to give my marriage my very best shot – you know that don't you? It would be grand if we could be together for the grandkids and the whole family.'

'I know, Dad.' Ursula put down her glass on the big refectory table so she could take his other hand to demonstrate her sympathy. Delicately, she said, 'I'm sensitive to possessive behaviour. It can be hard, when you're on the receiving end of it – can't it?'

He fidgeted. 'We're focusing on the positives, and the counselling has helped.'

Ursula glanced at their reflections in the kitchen window. No one had pulled the yellow blind and she could see his dear, patient, genial expression as if in a mirror, alongside her own uncertain one. 'She's talked to me about stuff the counsellor said.'

He grimaced. 'She's told me I must tell her when she's being unreasonable.'

In the reflection, Ursula watched her eyes widen. 'How's that working for you?' She switched her gaze to his face to try to read it.

'It's easier if I can avoid it,' he admitted carefully.

Ursula thought of all the years Stanley had gone to work every day at whatever office of the bank his role took him to, returning each night with time for each and every member of the family. He'd taken a greater share of being 'Dad's Taxi' than other parents, declaring good-naturedly that at least that way he knew his kids were safe. It made sense that he was also doing more than his share of making marital compromises now. 'Hmm,' she said.

He peeped into her face, his eyes twinkling. 'Hmm?' he repeated.

She cocked an ear to make sure the quiz was still in rollicking progress, then picked her words. 'Some people might call that "enabling".'

He snorted. 'Or being smart. Managing the situation for the greater good. Being receptive to her needs. Meeting her halfway.'

'Right.' It was as if her parents had swallowed a dictionary of relationship-mending phrases.

Perhaps sensing her cynicism, he reminded her, 'I was line manager to a lot of people, before I retired. I learned a long time ago that different people have different needs and should be managed in different ways. Some people respond better to a straightforward request, but others . . . well, you just have to work with them.'

She thought back over his relationships with her, Finola, Caden and Sorcha, gently teaching them, talking over knotty problems without ever forcing his solutions on them and could see how he might indeed have been flexing around everybody's differing personalities. 'Are you OK, Dad?' she asked gently.

'If we can carry on getting along OK, I'll be fine.' Stanley squeezed her fingers. 'I want things to work between your mother and me, and I want you to understand that.'

Being 'fine' wasn't exactly shooting for the stars, but Ursula returned the pressure of his fingers. 'I know, Dad. I remember how it feels to want a marriage to work.'

Chapter Three

It was nearly the end of May when Alfio finally made it home to Ortigia, having worked his notice as international comms office manager despite his boss Inigo being clearly dismayed to see him go. His furniture had been sold, as Residenza dei Tringali groaned with the stuff; his car had gone, too; and he'd given up his apartment. Alfio and Hettie had untangled their possessions, her quiet and subdued, him shocked and disappointed; her accusing him of changing the boundaries, him feeling he'd only tried to move their relationship up a level.

Had he been foolish to rush home over a bad dream? But his mother and niece were unwell. His mother and sister had come out of relationships badly. He should help. He and Hettie had been together long enough that it was natural he'd invited her to come too.

But here he was, arriving alone – and without notice, because he knew that if his mother had received advance warning that he meant to give up his life in Spain to help her, she'd have given him hell. He'd asked the taxi driver to drop him off in Via Duca degli Abruzzi so that he could wheel his suitcases across the courtyard behind Residenza dei Tringali and through the double doors that were so practical for deliveries. In the kitchen, he halted to gaze about the enormous, high-ceilinged room that, along with a short hall, formed a bridge between the family apartment and the public part of the hotel. A large central island functioned both as workstation and table. Sinks, fridges, cupboards and work surfaces lined the clean white walls. Stainless steel was everywhere, like any professional kitchen, and it was the only place in the building where the original tiles had been covered over. Small, deep windows were set either side of the double doors.

It was nearly midday. Breakfast for guests would be over and for now the kitchen was quiet and clean. He caught the sound of voices from the other side of the hall that led to the lobby and envisioned general assistant Nino helping a guest with the automated check-in machine that Nanda had had installed a few years ago, or carrying luggage up the central staircase.

Fully serviced hotels employed an army of staff in order to offer lunch, dinner, room service, minibars, porters and a twenty-four-hour reception, but the semi-automated business model at Residenza dei Tringali meant that the family and a modest staff could run the entire three storeys. Reception was only open from seven a.m. to seven p.m. and the sole meal offered was a cold but generous breakfast.

What would Hettie have made of the family concern? Would she ever have lent a hand?

Probably not.

Not only was Hettie good at ordering her life to contain more leisure than work, but she spoke no Italian. Even in Spanish she knew only simple phrases and swear words, proud that she could get by with the minimum. She was so sure that the only language anyone really needed was English that she went out with missionary zeal to teach it to others, choosing hot countries her skin was unsuited to and then turning pink and freckled. He refused to acknowledge now how attracted he'd been to that pale, satin skin.

In a few moments he'd look for Mamma, his sister Nanda and baby Marilù, but first he stood and drank in the feeling of being home for more than just a short visit, breathing in a sense of belonging along with the lingering aromas of cheese and herbs, coffee and pastry, familiar for as long as he could remember. Residenza dei Tringali had been in his family since his great-grandfather's day. Under Italian inheritance law, he'd owned one-quarter of Residenza dei Tringali since the death of his father, but his mother and sister ran the hotel. Even though they'd taken advantage of technology to streamline everything possible, it was a big commitment.

Suddenly, a woman barged in through the doors from the courtyard, letting them swing behind her, two jute bags clutched in each of her hands. With a loud 'Phew!', she dumped the bags on the floor and flexed her reddened fingers. Alfio gazed at her. If she was a member of staff, she wasn't one he'd met before. He might not remember whether those servicing the guest rooms each day were currently named Maria or Anna or Giuseppe or Eleni, but definitely none of them was tall with a jagged blonde haircut and body art swirling up one of their arms to vanish intriguingly into the sleeve of a blue T-shirt.

The woman glanced at the door to the family quarters, which stood slightly ajar, and called out in badly accented Italian. '*Ciao!* Milk and juice. Your food. Pastries and bread ordered for tomorrow.' After pulling open the door to the enormous stainless-steel fridge, she stooped to gather cartons of fruit juice from one of the bags then stretched to stow them at the top. The movement made her shorts ride down and her T-shirt ride up, awarding him a view of the waistband of what was obviously a thong – yellow, the colour of sunflowers.

Alfio blinked.

The woman swung back to the shopping bags and then jumped as her eyes fell on him for the first time. 'Shit on a stick,' she gasped in English as she clutched a hand to her chest. 'Who are you?'

Alfio spoke English as proficiently, if not better, than he spoke Spanish, but he felt a stab of annoyance that she had blundered into his family home – yes, pink-skinned, freckly and smelling of a suntan lotion a lot like the one Hettie had worn every day – and challenged him in English.

'*Buongiorno. Chi sei?*' he asked coldly, using Italian to ask her who *she* was.

'Oh.' She flushed as she floundered for words. '*Non so molto l'Italiano.*' He hadn't really needed telling that she didn't speak much Italian. At least it wasn't '*Solo Inglese*', which was all many tourists knew. With a wary glance his way, she hurried to the apartment door to push it open further. 'Agata? Nanda? *C'e un signore.*'

He supposed he ought to give her marks for trying to speak the language of Sicily, as Mamma and Nanda both spoke good English, but his attention flew to the door as it was thrust open and his mother emerged, less drawn than on his visits to see her since her operation a month ago, but still paler and more lined than he'd have liked, despite her smart haircut and well-cut clothes. Until recently, she'd never looked her sixty years.

'*Un signore?*' Agata halted in her tracks as her eyes lit on him, then she launched into a motherly mixture of welcome and scolding. 'Oh, Alfio, I didn't know you were coming home! Look how long your hair's grown. And you are too thin.'

Nanda rushed out of the apartment on Agata's heels. 'Alfio? Why didn't you tell us you were coming?' Baby Marilù stared at him from solemn dark eyes as she bestrode her mother's hip.

Within moments, Alfio found himself swept through the door into the salon, amongst the familiar heavy wooden furniture and oil paintings that hadn't changed in his lifetime.

Behind him he heard the fridge close, and a faint, English: 'See you later.'

When he'd heard the door to the hallway open and close, too, he gently kissed Marilù's soft forehead, noting slenderness and frailty where he might have expected baby fat. He ushered his mother to a tapestry armchair, not liking the lines of fatigue around her eyes and the extra silver threads in her dark hair. 'Who's she?' He jerked his head towards the now empty kitchen to indicate the recently departed blonde woman.

Agata looked wrong-footed by his question. 'Ursula. She's helping here for the summer. She's efficient and friendly. We like her.'

'Very much.' Nanda nodded enthusiastically. Alfio's junior by two years, she, too, looked exhausted, no doubt from the demands both of the hotel and of Marilù, who hung on to her mother like a baby chimp. Inwardly, he cursed his absent brother-in-law, Mason, for dumping his wife while she was pregnant, leaving Nanda to give birth alone. *Bastardo*. Mason hadn't been to see his baby, not even when she'd developed a digestive issue. *La bambina* needed a medical procedure, which was scheduled for Friday, just five days away. The two women had been left battling on their own.

Alfio's mind returned to the issues of the present. 'There's enough money to pay this Ursula?'

Agata looked pleased. 'We don't pay her because we made an arrangement. She lives here in return for working till noon. She handles breakfast, shopping, orders and deliveries.'

'I see,' he said slowly, his stomach hollow. These were some of Agata's former duties – which Alfio had charged home intending to take over, along with whatever he could do to support Nanda. He rubbed his chin, which was rough with stubble as he hadn't shaved before his early morning flight. He'd intended his arrival to be not just a surprise, but a loving gesture, a fulfilment of what he'd dreamed so convincingly his father Domenico wanted. Now it was beginning to dawn on him that perhaps he could have believed his mother and sister when they'd assured him that they would find a way to manage the hotel in their current tricky circumstances.

He'd changed his entire life because of a bad dream . . . including splitting up from Hettie.

Nanda only underlined his thoughts when she asked, 'How long will you be here, Alfio? Marilù has your room, but I can move her cot beside my bed for a short time.'

A flash of dismay crossing her face, Agata shook her head. 'Marilù doesn't sleep well near you, Nanda.' To Alfio, she explained, '*La bambina* senses her presence so wakes and cries for attention. Nanda needs as much sleep as she can get. We both do,' she added feelingly. The apartment, though comfortable, wasn't large, and a crying baby would probably wake them both.

Alfio looked from his niece to his sister to his mother, feeling foolish. 'I've come home indefinitely, to do the things you can't do,' he admitted, wincing as he caught blank astonishment on their faces. He took his mother's hand as he tried to explain. 'You're still recovering, and Nanda deserves more time to rest, too, with Marilù being unwell. Your man friend didn't help you as he'd promised, so I wanted to do this for you.' He knew the name of the man friend, but he didn't want to sully his lips with it. For several months prior to her surgery, Agata had seemed happier than any time in the past twenty years, quietly building a new relationship and telling her family little but that things were going well – so well the man was coming for the summer and would be here to do all the things she couldn't after her surgery.

And then suddenly it had ended, and, instead of excited and sparkling, Agata was pale and withdrawn.

Now he read dismay in her gaze. 'That's generous, Alfio. But what about your job? And we have Ursula.'

'Let me worry about my job. You can let Ursula go and I'll take over her duties.' He ignored a flash of guilt at disposing so summarily of someone's method of subsisting.

His mother's eyes widened. 'But I couldn't do that,' she said swiftly.

'Why?' He frowned, perplexed at such an emphatic reply.

Agata paused. Then her face tightened in a stubborn expression he knew of old. 'Ursula is helpful, has been here three weeks already and knows her job. We have an agreement. After working all morning, in the afternoon she studies with a *ceramista* who she selected carefully—'

He flung up an impatient hand. 'Her studies are not our problem.'

'Alfio!' Agata halted him with what he felt was undue finality. 'She more than keeps her side of the bargain, even things she doesn't have to do, like shopping for the family, and she often makes our dinner. I was tired. Her coming here was easy to arrange and she costs us only the price of her food.'

While he let this information sink in, Alfio studied his mother, the shadows beneath her eyes and the hollows in her cheeks.

He switched his attention to Nanda and her visibly underweight six-month-old baby. As if sensing his concerned gaze, Marilù began to cry. Nanda gave an apprehensive squeak and made to rise, but it was too late. Poor little Marilù threw up over her mother like a human geyser, and then her cries gathered force. With a look of apologetic, weary resignation, Nanda managed to contain the mess by looping up her top over it, before disappearing into the bathroom with her daughter.

'The truth is,' Agata said, as if he'd raised a fresh objection, 'I'm glad I said yes to Ursula. Nanda is finding it hard to cope with Marilù's illness.' Sorrowfully, she shook her head. 'Such a baby to be facing surgery. And with Mason leaving—'

'*Bastardo*,' Alfio responded, automatically.

His mother didn't contradict him. '—Nanda's exhausted. It's all she can do to look after Marilù.'

Despite the presence of Ursula, Alfio began to feel he'd done the right thing to come home after all. 'I'm here now. The hotel can use me.'

But Agata shook her head, looking troubled. 'You never wanted to be a hotelier. You said that right from being a small boy.'

'True,' he acknowledged. 'But I shall stay for a while,

while the surgeon solves Marilù's difficulty, and you regain your strength. Then I'll look for a new job, maybe here in Sicily, to be closer to you.'

His mother blinked. 'Why won't you return to your present job?'

Alfio felt suddenly like a small boy found out hiding something he knew he'd get in trouble for. A defensive note crept into his voice. 'I left it.'

'Not just so you could help us? Oh, no, Alfio,' Agata remonstrated, clutching her forehead. 'I assumed you meant that you'd taken a few weeks' leave. You know what the employment market's like in Sicily.'

'You don't need to worry,' he replied heartily, skirting this very real issue.

Agata treated him to a frown. 'What does Hettie think about all this?'

He couldn't suppress a sigh. 'That relationship is over.'

'Because you came home?' Agata's voice had risen a pitch. 'Why not ask me before you gave up everything?'

'Because you would have said you were fine,' he shot back. 'Even if you were producing breakfasts on your knees, you would have said you were fine.'

Her frown became a glare. 'I *am* fine because I've arranged things with Ursula. Get your job back. Talk to Hettie.'

He rubbed his nose. 'Not possible.'

'*Merda*,' she muttered under her breath. Alfio probably hadn't been meant to hear but he had to agree. *Shit*.

He gave her hand a reassuring squeeze, feeling that a little of the flesh had melted from her bones. 'I'll stay in an attic room.'

'Ursula has the one with the balcony,' Agata retorted warningly.

42

He fought the urge to snap that Ursula would have to swap to the one without the balcony. 'Then the other one,' he answered patiently.

Agata vented a gusty sigh. 'I'd better make lunch.'

'I'll do it.' He remembered that he'd seen blonde Ursula stocking the fridge.

When he went back out into the kitchen to investigate, he found cheeses and fresh Parma ham, along with salad leaves and big red tomatoes. A round crusty loaf waited in the bread bin. He was pulling the simple meal together when Nanda appeared, freshly showered, her long, dark hair whisked up behind her head. She, at least, hugged him and said, 'Mamma has told me what you've done. You shouldn't have, but it was good of you.' Then she glanced at the crusty bread and reopened the bread bin. 'Ursula will have bought soft rolls for Marilù. She can't eat the *pagnotta del dittaino*.'

He hadn't thought of that, and felt unreasonably irritated that this Ursula obviously did.

After lunch, he left Agata, Nanda and Marilù all hoping for naps and dragged his two suitcases towards the stairs, sure they were heavier now than when he'd arrived. He paused to pass a few words with Nino. The middle-aged general assistant had settled himself in the cool of the small office behind the old-fashioned mahogany reception desk. Nino was great with guests but not so good with computers or admin tasks, so nobody minded if he whiled away quiet times by playing games on his phone within easy earshot of the lobby. In return, Nino didn't worry about a set schedule for breaks, so Agata and Nanda weren't troubled by too many guests dinging the reception bell.

'*Ciao*,' Alfio said, when he'd enquired politely after

43

Nino's health and could move on. Residenza dei Tringali was quiet. Probably most of the guests were out in the sunshine, enjoying lunch at pavement cafés or sweltering on boat trips.

He paused and gazed up at the long flights of marble stairs stretching above him towards the vaulted white ceiling. He'd carted luggage up those stairs since he'd been big enough to do so. The hotel had no lifts. Alfio knew the nearby Grand Hotel Ortigia had a lift all the way to its roof terrace, but they'd been able to position it on the side of an existing inner courtyard. Residenza dei Tringali, being L-shaped, had only a rear – and unsuitably positioned – courtyard. Domenico had taken his role as custodian of Residenza dei Tringali's gracious traditional marble and tile seriously, yet had been prepared to sacrifice a little of the lobby to create a lift shaft. The authorities had refused permission.

With a sigh, Alfio hefted a suitcase in each hand and began up the first curving flight of stairs, unworried by having no free hand to grip the iron balustrade. Each grey-veined marble tread felt like a familiar friend as he climbed from ground floor to first, first to second, second to third, then shouldered his way through a plain door marked *privato* to a narrow, more modest wooden staircase to the attics.

On the landing, he paused for breath, noting that the right-hand door, the one to the room with the balcony, was closed.

He opened the other door. It hadn't been locked but then no one was likely to want what was inside – a single metal bedframe with a faded mattress, a bare window and a couple of coats of dust. Leaving his suitcases at the door, he jogged all the way back downstairs for

44

cleaning things, pausing on the way up again to raid the linen cupboard.

His new abode was going to be a come-down after his sunny apartment in the suburbs of Barcelona – 'Barca', Hettie called it, as if the word Barcelona was too complicated to bother her British tongue with.

Well, he wasn't in 'Barca' now, he thought resignedly; he was in Ortigia. And in the worst room in the house.

After the son of the household's unexpected appearance followed by his vanishing into the family apartment, Ursula had grabbed a bottle of water, then headed out of the kitchen to climb the many flights of stairs to the attic. She ought to have wonderful glutes by the end of this summer, if nothing else.

In her little room, she pulled the shady curtains aside to peep out over the rooftops. Though she hadn't been in Sicily three weeks yet, Ursula loved Ortigia, the *Città Vecchia* or Old City and its bridges spanning a canal of blue seawater. She loved the Sunday morning tenor clamour of church bells and the daily market, the sheer number of boats moored in the bay and the marina, and the railings that ran all around the island, as if acknowledging that the views were too wonderful to hide with walls. Her balcony was no more than the flat roof to a bay window in the angle of the L-shaped old building, enclosed with a plain iron railing. It faced inland rather than over Porto Grande marina, but received the perfect combination of morning sun and afternoon shade. From up here amongst the birds, she could even glimpse the topmost part of the cathedral, or *il Duomo*.

Letting the curtain fall back into place, she kicked off her flip-flops in favour of comfy trainers ready to head off for Fabio Ceramiche, the studio of her teacher, Fabio Iacobello. Every day, she looked forward to learning more about ceramics painting and felt encouraged by the fact that Fabio, a crusty guy she thought must be in his sixties, was taking a special interest in her work.

And thinking of crusty men, what was with Agata's darling son? A right grumpy guts compared to his mum and sister, from what Ursula had seen so far. Still, she thought to herself as she stowed her water bottle in her bag, she'd probably have little to do with him, and his surprise visit was lovely for Agata and Nanda. They mentioned him often, and the great life he lived in Spain. They missed him, just as her parents missed her, so she'd give the family space to enjoy the prodigal's return. The hotel would be busy until the end of October, so she had plenty to occupy her – putting out breakfast, decanting milk and juice into jugs, handling the enormous freshwater containers, taking deliveries, cleaning down the kitchen and shopping. She also fed the skittish stray cat that sat on the courtyard wall. Ortigia had many strays. People put out food for them or made them little shelters. This one had a distinctive, patchy coat so Ursula had named her Camocat and was trying to gain her confidence with kitchen scraps.

She slung her bag crosswise over her body, then hurried into the corridor and down the stairs from the attic, slowing to admire the beautiful stairwell she emerged into, where the walls were painted a soft buttery yellow and the ceiling and ornate plasterwork white. Then, her bag bobbing, she ran all the way to the foot of the final flight to where the marble floor tiles of the lobby shone and barely a crack marred their soft white and grey. Heavy wooden chairs upholstered in powder blue stood in small groups, and a grey-haired guest sat reading in one of them. Ursula glanced over to the large, old-fashioned reception desk and waved at Nino, who seemed almost part of the furniture himself. '*Ciao*,' he called.

'*Ciao. Vado in città.*' *I'm going to town.* She ran out of the main entrance and down the steps to Viale Mazzini, drawing in her breath at the sudden heat outside. It wasn't quite June yet and Nanda said that July and August would see forty degrees Celsius, so she'd better get used to it.

The red Hop-on Hop-off bus had stopped by the car park on the other side of the road, its windscreen reflecting the sun. Designed for tourists, it ambled from one sight-seeing point to another before it left Ortigia via the older bridge, Ponte Umbertino, and then ambled about the main city of Siracusa. She'd used it a couple of times when she'd first arrived, to see the sights en route to the studio, but now she preferred to walk the mile or so along the streets lined with pink oleander trees to Piazza Brancaccio off Viale Teocrito.

It was a hot walk, across the centre of the city, with unhelmeted riders on scooters weaving through the traffic and pedestrians automatically choosing the shady side of the street. Piazza Brancaccio was a stone square not far from the great concrete Basilica Santuario Madonna delle Lacrime, the shape of which made Ursula think of a woman in a conical pleated dress with a flirty hemline. Over the years, urbanisation had crept up on the old square so that it now looked like an elderly relative at a gathering of younger family – old and grey but still beloved. Made up of low, stone buildings like Fabio's studio, a café bar stood diagonally across the bumpy pavings with a small grocery shop in another corner. People filtered down from nearby apartment blocks to meet beneath the white umbrellas of the café bar and watch the central fountain dance, tubs of red geraniums at its feet.

Fabio Iacobello was also a regular at the bar. With the kind of spare tyre that spoke of eating all the wrong food, he was grizzled and grumpy, but a kind heart lay beneath his gruff manner. As he had told Ursula on her first day, since his wife had died a few years ago he'd lost his mojo for creating his own artisan ceramics and instead ran courses to pass on his skills. His past work, mainly ornamental heads that showed his prowess with clay as well as glaze, stood around on shelves. The short course Ursula had taken with Lucia in Umbria had been all about commercial ceramics – plates and jugs and everyday items – and she was more interested in those at the moment. Maybe one day, she too would try her hand at creating the heads of the King and Queen of Greece, the style of sculpture that was so popular on the island.

On the second day Ursula had worked with Fabio in his cool studio, he'd informed her that she wasn't on a course with him. It had been a surprise, as she'd certainly enrolled on one. But, in his growling, heavily accented English, he insisted she was not like the others, either beginners or what he called 'hobby students', who would drift on to some other pastime before too long.

'I no had someone worth training for long time,' he'd told her. 'I mentor you. You build skills.'

Building skills usually meant sitting on a wooden stool with a tile on a turntable on her workbench, repeating a simple design until it was consistently formed and regularly spaced, practising with brushes of differing sizes and shapes. He waited until, slowly, carefully, she could achieve a perfect border of a certain design, then he'd snatch up a fresh tile and paint the same design himself, saying, 'Quicker,' as his brush danced across the surface.

Ursula learned to persist on tile after tile until he took one off her and put it ready for firing. The kiln was expensive to run so was only switched on when full. Then it burned for twenty-four hours, and every door and window of the studio stood open to let out the heat. Ursula never got tired of the thrill of the tiles emerging from the kiln, patterned with red and blue, the previously matte glaze now glossy and catching the light. Recently, he'd set Ursula to painting sunflowers, which she'd thought she'd already mastered under Lucia.

'In Umbria?' Fabio had demanded, as if no one from Umbria could even approach the necessary skill set.

Today, Fabio had a group of six hopeful students at the large workbench – four young women who looked as if they might be art graduates and two middle-aged men – but he broke off when he saw Ursula. 'Sunflowers, like before,' he instructed her succinctly. A tile stood ready for her on the rotating stand on her small bench, a dozen more, virgin and white, stacked alongside. After offering him and the students a cheerful greeting, she sat down to create a sunflower centre with a fine brush dipped in both black and brown glaze. 'Not dab, touch,' grumbled Fabio before he turned back to his class.

As she touched, touched, touched, reloading the brush and touching some more, Ursula's mind drifted to tall, lean Alfio Tringali, with his mop of dark curls. He'd stared at Ursula so hard that each dark iris had seemed to glow, as if he was . . . well, what? Annoyed? Astonished? Hostile? Maybe he didn't like women with tattoos. Or maybe he didn't like women. Or maybe he just didn't like her.

Her brush paused above the tile as she frowned

thoughtfully. If she carried out her earlier resolution to leave the Tringali family to their own devices this evening, would Alfio think to cook, or would he take it for granted that his mother or sister would take care of that? Unfortunately, Agata found meal preparation exhausting and Marilù would have a screaming fit if Nanda put her down for long enough to do it. Agata couldn't hold a kicking, screaming six-month-old. Her tricky hysterectomy only a month earlier had caused complications involving stents into the kidneys, which had left bruising that was slow to heal.

Ursula would talk to Nanda, she decided. They were a similar age and got on well. She could say something like: 'I'll make pasta and pesto and salady things, then I'll leave you Tringalis to enjoy each other's company.'

Agata's surname was actually Greco, as in Italy women didn't take the man's surname upon marriage, but when speaking of the family or the couple, it was usual to use the man's name.

Women keeping their own name was a great idea, she mused, breathing in the sharp smell of the glaze and listening to Fabio talking to his group in rapid Italian that she hadn't a hope of following, but which rose and fell pleasantly on her ear. If Ursula had kept Quinn, she wouldn't have had to go through the chore of changing back to it when she and Stephan ended things. Or he ended things and she tried to *end* things. She winced to remember being so miserable that she'd actually slugged down a handful of pills.

She bent her head over a new tile. It made sense to paint lots of sunflower centres in one go, because moving on to the petals meant pouring out fresh glaze.

Fabio came over to examine her work and grunt approval, his pot belly wobbling over the waistband of his shorts. 'OK.' He reached down to pick up the tall plastic bottles of liquid glaze in sepia, ochre and lemon. 'You remember petals from yesterday?'

Ursula nodded, reaching for a square-ended brush, miming dipping each corner. 'Two colours on every stroke.'

'Good.' He frowned at her, which seemed to be his way of showing approval. 'Show me.'

She took up a fresh tile so as not to risk spoiling the centres that had just been passed 'OK', dipped a corner of the brush in the sepia and one in the lemon, then with a press, twist and flick, produced a perfect streaky, textured sunflower petal.

'Good,' he said again, and waved at the waiting tiles sporting sunflower centres. 'You go on now.'

Ursula felt as if she'd won an award. With a rush of triumph and satisfaction as she gazed at a tile, she envisaged exactly how the sunflower petals were going to lie, then, against the background hum of conversation from the rest of the room, she began to wield her brush.

Chapter Four

Early next morning, Ursula stepped out onto her balcony, the first coffee of the day in her hand – instant because she had a kettle in her room but not a coffee machine. Then she halted.

Alfio Tringali was perched on the broad sill of the next window, set at an angle to hers owing to the L-shape of the building, gazing at a blue sky washed pale by the recent dawn. His jaw was rough with morning stubble, his dark curls brushed off his forehead by the breeze. Slowly, he turned to look at her. '*Buongiorno.*'

'*Buongiorno.*' Aware that she sounded stiff, she tried to add a smile. It wouldn't quite form. She was used to this space being hers, but his window ledge was so close that he could easily have reached out for the black iron railing and clambered over it onto her balcony. As the son of the house, if he decided to share her little eyrie above the courtyard, she could do little to prevent him, not even if she could summon the Italian to say, *Hey, can we talk about boundaries here?*

Usually, she lounged on a wooden chair, feet up on the

railing, watching the sun caress the tiled roofs and stone buildings of Ortigia as she sipped her coffee. It was her moment of peace before the day began, and it didn't include anyone observing her.

As if reading these ponderings, Alfio gave a short nod, swung his legs back indoors and vanished into the depths of his room.

Ursula exhaled and took her customary seat. But Alfio stayed in her mind, as if he were watching her. He could be, standing back from his open window, invisible to her but with a perfect view . . . She shook her head, trying to vanquish such unsubstantiated suspicions. He was Agata's son, for goodness' sake. Agata and Nanda loved him dearly and talked about him all the time. He was no danger.

But his room appeared to be next to hers. If she'd thought about what lay behind that door, she'd have assumed it to be the many water tanks and pipes necessary for the guest rooms rather than another bedroom.

In her pocket, her phone buzzed. She took it out and was surprised to find a message from a Brighton friend, Charlotte. Charlotte and Drew were what Ursula thought of as 'couple friends', who belonged to the days of Ursula-and-Stephan. She hadn't heard from them for over a year. Frowning, she opened the message. *Hi stranger,* she read. *Hope all's OK. Steph asked me to ask you if you know where his signet ring is, the one that was his grandpa's. Char xx*

Irritation washed over her. From most people – even an ex – it would be an innocent enquiry. From Stephan, though, trumping up reasons to get others to contact her wasn't new behaviour. It was as if he sent messages within the messages. *Think we're divorced and everything's settled, eh? Blocked me, have you? You can't keep me out of your life that easily.* She could imagine him getting round Charlotte in his rueful, boyish way. *No point messaging her myself. She took the divorce so hard we can't carry on a civilised conversation. I don't know where Grandpa's ring could be if she didn't take it. It's valuable . . .* Insinuating, but not quite saying, that she'd stolen it.

Rapidly, Ursula tapped out a reply. *Hi, I'm fine, hope you are. No idea about the ring as have zero of Steph's possessions.* She paused over whether to add a kiss. The message was chilly without but if Charlotte was going to play go-between for Steph, then, yeah, chilly seemed appropriate. She sent it without a kiss, checking the time before slipping her phone back in the pocket of her shorts. The UK was an hour behind so that made it just after five a.m. Why was Charlotte up at the crack of dawn?

Irritatingly, her phone buzzed with another message before Ursula had drunk half her delicious coffee. Charlotte again. *If you find it let me know and I'll pop round for it, if you like. Xx* Ursula snorted. 'Yeah, right.' Was Charlotte fishing for her address? Had she – or Steph? – been to her flat and found her gone? That would explain Steph making this indirect contact.

She answered: *I don't have it.*

A reply came right back. *It's just that it's valuable.*

Jeez. Ursula swigged down the last of her coffee and rose, her early morning peace destroyed. She slid her feet into flip-flops and prepared to meet the day, trotting down the several flights of stairs, across the marble floor of the lobby and through the hall to the kitchen. After washing her hands, she began pouring juice and milk into lidded jugs.

54

Alfio arrived soon after and murmured, '*Buongiorno*,' again, as if he hadn't already seen her. She answered with a sunny smile, but he didn't smile back. Oh, well. If he didn't speak English and her Italian was shite, that suited her fine. She'd taken her dinner to her balcony last night to let the family eat together, and she could do so every night of his visit.

She was almost ready to carry the first jugs along the hall and into the breakfast room, an elegant room off the foyer that sported gilt plasterwork and a black marble mantelpiece, when her phone rang. The screen read *Charlotte*. Swiftly, she declined the call. The phone rang again. Alfio's gaze flicked in her direction, and he smiled and nodded as he made a rolling gesture with his hand, as if to indicate that she was free to answer. Reluctantly, she did so. Charlotte might only persist, otherwise.

'Aha,' chimed the giggly voice. 'You've run away with the treasure.'

Wow. Charlotte was tipsy. That explained the early call but . . . oh, yeah. It was Spring Bank Holiday in the UK, she remembered. They'd probably had a boozy barbecue last night and had yet to go to bed. 'What?' Ursula demanded, past even pretending to be pleasant. Residenza dei Tringali didn't provide hot breakfasts, but the pastries would arrive any moment and breakfast had to be ready by seven. Tucking the phone between ear and shoulder, she began sliding the jugs onto a tray.

'Single ringtone, so you're not in the UK or Ireland,' Charlotte crowed. 'Ergo, you've left the country with Steph's heirloom.' Charlotte put on a gruff voice like a cartoon villain. 'So, where are you? And what have you done with Stephan's ring?'

It was obvious that Charlotte was joking, obvious that

she was drunk, but the accusation really, really pissed Ursula off. 'I have no use for Stephan or his ring,' she said shortly.

It would have been easy to end the call, but she waited, something in her wanting Charlotte to show some loyalty to Ursula by bursting into giggles before saying, *Oh, I know, I know. But Stephan insisted I ask you. Isn't he a twat, sometimes?*

Instead, there was a muffled conversation, as if Charlotte had put her hand over the mic, then she returned, suddenly sounding uncertain. 'Erm . . . Stephan says go screw yourself.'

So, he was actually there, with Charlotte? She pictured Drew, too, all of them drinking and talking about her behind her back. Sweetly, she answered, 'But if I could screw myself, I'd never have had any use for a prick like him.' Gaining some satisfaction from the juvenile comeback, she ended the call with a stab at the screen, thinking how sad it was that people who used to be her friends were being gradually gathered in Stephan's end of the playground.

She saw Alfio gazing steadily at her and gave him a quick smile to make up for her tone on the phone. Then she began to run the milk and jugs into the graciously styled breakfast room.

When she hurried back into the kitchen, Alfio looked up from his task of loading small jars of conserves into a bowl. In perfect English, he asked, 'Is everything OK? That call sounded as if it might be upsetting.'

Heat flooded her cheeks. Damn. She'd jumped to the conclusion that he didn't speak English just because he hadn't so far. That was why she'd felt able to let loose on the phone, forgetting that Nanda had once told Ursula

56

that their father had been keen on them all having language skills because it helped with the hotel. She cleared her throat. 'Um, fine thanks. Sorry. Bit sweary, there.' She grabbed bowls and plates and carried them in the breakfast room to place on the sideboard, which was topped with a marble slab to keep things as cool as possible. Alfio followed with the conserves and a tray of cutlery. He opened the sideboard, withdrew a stack of neatly folded yellow tablecloths and began floating them over tables with an expert flick of his wrists.

When the kitchen doorbell rang, Ursula raced back to receive the bread, pastries and small cakes. Alfio returned to take from the fridge the meats and cheeses she'd shopped for yesterday and arranged them on a platter that had a cover. The coffee machine was on, and Ursula was adding the last napkin to the table placings just before the hands of the big wall clock moved to seven.

A couple with a daughter entered promptly. 'Good morning. *Buongiorno*.'

When the little girl's gaze fell on the tray of food, her mouth made a perfect O. 'Ooh, cake for brekkie!'

Ursula laughed, forgetting her bitter thoughts about Charlotte and Stephan. 'It's perfect, isn't it? *Perfetto*.'

As the morning progressed, Alfio continued to work alongside Ursula, silently clearing tables after guests had finished their meal, and then re-laying them. He knew he was being offish, and that Ursula had done nothing wrong except be here at the hotel, ensconced in the role he'd planned for himself and occupying the better of the two attic rooms. She carried out her tasks with speed and efficiency and couldn't have made it plainer that she normally managed the breakfast alone if she'd written him a note. Or inked it on her skin – she had one arm free of leaves and flowers and clever, swirling designs, after all.

Her dismay had been almost comical when she'd stepped onto her balcony this morning and found him on his window ledge. Although he'd been enjoying his unorthodox seat perilously close to thin air, it would have been creepy of him to stay once she arrived . . . yet leaving had irritated like crumbs beneath his skin. If it was unreasonable to be irritated about something so small, well then, he was unreasonable.

Breakfast ended, they moved into the kitchen and she bustled around him, checking cupboards and the fridge, tapping at her phone to make what appeared to be a shopping list.

He wondered who'd phoned her earlier and provoked her aggressive reply. She so obviously hadn't wanted to tell him that he'd found himself wanting to know. Without examining his motives, he asked, 'You are sure you are OK?'

Her head shot up. 'I'm sure. Why?'

He shrugged. 'You were obviously upset with someone, earlier. On the phone.'

Her blue eyes remained trained on him for several thoughtful seconds. Then she replied, 'It would be more accurate to say I was upset *by* someone.'

As he mulled over this distinction, his thoughts were interrupted by a delivery of the bottled water they placed in guest rooms and made available with breakfast. He got to the door before her, feeling better suited to haul the packages around, but the deliveryman looked past him. '*Ciao*, Ursula.'

'*Ciao*, Peppi,' she called back, reached around Alfio and began hefting cartons of forty bottles each.

Irritated now that she hadn't left him to the heavy job,

he hesitated, but then the reception bell sounded. This meant that Nino wasn't manning the desk, so Alfio set off to answer the summons. After he'd attended to a Dutch couple at the huge mahogany desk over which his family had been presiding for years, he returned to frown over the fact that Ursula had already stacked the water in a small, dark offshoot of the kitchen that had probably once been for wine. Then he caught her uncertain, wary look. It made his conscience twang. Whatever he thought of her being here, he represented his family and should make an effort. He smoothed his frown away. 'In which part of England do you live?'

She crossed to the sink to wash her hands. 'Brighton, on the south coast. At least, I did.'

'It's unusual for Mamma to have British staff,' he essayed, trying to think of a time when she had.

'I'm not British. I'm Irish. Quinn is a common Irish name.' She tacked on a smile.

He paused, realising that, yes, her accent was quite different to Hettie's. Then he shrugged. 'But you live in England.'

'You live in Spain.' She raised her eyebrows. 'Still Italian, though, yes?'

He gazed at her, unsure whether she was being prickly or teasing. She had a strange, guarded manner sometimes, looking at him as if expecting him to give a wriggle and transform into a snake. 'The Irish don't like to be British?' he probed solemnly, knowing the difference but waiting to see if she laughed or scowled.

She did neither, merely explaining, as if she'd explained it many times before, 'The Republic of Ireland is not British. Northern Ireland is British. The Irish have links both with Britain and with Europe.'

'I see.' He reached into the fridge for two bottles of water, handed one to her then pulled out a stool from beneath the central island and sank down onto it, trying to make the atmosphere more relaxed. 'Is your family in Ireland or England?'

She smiled suddenly. 'Loads in Ireland – parents, siblings, aunts, uncles and cousins. Second cousins, third cousins,' she added. 'A few cousins in England.' She paused and drank deeply from the bottle of water.

He watched the movement of her throat. 'Mamma didn't tell me how you came to be working here.'

She licked her lips and returned the lid to the bottle. Her mouth was moist now and his attention was held by its glistening pink. 'Agata has probably told you that when she was young, she visited Swords near Dublin, where we live, and made a friend who she kept in touch with. Funny to think of her being there before I was born.' The pink lips smiled. 'My family's church has a helping-hands scheme, which my aunt's involved with, and the opportunity got through to me that way. I had plans to go to mainland Italy but when this came up, I found a great master of ceramic painting to work with and learn from – Fabio Iacobello. His studio is near Viale Teocrito in Piazza Brancaccio. Coming to Sicily has worked out well.'

He suddenly realised he was watching Ursula's mouth and managed to lift his gaze. 'It is only really in the past year that Mamma has spoken of visiting Ireland when she was young—' The reason Agata had talked about Ireland recently clanged into his mind and his voice caught in his throat. He heard an echo of Ursula's earlier comment: *Quinn is a common Irish name*. 'Did you say your surname is Quinn?' he asked slowly.

Puzzlement entered her blue eyes. 'Yes.' Then, frowning: 'What of it? I'm getting the distinct feeling that you have a problem with me, Alfio. Tell me if I've caused offence.'

His breathing quickened. Was this woman connected to his mother's recent love affair? To give himself time to study her, to think, he demanded testily, 'Are you always suspicious of people?'

'Only men,' she answered, with patently false affability, but looking at him as if he was off his head. She checked her shopping list. 'Be sure to tell me if you have a complaint about my work.' After knocking on the door to the family apartment she vanished inside for a minute, then returned, tucking euros into her pocket.

Only pausing to pull empty bags from a cupboard, she said, 'I'm going to the market. *Arrivederci*.' He didn't miss her pointed use of the formal goodbye rather than the more friendly '*Ciao*'. She strode out into the courtyard. A few moments later, though, her voice floated back to him, softer and more friendly. 'Hiya, Camocat. Are you skulking around out here doing your urban commando thing?'

He edged sideways a couple of steps to peep through the open door and saw that she'd paused before a slender cat that sat atop the wall. Ursula's blonde hair blazed in the morning sun and the cat's patchy coat looked drab in comparison. Warningly, he called out, 'Sometimes the feral cats will scratch you.'

She barely glanced back. 'Sometimes people deserve it.' Then she hefted her collection of bags and edged past Nanda's little purple Fiat before disappearing through the open gates.

The cat gazed at him smugly, as if to say, *She doesn't like you.*

The cat was right. Alfio knew he'd come across like a

jerk as shocked suspicion had ripped into him. But now he must discover whether his suspicions were correct.

From behind the apartment door, Marilù began to cry, as if foretelling that trouble was on the horizon. He followed the thin wail into the family area, where he found Nanda pacing the floor while the baby stirred uncomfortably in her embrace, her curls springing from her head in all directions – much like his own did in the mornings. Agata looked on from the depths of a large armchair.

Alfio crossed the rug to crouch at his mother's feet. 'Is this Ursula something to do with your Stanley?' Behind him, he was aware of Nanda's motherly crooning coming to an abrupt halt.

Agata blinked. Then she squared her shoulders. 'Ursula is Stanley's daughter,' she admitted calmly.

'*What?*' Alfio hissed. 'That *bastardo* hurt you. He made promises he didn't keep. And she's his *daughter?* Why the hell would you want her here?' When he encountered reproof in his mother's expression, he paused to calm himself. 'She thinks it's OK, what her father did? Promising to come here and help you over this difficult time, but instead returning to his wife?'

Agata's gaze slid away. 'She doesn't know. It was Stanley's brother who suggested she come here, thinking he was doing everyone a favour. Ursula had lost her job and her apartment through no fault of her own. The arrangement helps her, and it helps us. I do not want you to let the secret out to Ursula, Alfio. My relationship with Stanley is over.' Only the merest tremor as she said the final few words hinted at her distress.

Her wounded dignity wrung Alfio's heart. 'Ursula is carrying out her father's promise without knowing? And her uncle arranged this?' he demanded incredulously.

'You make it sound like a conspiracy, but it was just circumstance.' Agata gave a pained smile. 'Stanley telephoned to explain that his brother got carried away and suggested it to Ursula, and that it was Stanley's first instinct to put a stop to it. But he paused and asked what I wanted. I suspect he thought I'd say, "Stop it happening," but Nanda and me, we were both so tired.' Apprehension stole over her face. 'Try and understand, Alfio. His daughter needed a place to live and a way to support herself while she studied, and we needed help.'

The words rang inside Alfio's head. *So tired . . . needed help.* Despite his enquiries, they'd refused to admit it until he'd actually come home, choosing instead to let him live his life without bothering him with their problems. Abruptly, his angry indignation drained away. Nanda and Agata had simply done what they had to in order to keep going.

He straightened up and turned to his sister, who was staring at him, eyes huge, looking so tired and strained that Alfio's heart ached. He didn't need to ask if she'd known who Ursula was, too. That she had was written in her face. He held out inviting arms towards his restless, grimacing niece. 'Will you come to Zio Alfio, Marilù?'

Although she'd accepted a few cuddles from him yesterday evening, Marilù shrank away.

Agata smiled wanly. 'She just wants her mamma.'

'Only a few days until the surgery,' he reminded his sister gently, reaching out to stroke Marilù's tiny fingers where they lay on Nanda's shoulder, feeling glad that even if things were tight with the hotel this season, the family could still afford private medical insurance. The baby's problem stemmed from a thickening of muscle between the stomach and the small intestine, causing her to vomit like Etna erupting. The muscle would have to be cut to allow her to digest her food and gain weight, but it was hard to think of such a little scrap going under the scalpel. He'd been surprised to hear that Marilù was in the care of a local hospital rather than one of the big specialist places . . . but, of course, Nanda would have tried to stay near to Agata, too, not knowing that her big brother would finally show up to share the load.

'Yes,' Nanda murmured and caressed her daughter's back. 'In some ways I want those five days gone. But also I dread Friday arriving.'

'I'll drive you to the hospital and stay with you while Marilù's in the operating theatre,' he offered. A day-long task, it would be too much for his mother. Alfio slipped his arms around his sister and her baby, hating and despising the man who'd left his wife to cope alone.

Perhaps Nanda was thinking of this desertion too because her lips trembled for a moment before she smiled. 'Thank you, Alfio. Ursula will deal with the breakfasts.'

Annoyingly, Alfio found he was grateful to Ursula Quinn, despite who her father was. Agata was in no fit state to try and cope alone.

Chapter Five

The shopping and her other morning tasks complete, Ursula was glad to leave Residenza dei Tringali – and Alfio – behind. She'd had enough of moody men.

When reading about Sicily before setting off on this odyssey, she'd laughed at a cynical caricature of Sicilian Man as smouldering, grumpy and autocratic, but Alfio was showing signs of fitting the stereotype. Sicilian Man had also been deemed an amazing lover, but Ursula had no plans to put that to the test.

She hadn't slept with a man since Stephan.

Two years.

She missed sex. Yeah, she did. She'd considered the traditional post-break-up sex but hesitated. Stranger sex? A hook-up? Either were easy to arrange in the clubs of Brighton – but that was where all her troubles had begun. The memory made the sun feel hotter than it was.

Given that she was passing close to what Nanda had assured her was the best gelateria in Siracusa, she treated herself to a cone of *frutti di bosco*, a delicious confection of ice cream and mixed berries. She ate it as she crossed

Ponte Santa Lucia, known as *il ponte nuovo*, the new bridge, by virtue of it being less than twenty years old. Rowing boats were moored along the edges of the canal beneath her, each one a patchwork of colours such as green, apricot and yellow. The stone arches of the older bridge, Ponte Umbertino, ran parallel, with an irregular-shaped quay that was part of the Archimedes monument between the two, causing the canal to divide around it. On the other side of the bridge, she bought a couple of slices of pizza from a kiosk to complete her dessert-first lunch as she followed Via Malta, lined with pink-blossomed oleander trees that overhung dusty cars and scooters. Her feet carried her along hot pavements as she enjoyed the coloured buildings and window boxes frothing from wrought-iron balconies.

She crossed a park to Piazza Pantheon where stood the elegant, columned cylinder of the church of San Tommaso, where broken, ancient columns studded its grounds. The past and the present gently coexisted in Siracusa – the remains of Apollo's temple stood beside the daily market in Ortigia, and ruins of she didn't know what stood near one of her favourite ceramic shops.

The wind caught her hair and blew it into her face as she crossed a busy road where the traffic only intensified the late May heat. She took her water bottle from her bag to refresh her during the half-hour slog along broad, busy streets that ran up a slight incline. Eventually, she reached Piazza Brancaccio, where Fabio Ceramiche filled half of one side of the square – studio below and his apartment above.

The studio door stood open, and she was glad to step into the coolness, windows high in the walls allowing in the light but diffusing the heat of the sun.

Fabio awaited her at the smooth wooden bench she'd made her own. He scratched his beard and frowned. '*Buongiorno*.'

She took no notice of the frown, a furrowed brow being his default expression. 'How are ya?' she replied with a grin.

He beetled grey brows at her. 'Is that English?'

'More Irish.' She kicked off her sandals to cool her bare feet on the stone floor and shrugged into an overshirt that had begun life white but now was brushed with glaze of every colour.

Fabio frowned. ''Ow ayya?' he repeated experimentally.

'Grand,' she answered approvingly.

A class began to filter in, and Fabio greeted each entering student with a straight-faced, ''Ow ayya?' which earned him odd looks from the Italians.

Fabio might look as grim as a gargoyle, but Ursula had quickly discovered the humour and soft centre beneath. Now that he lived alone, his daughter living elsewhere in Sicily, he spent his time precisely as he wished. He did most things as he wished. 'How ayya?' she echoed gravely, enjoying the bemusement on the faces of those who found their stools at the other workbench.

Soon, the students all had paintbrushes in their hands and Ursula was able to relax and forget moody-guts Alfio Tringali. Under Fabio's eagle eye, she produced six – six! – thick white plates with blue borders and sunflowers in the centre. Fabio accepted five of them for firing.

Ursula nearly fainted in shock.

It was much later in the afternoon when she re-entered the courtyard. The stray cat sat on the wall, green eyes gleaming as she watched Ursula approach. 'Hiya, Camocat.'

Ursula put out a hand to stroke the mottled fur, but when the cat shrank from her touch she let her hand fall again. 'I'll put out scraps after dinner. Keep your eyes peeled.' Camocat looked away and sighed, as if thinking that was a long time to wait. Ursula might have been fooled into finding the hopeful feline something immediately, had she not bought cat food from her own pocket and left it out only this morning. The empty bowl nearby was proof.

With a light, 'Ciao, Camocat,' she swung her way into the hotel, expecting to find the kitchen empty and clean, just waiting for her to set to with the evening meal. What she found was Alfio lounging at the table, frowning at his phone screen.

'Ah,' he said, pocketing the phone, as if he'd been waiting for her to appear. 'Can we talk?'

Ursula eyed his white T-shirt and trendy skinny shorts in dull blue. He'd shaved off his stubble, which made him look younger and less glowery. 'Problem?' she asked stiffly. She knew Agata owned half the hotel, and her children owned the other half between them. If Alfio was going to be as much of an arse as he had been this morning, he could prove a serious fly in Ursula's summer ointment.

When he shook his head, a curl broke free. He shoved it back from his forehead. 'I'll make a meal tonight for myself and Mamma. Agata,' he added, as if Ursula might have forgotten who his mother was.

'OK,' she said, cautiously. Was this a big fat hint that she was imposing on the family? Although she usually ate with Nanda and Agata, she'd be happy to eat upstairs. 'You're OK with me getting my own meal, though? That's kinda the deal – which I have with your mother,' she added, for avoidance of doubt.

He frowned. Then his eyes lit up in the most natural,

engaging smile she'd yet seen from him. 'I have given you the wrong impression. In fact, I am hoping for a favour.' As if in justification, he added, 'My mother and sister tell me that you are kind.'

It gave her a warm feeling inside to know that the two Sicilian women she'd come to like had said nice things about her. Still, she was cautious about admitting to kindness until she knew where the conversation was going. 'Sometimes.' If he wanted her to extend her hours he was out of luck, because her afternoons with Fabio were the point of her being in Sicily. Even at weekends, when Fabio didn't hold classes, she was allowed to turn up to be growled at and put right on every brush stroke.

Alfio pulled out a second stool from under the counter and, after a moment, Ursula realised it was an invitation and sat down, wondering at his pleasant manner. Was he always this unpredictable? 'Please,' he said, 'would you invite Nanda for a meal with you this evening? Mamma and I will babysit. Soon Marilù must go to hospital and an evening out first would do my sister good.' He grimaced, and pulling a face made him seem more human. 'Nanda is so protective of Marilù and—' he paused, as if hunting for the right word '—dutiful, that if you could hint you need a night out and don't want to go alone . . . ?'

Ursula was surprised, but pleasantly. The tiny deception Alfio was suggesting obviously sprang from love and concern for his sister. It was the type of thing Finola or Sorcha would have done for Ursula. Even Caden might, if he'd been feeling particularly empathetic. 'Sure. I like Nanda. I'd have suggested something similar before, but it wouldn't have been fair to leave Marilù with Agata, as she can't pick her up when she cries.' Dinner out would be fun for Ursula, too. None of the students she'd encountered at Fabio Ceramiche had turned into friends, not so much because her Italian was no good but because Fabio taking a special interest in her meant that she tended to work alone. There had been little time for her to develop contacts in Sicily other than the Tringali family and Fabio, and she'd occasionally felt envious of the many laughing, chattering groups in bars and restaurants.

With a grave twinkle, he observed, 'Luckily, I have the strength to lift a six-month-old child.' Then he extracted something from his pocket and held it out to her. 'Allow it to be my pleasure.'

Still absorbing the fact that he'd made a joke about being able to lift a baby, it took her a second to realise he was offering her two fifty-euro notes. 'Oh, no thanks,' she said promptly. Then, because he hadn't been even slightly grumpy during this conversation, she added with a smile, 'I have a thing about paying my own way and I'll enjoy being out with Nanda anyway.'

'I understand.' He put the notes away.

Inwardly, Ursula was impressed. Stephan would have probably snapped, *Can't a man make a perfectly nice gesture without threatening your feminist principles?* Whereas Alfio had indicated his appreciation of there being a financial implication to the favour he'd asked, but then accepted her polite refusal.

In her new life – her post-Stephan, post-divorce, post-overdose life – Ursula kept control of everything possible, especially concerning men she didn't know well. This was not, as Colleen sometimes suggested, a feature of anxiety or depression. It could even be considered a sturdy strategy for *avoiding* anxiety and depression.

'Ursula?'

She realised Alfio must have been speaking. 'Sorry? I was miles away.'

He paused, as if taking a moment to understand the idiom, before going on politely, 'Is it OK to suggest this to Nanda now? It is almost six o'clock.'

'Sure.' She followed him as he went to the polished, dark wood door into his family's home, noting that although she was five feet ten, he was taller.

Politely, he opened the door and ushered her in. For once, Marilù was kicking contentedly on the floor rather than hanging around Nanda's neck, so Nanda was tapping at a laptop while Agata watched the news on the television. All three looked as relaxed as Ursula had ever seen them. 'Nanda,' Alfio began, as they all looked up at the opening of the door. 'I met Ursula in the kitchen. She wants to ask you something.'

Ursula went along with his ruse. 'Just wondering if you'd take pity on a stranger in town and come out for a bite to eat tonight,' she said. Then, realising that 'a bite to eat' translated literally, would sound odd, clarified, 'Go out for dinner, I mean. Your brother has agreed to babysit.'

Immediately, Agata – was she in on Alfio's plan? – chimed in. 'That will be good, Fernanda. You need to relax, and I will be here with Marilù also.'

Nanda looked so surprised that Ursula's heart twisted, knowing the poor woman had barely had an hour away from her baby since the birth, seeing as the bloody husband had skipped. She watched Nanda glance at Alfio, as if assessing him. *You said this? Do you think you'll manage?*

Alfio apparently read the same doubts, as he sank down onto the floor beside Marilù and tickled her chin. 'We'll be fine while your mamma eats a nice meal, won't we, *piccolina*?'

Marilù gave him a four-toothed grin, a smile almost as

71

rare and attractive as his own, Ursula thought. Between her curls and his, the family resemblance was obvious.

Nanda smiled, but said tentatively, 'Just here in Ortigia, perhaps, Ursula? Then I can return if Marilù needs me. And I would like her to be asleep before I leave.'

'Sure,' Ursula agreed equably. 'And we needn't stay out late.' They arranged the details, then Ursula did the mammoth stair run to her attic room, enjoying the airy vaulted stairwell, greeting guests who were either coming or going. They were usually a relaxed, independent crowd because Residenza dei Tringali was popular with the TripAdvisor type who wanted nice accommodation in a great spot but not the nannying that package tour operators went in for.

Once in her room, she took out her phone and flopped on the bed to call her friend Zia in Umbria, central Italy, who was almost obscenely happy with her handsome Italian husband Piero. 'Ursula,' Zia answered the call excitedly. 'Are you still enjoying Sicily? Do you think you'll get away to visit us?'

'In a week or two, maybe,' Ursula replied, smiling just at the sound of her old friend's voice. 'I haven't discussed it yet because the family's worried about the baby's surgery, but the son's here for a while so maybe he can do my jobs if I come.' Time off had never been thrashed out in her arrangement with Agata, but it seemed to her that her request would be a reasonable one. The next half-hour flew, as she told Zia about Fabio and her progress painting sunflowers, and Zia shared details of the swelling breasts and nausea that were characterising her pregnancy.

Then Ursula caught sight of a small, cracked black enamel clock that graced the top of her chest of drawers. 'Whoops,' she exclaimed. 'I'd better shower and change because I'm eating out tonight. Not with a man,' she added, as Zia made an interested noise. 'With Nanda.'

'Disappointing,' Zia complained, before laughingly ending the call.

Ursula got ready, dressing in a red and blue dress she knew suited her. She even put on make-up, which she hadn't done since she arrived.

The evening should be fun.

Nanda was ready just after eight and she and Ursula stepped out into the warm Mediterranean evening. The sea road was one of Ursula's favourite walks. The marina's floating finger pontoons were arranged like a capital letter E where yachts, fishing boats, motorboats and tour boats rolled at their moorings. The fishing boats were especially fun, their generous cargo of coloured floats making them look as if they'd got in the way when some giant hand had been beading.

By far her favourite part was past the marina car park, the wide expanse of paving with cafés under tall trees on one side and the grander boats on the other. The paving was popular with those on electric scooters or bikes that contrasted sharply with the billionaire's playground of superyachts. Some of these stunning floating palaces in grey or white even had security details guarding gangplanks while passengers lounged on upper decks, watching pink dusk fall over the sea. It was fun to check out the home ports lettered on the boats' paintwork, often Douglas on the Isle of Man or Valletta, Malta, and Ursula was fascinated by mooring floats that looked just like plugs from the most enormous sinks.

She turned to Nanda and inspected her well-cut pedal pushers, red top and silver mules. 'You look great,' she said, thinking Nanda could use some encouragement to relax and enjoy a couple of hours off as she'd checked her phone already and they hadn't moved more than a hundred yards from the hotel. It must feel odd to entrust your sick baby to others when you usually spent much of every day tending her yourself.

Nanda gave a self-conscious pat to her dark, upswept hair. '*Grazie*. So do you. This is the first time I've seen you in a dress, I think.'

'First time I've been out properly since I arrived,' Ursula responded, shoring up the slight distortion of the truth she'd agreed on with Alfio. She went 'out' to Fabio's, to the market, to walk or swim; she'd paused at cafés for coffee or beer; but never before 'out out'. 'Where are we going?'

'Not Piazza Duomo,' her friend said decidedly. 'It is for the tourists. We'll go a little further on.' She steered Ursula between the trees to an arch and a set of stone steps that climbed to the street above, which Ursula had only reached before by going through a different, much larger and older arch near the hotel and climbing a steep hill. Here, a row of three-storey, balconied buildings, of faded yet imposing grandeur, gazed over the terrace railings to the bay and the boats below.

Nanda turned into a paved street that was no more than eight feet across, and led the way onwards to another narrow street filled with shops, none of which had yet closed. Many sold ceramics, but they were those designed to appeal to tourists: cheap, cheerful and mass-produced off-island. The ever-popular ceramic heads were much in evidence, from egg-cup size to plant pot. She lost count of the turnings she and Nanda took and the pavement cafés they passed, filled with diners. The restaurant where they eventually ended up was called Trattoria del Mare, a stone structure with a roped-off enclosure of wooden tables and chairs outside. When Ursula caught a glimpse of sea down one of the nearby streets, she realised they had almost crossed the island – not hard as it was little more than six hundred metres at its narrowest point.

Nanda selected a table and began a conversation with two members of serving staff. Ursula only caught occasional references, mainly to '*Mamma*' and '*la bambina*', both of which occasioned concerned expressions. Ursula studied the menu, in no hurry to cut the conversation short while her new friend was so evidently enjoying the simple pleasure of catching up with people she knew.

Then Nanda introduced Ursula, switching to English to say, 'Ursula's helping us this summer. She is very kind.'

Ursula smiled and said, '*Buonasera*,' though feeling slightly uncomfortable about everyone running away with the idea she was kind. She just considered herself a normal human being.

When, at length, the servers returned to serving and Nanda had chosen *pasta alla Norma* and Ursula vongole, and a bottle of Nero d'Avola red had been positioned before them with glasses that glittered in the lights of the restaurant, Nanda glanced around at the busy tables and smiled. 'Thank you for suggesting this. I just worry, worry, worry about Marilù and the *ospedale*.'

Ursula gave her hand a consoling pat. 'Of course. She's so tiny. But the surgeons will be skilled at the procedure.'

Nanda nodded, her fringe lifting in the breeze. 'And Alfio is now coming to the hospital with us. That makes me feel better.'

For the first time, it occurred to Ursula that Alfio had timed his visit for this very reason. Ah, maybe he wasn't so bad. She saw suddenly how she, too, could help. 'I can keep Agata company during the day on Friday, if you like. Fabio has told me to draw a few of my own designs and I can do that at your place while you and your brother are with Marilù.'

Instantly, a smile blazed over Nanda's face. 'Ursula, *grazie mille*. Nino has changed his day off so that Mamma does not have to deal with reception, so now I do not have to worry about her.'

Focused on her own duties in the kitchen and breakfast room, Ursula hadn't even considered reception. A lot of the guests were Brits or Americans, but Sicily was popular with Italians and Maltese, too, and she was severely limited with anyone who didn't speak English. 'Perfect. It's great that your brother can go with you.'

Nanda tilted her head. 'You say "your brother" as if you do not know his name.'

Ursula was taken aback. 'Alfio, of course.' Was she really so off men that she didn't even want to award one the common courtesy of using his name? But she used Fabio's name, and also that of Peppi the water delivery guy. Maybe it was only men of her own age? That instinct to keep them at arm's length?

'There is no man in your life?' Nanda asked curiously.

'There's not,' Ursula confirmed, then noticed the way the surrounding tables were filling up. 'This is definitely a place for the locals, so I'm looking forward to some fabulous food.'

'Oh . . . or a woman?' Nanda persisted, evidently not intending to be sidetracked into a conversation about their fellow diners.

Ursula shrugged the question away. 'No romantic partner,' she said. 'I'm happily divorced.'

With a sympathetic moue, Nanda topped up Ursula's

wine glass. 'I used to be happily married. My husband changed when I was pregnant. It was . . . a shock.'

Ursula took a moment to sip her rich, full-bodied wine. She'd known there had been a husband, that he was English and was called Mason, but neither Nanda nor Agata had said much more. 'Didn't he want to be a father?' Surprise pregnancies happened to lots of people but most coped, once the initial shock was over. They fell in love with their child, and everyone lived happily ever after.

Their meal arrived amid renewed conversation from the server, a woman with her dark hair in a ponytail. Nanda waited until they were alone again before she answered. 'It was strange.' Her voice was pensive. 'Mason and me, we were happy, but the pregnancy was not planned. As my body changed, so did he. He said I no longer attracted him.' Tears glistened in her eyes. 'He was confused and upset by his own reaction, he said, but had no control over it.'

'Oh, Nanda.' Ursula's heart wrenched at her new friend's bleak expression.

'It happens.' Nanda lowered her voice, although the chatter of voices and clinking of cutlery on plates around them must surely have drowned her out. 'Some men go off women during pregnancy. It broke my heart, but I read that it is in here.' She tapped her head. 'A confusion with feelings about mothers; that a man should not feel lust for one. And Mason did not wish to be a father after all.' Her lip wobbled.

Ursula thought about her brother Caden and brother-in-law Dec, who were both mad about their kids. Boring about them, even. Her blood boiled on behalf of this lovely, hurt woman and her helpless child. 'And he left you with a sick child and thought that was OK?'

Nanda stared at her meal, steaming gently on a white

plate. 'He had been back in England for months before she was born.' Her laugh sounded artificial. 'Alfio, he says Mason is weak because he is British. Alfio has left his girlfriend behind in Spain, and she is British too.' She picked up her fork.

Ursula grinned, glad to see a defiant tilt to Nanda's chin. 'I didn't know that about the girlfriend. He thought I was British, so I expect that's why he was so grumpy when we met. I should have explained that my British husband turned his back on me. Maybe we would have got along better.' It was easier to joke about the situation than show Nanda how raw the past couple of years had left her. Instead, as they began to eat, she recounted how she'd left Ireland for England and later visited the Italian region of Umbria, two summers ago, when her friend Zia had been searching for her Italian father. 'Zia found her family, though her father turned out to be far from perfect. I began my interest in ceramics there.'

The conversation moved on to easier subjects. Ursula chatted about her work under Fabio. Nanda, sufficiently relaxed to order both dessert and coffee, talked about her days at university and how she, rather than Alfio, had always been the one to want to carry on Residenza dei Tringali. 'I do not regret, even though I did not expect to be a single mother,' she added.

Not long after, Ursula noticed Nanda checking her phone more often, so affected a yawn. 'Shall we pay? We both have early starts tomorrow.'

Nanda, looking relieved, signalled to a server and soon they were heading back beside a sea so calm that it looked to be made of black oil, reflecting all the lights of *Città Vecchia*. The boats seemed to skate about the surface at their moorings.

Once past the marina, they crossed the road, which was quiet at this time of night, and followed four guests up the steps and through the entrance with 'Residenza dei Tringali' in gold script above. Obviously footsore, the guests joked with them about the stairs before groaning their way up the first marble flight.

Nanda waited until they were out of earshot. 'Last year, a drunk guest fell on the stairs and broke his pelvis. His travel insurance company tried to blame us, but we sent evidence of guests being clearly informed that we have no lift and pictures of the handrails and safety notices. They accepted that drinking alcohol was a risk the guest took upon himself.'

'You're obviously on top of the job,' Ursula observed. Then she added, 'I'll just come into the kitchen to check whether I switched on the dishwasher at the end of breakfast. Then I'll head up to my room.'

They found Alfio reading at the central island, a glass of grappa and the baby monitor at his elbow. He studied Nanda and then smiled, presumably pleased by what he saw. 'Mamma and *la bambina* are both sleeping.'

Nanda dropped her arms around his neck in a sisterly hug. '*Grazie, grazie,* Alfio.' Then she gave Ursula a hasty peck on each cheek and took the baby monitor into the apartment.

Alfio gestured politely to the grappa. '*Un digestivo,* Ursula?'

Ursula eyed the open bottle. 'Not for me, but thanks. Nanda seemed fine, by the way. Great for her to have time off. It was a good idea.'

Without giving him time to say more than brief thanks for her part in the evening, she checked the dishwasher had run then left, hoping he didn't come to his room just

79

yet because she wanted a few minutes on her balcony, one eye on her Kindle and the other on the bats that flitted across the night sky.

She'd enjoyed her foray into Ortigia's nightlife, but now she was ready for peace – and somehow, Alfio Tringali and his searching manner never made her feel peaceful.

Chapter Six

On Friday morning, Alfio was awake even earlier than usual in the cramped single bed that was all that would fit into his room, aware that he and an understandably nervous Nanda were scheduled to get Marilù to the hospital at seven a.m. ready for surgery.

They were to take Nanda's car. If he stayed in Sicily, he'd buy his own. *If*. He stared at himself in the mirror above the basin as he shaved. What would he be doing now if he'd never decided he should come home? Never had the nightmare about Papà? Never begun the conversation with Hettie that had led to them breaking up? He wouldn't be supporting Nanda through this; that was for sure. And she needed – no, *deserved* – his support.

He dressed quickly, gathered up his wallet and phone and then jogged down the familiar stairs, knowing every bump and dip in the grey-veined marble, crossing the lobby, the hall and the empty kitchen before entering the apartment and hearing a whimpering cry from behind the door of his old room, and Nanda's answering coo.

Poor little Marilù, who must always feel weak and empty when she couldn't keep food in her tiny stomach. A few unpleasant days lay ahead for her, but then she should make progress.

If Mamma would improve too, he could reassess his life and decide what to do next. He'd allow a month, he decided, needing to bring purpose to his life in place of his current aimlessness. A month should give him some idea of how things were going. He'd make himself useful doing the jobs that Mason used to do, like replace the mortar coming out of the courtyard wall and grout from the floors of the upstairs landings, help Nanda in the office and on reception. He might even paint his room to cheer it – and himself – up.

He paused. How long could Nanda and Agata keep the hotel going, after this difficult summer?

Might they agree to selling up now? If so, he might stay to help ensure the hotel was back on its feet financially and therefore more attractive to buyers. It would mean a couple of years out of his life, but it was possible . . .

He looked around at the salon he'd known all his life. Would leaving the hotel free up the Tringali family to live lives of their own choosing?

Or would it destroy their anchor to Ortigia and Sicily? To Domenico, who had loved them all? Domenico's parents had helped look after Alfio and Nanda, as Domenico and Agata had taken over the daily running, and Alfio had nothing but good memories of the couple. Would he lose the feeling of connection he still had with those loving grandparents?

Interrupting his thoughts, the door to Marilù's room opened and Nanda emerged, an overnight bag on her shoulder as she'd be staying with Marilù. On her other shoulder, the baby cuddled up to her mother's neck, pale and unsmiling.

Seeing the bleakness of Nanda's expression, Alfio abandoned thoughts of winding up the family business and pinned on a big, encouraging smile. 'Time to bring good health to this little one, yes?'

Nanda nodded, pale and anxious. '*Sì*. It's time.'

Agata came out of her own room, a light wrap over her nightclothes, her normally neat hair messy.

'You didn't need to get up,' Alfio chided her gently, though he knew his mother probably hadn't slept any better than he had.

Agata pinned on a smile as falsely cheerful as his own. 'I want to say goodbye. Be good, Marilù, and soon you will be well.' She stroked Marilù's cheek with the backs of her fingers and the baby smiled.

Alfio and Nanda kissed their mother and went out to Nanda's car, which didn't look as if it had been washed for a year. Sicily was dry and dusty in summer and few people wasted water on a vehicle that would be dirty again in a week.

Nanda was shaking, and handed him the key without protest while she slipped Marilù into her car seat.

Once they were pulling out of the courtyard into Via Duca degli Abruzzi, Alfio glanced across at his sister's set face. 'Have you told him what's happening?'

He didn't have to clarify who 'him' was. Nanda nodded. 'He messaged to say he hoped it went well.' Her hair was loose today, hanging dully past her shoulders.

His hands tightened on the wheel. 'No call?' *Bastardo*.

'We don't call. You know that.' Nanda turned to gaze out of the window as the buildings of Ortigia passed by.

Alfio could have cried to think of the scrap of humanity

in the car seat behind him, who'd spent most of her short life unwell. One day, that little innocent would realise that her papà didn't want her. Nanda would be the one to deal with that, just as she dealt with everything. 'He should make an exception when his daughter is going to hospital.'

Nanda gave a long sigh. 'He sends money.'

Alfio snorted.

So began a long, stressful day. Once they'd parked the car and found their way in the sterile corridors of the hospital, Alfio stayed close while Nanda underwent the procedure of admitting Marilù by her full name of Maria Louisa Robertson. She became increasingly wobbly as tiny Marilù was examined, stripped to her *pannolino* – for which the English word was the faintly comical 'nappy' – and answered what felt like the same questions from different medical professionals and repeated several times that Alfio was Marilù's uncle, not her father.

He was glad to be there to hold Nanda's hand as they finally wheeled her baby away, because she shouldn't be alone. Then they waited in a cubicle-sized room, Nanda withdrawn and silent.

Alfio's mind circled back to his earlier thoughts. Even if Agata conquered her current issues, she couldn't go on at the hotel forever. What then?

Alfio had never wanted to be a hotelier.

It had been planned that Mason would one day leave his job and take over from Agata to run the place with Nanda. Would Nanda want complete responsibility for Residenza dei Tringali, even when Marilù was older and in better health? Agata had carried on alone after losing Domenico, but Alfio had been eighteen and Nanda sixteen. Alfio's grandparents had still been around. They'd all shared one grief; and they'd pulled together.

84

Well, the others had, he thought uncomfortably. Alfio had gone to university.

Today, he couldn't be anything other than glad that Ursula Quinn had come to Residenza dei Tringali, no doubt clearing breakfast at this very moment. Otherwise, he and Agata would have had to decide who was to come with Nanda and who to look after the guests, though Agata wasn't really fit for either task. It was hard to know who they could have asked to take over breakfast duties, unless they could have trained someone from the cleaning staff. Their workforce was cut to the bone.

He pictured his mother's pallor as she'd waved them off earlier, a brave smile overlying her worry. She'd lived with Marilù, her *nipotina*, since the baby was born, when Nanda gave up her apartment and moved in so she and her mother could support each other.

If only Agata's recovery from her own health issues wasn't so slow, he thought. She was still drawn and lethargic. Fear quaked through him in case there was something that wasn't healing inside his mother, or something fresh brewing up. Agata had been both parents to him since he was a youth and the idea of losing her clawed at his heart.

She hadn't even found love again until Ursula's father, and he, Stanley, had hurt her.

Abruptly, he asked Nanda, 'Did you ever meet Ursula's father? Mamma said he has visited her in Sicily.'

She shook her head. 'I was dealing with Mason leaving the first time and the second time I was a few weeks from giving birth.' There was a snap in her voice that told Alfio that now was not the time for this conversation.

He subsided. He was here to support Nanda and *la*

bambina, not work himself up about Stanley Quinn or Residenza dei Tringali. The past couldn't be changed, and it wasn't quite time to plan the future.

Time dragged by. Alfio left the waiting room to hunt down coffee and Nanda's fingers shook around her cup when he passed it to her. To distract her from her anxious thoughts, Alfio said, 'You enjoyed your evening out with Ursula? You must have felt as if you were in prison lately.' He knew that she didn't take Marilù out much, because the baby could normally be counted on to throw up over herself and her buggy.

Nanda swallowed a sip of coffee. 'She's a nice woman. It was good of her to stay with Mamma while you're with me. We should get her a gift.' Then she smiled. 'Not too expensive, or she won't accept. She's firm about things like that.'

He remembered Ursula refusing the euros he'd tried to press on her to pay for her evening with Nanda. 'She does seem prickly.'

'Prickly?' Nanda's dark eyes widened as they turned on him. 'I think she finds it difficult to trust. Probably it comes from whatever happened with her husband.'

He hesitated. Had he known there was a husband? His life had been so disjointed and odd lately that he may have assumed Ursula to be single, as she was alone in Sicily. 'She's married?'

'Divorced.' Nanda screwed up her forehead. 'I think she's bitter about it, though she hides it. I wouldn't be surprised if she hides a lot. I suspect Mamma knows more, that Ursula's father told Mamma some things, and that's part of why she said "yes" to her coming to us.'

He mused on this. 'That does sound like Mamma.' He sighed. 'I thought Mamma was going to be happy with this Stanley. I resent him for letting her down.'

Nanda put down her coffee, hugging herself as if cold, though the room was stuffy and hot. 'I thought I was going to be happy with Mason. You thought you were going to be happy with Hettie. We can't be angry with them all.'

'I can,' he declared with a comical grimace.

At least that made Nanda laugh. Then, finally, a smiling nurse entered. 'Would you like to come down with me to collect your daughter? The operation went very well. She's awake but sore, so don't worry if she cries. She'll soon be much better.'

Nanda jumped up as if her heels were springs and abandoned Alfio, wiping her eyes on the backs of her hands as she hurried out in the nurse's wake. He remained in his seat until such time as he was called to rejoin Nanda and Marilù.

While he waited, Nanda's words floated back to him. *You thought you were going to be happy with Hettie.*

He wondered what Hettie had thought.

It was late afternoon when Alfio finally left the hospital smells behind and drove home in Nanda's small car, its size suited to the narrow streets of Siracusa.

Nanda's shoulders had relaxed, and though her brow puckered when Marilù cried or grasped at the tube in her nose that was feeding her, the nurses had shown her how to cradle her baby to avoid the small incisions. Marilù had already had a feed of some modified solution and hadn't vomited at all. It was illogical to call planned surgery 'a miracle' but it felt like one.

Alfio couldn't believe how tired he was. All he'd done was sit about in hospital rooms and corridors, periodically updating Agata by text. Now, after battling the traffic between the hospital and Residenza dei Tringali – which took longer than mere distance indicated it should – he parked in the courtyard and crossed to where the double doors to the kitchen stood open.

He stepped in, letting his eyes adjust to the artificial light. His mother was seated at the counter flicking through some books, while Ursula, in a cotton dress, washed salad leaves at the sink.

The instant his mother noticed him, she broke off the conversation. 'Alfio, Marilù is still doing well?'

He crossed towards her and kissed her cheeks. 'She just needs to heal, and you can visit her tomorrow,' he confirmed. He glanced at Ursula with a smile. '*Buonasera.*'

'*Buonasera*,' she returned, flicking a lock of blonde hair from her face. 'I didn't get all of that Italian but I'm glad Marilù's going to be all right.'

Agata returned to her stool, and Alfio dropped onto the one beside her, watching as Ursula continued slicing tomatoes and shredding basil, tossing the gleaming red and green together in olive oil, dropping handfuls of rice into one pan and frying chicken with mushrooms and onions in another. A heap of Parmesan shavings stood beside a pot of cream. The aromas stealing across the kitchen were delicious.

His stomach and his conscience suffered simultaneous pangs at how prickly their previous conversations had been, and how much of that was his fault. It was about time he gave her the benefit of the doubt and accepted that not only was Ursula not responsible for her father's sins, but that she had no idea what they were. 'Dare I hope there's enough food there for me, Ursula?' Her name felt full of curved syllables on his tongue.

She glanced over her shoulder. 'I made plenty for us all. It'll be ready in twenty minutes.'

He was accustomed to eating much later but there would be no complaints from him. Her movements were quick and economical, her legs tanned where they showed beneath her light denim dress, her feet bare, her nails painted blue. As she reached across the counter for something the broad strap of her dress shifted, allowing him a glimpse of tiny pink jewels inked on her skin. Her tattoos were therefore not confined to those swirling up her arm. Where else, he wondered?

His mother gave him a sharp nudge. 'Look.'

He dragged his gaze away from Ursula and turned it instead to the books his mother had been perusing, which were full of pencil sketches of sunflowers and lemons. Finely executed dark patterns ran along the lower edge of each page, swooping lines and sharp angles that created intricate knots.

With a jolt, he recognised the patterns and motifs. His gaze flew to Ursula's body art. The designs looked to be created by the same talented hand. 'Did you draw these?' he demanded in astonishment, and then wondered at his own surprise. If she was studying painting on ceramics, then it made sense for her to have artistic ability.

She paused, tomatoes in a dark blue dish in one hand and salad leaves in a white one. 'Yes. It's my homework from Fabio – making traditional designs my own.'

'They're good,' he said inadequately, eyes drawn back to the sketchpad before him.

'*Fantastico*,' Agata corrected him.

'*Fantastico*,' he echoed. 'You're an artist in England? I knew you were visiting a ceramics studio while you were here but somehow, I didn't realise . . .' He tailed off, seeing that no one without serious talent would go to the trouble of moving her life to another country to study. Agata had told him quite a bit about Ursula, but all he'd listened to was who Ursula's father was.

'Since uni, I've been a tattoo artist.' She turned back to the hob to stir the rice and then take down shallow bowls with wide rims from a cupboard. She caught his gaze on her arm and grinned. 'I didn't do my own tattoos, obviously, but Lou, my boss, did them from my designs. You're shocked?'

No. Fascinated. But he answered with a more neutral, 'Surprised. I have never talked to a tattoo artist. I suppose I thought you bought in templates to apply to the skin and ink over. I did not consider talent.' Lately, he didn't seem to be thinking clearly at all.

'My designs have always been bespoke and freehand.' With a swish, she took the pan of chicken and mushroom from the heat to slowly stir in the cream and then the cheese.

He tried to imagine her with one of the drill-like contraptions he'd seen tattooists use on television, stooping close over the skin of strangers. Making them bleed. It went with what he'd seen of her personality – creative and sensitive, but prepared to do what was needed, like standing up to him when he'd been awkward. While she drained the rice and combined it with the sauce, he continued to turn the pages, comparing her sketches with the designs in the reference books also open on the table, faded and dog-eared with age.

Ursula carried over the food. 'The reference books are Fabio's. I've been allowed to borrow them if I treat them as if they're made of spun gold.'

He had never come across spun gold, but he presumed it must be both delicate and valuable. 'You must return them to him?'

Regretfully, she nodded, setting out the three flat bowls and offering a serving spoon to Agata. 'Fabio's students refer to them, but the books aren't usually allowed out of the studio.'

Nanda had said they should buy Ursula a gift. Now he knew what it should be. 'They're very expensive?' he queried, remembering that Nanda had also said that Ursula wouldn't accept anything too valuable.

'Just difficult to replace, maybe.' She nudged the risotto dish his way to indicate that he should serve himself and picked up her own food, taking a step towards the door.

Noticing, he said, 'You are not to eat with us?'

'I thought you might prefer to be alone with your mother.' Her gaze shifted away from Alfio as she spoke. He knew that she'd eaten with the family before his arrival, and it gave him a chilly feeling to realise that he must therefore be the reason she'd been taking her meals up to her room. He had, to quote an accusation Hettie sometimes levelled at him, been acting like an overemotional jerk.

'Please,' he said, feeling like a clumsy teenager. 'Join us.'

Ursula still hesitated.

'Sit, sit,' broke in Agata, gently scolding. 'You have prepared a lovely meal. Let us enjoy it together. Alfio, the wine.'

He rose and fetched a bottle of red wine from another of the cool nooks that led off the kitchen and, after a second, Ursula took a seat. 'OK. Thanks.'

He poured the wine, allowing himself only a small measure as he expected to return to the hospital that evening to give Nanda a meal break.

They ate, Agata and Ursula talking about the next day's shopping and how to vary the bakery order. It was soothing, in its own way, the business of the hotel going on as ever, even though those conducting it might change.

In a pause in the conversation, he smiled at Ursula. 'This risotto is delicious. Are you sure you don't have Italian blood?'

She rolled her eyes. 'Not unless there's something vital that my parents aren't telling me.'

A momentary pause. He caught his mother's widened eyes. No, Ursula couldn't know about the liaison between their parents, or she would surely have steered away from such a comment.

After the meal, Agata made espresso. Nanda called to tell Alfio that Marilù was sleeping in short bursts. 'I'll drive back now to watch over her while you eat,' he said, relieved to hear some of the worry had left his sister's voice. He passed the phone to Agata so she could hear further assurances that Marilù was doing well, while he drained his cup.

Then he saw Ursula slip away into the courtyard. Curious, he followed her and found her watching the stray cat eat delicately from a bowl. She was a little like the stray cat herself, he caught himself thinking, her with designs on her skin and the cat with a coat of patchy colours, both slender and graceful. From the matching glances they threw his way, both were wary, too.

Ursula's voice carried on the still air of dusk. 'I'm only giving her kitchen scraps – the bits of chicken off the carcass.'

'She's welcome to them,' he said, feeling faintly surprised that she'd sound defensive about such a small matter. Then his conscience twanged again. He'd been short with Ursula so many times that now she was waiting for him to find fault. He paused to lean on the car roof, the key dangling from his hand. 'Thanks again for staying with Mamma today. It took the weight off our minds while we focused on Marilù. And please join the family for meals, just as before I arrived. You are welcome.'

'Oh,' she said. 'Thank you.'

As he said goodnight and got into the little Fiat, he wished she hadn't sounded so surprised.

In the narrow streets he knew so well, he wove through traffic that had thinned into evening mode, with people strolling the pavements and tables outside brightly lit bars. He let down the windows and propped his elbow on the opening, enjoying the warm air. It was, despite everything, good to be home.

Back inside the hospital, he made his way quickly through the corridors to the children's ward where Marilù lay, squirming slightly in her sleep, the feeding tube running into her tiny button nose.

Nanda rose, stretching her back. Her hair was dishevelled, and her trousers creased, but her fatigue looked a healthier kind of tiredness than the pinched anxiety of earlier in the day. He smiled down at her and then his niece. 'It's easy to love your tiny daughter. She's beautiful. Soon, she'll be able to enjoy food and have a fully belly, like anyone else.'

With a laugh, Nanda hugged him. 'I will only be happy when she's fat.' Then she left for a well-earned break, clutching her phone and leaving him with firm instructions that he should call if Marilù woke and cried.

Alfio took his sister's vacated seat and fished out his own phone, opening the web browser. He found a bewildering offering of books about ceramics, none of them bearing any resemblance to the aged volumes he'd seen today. He performed a different search, this time looking for a Fabio Iacobello who taught ceramics in Siracusa.

He needed to find out how to buy the right book for Ursula.

Chapter Seven

Ursula had stayed away from Fabio's studio over the weekend so that she could support the Tringalis while one family member or another was at the hospital. Now, Monday, she left the sunlight behind as she slipped quietly inside the studio, trying not to disturb the class of five in progress. The other students glanced at her as she took up her place at the workbench that she'd made her own, beneath one of the high-set windows. She knew no one in this group. Her cohort had come and gone, while she followed her own programme under Fabio.

As soon as she took out her things, Fabio finished with a thin, dark, middle-aged female student who glumly binned one white tile and took up another, and then he lumbered across to take Ursula's sketchbook from her. '*Buongiorno*,' he rumbled. Slowly, the pages turned in his large hands as he inspected her designs, no doubt preparing to give her a thorough critique, she thought, as she unpacked the reference books that he'd lent her and replaced them on a shelf, careful not to add fresh marks to their scuffed covers.

Gruffly, he asked, '*E la bambina?*'

Ursula, having known the big heart beneath his cantankerous crust would mean he'd enquire, had readied an answer in Italian. '*Sta migliorando. L'operazione è andata bene.*' She's improving. The operation was a success.

His eyes smiled. '*Bene.*' Minutes passed as he moved forward and back between the pages, studying each drawing several times. Ursula found her heart speeding, as if she was back at school or university. Even the other students had fallen silent, casting looks her way, plainly curious about the status of the blonde foreigner. Dust motes danced in the sunlight that streamed in through the windows and it felt as if the whole room was holding its breath.

Then Fabio burst into a roar of laughter, making Ursula jump. He tapped the paper and pointed to her skin. '*I tuoi tatuaggi!*' Your tattoos. 'Good, very good.' Another laugh rumbled out, jiggling his capacious belly.

Ursula laughed, too, gratified that he'd caught the way she'd chosen to bring something of herself to the traditional subjects for ceramic painting and charmed at hearing laughter pour from this growly bear of a man.

With a mixture of Italian and English and a few recourses to Google Translate, they discussed the drawings. He checked that she was the originator of the designs inked on her skin and was therefore not 'borrowing' anyone else's work. In the creative industries, it was OK to be inspired by someone else's design but disrespectful to steal it.

Finally, they decided on a design to transfer to a bowl that was shallow with a broad rim, like the ones they ate pasta from at Residenza dei Tringali. Lemons and leaves would go on the flat interior of the bowl, and her pattern based on triquetra knots would form the border. The triquetra was a circle linked through a motif of curves meeting at three corners, a symbol of strength.

'Very complex. Very good,' Fabio said, which was positively gushing by his standards.

For the rest of the afternoon she was absorbed, taking painstaking measurements so her linked triquetra knots would be perfectly even, and then practising on paper. Suddenly, she realised that only she and Fabio were left in the cool studio, and she hadn't noticed the other students leaving. She stopped and stretched. 'Wow, it's nearly seven in the evening. I'm surprised you haven't thrown me out, Fabio.'

Fabio shrugged, though he cast a longing look at the bar across the square where Ursula knew he often took his evening meal.

After tidying her workstation, she swung her bag on her shoulder, feeling light with joy that Fabio had liked and enjoyed her designs, and filled with a sense of accomplishment that she'd soon be able to try the whole design on a bowl for Fabio's critique. It didn't matter that dinner would be late at Residenza dei Tringali tonight – late for her, anyway. Italians seemed happy to eat well into the evening.

'*Aspetta*. Wait,' Fabio rumbled. With a curiously pleased expression, he brought out two ten-euro notes from the pocket of his old denim shorts and then handed them to her.

She frowned down at the brown banknotes in confusion. 'What's this for, Fab?'

His eyes twinkled. 'The five plates of yours I fired. I showed them to the owner of a shop in Ortigia and she bought them. It is your money.'

Oh. Ursula felt like a deflating balloon, all the pleasure

and fulfilment leaching from the afternoon. She sank back onto her seat. 'What are the rules about this?'

'Rules?' He squinted at her, plainly puzzled.

She tried to explain. 'If I'm under your tutelage, do you automatically own my work?' When he frowned in perplexity, she took out her phone to try to overcome the language barrier. Pulling up a translation app, she typed: *If they were my designs, painted by me, on materials I'd paid for, didn't I own the plates? Or did you own them because you supervised me?*

Fabio rubbed his chin as he read the Italian translation. He nodded in comprehension but then shrugged, his hands spread wide. 'The money.' He indicated it. 'All the money for you. Your money for your plates.'

'I know.' She turned to the translation app again. *I'm not saying you cheated me. It's about choice. You took my choice away, because you didn't consult me.*

Understanding dawned in his eyes, and with it sorrow. Stiffly, he said, '*Mia dispiace. Hai ragione.*' *I'm sorry. You're right.* 'I should ask you, but I think it will be a good surprise.'

Ursula forced a smile. 'Of course. I understand. Thank you.' After a moment's consideration, she took the money. It would make the tension worse not to and, if nothing else, the modest nature of the payment would remind her that she'd have to get a hell of a lot faster at painting plates if she ever wanted to make enough money to live on.

It was a subdued goodnight, and then she crossed the square to Viale Teocrito on a homeward journey that felt a slog tonight. Finally reaching Ponte Santa Lucia, she paused on the bridge to watch the sunset setting fire to the water of the marina and painting yachts and motorboats in hues of pink and lavender. Two men and a woman were busy on board a fishing boat tied side-on to the quay. A ferry moored at the mouth of the canal looked workmanlike and white uniformed figures were waving passengers on board.

Her heart was telling her that she could have handled the Fabio situation more graciously. A lot more.

Uncertain and unsettled, she tried to order her thoughts. She still paid for tutelage, though it was a modest sum now, but in her view, and in law, she felt firmly in the right.

On the other hand, the older man had been nothing but kind to her in his brusque, growly way . . . and she'd upset him.

It might have been better just to smile and be pleased at her first sale. He'd meant well—

No, she scolded herself. Smiling and being pleased was a cop-out. It was out of order to sell other people's original work unless the creator was clearly an employee. Ursula *wasn't* employed by Fabio. She *had* created the plates. Disposal of them was her decision.

But uncertainty was a chilly companion.

Slowly, dragging her feet, she completed the last few hundred yards to the main entrance of Residenza dei Tringali, finding Alfio at the big reception desk, hair tousled as he stared at the computer screen.

'*Buonasera,*' she said, as she passed him en route for the kitchen, intending to get straight on with the meal.

'*Buonasera.*' He smiled. He was getting quite good at smiles, now. 'I'm hoping you like lasagne because I've made enough for us all. *La bambina è a casa.*'

Her spirits rose a notch. 'Marilù is home? And you've cooked?'

'I cook.' He assumed a mock-injured air. 'Perhaps very well.'

Ursula swung her bag from her shoulder – much lighter without Fabio's reference books – and said, hastily, 'Of course. Sorry.' Then her phone began to ring. She took it out and read the screen. *Unknown number*. 'Crap,' she muttered. Then, seeing Alfio's black brows lifting, she added, 'It's an unknown number. I never like to answer them.' After going to all the trouble of blocking so many people from the old days, she meant.

After that annoying call from Charlotte five days ago, she'd blocked everyone she used to know in Brighton who might be considered friends of Stephan – which really only left a handful of her own friends such as her old colleagues: Lou, Cali and Radic. Stephan intruding via Charlotte had made her feel watched, especially as Charlotte had noticed the ringtone that Ursula wasn't in the UK. She couldn't imagine how anyone would track her to Siracusa, but shutting off avenues of contact still felt right. Why shouldn't she make herself feel as comfortable as possible in Sicily?

'Then don't answer,' Alfio suggested easily. 'Probably advertising.'

'Yeah. You're right.' The ringing stopped and she stuffed the handset back in her pocket. By the time she'd made her attic room and thrown her bag on the bed, however, the unknown number had tried twice more. She sighed. When it rang a fourth time, she caved in and answered with a discouraging, 'Yes?'

'Ursula,' said a familiar voice, the friendly, eager, female voice that belonged to her ex-mother-in-law. 'I've had ever such a job getting through, dear. I've had to borrow my friend Carole's phone. There must be something wrong with mine.'

'Hello, Claudia,' Ursula murmured, silently cursing Claudia's problem-solving skills. Ursula had had no compunction in blocking Stephan's relatives. His parents lived in the north-east of England, right up past Newcastle, a long way from Brighton, so it wasn't as if they'd formed a close enough relationship to remain friendly when her marriage ended badly.

Now, after polite enquiries about health, Claudia got down to business. 'I just wanted to talk to you about my dad's ring, pet.'

Ursula jumped in. 'I don't have it. I'm sorry if Stephan's mislaid his grandpa's ring, but I don't have it.'

'You see,' Claudia steamed on blithely, 'it's valuable. I gave it to Stephan when he graduated from university. We must have it back.'

'I. Don't. Have. It.' Ursula ground her teeth.

'If you'd just check—'

'There's no point. I've never had it. Stephan always kept it in a box of his own things. I'm sorry, but I'm afraid I have to go now,' Ursula gabbled. 'Bye.'

She ended the call, hurled the phone onto the bed and vented a long, loud string of swear words, ending with an infuriated: 'That gobshite.'

It took her a good ten minutes to calm down. Then she remembered being promised lasagne and opened her door.

Alfio's door opened at almost the same moment. He quirked one eyebrow in her direction. 'Are you OK?'

She quirked an eyebrow of her own. 'Any reason I shouldn't be?'

'No.' He shrugged and motioned her to go ahead of him on the stairs. 'But I wonder what a "gobshite" is.'

Heat rushed to her face, and she had to stifle a giggle.

101

'Ah . . . you heard me swearing. Sorry. I suppose a gobshite is someone who talks shit.'

He laughed, then moved up alongside her as they reached the wider staircase, wishing '*Buonasera,*' to a woman wearing a blue backpack and a weary frown, presumably wending her way back to her room after a long day around the historical sights of Ortigia.

It wasn't until they'd nearly reached the lofty lobby with its ornate light fittings that Alfio spoke again. 'I do not want to intrude, but twice I have witnessed you receive a phone call and be upset. If my family can help you, please let us know.'

It was probably because he offered his family's services rather than suggesting himself as the purveyor of strength and support, but Ursula found herself responding. 'My bloody ex is trying to wind me up via friends and family. Annoy me,' she clarified, in case 'wind me up' wasn't plain enough English.

'Ah,' he said, understandingly, as they swung around the foot of the mighty staircase and headed past the breakfast room, in the direction of the kitchen. 'We all have at least one ex we still think of.'

'I don't think of him,' she protested. 'At least, I don't *want* to think of him, but he keeps finding ways to force his way into my head. Exactly what he's bloody after.' In some ways, she wished she had his mouldy old ring so she could send it back to him and shut him up.

'Rude of him,' he said solemnly, holding the hall door for her. Once in the kitchen, he went straight to the stainless-steel oven, from which issued a mouth-watering aroma of cheese and herbs.

Agata emerged from the apartment with her usual calm

102

smile. 'We are to eat, Alfio? The smell of lasagne is driving me mad.'

Alfio turned away from the oven, oven cloths in each hand, cradling a large orange dish topped with melted cheese, rich tomato sauce bubbling through at the corners. He placed it at the centre of the island, but Agata motioned him towards the apartment. 'I have laid the table in the apartment to celebrate Marilù's homecoming.' She held the door open expectantly, so Alfio picked the dish up again and followed. Ursula did the same.

The dining table, through an arch to a room off the salon, proved to be covered in a snowy tablecloth, and Ursula made a mental note to lean well over her dish so as not to freckle that impressive field of white with tomato sauce. Yellow napkins made a pretty contrast to gleaming cutlery and glassware. Red and white wine stood in the centre of the table – Ursula nudged the white away from the lasagne dish as she liked hers cold – and delicate white plates with elegant gold borders stood at each place.

Nanda appeared, closing a door quietly behind her. 'Marilù is sleeping,' she whispered. Then, to Ursula, '*Buonasera*. I am glad you can join us. We are so grateful that you changed plans to help Mamma while we had to be at the hospital.'

Alfio, who'd vanished back into the kitchen, reappeared, balancing bowls of salad and bread on his hands like a waiter. 'We all thank you,' he said formally.

'I will be well again soon,' Agata murmured, as if feeling that she wasn't keeping her end up by needing someone else to undertake her duties. She'd already taken her seat, though, as if her legs were glad to be relieved of her slight weight.

Ursula sat too, feeling conspicuous under their combined scrutiny. 'Don't mention it. Glad to help.'

Agata, however, clearly wasn't minded not to mention it. She regarded Ursula with a sweet smile. 'It was not the arrangement that you give up your afternoons to us as well as the mornings, and many evenings you cook as well. We have for you a small gift.'

Ursula glanced around at them all in surprise, feeling her cheeks heat. None of them had begun the delicious-looking lasagne that was steaming in the centre of the big table. 'Ah, that wasn't necessary, honestly.'

But Nanda produced a square, flat object wrapped in delicately printed wrapping paper and Ursula couldn't suppress a 'Wow,' at the sight of such a prettily wrapped gift. Trying not to damage the ribbon or paper overmuch under the weight of three expectant gazes, she slipped her finger under the tape. Inside she found a black box. And inside that was a slightly scuffed, lovingly used book on Sicilian ceramics, similar to those Fabio had lent her. The scent of the old paper tickled her nose even over the rich smell of lasagne. 'Ohhhh,' she breathed. 'That's fantastic.'

'Fabio Iacobello told us the shop to buy it from,' Nanda said, pulling the lasagne dish to where Agata could reach it. 'Alfio found him on the internet.'

'Thank you all so much.' Ursula opened the cover and looked at the stream of Italian on the inside flap. 'My language skills aren't up to reading this yet, but it's the pictures that will be valuable. Really, you needn't have but I'm very grateful.'

Agata pushed the salad bowl closer to her. 'A used book is an odd gift, I think.'

'But perfect,' Ursula hastened to assure her as she carefully returned the book to the protection of the black box.

'When I asked Fabio about books like this, I thought he said they were expensive.'

Alfio took up her plate and cut a slice of lasagne onto it, obviously growing impatient waiting for her before he felt able to serve himself. 'Translation issues, perhaps? No doubt he thought you meant a new book.'

That made sense, though Ursula said, 'Or perhaps he had a poor idea of how much money I have.' They all laughed, before settling down to their meal.

Helping himself to Parmesan, Alfio told his family, 'Ursula has taught me an Irish swear word. Gobshite.'

'The UK uses that word too,' she admitted with a twinkle. 'But I think it was ours first.' She explained the meaning, and Nanda and Agata laughed.

Relaxing as they chatted, she enjoyed herself even more than she had when she and Nanda had eaten at Trattoria del Mare at the beginning of the week.

She supposed she wouldn't see her own family this summer, so it was lovely to be included with the Tringalis.

It was late in the evening and Nanda was now Alfio's only companion in the dining room.

Agata had been ready for bed at ten and Ursula had seemed to take it as a signal that she should go to her own quarters. She was always up at six to deal with breakfast, of course. Alfio usually got up early, too, as Nanda couldn't leave Agata and Marilù alone together. Nanda was fading yet had declared herself too tired to move. Alfio was just beginning to think about his own bed when his phone rang, and his heart put in an extra beat.

It was the ringtone that he'd allocated to Hettie.

Hettie and Barcelona seemed far away. It was only a

week ago that he'd come home to Sicily but, including the month it had taken to wind up his life in Spain, it was over five weeks since he'd heard from the woman who'd shared his life. '*Scusa*,' he said to his sister. Wanting to take the call without being overheard, he said into the phone, 'Just a moment,' before leaving through the kitchen, the hall and across the lobby to the main entrance onto the seafront.

Over the road was a bench, and he sank down onto it, looking into the marina through the few cars left into the car park. 'This is unexpected,' he said into the phone, feeling odd to be speaking to Hettie again.

Hesitantly, she said, 'I just want to talk to you.'

'I'm flattered,' he muttered.

A pause. Then she said in a small voice, 'And by "flattered" you mean angry? About what happened, I mean.'

He pictured the doll-like blonde curls and blue eyes that he'd fallen for. 'You're entitled to end a relationship,' he said stiffly. 'It took me by surprise, I admit.' Understatement. He'd been stunned. Broken-hearted? Perhaps not, but it had sent him reeling. He waited, silently, for her to continue.

Hettie drew in an audible breath. 'I'm just going to say this, OK? I think I might have been hasty. I'm missing you. Maybe ours was the one relationship that was worth giving things up for. I should have tried.'

In the loud silence, Alfio processed her words, rehearing them in his mind. He looked out over the lights of the marina and the sea smoothly lapping at the boats, listening to the scratchy sound of the movement of the rigging. He'd grown up with the sea in all its moods, swum, fished, rowed or paddled. It was unpredictable, as they'd all discovered when it had taken Domenico's life. Hettie was unpredictable too, but when she'd left their relationship – hurled herself out of it as if leaping for her life, in fact – it hadn't ever occurred to him that she'd change her mind. 'What things would you be giving up?' he asked curiously.

'You know,' she answered, as if he was being deliberately obtuse. 'Freedom and independence. The single life.'

Her answer nettled him. 'I thought we were in a relationship, so I had not realised you had been single recently.' When she didn't answer, he added, 'Or that you would see being with me as giving up what you value.'

Another silence. Then Hettie ventured, 'Have you missed me?'

Alfio pondered. 'At first,' he answered cautiously. Then, in the whirl of arriving back in Ortigia, helping Nanda with Marilù and trying to find a role for himself at Residenza dei Tringali, it had been much less.

In a low voice, she said, 'I miss you. I'm not over you. I've tried to be.'

'Yet you use freedom and independence as weapons,' he snapped. It occurred to him fleetingly that Ursula used them as defence. Did women really *need* to keep pointing these things out as important? The suspicion that they did, while his gender took them for granted, went some way to making him add more gently, 'I do not think I have ever tried to take those things from you.'

Hettie groaned aloud. 'I'm a commitment-phobe. When you suddenly suggested I go off with you to your home – I suppose it scared me. But being without you has been horrible.'

A group of people wandered by, chatting. Two called goodnight, broke away and strolled up the floating pontoon to a motorboat. The rest carried on, to be swallowed up by the darkness. Cars swished along the road behind Alfio, and one sounded its horn. The humid evening broke sweat across his brow and he wiped it absently. 'I'm still in Sicily, Hettie.'

After a pause, she asked, 'Will you come back to Barcelona when your mother's better?'

He knew the answer to that, at least. 'I don't know.'

'If you did . . .' She took an audible breath. 'Can we start seeing each other again? See how it goes? Your mum will get better, right?'

Hurt tugged at his insides. Now she wanted him? After all the upset and upheaval? 'My mother has someone to help, but her health is still not good and Marilù still recovers from surgery. We could find ourselves in a similar situation in the future. And I would come home again. Would you come with me?'

She sounded taken aback. 'Well . . . suppose *my* mother needed *me*? Would you move with me to live in England?'

He rose to his feet and moved closer to the boats, as if their moonlit serenity might bring comfort. 'Good question.' He liked countries with hot summers and mild winters. England didn't fit that bill, to his mind. He thought his way through another silence. *Would* he have gone to the UK with Hettie if their situations had been reversed? Found another job there? 'I do not know,' he admitted at last.

Instantly, she abandoned the hypothetical England question. 'I want things back to how they were.'

'For me,' he replied, 'it is not so clear.'

'Will you at least think about it?' she asked, her voice small again.

'Of course.' It would be hard not to think about such an unanticipated option. After saying goodbye and ending the conversation, he wandered around the corner and along the canal, watching traffic flowing over the bridges, thinking about bright, pretty Hettie, outgoing and fun. The tourist season was picking up now it was June and couples wandered hand in hand. The restaurants and kiosks were all open and holidaymakers were drawn to their light like moths.

Go back to Barcelona?

To Hettie?

He turned and retraced his steps around the corner to gaze at the three storeys and tiled roof of Residenza dei Tringali, the modest hotel of only forty-four guest rooms that the families of his great-grandfather, grandfather and father had built up, and his mother had driven along since Domenico passed away. Alfio had never seen it as his future. Once Agata had regained her strength and was allowed to attempt heavier work again – and the hotel had hopefully enjoyed a busy season and refilled its bank account so they could employ more help if needed – it seemed his old life was available again. He'd been replaced in his old job but with his language skills and communications experience, he was sure there were other roles in Barcelona for him. Another apartment to rent, another car to buy.

The same girlfriend.

After waiting for a break in the chain of headlights of passing cars, he sauntered across the road and indoors. A guest had left a note on the reception desk about a rattling window in their room. He left it for tomorrow, and mounted the stairs, tired but not sleepy.

His little room was not bright and colourful, but the bed was OK, for a single. The space was too small to let out to guests and he was getting almost fond of it as it demanded little of his energy but offered a beautiful view of the moonlit old city that sparkled with lights.

Through the window, a movement caught his eye and he saw Ursula seated on her balcony, feet up on the railings, sketchpad on her lap. Her pencil was idle as she stared out at the view. For several seconds, he watched her, the way her hair hung, longer at one side than the other. Her body art was a filigree over her pale skin. Hettie had had a small flower tattoo on one shoulder, but nothing so bold yet as pretty as Ursula's ink.

There was something about her stillness and her blank stare that spoke of sadness.

Without knowing he was going to do it, he stepped closer to his window and slid it up.

Ursula's head swivelled his way. Her wistful expression vanished as she smiled. 'It's a beautiful night.'

'It is.' He swung one leg over the broad window ledge and left the other in the room, bestriding the wall of the house. For several moments, they each gazed at the moonscape, a study in shadow and light. He said, 'I expect you know that once this area was Greek. Ortigia was an outpost. A fort.'

She nodded. 'I read about it before I agreed to "meet"—' she made air quotes with her fingers '—your mum on the video call.'

It was strange to be sitting a couple of metres apart but separated by a length of wrought iron and a small open space. He could have reached for the railing and clambered onto her balcony without much trouble. Of course, he wouldn't, not without an invitation.

Referencing her earlier phone call from whoever had made her vent that impressive string of swear words, he said, 'It must be a night for unexpected phone calls. My ex-girlfriend from Barcelona has just called me.'

She tilted her head. 'Really?' Then, with a smile in her

110

voice because she was repeating his words to her, she enquired solicitously, 'Are you OK?'

He grinned, to show he'd got the allusion, but elected to take the question seriously. 'Just confused. We ended, and now she wonders if we made a mistake.'

A small frown curled her brow. 'And what do you think?'

Simply, he answered, 'I do not want to feel like a stone around her ankles.' He enlarged on the statement by summarising Hettie's comment about independence and freedom.

'That would be uncomfortable,' she answered, turning to stare out at the city again.

He wasn't sure if she meant wearing a stone or feeling you were one. Either way, she was right. Absently, watching her profile, he said, 'It seems I could have my life back in Barcelona, with Hettie.'

She screwed up her face as she swung back to him. '"Have your life back"? Surely, your life is still in Spain? Nanda told me your relationship had ended but that doesn't affect your job, does it? You're just here for a visit, right?'

He froze, realising that he'd never explained that he'd come home on the expectation of filling the role that she currently held. It would have been awkward. She didn't know the story of her father and his mother, and Agata didn't want her told. Not enjoying the feeling of needing to hide things for others, he prevaricated. 'I'll stay as long as I believe to be right.'

Her stare was unwavering. He could almost hear her brain working. 'But what about your career? Agata and Nanda, they both told me that you had a good job in Spain. A good life.'

111

He nodded. '*Sì*.'

Then her voice dropped, becoming soft and sympathetic. 'Ah, your girlfriend. She ended things and you didn't want to stick around? You left your job? That's crappy, if she's just now changing her mind.' Her hair gleamed palely in the moonlight. It was too dark to see the colour of her eyes, but he knew them to be a particularly bright, deep blue, like the sea on a sunny day.

Touched by her sympathy, he opted for a truth, if not the whole truth. 'It was a good time to come here for a while to be with my family. There are other jobs.'

Her voice remained rich with understanding. 'Sometimes, home's just where it feels best to be. I went to Ireland when my job and my flat vanished almost simultaneously. If I hadn't, I wouldn't have heard about this set-up here with your family,' she added.

Did he still wish she *hadn't* heard of the opportunity to come and help his family? He'd got over his initial prejudice against her, now, and appreciated that she did more than his mother could ever have hoped for. 'Our lives are made up of chains of events,' he agreed.

She regarded him gravely. 'Are you happy at the chance to take up where you left off with your girlfriend?'

'Relationships are not that straightforward,' he countered. 'I feel . . . disturbed that she views a relationship with me as a sacrifice of freedom. Offended,' he added, as a more precise word came to him. 'She did not break my heart. Just bruised it.'

Ursula nodded, then stretched, making him imagine her willowy body shifting beneath her clothes. 'I'd better be getting some sleep.'

'Yes, goodnight,' he answered. He watched as she collected her pad and pencil and slipped through the tall glass door to her room, closing it behind her, then he sat on, perched on his attic windowsill, thinking about Hettie and her view of him.

Eventually, he, too, took himself off to bed, only to lie awake, watching the curtains around the open window dance sinuously in the breeze, while he wondered what he wanted. And whether Hettie was it.

Chapter Eight

A lot of guests were checking out of the hotel. It was Nino's day off, so they kept Alfio busy helping with luggage, but early departures made it possible for Ursula to have the breakfast room and kitchen cleared promptly. After collecting money and shopping bags, she stepped into the courtyard and the blaze of the sun and found Camocat on the wall. 'Well, hello,' she said. 'Wait there. I have something for you.' Back in the kitchen, she grabbed some milk that had already been out for breakfast once so couldn't be set out again, and the end of a pack of grated cheese. Camocat loved cheese.

Outside again, she found the feline had come off the wall to meet her, carrying her tail behind her like a flag. 'Progress,' Ursula said softly. 'You're not quite so wary now, eh kitty?'

Camocat gave her a sidelong look and hunched over to nibble at the cheese, clearly ready to vanish if Ursula made the wrong move. Ursula stood perfectly still, but even so, Camocat suddenly startled and raced vertically up the wall and over the top.

Oh, well. Mistrust could stop you from being hurt. 'I'll leave it for you,' Ursula called after her, gathering up her bags.

At the bakery, she gave the week's order of bread and pastries, practising her Italian and making the woman behind the counter laugh at the way she pronounced *cannoli*. After pausing at a kiosk on Piazza Pancali for a lemon granita, next on her itinerary was the market. The slushy, tangy ice was cooling as she wandered up and down the aisles of clothes and souvenirs before moving on to the fresh food section, where fresh fish and meat vied for her attention alongside colourful fruit, vegetables and heaps of spices. Soon her bags were filled with juice, milk, cheeses and cooked meats.

All the time, though, her thoughts wandered to Fabio and the tension that had developed between them. Yesterday evening, alone on her balcony, she'd had time to reach the conclusion that she'd blown things out of proportion. Maybe she took after her mother more than she'd thought. Her dad would have found a way to put his point across with an easy smile and without causing an atmosphere, she was sure.

Thinking of her parents made her realise that she hadn't talked to them for over a week. When she got back to the hotel kitchen, she saw that the door to the family apartment stood open, as it so often did. She filled the fridge, calling through to report to Agata in her somewhat stuttering Italian that her shopping trip had been successful. Then she switched to English. 'OK for me to FaceTime my family from the kitchen, please, Agata? The Wi-Fi router upstairs is on the blink again and I'm about at the end of my phone data for this month.'

Agata appeared in the doorway, her smile more reserved

than usual. 'Nanda and I will take Marilù out in her buggy. It will be good for you to have privacy.'

Ursula halted, feeling now as if she ought not have asked. 'I didn't mean to inconvenience you. I'll wait for the router to be fixed or buy more data. I just thought that as I was finished early this morning—' and she wasn't sure how Fabio was going to receive her, after her annoyance with him the day before, so it was tempting to delay having to see him again '—I'd do it here. Not to worry, though.'

But Agata brushed away her objections. 'No, no. Now is good to go out, while it is not as hot as afternoon. The doctor has reminded me I should walk a little every day and Marilù will enjoy some air. She is a more happy baby, now, yes?'

'I hardly hear her cry at all,' agreed Ursula. No doubt having overheard the conversation, Nanda brought Marilù out. The child was beaming from her mother's arms, her dark curls caught into a green ribbon atop her head. Though it was only a few days since surgery, she was visibly happier and more comfortable. Ursula stooped to kiss the baby's forehead. '*Bambina bellissima.*'

Everyone laughed as Marilù cooed back and then wrinkled her nose like a rabbit. Minutes later, baby, mother and grandmother were strolling out through the courtyard, Marilù under a sunshade in her buggy and trying to pull her toes into her mouth with her little, starfish hands.

Ursula fetched her laptop then settled at the centre island, slightly out of breath after the stairs. Soon she had both parents on screen, side by side at the kitchen table, the background an orderly row of pans hanging on the wall.

'Seeing the house makes me feel homesick,' Ursula

116

declared, knowing they loved to hear that she still felt affection for Swords. 'You both OK?'

'Ah, we're fine.' Colleen beamed. 'I've had my hair cut again. Dad says he likes it, but I think it's too short this time.'

'It's smart,' Ursula reassured her. The conversation cycled through whether Stanley's hair needed cutting too – Colleen said yes, Stanley said no – little Kira, baby Eoin, and whether Ursula was still enjoying Sicily. Wasn't that an enormous kitchen she was sitting in?

'Sure, I am, and yes, it is a lovely big kitchen because it's the one for the hotel.' Ursula told them about getting finished early today, her ceramic designs, and how much Fabio had liked them. She didn't add, *But now I feel as if I'm the idiot for getting shitty with him instead of explaining why I felt as I did when he sold some.* Soon she'd go and make peace, she thought, as she asked Stanley if he was OK, because he seemed exceptionally quiet.

Then the door from the hall banged open and Alfio burst in. 'Ursula, do you know—' He jolted to a stop as if his flip-flop had caught in a grate. 'Sorry. I did not realise you were on a call.'

Ursula twisted around on her stool, flushing. 'It's just my mum and dad. Agata said it was OK to FaceTime from here because of the Wi-Fi needing attention upstairs. They've taken Marilù out for a stroll. Agata said it would give me privacy, though it wasn't necessary,' she added, because he looked so stiff, his eyes so wide as he stood gazing at her computer as if it was a spaceship that had landed.

Then his gaze shifted to her. 'Did she?'

He sounded so odd that Ursula felt obliged to say, 'If

117

I'm in your way or you need me for something, I can call my parents back later.'

'No.' He took a breath and shifted on his feet. 'Um, it was not important.' He turned on his heel and returned the way he'd come, the door swinging shut behind him.

'Who was that? Are you in trouble?' Colleen demanded, her eyes wide with alarm.

'Alfio. He's the son. I think it's OK.' Ursula did continue the call, but even as she listened to Colleen's plans for entertaining Kira every day after school when September finally arrived, she kept listening for Alfio to return, disconcerted by how strange he'd seemed. Maybe she shouldn't have asked to make the call, because Agata and Nanda had bolted outdoors, and Alfio had looked as if she'd thrown a scorpion at his feet.

It felt like time to wind the conversation up. The good-byes inevitably took five minutes longer, as Colleen remembered something she'd meant to tell Ursula, and Ursula realised again that she'd hardly talked to her father. 'You are OK, Dad?' she asked again, fingers already hovering over the 'leave' button, but aware that he'd left almost all the conversation to his wife and daughter.

'Of course,' he said with a hearty smile. 'But you need to get along to your class.'

'I do,' she agreed. Her eyes strayed to the clock in the corner of her screen, which told her that she wouldn't get to Fabio's as early as usual. Part of her would have liked to ask her dad for lessons on getting her point across without pissing people off, but she knew Colleen would just jump in and say that Fabio had asked for it, selling Ursula's gear without consulting her. She ended the conversation and raced up the marble stairways to leave her laptop in her tiny sanctuary in the attic. She must make

118

peace with Fabio. It wasn't his fault that she had swarms of bees in her bonnet about men trying to run her show.

She sighed as she clattered down the stairs again, a sunflower-strewn bag slung over her shoulder, and grabbed an apple, a banana and a bottle of water to lunch on as she hurried along. Though she chose the shady side of the streets, sweat beaded on her hairline and the scent from the oleander trees was almost suffocating. Dust swirled, and she wondered how long it would be before Sicily saw rain.

Finally, after passing the enormous reeded cone of the basilica and rounding the corner, she turned off amongst the old buildings that formed Piazza Brancaccio. Then she halted.

The big wooden door to the studio, which always stood ajar, was shut.

The old paving seemed particularly uneven beneath her feet as she trailed closer and tried the battered brass door-knob. Locked.

There was one window at Ursula's height, beside the door. She peeped through it. No students gathered around the big workbench, their turntables before them. No Fabio sat waiting to greet her in his rumbly voice. Biting her lip, she backed away so that she could look up at Fabio's apartment above. What if he was ill? The only phone number she had for him was for the landline in the studio, so it was, presently, useless.

Disconsolately, she turned away.

Then she saw him, calmly observing her from the shade of a parasol outside the bar opposite. Two men sat at his table, as grey and grizzled as he. Relief flooded through her. 'Fabio!' She raced across the bumpy stone of the square. '*Buongiorno*,' she panted, as she arrived where the

119

men sat at a table piled with empty coffee cups and full beer glasses. 'So glad to see you're OK. I was worried when I saw the studio shut.'

Gravely, Fabio inclined his grizzled head. '*Buongiorno.*' His companions, too, uttered the habitual greeting.

Fabio filled the entirety of the iron chair he sat upon, looking settled and comfortable and not in a hurry to shamble across the piazza and open his ceramics studio.

Ursula knew he was hurt. He'd taken a special interest in her, he'd let her turn up out of hours, he'd advised the Tringali family on where to buy that beautiful book. With an exhalation, she dropped down at the unoccupied seat at the table. '*Mi dispiace*, Fabio. I shouldn't have been so angry.'

As one, Fabio's two friends rose silently and drifted over to join another table, apparently knowing enough English to judge this conversation not for them. Was Fabio going to tell her that she shouldn't bother turning up at the studio anymore? Dismay almost swamped her, not because she'd lose access to her newfound love of ceramics, but because she'd lose something she'd come to value more – Fabio's friendship. Her resolution not to be bossed about by a man had caused her to be cold and cutting to one who'd been kind to her.

She sighed. 'I want to explain. My Italian definitely isn't up to it, so I'll speak in English and then we'll let Google translate whatever you miss. It's all about the ending of my marriage because of something I couldn't help, but my husband couldn't or wouldn't see that.' She didn't delve into detail. 'He began to take decisions away from me, as if I'd shown myself to be incompetent to run my own life. When we finally split up, I swore that no man would ever take choice away from me again.' She gazed over the sleepy square, at the parents with babies in buggies and children running around the dancing fountain, the older people enjoying meeting with friends. It was a lovely focal point for the neighbourhood.

'I guess I have to learn how to find the balance between being a pushover and turning on people,' she admitted. 'You've been a great mentor, and I must have seemed ungrateful when you had tried to do something nice. You were excited about my first success, and I poured cold water on it.'

Fabio responded with silence.

Despondency swept over Ursula. 'I had a lot of trouble when my marriage ended,' she added, really talking to herself, now. 'Fear of the future swamped me. I came to Sicily to get a long way from my past.'

Finally, Fabio stirred. 'I think we apologise to each other. I think I do a favour but is only a favour if someone wants. Forget the husband. You want limoncello?'

She turned to stare at him in surprise that he'd got so much of the gist of her confession. His eyes were twinkling back at her in a signal that he was prepared to put the episode behind them. She laughed, knowing his weakness for sweet things. 'That sounds grand.' Fabio called for two glasses of limoncello and his friends at the other table turned and grinned, as if realising whatever the trouble had been it was now over. Ursula ordered little cakes, too, remembering that limoncello was often eaten with dessert, if not as a *digestivo*.

The bright yellow liquid arrived in frosted, small, stemmed glasses with a selection of cakes and Ursula thought, as she relaxed over the ice-cold syrupy sweetness, that she was happy here, with this growly old man who looked as if he never ironed his clothes.

Fabio stretched out his chunky legs and folded his hands on his rotund belly. 'You go after summer? England? Ireland?'

Ursula twisted in her seat, leaning on one elbow. 'I suppose so. I haven't planned, yet. I must be practical and look for a new way to earn my living, or return to the tattoo parlours, which I'm sick of, really.' And the teaching course her mum had been so keen on didn't feel one bit appetising, not compared to creating every day in the cool studio.

Fabio gazed across the square to his premises as he reminded her, 'I have not made pieces to sell for five years. My wife, she died. Without her, I tell other people how to work, and get old and cross.'

'I'm so sorry,' Ursula murmured. His simple words made her newly aware of his grief.

He tossed back the dregs of his limoncello. Then he leaned forward suddenly, making Ursula blink. 'Your work, it excites me. Designs with this.' He gesticulated at her body art. 'I like to put a range together, you and me. I think about this. We call it "*Il Tatuaggio*" and each piece has tattoo design border. It is good. It is unusual. It is commercial.' He pronounced the last word with relish.

Heart beating hard all at once, Ursula gazed at him. 'Really? Like a partnership? You and me? Am I good enough?'

'*Sì*. I help if you need.' He gestured expansively. 'We have bowls, plates, jugs. You design. Make specimen pieces for me to get orders from shops – with your agreement,' he added deliberately, waggling his thick grey eyebrows.

'Fabio,' Ursula breathed. 'That would be fantastic. *Fantastico!* Lemons, grapes, ivy, flowers, all different arrangements with each style of border.'

Judging by his unusually broad smile, Fabio was pleased by her enthusiasm. 'Summer project. Talk in autumn. Maybe stay?'

'Maybe,' Ursula breathed. 'I'd have to have somewhere to live and be able to support myself while we see if I can make enough money from ceramics.' Or could she rent the room with the balcony from the Tringalis? At least for winter? She'd love that because she felt safe there, especially since Alfio had become friendly. By spring, when they might need the room for a new staff member, she'd know if the project was going to be viable and might even afford a proper apartment.

'This is *thrilling*,' she declared, glancing around for a server so she could order more drinks – blood-fizzing, spine-tingling excited.

She might stay on this lovely island . . . far away from Stephan and the people he kept trying to use to contact her.

At Residenza dei Tringali that evening, she prepared a cold meal, with prosciutto and sliced chicken. Alfio chose a rosé to go with it and they gathered around the kitchen island. Marilù was still awake, but content to roll around on a mat on the floor. She seemed to have come on a month in the few days since leaving hospital.

'Something amazing's happened,' Ursula burst out eagerly, as soon as they were all seated. 'Fabio wants to work with me.' As she expanded and expounded, her words fell over each other. 'I thought he'd say I'd been too obvious, using my body art when he said I had to put something of myself in the designs. But he loves the concept.'

'That is very good. Very good,' Agata approved. 'You

123

are a true artist. Soon, you will be too important to make breakfasts.'

Ursula laughed. 'I'm not trying to welch on our deal. Go back on our agreement,' she clarified, as she saw Agata's brow knit over 'welch'. 'In fact, if I stay on after summer, I was wondering whether I could rent my room off you, at least until I get some idea of whether my work will earn enough money.'

It was Alfio who said, 'It is considered too small to be a guest room. There are rules.'

For a moment, Ursula was crestfallen. 'Oh. I hadn't realised. OK, let's see how things go. Or, if Agata and Nanda have enough work for me in winter, we could continue exactly as we are.'

'That is true,' agreed Nanda, buoying Ursula's spirits anew.

Alfio had served himself with thin slices of prosciutto, like dark pink petals on his plate against the green leaves, red tomatoes and yellow peppers of chopped salad. 'What will your parents think if you stay?' he asked.

She shrugged. 'I left home when I was eighteen, so I don't think they'll be upset. Sicily is further from Ireland than England is, but they can still visit. More clients for your hotel,' she added. Then, seeing a strange expression dawn on his face she amended hurriedly, 'I'm not asking for special rates, of course.'

As if it knew she was talking about family, her phone rang, and she saw *Finola* on the screen. 'Ah, my sister,' she said. 'I'll take it outside.' Relieved to have a reason to avoid the sudden atmosphere, she swooped up her wine and plate and was soon perched on a wooden box that had found its way into the courtyard. 'Hiya, Fin. How are ya?'

124

'Grand,' responded her sister's composed voice. 'But there's something I want to tell you.'

As she'd left her fork behind, Ursula began to pick at her salad with her fingers. 'Go on.'

'Mum had quite a go at Dad.' Finola groaned.

Ursula's appetite faded. 'Oh.'

A sigh, long and drawn out. 'It began with a "who's the most favoured granny?" thing. Y'know, Dec's mum asked to have Kira because they had an old friend visiting. Mum and Dad had been going to take her to the park. Dad said they could take her any time but my in-laws' friends were only coming for the day. Mum got all tight-lipped and started with: "We know we're second in the queue, then."'

'Shite,' said Ursula. 'I thought she'd stopped with that carry-on.'

Finola snorted. 'Exactly. *And* didn't she tell Dad to point it out when she went back to her old ways? So, he tried, really kindly, to say they could take Kira on Sunday instead of Saturday, and she snapped at him that he was never on her side. Then she saw how we were all staring at her and seemed to come to her senses. She tried to laugh it off, like she'd been joking, and said of course they didn't mind.'

Ursula considered as she nibbled a leaf of chard. 'So, she isn't over the insecure point-scoring thing. Is an occasional lapse excusable? Or is it not occasional?' Here in Sicily, she was insulated from the realities of her parents' relationship. 'On FaceTime this morning, they looked solid enough, side by side at the kitchen table, talking about their grandkids.'

Finola sounded dubious, and Ursula could picture her rubbing worried fingers through the sensibly short hair that worked for her busy lifestyle. 'I don't know, because I'm not there twenty-four-seven. Although it sometimes seems like I am.'

'Ah.' Ursula detected the aggrieved note in her sister's voice. 'How often do you see them?'

'Once or twice a week, because Mum likes to see Kira. But when they start having her every weekday after school and part of the school holidays, it'll be even more. It's getting me down in advance.' Finola tried to laugh, but it sounded hollow.

Ursula couldn't imagine seeing her parents every week. A week or a weekend every few months had been her norm. That was the difference between living locally and not.

'I'm disappointed, too,' Finola went on.

Ursula had to hurry her thoughts to catch up. 'In Mum?'

Finola paused. 'I suppose. And Dad's so quiet.'

'He was when we talked this morning.' Ursula's bum became uncomfortable on the rough wood of the box, and she got up to pace, glancing up when she got to the gate, from which point she could see a sliver of her balcony railing. 'Are you resentful about being the one so close to Mum and Dad with me here and Sorcha more interested in Instagram and TikTok? I suppose Caden ignores the emotional stuff so probably wouldn't notice if Mum had a strop about Baby Eoin and his in-laws.'

'He doesn't notice. Bree said so.' Finola made a grumpy, humming sound. 'I don't know how much I'm resentful and how much I just hadn't anticipated. When they said they'd get back together I was delighted, of course, and to get free childcare . . . Well, that saving would pay for a lovely holiday. But there's definitely some rough along with the smooth. Anyway,' she added, wearily. 'How's life in sunny Sicily? Are you Cinderella scrubbing floors all day? Or Naomi Campbell, jetting around?'

'I work pretty hard from six-thirty a.m. to twelve, but I'm having a great time, really,' Ursula admitted apologetically. Feeling traitorously happy with her lot, she once again recounted Fabio's idea that had filled her with twinkling joy. 'So, I might stay on,' she said, judging that she might as well get it out in the open.

At least Finola didn't sound too surprised. 'I knew you wouldn't come back. You've been away too long. That Cillian Murphy one – that actor who made it big in *Peaky Blinders* – he said it's very Irish to move away but eventually come home. Not sure he's right so far as you're concerned, though. You've only done the moving away part.'

Guilt gnawed through Ursula's previous good mood. 'I'm sorry you're feeling put upon, Fin. Because Mum and Dad made their reunion seem all about the grandkids, it draws you and Caden in. But Bree still being on maternity . . . well, it's mostly on you.'

Finola agreed resignedly. 'You chose your life, and I chose mine. I feel better now I've had a good moan.'

When the call ended, Ursula retrieved her plate and chewed a piece of prosciutto that now seemed tasteless. As her sister now knew her new plans, she'd better call the folks again soon and tell them, too. When she spotted a pair of eyes watching her, she realised it was Camocat, her coat doing a great job of making her invisible in the shadows. 'Here you go,' she said, and threw the last of the prosciutto towards the hovering feline.

On dainty paws, Camocat picked her way through the weeds that flourished in the cracks of the paving and assumed the hunched position that allowed her to keep her gaze on Ursula as she ate.

Ursula sat on over her glass of wine, watching the pale eyes. It was only when they blinked and vanished that she realised Camocat had moved, reappearing like magic as a silhouette on top of the wall. 'Good trick, you ninja,' she murmured.

After nibbling at her salad and finishing her wine, she returned indoors to discover that someone had cleared up the kitchen and loaded the dishwasher. Feeling too antsy to spend the entire evening on her balcony, she decided on a walk in the beautiful warm evening, admiring the boats and watching people herding around between restaurants and bars. She ran upstairs for her purse in case she decided to stop for a drink and happened on Alfio exiting his own room. He gazed at her so curiously that she realised her forehead had puckered in a giant frown and so she smoothed it out.

'I'm going to meet a few old friends at a bar here in Ortigia,' he said. 'Would you like to come?'

Taken by surprise, never having received any such overture from him before, Ursula almost refused as a reflex. But then that reaction seemed stupid, as if she was still letting Stephan make her choices, in a way, by making her wary of all men – even this one, who occupied the room next to hers without any hint of taking advantage of their enforced proximity. Once he'd got over his funny mood on arrival – which, in retrospect, might have been caused by the recent demise of his relationship – she'd warmed to his pleasant manner and quiet intelligence. And his dark good looks, she admitted to herself, and the way his brown eyes changed from a peaty whiskey colour to dark chocolate, according to his mood. 'Why the hell not?' she answered affably. 'Let me just get some dosh.'

From Alfio's perplexed expression, she could tell that

'Why the hell not?' wasn't a response he was familiar with, but he waited while she grabbed her purse.

Soon, they were walking through the velvety warm twilight, enjoying the salty breeze that blew in off the sea. They paused at the floating pontoons to watch a sleek grey sailboat come into the marina under motor power. Ursula thought a small orange rubber inflatable boat had intruded on the yacht's right of passage until she realised it was a pilot, leading the way past the excursion boats to a vacant berth. A man on the pontoon kept his eyes on the yacht's sides and fenders while the pilot boat, like a dancing gnat, whizzed side to side in front of his more ponderous charge, even putting its soft rubber nose against the sailing yacht's side to nudge it clear of the vessel in the next berth.

Ursula glanced at Alfio and saw a faraway look on his face. As if sensing her regard, he glanced at her and smiled. 'Papà kept his boat here, until . . .'

'Agata and Nanda told me,' she said sympathetically. 'I'm very sorry you lost your dad.'

'I was supposed to be with him.' His voice was barely louder than the sighing of the breeze. 'I often fished with him, and Nanda and Mamma too, sometimes, if my grand-parents could look after the hotel for a day. That day, I had a virus and couldn't go. There was a summer storm. It was an old boat. Like that.' He pointed out an old-fashioned vessel, a tub with a cabin on top. 'His boat turned over and he was trapped inside.'

Ursula laid a hand on his bare forearm for an instant, then awareness of the warmth of his skin and the brush of his body hair whooshed through her and she removed it again. Wow. That had been a . . . a thing. A proper frisson. It took her by surprise so much that she almost returned her hand to his arm to see if happened again.

Showing no sign of feeling anything, he gave her a quick smile and turned to follow the quayside where the superyachts were moored, the broad hardstanding alive with people on foot or on scooters, the restaurants glittering with light beneath the trees. In a gap stood a shiny carousel and a few other rides for small children. A street performer looked as if he was juggling with handfuls of fireflies, and it took Ursula a beat to realise they were balls filled with tiny sparkling lights.

Further along the marina, they were forced to detour around a fenced-off area at the foot of the gangplank belonging to one of the bright white superyachts. With a glance at the towering, chrome-edged decks, Alfio said, 'I read that the world would support billions, if not for the billionaires.'

She considered the idea as they passed more floating palaces, liking the glimpse into his world view. 'I wonder if it's true?'

He shrugged, his hands in his pockets. 'They spend some of their money here. Ortigia likes rich visitors.' He looked relaxed in his usual outfit of flip-flops and shorts, and perfectly at home, the breeze running its fingers through his curls. She knew that Agata thought his hair too long, but Ursula was sure that the glossy coils framing his lean, handsome face were responsible for some of the looks cast his way by groups of women strolling by. She wasn't the only one who'd noticed his attractions, and his typically Italian talent for making shorts look like the coolest of fashion statements only added to his appeal.

At the end of that part of the marina they had to veer around the *zona militare* where a coastguard's boat was moored, and then they passed through a patch of trees and some souvenir stalls and emerged near a beach club playing music. Alfio nodded at it. 'We can tell today is a weekday as they play soft music. Friday and Saturday, it is like a nightclub.' They rounded Fonte Aretusa, its khaki water illuminated all around, then Alfio turned inland and led her to a different area to that where Nanda had taken her, down the island rather than across, narrow street following narrow street. Where the route widened into a piazza, he tracked diagonally across, ignoring an oncoming car which, as if recognising that this was not the kind of pedestrian to be intimidated, slowed.

'These roads look as if they were constructed for horse-drawn carriages. You live in a wonderful place,' Ursula observed. She was still thinking of that *zing* when she'd touched Alfio's skin and wondered if the same would happen if she touched him again.

'True. My family is fortunate in many ways. Not only do we have a hotel in this lovely place passed to us, but we like each other enough to co-operate in the business.' Alfio took yet another narrow street, one that sloped steeply down, balconies almost seeming to touch overhead. A great bougainvillea formed an arch, moths pulsating between it and nearby lights, while a constant stream of people passed beneath.

'My family like each other, too. Mostly,' she added, stepping aside to let a group by and thinking of the unsettling conversation with Finola about Colleen being tricky again.

'Lots of people called Quinn, the Irish name,' he commented.

Surprised at him remembering her telling him that Quinn was Irish, she said, 'Yes, it's common where I come from.' They stood aside to let a bicycle pass them, its thick tyres no doubt designed to absorb the bumps in the paving, very close for a moment before setting off again.

Courteously, Alfio ushered her around a corner. 'Tringali goes back to when we were Greek and means "commander of soldiers". If you mix the languages, you could say Residenza dei Tringali means residence of the commanders, but I think my great-grandfather just thought it made an imposing name. Here we are,' he added, as they arrived at a row of tables and chairs at a point where the hill levelled.

The bar, Ferramenta, was tucked into the ground floor of a narrow stone building. Most of the tables were already occupied. A man of about Alfio's age waved. 'Alfio! *Amico carissimo!*'

Alfio made a beeline for him, slapping his shoulder and shaking his hand. 'Rocco!' Then he turned to the other man at the table, 'Giovi!' and treated him to the same hearty handshake. 'Let me introduce you to Ursula, who is helping Mamma this season. She is a Brit.' He grinned mischievously at her.

Ursula refused to rise to the bait. '*Buonasera. Sono irlandese e il mio italiano non è molto buono.*' She had it down pat to tell people she was Irish, and her Italian wasn't very good.

Both men shook her hand, less violently than they'd shaken Alfio's. Sheepishly, Rocco said, 'My English is . . .' He made a sawing motion with his hand.

Giovi nodded, as if his own situation echoed Rocco's.

'I will translate.' Alfio pulled out a chair for Ursula, brushing against her as he slid onto another and signalled to a server. *Yep, there was that tingle again . . .* In no time, their drinks were placed upon the round tabletop and they were involved in an exchange of information in a mix of Italian and English. Alfio explained to Ursula that Ferramenta had once been an ironworks. Rocco told her he lived and worked in the centre of Siracusa, while Giovi explained he was visiting his parents with his wife and children. His home was now in the north-west of the island, quite near Palermo. Both men had been at school with Alfio.

'Alfio was bad boy,' Rocco told Ursula solemnly, while his dark eyes twinkled.

'He did not wash,' added Giovi.

'I was perfect,' Alfio corrected them, his melting brown eyes alight with laughter.

Ursula laughed too, enjoying the banter that only added to the noise of the bar and the chatter of people strolling by. It was an *area pedonale*, as depicted by a picture of a person on foot, but no car would fit down the street anyway.

Rocco asked Alfio something in Italian. Alfio replied, and Rocco and Giovi looked impressed, then Alfio turned to Ursula. 'They admire your beautiful body art. I told them you're a tattoo artist.'

She nodded, making a gesture over her shoulder, indicating the past. 'I used to be. I haven't checked whether I'd need a licence here, but I've had enough of tattoo parlours, really. I'm here to learn about painting ceramics.' Her heart gave an excited skip at the thought of her summer project, which might turn into something long term.

They chatted amiably, mostly via Alfio, while they each drank a couple of beers, then Giovi looked at his watch. 'I go home, now. My pleasure that we meet, Ursula.'

Rocco nodded. 'And I have a person waiting for me.' He winked, which made Ursula think the 'person' would be someone female.

A flurry of farewells followed and soon the two men

were striding back up the slope before vanishing around the corner of the street. Ursula's beer bottle was still quite full, and Alfio ordered another for himself. She found she was pleased that he was evidently in no hurry to leave, even though his friends had gone. It had been a good evening and, for the first time in more than two years, she was actively enjoying the company of a man.

That was something she wouldn't have anticipated – especially not this man, when he'd first come home. He'd definitely improved for the knowing.

'You are smiling now,' he observed. 'Earlier, you looked upset. I hope you did not have bad news in your phone call.'

It was carefully phrased as a comment that Ursula could shrug off rather than a question, but his interest seemed so genuine that she saw no reason to be cagey. 'It was my sister Finola. She's the eldest of us – I have another sister and a brother.' She hesitated, but why not chat the situation over with Alfio? Her parents were unknown to him, after all, so it couldn't matter if she aired their business. She took a slug of her beer. 'Last year, my mum and dad separated. It wasn't comfortable for us, but what can you say to your parents? "Stop being so human. Although I've lived my own life for fourteen years, I always thought you'd be there, together, if I wanted you"?'

He blinked, perhaps surprised, and his dark eyes fixed on her, as if she'd caught his attention, so she continued. 'In April, they reunited, which was a surprise. They said they want to be together for the family, especially the grandchildren. From September they're to look after my niece after school, which means Finola's kinda involved with them as they try and make a go of things again. It makes her Johnny on the spot.'

His eyes widened. 'Johnny . . . ?'

She grinned. 'It's a daft expression, isn't it? It means the person who's there, dealing with a situation in person.'

His face cleared. 'I understand. Did she hope you would return home?'

Ursula was shaking her head before his sentence was half out. 'I've spent all my adult life away.'

He knitted his brows. 'There must have been a reason for your parents to separate. Perhaps one had found a girlfriend or boyfriend.'

She remembered what Finola had said about their dad maybe meeting someone while separated from their mum. As there was no evidence either way, she answered, 'We're told the problem was Mum's insecurities. She's wonderful most of the time, but then in certain situations she turns possessive and overly sensitive. Dad's much easier. Everybody likes Dad.'

'I don't,' he said unexpectedly.

Ursula laughed, giving his shoulder a friendly nudge, though it couldn't have been a hard nudge because he barely moved. 'OK, people who don't know him, can't like him, can they? But they can't dislike him, either.'

He hesitated, then nodded. 'I see your point. So, if things do not work for you in Sicily, you will return to England.'

Thoughtfully, she answered, 'I could, but I'm not keen to.'

'Because you are divorced?' he murmured. 'Nanda told me.'

Ursula had to strain to hear him over three men at a nearby table becoming very vocal about something, so edged closer to his warmth, picking up a whiff of soap or shower gel on his skin. 'More or less,' she admitted. 'I'm not keen on living near my ex-husband. As it is, he tries to get news of me via friends and all kinds of mad stuff.'

'Then he must regret the divorce.' Alfio upturned his palms as if this was the only answer. His hands were large but lean.

'Ha,' she snorted. 'Divorce turns some people into monsters, and that's what happened with him. Only his negative qualities remained. He regrets me being OK without him.' She was aware of talking more freely than usual. Maybe it was the beers on top of wine at dinner. Or maybe it was Alfio proving such a good listener. Conversation was human, wasn't it? It was how people made sense of things. Still, she was surprised when she heard herself volunteer, 'I have rules about who I drink with, and where. I get unopened bottles where feasible, I take alcohol in public places, but I avoid clubs.'

Alfio looked baffled, gazing at her as if expecting more.

She flushed at the realisation that her train of thought had jumped tracks from divorce to what had triggered it. She took a steadying breath. She'd mulled over the end of her marriage with other people, of course, but maybe she had to get it out every now and then, like a boil needing to be regularly lanced. 'My marriage ended,' she explained slowly, 'because three years ago I was at a nightclub, and passed out. A stranger carried me home unconscious. My husband, Stephan, he reacted by deciding that I'd got drunk and cheated on him with the man.'

'He thought the man would have sex with you and then deliver you home unconscious to your husband?' Incredulity laced Alfio's voice.

'It's an unlikely picture, isn't it?' Ursula replied, grimly, remembering the shock of coming round to find Stephan hanging over her, his usually loving face suffused with anger as he accused her of 'shagging that man'. 'I rang round the friends I'd been with that night, and they said

136

I'd just disappeared from the club, and agreed that I'd only had a couple of drinks.' The old feelings suffused her; disappointment in Steph combined with frustration at the way her memory had failed. 'But Stephan refused to entertain any possibility other than that I'd been unfaithful. I moved in with my friend Zia while I tried to work things out.' She winced as she remembered how she'd exploded with hope each time Steph had rung 'to talk', even when, time and again, 'talking' meant 'trying to get Ursula to admit she's cheated'.

Alfio's mouth quirked at one corner. 'Zia means "aunt" in Italian.'

She gave a small smile. 'Yeah. There's a whole story behind her name. She lives in Umbria now, and I was there with her when the same man returned to tell Steph that on the night I was "drunk", another woman who'd been at the same club had been found naked and unconscious in a local park, the victim of drug assault. So, had some rat-bastard spiked *my* drink, too? It made sense of the strobe-like memory flashes, of noodly legs and a foggy-brain hangover that lasted days. At that point, you'd think Steph would have seen that I was a victim, not a cheater, but it took ages for him to come round to that. Looking back, I think I even went along with being forgiven – perhaps out of some residual fear that I'd done what he originally accused me of. We had a brief go at trying to make our marriage work, because we'd been happy once, but Stephan still brooded. He wanted someone to be accountable and I was the only one available. Eventually, I confronted him about a particularly unacceptable piece of behaviour. He locked me out.'

'Emotionally?' Alfio hazarded, slanting his dark brows.

'By using his physical strength to shove me out of the

door of our home and throw the bolts, not caring whether I could find a roof over my head that night.' The memory of her trying to hurt herself hovered, but she decided that Alfio didn't need to know. Everybody who *did* know saw her as weaker than she was as a result. It would be good to have a clean sheet in Sicily, and have people value her for what she was now, rather than what she'd once done. She finished her beer and rubbed her forehead, the horrible memories creating a physical pressure. 'At first, I thought well of the man who'd seen me home. I used to refer to him as the White Knight, because I thought he'd rescued me, seeing me in a bad situation and getting me to safety.'

Alfio's arm was against hers now, as he listened intently. It was warm and comforting. 'You no longer think well of him?' A question hung in his eyes.

A familiar heavy lump settled in her stomach, that mixture of anxiety and vulnerability that had ruined many a night's sleep. 'No,' she answered simply. 'Why didn't he tell the staff at the club that a woman was unconscious? Or try to find out who I was with? He told Stephan that I'd given him my address before I passed out, but who knows? He could have been watching me for a while, because I'd been to that club with women friends a lot. Maybe he'd followed me home before . . .'

Alfio grabbed the attention of the waitress as she steamed by. Ursula prepared to stop him if he meant to buy her another beer but caught the words *acqua minerale* and realised he was ordering water.

She returned to her story. 'I've researched drug assault. People assume it's about rape but it's not always, and I don't believe that happened to me – though I don't know what else might have taken place.' She left him to join up the dots: that women generally knew if they'd had full sex, but lesser invasions might not leave traces. 'Roofying someone can also be about power and making them totally helpless and vulnerable.' A shiver ran over her at the images that conjured up.

The water arrived and, in silence, Alfio watched the waitress put clean glasses before them. When they were alone again, he murmured, 'And your husband blamed you for this?' He shook his head disgustedly. 'That is incredible.'

'It's been hard to cope with that,' she admitted. 'But I survived it all, and I'm stronger because I did.' But she felt tired, weighed down by the unresolved issues in her past.

She checked the time and by unspoken consent they drained their drinks and prepared to leave.

A few minutes later, as they walked back beside the sea where the city lights scribbled their reflections on the calm water, she turned the conversation to him. 'I've talked about myself too much. How about you? Any progress with Hettie?'

He shook his head, making his curls dance. 'We have not been in contact again. I suppose we are both still thinking.'

She held her hair back to stop the breeze from brushing it into her eyes. 'Trust's a funny thing. It can be hard to get back.' Realising he hadn't mentioned not trusting Hettie so Ursula was implying something negative about a woman she didn't know, she added, 'Still, trying again works for some people.'

They arrived at Residenza dei Tringali, a gust of wind off the marina almost blowing them up the front steps. In silence, they crossed a quiet lobby and climbed each flight of marble stairs. When they reached the doors to their rooms, Alfio paused and looked at her keenly. 'Will you be OK alone tonight, after telling me about the drug assault? If you prefer to be near other women, I can open the apartment so you can sleep on Mamma's sofa.'

Incredibly touched at this evidence of empathy, Ursula felt tears prickling. 'I'll be fine,' she said huskily. 'I usually try to leave the past in the past. It's just that Stephan's been bugging me, lately. He keeps trying to get people to contact me, saying I ran off with a ring of his grandfather's. I have done no such thing, of course.'

Alfio propped one shoulder against the doorframe. 'If he wants to keep contact, maybe he still sees you as his.'

She snorted. 'Big mistake.' She almost added *huge*, like Julia Roberts in *Pretty Woman*, but wasn't sure he'd get the allusion. 'I belong to me and me alone. And I'm pretty sure I've cut off all avenues of contact, now.'

'I hope that gives you peace of mind.' He straightened and took a step towards his door, his gaze lingering on her. 'Goodnight.'

'It does. Goodnight,' she echoed, and – after he gave her a final smile that made her feel as if the building had tilted slightly – they went into their respective rooms.

But then, as if Stephan had been listening in and waiting for the perfect moment to intrude, Ursula's phone rang and as soon as she picked up her brother Caden boomed, 'What the fuck's up with your man?'

'What man?' Ursula asked warily, her mind still half on Alfio.

'Stephan bloody Shuttleworth,' he snapped. 'He's only guessed my email and contacted me with some tale about something you're meant to have stolen off him.'

Black fury rimmed the edge of Ursula's vision. 'He *what*? How the hell does anyone guess your email?'

Her brother sounded scornful. 'It's not hard if you work

140

for a big corporation, is it? First name dot last name at name-of-company dot ie.' He stopped short.

'And how would he know what company you work for?' she demanded silkily.

'Well,' he said defensively, 'I suppose it's on my socials. We just did a sponsored sleep-out in support of a home-less charity and we all posted about it.'

'Socials,' she scoffed. 'A bloody gateway into your life – that's what social media is. Why do you have to blab your activities all over Insta?' Facebook, Twitter, Instagram and Snapchat were things of the past for Ursula, and she'd never even begun with TikTok.

'Have you stolen his crappy jewellery?' he demanded.

'Of course I haven't,' Ursula snapped.

'Then I suggest you warn Sorcha because she's the famous influencer in the family. She'll be next.' Caden even managed to sound virtuous, as if he hadn't been the one to give Stephan a lead to seize on.

Ursula didn't let him off the hook. 'You didn't answer his email, Caden, did you?'

Silence. Then, reluctantly, Caden muttered, 'I might have told him to fuck off with himself.'

'Which means he knows he got the right email address.' She groaned. 'Block him, right? And don't talk to him again. And can you set your socials to private, or some-thing?'

'OK,' Caden agreed sheepishly. 'Isn't Stephan the biggest arse, though?'

'And so are you, for falling for his game,' she told him, with severe honesty. Nevertheless, when the call was over, she did take Caden's advice and call Sorcha.

Sorcha greeted her warning with scorn. 'Don't you get that I know my shit? My channels are about hair, not laying my daily diary open for anybody to see. Honestly, Caden thinks everyone's as much an eejit as him.'

'You probably know your shit better than the rest of the family put together,' Ursula allowed, 'but you've blocked Stephan from everything anyway, right?'

'Yes, yes,' Sorcha answered impatiently. 'Have you had a new cut while you've been in Sicily?'

Ursula pulled at the longer section of her hair to study the condition of the ends. 'No, it's kinda ragged, now you mention it. I'll find a salon. I can ask Nanda where to go.'

'Just hang on and I'll check out Siracusa on one of my forums,' declared Sorcha, enthusiastically. 'Italian women are chic, but are they alternative, like you?'

'Can Italian women be chic, as it's a French word?' Ursula settled down to a hair chat with the sibling on the rung below hers on the family ladder, which ended what had been an unexpectedly nice evening with Alfio on a far pleasanter note than thinking about her damned ex.

Chapter Nine

Nearly two weeks later, Alfio realised that though he was enjoying the company of his family, it was time to begin thinking about sorting out his life. It was mid-June, and he'd been back at Residenza dei Tringali for over three weeks.

His first step would be to discover how his sister and mother saw the future of the family hotel.

La bambina was making so much progress that Nanda had relaxed a lot, and at the weekend Ursula had returned the babysitting favour while Alfio and Nanda went out to a bar. Unfortunately, any ideas he'd harboured about initiating a serious discussion then had flown out of the window as he watched his younger sister exchanging news with old friends. He hadn't had the heart to introduce a difficult topic when she was the happiest and most animated he'd seen her since Mason had left. That arse, as Ursula might say.

Ursula.

Their conversation of the evening they met Rocco and Giovi had revolved in his head ever since. It bothered him that she'd had such a horrible end to her marriage. Worse, in some ways, his conscience was uneasy that he'd been unable to resist listening to her confidences about her parents when she had no idea about her father and Agata, nor that it was no news to Alfio that her parents had marital issues. Luckily, she'd laughingly taken completely the wrong view of him telling her darkly that he didn't like her father.

Now, it was Monday afternoon. Ursula was at Fabio Iacobello's ceramics studio and Nanda had taken Marilù to a follow-up appointment at the hospital, in no need of his support as the baby was gaining weight and more likely to laugh than to cry. He let himself into the family apartment and found Agata in an armchair, reading *La Sicilia*.

She set the newspaper aside and removed her silver-rimmed reading glasses. Her smile allowed him to see anew how her illness had etched lines around her eyes, denoting a frailty that simply hadn't been there a year ago. He hadn't had an in-depth conversation with his mother about the endless, debilitating bleeding that had prompted her hysterectomy, as Agata had let Nanda pass those personal details on to him. Had that made his concern for his mother appear less than it should have been? 'How do you feel?' he asked, taking the chair opposite hers and propping his feet on a leather stool that had probably been in this room since the Greeks owned Siracusa.

'Getting better,' Agata responded.

Alfio regarded her, trying to gauge how much weight she'd lost and whether she looked more than her sixty years. 'If anything,' he said gently, 'you looked better before your operation. Is that what you'd expect?'

Surprise flickered in Agata's eyes, and then exasperation. 'I need time to heal, that's all. And the recovery is slower than I'd hoped because of the problem with my kidneys. I am gradually beginning to feel more like myself.'

'Good. I have worried about you.' He tried a joke. 'Marilù has turned the corner, so you need to try and keep up.'

Love softened her eyes. 'I'm sure the doctor will be very pleased with Marilù. She puts on weight every day now and is a happy baby at last. Such a relief for Nanda. For us all.'

Alfio agreed. Marilù's frowns of discomfort had been vanquished. She laughed at peeping games or being tickled – under the chin, in case her little tummy still needed time to heal from the surgery. 'And you, Mamma? Are you any happier?'

Agata's eyes widened, as if taken by surprise by such a direct question.

Gently, he said, 'I noticed that you went out that time when Ursula FaceTimed her parents in the kitchen.'

Agata flushed. 'My doctor said I'm to walk every day. I need to regain strength.'

'I saw him on her laptop screen – Stanley. I didn't mean to, but I didn't know she'd be on a call and came in from the office.' Alfio remembered the shock of it, and Ursula flustered and puzzled by his reaction.

Instantly, Agata's eyes filled. 'Did he look . . . OK?' she murmured.

His heart went out to her at those few words – so sad, yet more concerned with that *bastardo's* well-being than her own. And suddenly Alfio remembered Ursula being plagued by her ex-husband wanting to keep a foothold in her life. Was Agata doing the same with Stanley? Even subconsciously, had she accepted his daughter here so that she'd hear news of him? Alfio didn't want to think that the answer was 'yes', because it told him that Agata's feelings for Stanley Quinn were very much alive.

He thought carefully about his reply. Frankly, he didn't care if Stanley Quinn was or was not OK . . . but Agata did, and he couldn't forget the light in Ursula's eyes as she talked of what a great guy her father was. 'He smiled because he was talking to his daughter.' Then, scrupulously, he added, 'He was quiet. Ursula's mother was talking.'

Agata gave a sharp, single nod. It made him wonder whether he'd been insensitive to mention Ursula's mother. But Agata had got involved with a man who had not been divorced, which was a risk . . .

Bluntly, he asked, 'Are you jealous of his wife?'

She blinked and her lips pursed in a way that told him he'd trespassed too far into her personal life. Stiffly, she said, 'Naturally. But she's his wife.' Then, as if to give him a dose of his own medicine, she began some trespassing of her own. 'It's weeks since you arrived. Do you know how much longer you'll be staying? Are you returning to Barcelona? Or will you get a job locally?'

Refusing to be put on the defensive, he smiled. 'I'll stay until I know you and Marilù are properly better, and then I'll decide.' He'd deliberately omitted to tell his mother or sister that Hettie felt she might have made a mistake. An old teacher had been fond of saying that no omission is accidental, so he suspected he was avoiding being asked whether he wanted Hettie back. Or did he not want to hear their opinions on Hettie's behaviour, because then he'd have to decide whether to stick up for her?

He wasn't ready to discuss her, was all he knew.

When a tap sounded at the apartment door, he rose to

answer and found Ursula on the threshold, looking summery in denim shorts and an olive-green strappy top. 'Ah, I didn't realise you'd be with your mum. I came to show Agata my haircut.' Her blonde locks were now shorn even closer on one side and the longer side ended in a more radical point than before. She hovered backwards, as if ready to slip away and come back another time.

Alfio stepped aside, to encourage her in. 'It looks great. I am sure she would like to see it.' He became a spectator from that point, as the blue-eyed Irishwoman laughingly struck a pose in front of his mother to afford her the full effect of her visit to a salon. He watched Agata smile and exclaim, '*È così moderno!*'

'I had it done on the way to Fabio's.' Ursula beamed. 'He asked when I'd have a hairstyle that's the same length all the way around. I don't think he likes *moderno*.'

Alfio did. The fresh cut exposed her face and neck just a shade more, drawing his eye. He smiled to himself, acknowledging that Ursula wore her hair to please herself, not any man who might notice the way the short side enhanced her cheekbone, or the long side softened her jaw.

It was sometimes hard to remember that she was the daughter of Stanley Quinn, the man whose appearance his mother had so eagerly anticipated.

The following morning, Alfio found himself in the kitchen at the same time as Ursula. She'd just taken a delivery from the laundry and stacks of snowy white sheets and pillowcases were spaced along the counter as she checked them against a list on Nanda's iPad, lips moving silently as she counted. A lock of her newly cut hair flicked across her cheek each time she turned her head.

147

'Cappuccino?' he murmured. He'd noticed that when she was attending to her morning duties, she rarely took time to do more than swig down a bottle of water.

Nanda emerged from the apartment. 'Me, too, please. Marilù is playing on the floor and Mamma is watching.' She made a little wafting motion with her fingertips, encouraging him into the breakfast room where the machine stood.

When he returned, a cup and saucer in each hand and one on his left forearm, as any self-respecting son of a hotelier could, he found Nanda talking to Ursula and he caught the name 'Mason'.

He raised his eyebrows in a silent question. Nanda said, 'Mason emailed to thank me for sharing the good report the doctor gave Marilù. He says he is glad.' There was a sad resignation in her eyes.

Ursula moved a stack of pillowcases aside. 'Will he visit her in the future, do you suppose?'

'We have not tackled the question of the future.' Nanda sniffed. 'I would like to forget him.'

Ursula discarded the iPad in favour of the cappuccino cup she took from Alfio with a word of thanks and regarded Nanda quizzically. 'My friend – you know, Zia, who lives in Italy? – she never knew her dad. She always thought there was a big mystery about him and felt odd, because of it. Her life might have been different if she'd known about him earlier. She found him when she was thirty.'

Nanda listened, frowning, her cup poised. 'Was it good, when she found him?'

Alfio found himself waiting for the answer, too, because, living alongside his sister at present, he felt more involved in her life than usual.

Ursula gave a short laugh. 'He's by no means perfect.' She paused to lick cappuccino froth from her lips. 'They have a relationship, though. More important is the rest of the family she found. She's now close to her grandparents and a great-aunt and uncle, as well as her half-brother and half-sisters. If she hadn't searched for her father, she would have missed out on all those relationships. People she's learned to love.'

'So.' Nanda pulled out a stool and sat, looking troubled. 'I see your point. Mason has parents, and brothers.'

Alfio glanced towards the apartment, where, through the opened door, Marilù could be heard crowing and Agata laughing in response. He'd been surprised how deeply he'd come to love his little niece, to regard her as a small human with big needs, connected to him by blood. Had Mason even told his parents that his daughter existed? If so, would they ever turn up to meet her? Alfio's mother's parents had died before he was born but he'd loved his father's parents, and they'd been a big part of his childhood life.

Absently, he watched Ursula put down her cup, then sweep the first stack of linen into her arms and stride towards the hall.

Waking up to the fact that there were several stacks left, he hefted the next into his arms and followed, up the marble staircase to the linen room on the first floor. Mason, Marilù and Nanda faded from his mind as he watched her behind as she took the stairs. She might be slender, but her curves were lovely.

His feet faltered. *Mamma mia.* He was noticing Ursula.

In the afternoon, he took up station in the office, checking bookings and dealing with emails, clicking through TripAdvisor to make sure no one had started a review fire for

149

him to put out with a soothing response. Occasionally, someone, having booked a hotel that was not full service, would complain that the hotel was not full service.

Presently, Nanda arrived, looking cool and self-possessed in a simple summer dress, her hair caught up in a red clip behind her head. 'Marilù is sleeping.' She deposited the baby monitor on the desk, a silent indication that if Marilù cried, Nanda would go to her. 'Thank God for Ursula this summer.' She dropped into the chair on the other side of the L-shaped desk so that they sat at right angles to each other, just as Agata and Domenico used to sit in the past, running the small hotel with efficiency and pride.

It was the ideal time to talk. If she looked reluctant or apprehensive, he'd stop, but Residenza dei Tringali was a family business, which meant family decisions. 'I've been thinking about the hotel.'

Nanda shrugged her eyebrows. 'What about it?'

Picking his words carefully, he said, 'What do you expect, going forward? You work with Mamma but we used to think that gradually, as she reached retirement, Mason would take her place.'

Nanda rolled her eyes scornfully.

'Sorry. We know that's not going to happen,' Alfio said sympathetically. 'What would you like to happen instead? I don't want you to think I'm trespassing on your territory, but I feel that I need to know more about the hotel's future before I make my own choices.'

Nanda frowned, propping both elbows on the desk and resting her chin on her fists. 'Mamma and I will carry on for now, I suppose, till she's older. If that's what she wants, anyway.' She puffed out a small sigh. 'But I suppose I've been avoiding thinking about it. We should ask her.'

'You might meet someone new, someone who'd want to work with you here,' he suggested. Nanda was pretty and bright. She'd certainly have no trouble attracting another man.

'Huh.' Another scornful eye roll. 'Or you might return and run Residenza dei Tringali with me.' Her tone suggested either eventuality to be unlikely.

'I agree that we should talk to Mamma. I just wanted to know your thoughts first.' He returned to his inbox feeling down. The conversation hadn't moved them on much, yet he wasn't sure what he'd expected – or wanted – from it.

That night, he made dinner, roasting vegetables with chicken pieces tossed in herbs. Marilù rolled around on the rug in yellow pyjamas, ready for bed after her final feed, while Agata and Nanda teased Ursula about the buyers who might want her work in their shops. Ursula laughed until she cried when Agata imitated a grumpy old woman who only wanted to pay one euro for any item. Alfio joined in the laughter, watching Ursula wiping her eyes on the backs of her hands and begging Agata to stop. '*No, smettila!*'

Tonight was evidently not the time to begin a serious discussion with his mother. Anyway, he could only make one decision at a time. And, watching Ursula laugh, the movement of her body and the lights dancing in her eyes, he realised that he'd just learned one thing about his future, at least.

And it was time to face that.

After the dinner things were cleared away, he went out, turning away from the marina outside the hotel, Porto Grande, and walking alongside the canal until he found a quiet bench overlooking the rowing boats moored in

151

the canal. Traffic swished past behind him and bursts of laughter floated his way from tables around the kiosks where young men gathered for a beer in the evenings. The salt on the air warred with the herby smell of cooked food from the nearest pavement café. He took out his phone and polished the screen on his T-shirt. Then he gazed at it, ordering his thoughts. Finally, he dialled.

'Hettie,' he said, when his call was answered.

'Alfio!' Hettie sounded half-pleased, half-apprehensive. After the usual social niceties, he sighed and said what he needed to say. 'Hettie, I do not think there is a way to go back.'

A silence. Then, all the pleasure gone from her voice, she asked, 'You're not returning to Barca?'

He considered for a moment. 'I don't know where my next job will be.' And he was unwilling to discuss his current confusing lack of direction.

Her voice became husky. 'I miss you. I wish I hadn't reacted as I had.'

'I missed you, too.' His use of the past tense had been inadvert, but once it was out, he didn't try to modify it. 'I put my idea to you the wrong way but, to use a phrase you taught me, there's no unsaying the things that were said. We want different things, no? I wanted to talk about a future together and discovered you were not committed.'

Her voice small, she protested, 'It was just a reaction, in that moment. We could talk about a future now I'm thinking straight.'

The water of the channel was dark in front of him, and he watched ripples fragmenting the reflections of the lights that lined both bridges, turning them into crazy patterns. Why hurt her by admitting that he no longer wanted that

152

conversation because his mind was on someone else? It was another blonde with English as her first language; more blue eyes to laugh at him. He suspected that nothing would ever come of it, not least because she saw no man in her immediate future. But that didn't stop him thinking of her, and he wasn't the kind of man who strung one woman along when another was on his mind.

At his silence, Hettie said suddenly, 'Let's give it a bit longer. I'll call you in a few weeks. Speak soon.'

Then she was gone, before he had a chance to decide whether to kill off any hopes that she might still harbour. He sat on in the dark, watching the eddies of the ever-restless sea, surprised by Hettie's reluctance to accept 'goodbye'. She'd hurt him by her shockingly bald rejection of his vision of their future together, but had she been rejecting the move to Sicily more than rejecting him? With the perspective of several weeks away from her, he could see that being woken from sleep by someone urging you to give up your job and all your friends and move to another country might prompt a blunt reaction.

He thought back to that night, the bad dream that had brought total conviction that he ought to come back here. It was disjointed in his mind, now, and it was hard to recall the near panic that had driven him.

Still. He didn't regret his return because he had more peace of mind over Agata, and he'd got to know Marilù.

It was just hard to see any future with Hettie. Despite her unexpected reaching out, he was sure she'd move on before long. And so would he.

It was just difficult for him to see his first step, and in which direction it would go.

Chapter Ten

The last day in June was a Friday. Alfio had to visit the Tringali family accountant, a chore for which Nanda and Agata had volunteered him. He wasn't sure why the meeting was necessary, as Nanda had correctly predicted that the accountant would gaze at him through her glasses and say that Residenza dei Tringali had been lucky to just about break even in the previous financial year, and that many local hotels were showing a loss. His pointing out that he felt the 'luck' had come from his mother and sister's good management and hard work had earned him a congratulatory smile, as if she was pleasantly surprised at his recognition of the fact. They discussed a tax efficiency she recommended, and he signed what had to be signed, and then he left.

Outside again, the sun felt especially hot as he walked back to Nanda's purple Fiat, because he'd worn trousers for the business meeting, rather than shorts. At least, as it was late afternoon, the shade in which he'd parked the car had remained. He drove past the old Olympic stadium and into Viale Teocrito, intending to avoid the nose-to-tail traffic of the much busier Corso Gelone. The studio Ursula visited almost every day must be close by and, even as he thought of her, he saw her, standing at the stop for the Hop-on Hop-off bus, her blonde hair blazing in the sunlight, the swirl of leaves and flowers standing out on her arm. A bulky backpack appeared to be dragging on her shoulders. She was on the phone but with scant regard for that, the traffic around him or the possible arrival of the red tourist bus, he pulled over beside her and lowered the passenger window. 'Ursula! Jump in. I'm on my way home.'

Hastily ending the call, she scrambled into the passenger seat, simultaneously struggling free of the backpack. 'Jeez, this is great. I was freaking baking there.'

He swung the car back into the traffic. 'I'm sorry I interrupted your call.'

'It was just my friend Zia. I'll talk to her later.' She secured her seatbelt and shoved her backpack between her feet. She beamed at him. 'Thanks. I would have had to go the tourist route on the bus, and it would have taken ages. What are you doing in the centre?'

She smelled of coconut, probably from her sunscreen. Alfio suddenly found it alluring, and the perfect accompaniment to her bright smile.

He turned up the air conditioning a notch because she looked so pink and overheated. 'I have been being bored by our accountant.' Then, spinning the steering wheel, he began to weave through the streets. 'You have had a good day?'

'I have. Fabio has fired the first of my range that we're calling "Il Tatuaggio". It was like getting a medal, I can tell you. I almost fainted with the excitement of it all.' She laughed.

155

He grinned, slowing to a halt behind a lorry that looked as if it might get stuck beneath the balconies of buildings either side. 'Mamma's right. You'll soon be too important to work with us.' Behind them, a driver tooted his horn to encourage the lorry to move.

'No way. Agata and I have a deal.' After a moment, she added more cautiously, 'Unless your family wants me to go?'

He knew without looking that she was no longer smiling. 'My family is very happy with the deal Mamma made.' Good manners might have prompted him to say something of the sort, but he found that he truly meant it.

'Grand.' Her smile returned and she continued to chatter about Fabio's studio while the lorry finally completed its delicate manoeuvre and Alfio drove them home, by habit glancing across the channel and into the marina as they crossed Ponte Santa Lucia, attracted by the never-ending sight of boats heading in or out of the marina.

He realised that Ursula had fallen silent while his attention had been divided between the road and the sea. To excuse his inattention, he said, 'I was just remembering watching the boats with my father, as a boy.' The car exited the bridge, and he turned off towards the back of Residenza dei Tringali.

'Do you sail?' she asked. 'Or go out on motorboats?'

'I can do either, but my family doesn't own a boat now.' He nosed the car through the gates that stood permanently open into the courtyard. He should paint them, he thought suddenly. They were a flaking green, and the hinges were dull with rust.

He parked the car, and after Ursula had had a conversation with the stray cat she'd befriended – what did she call it? Camocat? – they went into the kitchen, which was cool and empty at this time of day. Ursula slid her backpack down her arms and shot him a sidelong glance beneath her lashes. 'Can I show you something?' She looked almost shy.

Intrigued, he said, 'Of course.'

She settled the backpack gently on the kitchen island and unzipped it. Then she took something out, carefully unfurling the crinkled paper that had surrounded it. It was a white ceramic bowl. The inside base was painted with a circlet of lemons. The broad rim was decorated with the same pattern of interlocking shapes that made a narrow band around Ursula's left upper arm, threading its way through the leaves and flowers.

Slowly, he picked the bowl up, turning it over and reading '*Il Tatuaggio*. Ursula Quinn' on the underside. He turned it back to admire the fine brushwork. 'This is beautiful.'

She flushed prettily. 'I—I brought the first four for Agata. She's been so nice to me, the way she made me feel at home.' Uncertainty filtered into her voice, as if she was expecting him to dismiss the gift.

His heart melted at the gesture. 'She thinks *you* are very kind for coming, and for doing such a good job, and I think she will love your gift.'

Between them, they unpacked her backpack and unwrapped each plate, then Ursula took the stack into her hands and he strode to the apartment door. 'Mamma? Ursula has something for you. Come in, Ursula.'

Agata, who'd been reading, took off her glasses and peered at them both. 'Something for me?'

Ursula ventured into the room, glancing at Nanda, who'd just entered holding Marilù, who was babbling contentedly, one tiny arm hooked chummily around her mother's shoulder. 'These are the first of my new project,' she said, shyly. 'I thought you might like them.'

Agata's face was a mask of astonishment. 'For me?' she asked again. Wonderingly, she took the stack of heavy bowls onto her lap, turning each to catch the light. 'They're beautiful, Ursula. *Grazie mille, cara.* You touch my heart.' She lifted her arms to Ursula and Alfio stepped forward to swoop the bowls up so his mother could rise, hug Ursula and kiss each of her cheeks.

Ursula, pink with pleasure, returned the embrace.

Nanda put Marilù down so she could examine the bowls too, and soon Agata decided she was feeling stronger now and would cook. She declared, 'We will eat *coniglio alla stimpirata* from Ursula's beautiful bowls.'

'I will be your kitchen helper while Nanda feeds Marilù and bathes her ready for bed,' Alfio said promptly.

Ursula, still prettily flushed, said, 'Then I'll get a shower and change. See you later.' She looked relaxed and happy as she swung from the room.

Agata barely waited until she'd gone before she rounded on Alfio, her eyes smiling. 'She's a good, good girl. I told you she was kind.'

Alfio grinned as he reached down his mother's favourite heavy pan. 'You were right, Mamma. But she thinks it's you who's kind.'

Agata patted his cheek, as if he were five years old. 'Then everyone is happy. I'm so glad she came.' Her voice held a chiding note, as if to remind him that he'd been reluctant to see her at Residenza dei Tringali.

Alfio decided not to enter a conversation about whether he still wished Ursula Quinn gone. It was beginning to feel complicated.

*

An hour later, Ursula jogged downstairs feeling relaxed and buoyed by having had a lovely relaxing time completing the call to Zia that she'd been obliged to interrupt when Alfio picked her up from the bus stop. The result was . . . she now had something important to discuss with the family and harboured the tiny butterflies that came with wanting something without knowing quite how others would view it.

Downstairs, she found everyone gathering around the kitchen island apart from Marilù, who was already in bed. Ursula's recently fired bowls were laid at each place setting, pretty and glowing in the evening light and ready for the meal to begin.

Alfio carried a large black pan to the centre of the island, and then took off the lid to display a beautifully presented fricassee with fresh herbs scattered across the top. Agata followed with crusty bread and bowls of tuma cheese from southern Italy. Nanda made a round of the wine glasses, pouring glittering white into each.

As each person served themselves with many a compliment about the shiny new dishes they were eating from, Ursula decided to plunge straight in with her request. 'I hope you don't think the plates were a sweetener,' she began. Then faced with three blank faces, clarified, 'I mean, I hope you don't think I gave you the plates to make you agree to what I'm going to ask.'

Agata spooned tuma shavings over her meal. 'What are you going to ask?'

Ursula felt her face heat up. 'I'm, um, hoping to take a break. My friend Zia has invited me to visit her and her husband Piero in Montelibertà, in Umbria. I could take the ferry and the train.' She glanced around. 'We've never discussed time off, so I said I'd have to talk to you, first.'

Agata put down her fork and raised her hand to her cheek. 'Oh, Ursula, I have been treating you like family. You have worked almost every day.'

Ursula laughed at her horrified expression. 'Honestly, I like being treated like part of the family. But I would like to see Zia. She's been my best friend since we were students and it's because of her aunt that I got interested in ceramics.'

'You should take a week,' Nanda decided. 'I'm embarrassed that we've worked you so hard. Alfio will do your work.' She sent her brother a mischievous look, as if expecting him to protest.

But Alfio was already nodding. His eyes looked particularly dark as he sipped his wine. 'Happily.' He turned to Ursula. 'When do you wish to go?'

Ursula picked up her fork, suddenly starving for the fragrant meal before her. 'Is the end of July OK? It's the Montelibertà festival. There's lots of music, and we'll eat at lovely restaurants.'

'That will work well for us.' He glanced at his mother. 'The Ortigia Film Festival will have ended by then. It would be good to have Ursula's help during that, as the hotel is completely booked and guests from previous seasons are emailing to ask about cancellations.'

'I've seen the posters about the film festival,' Ursula put in. In such a hot country, outdoor events were common. Last week there had been a fashion show in Piazza Duomo, the pavings slippery in the heat and the nearby retailer she thought of as 'the colourful dress shop' doing a roaring trade in its clothes smothered in sequins, braids and tassels, much more affordable than the creations on the catwalk.

Nanda sipped her wine. 'The festival is in mid-July. The

160

piazzas are turned into cinemas and there are posters created by artists. It is an important event to give a chance to young directors. The hotel is not only busy, but guests also stay out later and drink more. They come back to their rooms all through the night and make a noise.' She added a smile. 'And they arrive at breakfast at the last minute.'

'I can see why you want me here,' Ursula answered with a laugh.

'We would appreciate it, if it fits with your plans.' Alfio took up his phone and tapped for a few moments. 'To travel to Umbria by train and ferry will take thirteen or fourteen hours. A flight between Catania and Perugia would be better, and the cost is the same.'

'Really?' Ursula took the phone he proffered and ate slowly while she scrolled through the options he'd called up. Flying did look a lot more appealing than a long land-bound trek.

'Alfio will drive you to the airport in Nanda's car,' Agata said, comfortably disposing of her children and their possessions. 'It is nicer than the train.'

As Nanda and Alfio seemed to see nothing wrong with this arrangement, Ursula thanked them. 'I'll ask Zia if someone can pick me up from Perugia airport. I'll book later.'

The conversation veered between homely topics such as the next day's shopping and more exciting things like Ursula and Fabio's plans for plates and jugs to match the bowls they were eating from. 'Fabio says oil pourers and serving dishes sell more slowly. We must think commercially.'

It was a lovely evening, probably the best since Ursula had been in Sicily. Nanda said that as Ursula had provided the bowls and Agata and Alfio the meal, she would clear up.

'I'll go out for a walk, then,' Ursula said. 'I feel too excited to read on my balcony tonight.'

Alfio finished his wine. 'I was thinking about going out, too. Can I invite myself?'

Ursula was nodding before he'd finished the sentence. 'Of course.' She wouldn't have minded walking alone, but it would be nice to have company. Especially Alfio's company. After their faltering start, things were now much more relaxed and friendly between them. When he'd invited her out with his friends to share the Sicilian night-life, she'd had a great time. Even sharing her worries about her parents and the sad story of the end of her marriage had made her feel lighter and less burdened, rather than depressed at reliving it all. He had been the perfect listener – interested and sympathetic.

Before long, they were once again stepping into the warm, velvety evening together, with insects dive-bombing them as if scenting fresh meat. Ursula had sprayed herself with repellent when she'd run upstairs for a small bag, so hoped it would do its job. They crossed the road and strolled over the marina car park to the sea, watching the boats bob and the water lap in a welcome breeze. She glanced at Alfio as they strolled side by side. 'I could have asked you about time off when we were in the car, but it was your mother who I made my deal with.'

His grin flashed in the dusk. 'Maybe I would have said no.'

Indignantly, she rounded on him. 'Would you?'

He threw back his head and laughed. 'No. We are all sorry that we didn't give you time off every week.'

That he and his family felt kindly enough towards her

162

to feel compunction at this small omission warmed her. She resumed her walk as music trickled over them from one of the biggest boats, an enormous thing with at least four gleaming decks. 'I was earning my afternoons at Fabio's.'

'Anyway,' he continued easily, his arm brushing hers with one of those *zing* things again as he swerved a group of people meandering along in the opposite direction. 'I am not important enough to make such decisions. Mamma is in charge, then Nanda, then Marilù, and then me.'

Smothering a giggle, Ursula tilted her nose in the air. 'I'm glad you realise it.'

He laughed. 'Tonight, you are very—' he whipped out his phone and consulted it, tapping the screen with his thumb '—pert.'

'Pert?' Ursula did giggle this time.

'Wrong word?' he guessed, moving close to her again, this time to allow a couple past them. His elbow brushed her upper arm. *Ooh, skin tingle . . .*

'It fits,' she admitted, thinking about how long it was since a man's skin on hers had evoked the response that Alfio's did. 'It's just not heard in conversation very much, I suppose.'

'What would you say?' He tilted his head quizzically.

'I'd say someone was sassy. Or cocky.' Hmm. She kinda wished she hadn't said 'cock'. She hurried on. 'I'm feeling "pert" because I've had a great day. Fab has passed my work as fit to go out into the world and now I know I'm going to see Zia. She's pregnant, so it's a lovely time, and nice of them to want me to have a share in it.' She gave a little skip. Her turn to brush against him, this time.

The lamps of the marina area and the noise of the nearby restaurants created their own little world around

163

them as he said, 'I like you like this.' His gaze felt warm upon her.

'Pert?' she queried, grinning.

He was smiling too, eyes glittering under the curls that fell over his forehead. 'Laughing. Smiling. Carefree. Teasing me. It's a side of you I have not seen so much.'

'Really?' she asked. 'Funnily enough, I was thinking the same about you. You seem less wound up than when I first met you.'

'The magic of Ortigia, perhaps,' he said. They rounded a beautiful dark pink building. After a few statues and the stalls selling costume jewellery, hats, crystals, fans, illuminated balloons and yo-yos, they passed into a small shady garden with massive trees, where aerial roots hung down like plaited beards amongst banana plants. At Fonte Aretusa, they joined a row of people hanging over the railings around the great basin of water, gazing at the illuminated statue of Alpheus chasing Aretusa, its bronze green with age. The brackish water filled was with strange, spiky, fluffy plants, the lantern light lying on the surface like floating clouds. White ducks paddled lazily, gazing up at the humans gazing down.

'Alpheus,' he said, pointing at the statue. 'Alfio, like me. You see, I am a god.'

Ursula snorted. 'A god up to no good, chasing poor Aretusa about.'

He shook his head in pretended sorrow. 'Aretusa got into the water wearing no clothes. She tempted me.'

'Ha,' she scoffed gently. 'Aretusa tempted Alpheus. Eve tempted Adam. It's never the man's fault.' But she could see why Aretusa might do a bit of skinny-dipping if there was a handsome god about.

They moved on, up a small slope and between a run

of restaurants and the railings that guarded a drop to the sea. Ursula circled back to his earlier words. 'If you haven't seen the carefree side of me, what have I been like?'

He stared out to sea, where the lights from passing vessels sparkled like carelessly flung diamonds on the waves. 'Reserved,' he said at last. 'Watchful. Not timid, but cautious.'

'Oh.' She paused to lean on the railings and follow his gaze to where a crescent moon painted silver tips to the waves. 'I suppose I've never been in this situation before. I've travelled on holidays or to visit Zia, but to take on a helping role in exchange for room and board . . . I had no real idea how it would work, but I assumed I'd be in the background.'

He turned and leaned his behind against the railings so he could look into her face. 'Is it working OK?'

'Teaming up with your family at the hotel has been better than I dared hope,' she answered frankly. 'And the ceramics part has been a dream. For Fabio to take a personal interest in me, and give me a real chance to make something happen, is just fantastic. I suppose I didn't think about the rest.'

'The rest?' His stubble had come through now it was evening, and it made his jaw appear hard and uncompromising as he frowned.

She tried to summon the right words. 'In the UK, when things were good, I went out a lot. When I was with Stephan we'd spend Sundays with friends, eating out, taking long walks, having a bit too much to drink. And Brighton's nightlife is brilliant. There's ton of clubs and bars to hit after a hard day in the tattoo parlour.' She realised that she'd barely thought about the clinical smell of the tattoo parlour recently. 'But the bad stuff that

165

happened, it did change me. I had moods. Some of the anxiety I'd had as a teenager came back.'

He was gazing at her, she could see in her peripheral vision. Gently, he said, 'You felt happy and safe in Brighton before this bad thing happened?'

'For a long time. That was why Steph's awfulness rocked me.'

They were almost, but not quite, touching as they leaned together at the railings, people chattering past, waitstaff threading between nearby restaurant tables. His voice fell softly on her ear. 'Why do you think it did not work when you gave him another chance?'

She didn't say that Steph had made it feel more like *him* giving *her* the chance. Now, she was ashamed of how eager she'd been. 'I wanted to believe in him, and that we'd return to how we were. Unfortunately, he raised his voice too much, took offence too easily, and always seemed to be waiting for me to make a mistake.' She paused before admitting, 'Or maybe those dark parts of him had been there all the time and I'd chosen not to see them.'

Alfio's dark brows knit as he considered her. Then he returned to her other comments. 'So here you have no social life?'

She blinked. She'd almost forgotten that she'd spoken of missing Brighton's nightlife. 'It's different here, but I take myself out for walks and stop at a bar for a beer.'

'Don't the men try and pick you up?' His brows quirked.

'Well, once or twice,' she admitted, though the tally was more. 'But I just smile and say no thanks.' Suddenly, she laughed. 'I sound like a saddo. Really, I'm happy in Sicily, away from . . . everything.'

He smiled, his eyes catching the reflection of a nearby

streetlight. 'Would you come for a drink with me, now? You can trust that I won't try and get you drunk.' When she didn't answer immediately, he added, 'You can drink lemonade, if you like.'

He was being so nice that she had to blink to prevent her eyes filling with tears. 'I don't mind drinking alcohol. Lemonade can be spiked as easily as a cocktail – not that I'm suggesting you would,' she added hastily.

With a wicked smile, he straightened. 'Then we might as well drink a cocktail.'

He led her further along the sea path and then turned into the maze of narrow streets to a busy, vibey bar. The street was pedestrianised, as all the narrowest streets were, and tables and chairs spilled out of the bar under dark green umbrellas threaded with fairy lights. A table amongst the locals and tourists magically came free as they arrived and Alfio promptly dropped into one of the chairs, disappointing a couple who'd also been making a beeline for it.

Consulting the cocktail list, Ursula chose Flaua Paua and Alfio Bloody Kimchi. The cocktails arrived, hung with fruit or mint and celery and decorated with twisted straws. As they sipped the colourful concoctions, Ursula used her phone to quickly book her flights to and from Perugia for the last week in July. The action – along with her second Flaua Paua – returned her to her earlier bubbling mood. 'So, tell me more about the Ortigia Film Festival,' she demanded.

Alfio grinned over his dark red cocktail. 'I've never been. It only began in 2009. It's more Nanda's thing than mine. Netflix is for me.'

'You're not very cultured,' she told him severely. Then she giggled. 'I'm more into Netflix, too.'

167

When the second cocktail had been drunk, Ursula began to yawn.

Alfio mock-frowned at her. 'You are not supposed to yawn at a man. It is bad for his ego.'

She snorted. 'Your ego is just fine.' She yawned again. 'I need to sleep.'

'Me, too.' He rose, pulling her to her feet, and he took them back a different way, winding through the streets that were quieter now it was so late.

They wandered over the slippery old paving of Piazza Duomo, the square at the highest part of the island where the Baroque cathedral loomed over them above the globes on the many armed streetlights. Unexpectedly, Alfio volunteered, 'I told Hettie that it is best we remain apart.'

Ursula turned to study him. 'Are you glad? Or sorry?'

He puckered his brow thoughtfully, but otherwise his face gave little away. 'It was the only result, really.'

She still said, 'I'm sorry,' but wondered about the unknown Hettie, who'd shared Alfio's life, let him go and now wanted him back. From the little she'd been told, Ursula couldn't find it in herself to feel much sympathy. She'd felt she owed it to herself and Stephan to try hard to save their relationship before finally giving up, whereas Hettie attempting to reverse her earlier decision seemed careless, as if she hadn't thought things through. Perhaps she didn't like sleeping alone, and that was why she was missing Alfio.

Ursula cast a covert look at him, lounging along with his hands in the pockets of his board shorts, and was unable to prevent a moment's speculation about what it would be like to sleep with Alfio.

Lost in her musings, it didn't seem long before they

arrived at the back of Residenza dei Tringali. Alfio had grown up in these streets of honey-coloured stone, of course. Every twist and turn among the monuments and ruins must be the norm for him.

Quietly, he unlocked the door. They padded silently through the kitchen so as not to disturb Agata, Nanda or Marilù, then through the hall to the foyer and up the stairs.

Ursula paused at the top of the uppermost marble flight to gaze into the stairwell, drinking in the white and grey marble and the heavy iron balustrades. 'I can't imagine growing up with all this.' She indicated the grandeur with a wave of her hand, her voice low in deference to any sleeping guests.

Alfio grunted. 'I admire it now, but Papà used to make me wash these stairs to earn my allowance. I hated the sight of them.'

She huffed a laugh. 'I think your friends Giovi and Rocco were right when they said you were a bad boy.' They turned and began the final climb to the attics, the narrow wooden stairs.

'But I did wash,' he pointed out gravely. 'I washed those stairs.'

At her door he kissed her cheeks, as if he'd been doing so for years. 'Goodnight.'

For a moment they were close enough for her to see individual spikes of stubble on his cheek and catch a whiff of his skin, overlaid with Bloody Kimchi cocktail. 'Goodnight,' she echoed.

She went into her room, where her bed waited invitingly. It was just bigger than a single, about four feet across, crammed against the wall. She thought about Alfio's bed being just the other side of that wall as a moth fluttered in the open window towards the light.

Something fluttered in the pit of her stomach, too. And *that* wasn't moths.

That was lust.

Chapter Eleven

The memory of that flutter lay within Ursula for the next eight days. It had been so long since she'd felt desire that she wasn't quite sure what to do about it, other than keep busy both in Residenza dei Tringali and in Fabio's studio. Apparently, though, her concentration was off, because Fabio frowned at one of her lemons and said, 'Melon, I think.'

Her travel arrangements to visit Zia just outside Montelibertà in Umbria were all sorted. Zia had said, 'Of *course* I'll pick you up from Perugia airport – I'm pregnant, not useless. Just tell me when. I cannot *wait!*' Ursula fizzed with equal impatience to see Zia again, happily ensconced on a rocky plateau above her husband's family's vineyard and next door to her great-aunt Lucia and great-uncle Durante. Since Zia had gone to live there, Ursula had managed a few lovely long weekend visits as well as the ceramics course with Lucia, but it would be wonderful to spend a whole week with her best friend, just chilling and catching up.

Now it was Saturday evening. Ursula ate dinner with

Nanda and Agata, Marilù beside the table in the highchair. At seven months old, she was making up for lost time as far as eating was concerned. Ursula ruffled her dark curls. 'You're scoffing that pasta down, Marilù. If you eat any more, you'll burst.'

Marilù wrinkled her nose and crinkled her eyes but didn't stop pinching penne pasta between her finger and thumb to transfer to her mouth. She had eight teeth now, and they were being put to good use.

Nanda smiled fondly. 'Soon she'll be as big as Zio Alfio.'

Marilù glanced around enquiringly.

Her mamma laughed. 'No, Zio Alfio is not here, *tesoro*.'

'He's gone out?' asked Ursula, wondering suddenly if he was with a woman. Tall, good-looking men had no trouble attracting them, after all. She tried to ignore a sudden sinking in her stomach.

'To see his friend Rocco,' Agata said. 'You met him, I think? They were at the same school.'

'Yes, I met him and Giovi,' Ursula agreed, now picturing Rocco introducing Alfio to local women. She told herself that it was none of her business.

When the reception bell sounded, Nanda rose to answer it, though reception was officially closed, while Agata entertained Ursula with stories of Alfio, Rocco and Giovi's schooldays. 'Domenico refused to take him out on the boat for a month when he failed an exam,' Agata declared. Then she smiled sadly.

Ursula knew the boat had been the one that took Domenico's life. She laid her hand on Agata's arm. 'Alfio and Nanda obviously loved their father very much. They've both mentioned him to me.'

Agata nodded.

Ursula waited for a moment and then asked, 'You haven't thought about marrying again, Agata?'

Agata looked shocked. Her smile this time was tremulous. 'Oh, I—' It took her a moment to gather herself to gasp, 'Once, I thought . . . but it was not to be.'

She looked so odd that Ursula was sorry to have brought the subject up.

Luckily, Nanda returned to finish her meal and the conversation moved on. Afterwards, Ursula cleared the table while chatting to Agata as Nanda got Marilù ready for bed, then she went upstairs, pausing en route to help an American couple who were wondering aloud how to book a taxi to Siracusa railway station tomorrow. As the phone the man was holding didn't look capable of accessing the internet, Ursula was able to supply a number the hotel often gave out and wish them a safe journey before resuming her path to her room.

She'd already mentally set aside time this evening for a cosy daughter-to-mother call, because yesterday she'd heard from Finola that her parents had had another tricky moment. 'They seem to save their squabbles for when I'm at their place,' Finola had sighed. 'Kira's beginning to be less enthusiastic about visiting.'

Safe in the knowledge that Alfio was out, Ursula went onto the balcony to call her mum.

'Hello, darlin',' Colleen's voice came, almost immediately. 'This is a fine surprise. How's Sicily?'

'Hot,' Ursula responded, with a theatrical puff. 'It was nearly forty here today. What's it like in Swords?'

'Sunny intervals, with showers,' Colleen answered wryly.

'Nothing changes, hey?' Ursula laughed. 'Is Dad there with you?'

'He's out at Gerry's, so we've time for a lovely chat,' Colleen said cosily. For the next half-hour, that's exactly what they had. Colleen had been out with ex-colleagues to see a film. Little Kira and baby Eoin were both growing like beanstalks. Uncle Gerry was his usual mad self and had bought a broken motorbike and wanted Stanley to help him mend it.

There was something so determinedly cheerful about Colleen's conversation that, eventually, Ursula ventured, 'Is everything OK, Mum? How are things going with Dad?'

'*Great*. We're out for Sunday lunch tomorrow,' Colleen cried enthusiastically.

Up on her balcony, looking out over the lights coming on as darkness fell, Ursula flipped up her eyebrows. Hmm. That didn't chime in with Finola's accounts of squabbles. Did Colleen not realise that sisters talked behind their parents' backs? Maybe not, as she had no siblings of her own. Gently, she said, 'You sound a bit strained, Mum.'

Then Colleen sighed. Ursula's stomach shrank as she waited for her mum to admit that the old arguments were brewing up all too often. But instead Colleen admitted, 'I wasn't going to tell you, if you hadn't asked. There's no need to worry, but it's Stephan,' she said, the name sending an unpleasant shock through Ursula. 'He's written to us. You can't block snail mail, can you? And we live at the same address we always have.'

Ursula's heart turned a violent somersault. 'Stephan's written to you?' she repeated stupidly. 'Why?' But even as she said it, she knew. 'Not his fecking mouldy old ring? Not only don't I have that, but I don't have much more patience. It's a ruse, Mum, a way of trying to get people to talk about me and what I'm doing. Honestly, it's tanta-mount to stalking.'

174

'I know,' Colleen said pacifically. 'We haven't answered, and I've thrown the damned letter in the bin.'

'Oh. Good.' Ursula felt her shoulders relax. 'Just do exactly that if he writes again.'

'Only . . .' Colleen drew out the word. 'The letter said he might be coming to Dublin soon and could call by—'

'Fuck*sake*,' Ursula exploded, not caring that it was a rule the Quinn children followed not to swear in the hearing of Colleen. 'He'd just better not.' She stopped to breathe hard, her heartbeat hammering in her ears. 'I doubt he will,' she said more calmly, after a few seconds to think. 'But just suppose he turns up, you can tell him that I'm going through *all* my possessions in *great* detail, to check again that his grandpa's ring is not here with me. Then you can tell him to clear off and never come back and never contact you *ever, ever again*. OK?'

'Yes, darlin', Colleen replied soothingly.

Ursula let out a strangled laugh. 'I'm sorry. I didn't mean to give out to you. He just makes me so mad I could scream. Let's not talk about him anymore. Tell me more of your news, instead.'

Colleen sounded relieved. 'In a couple of weeks, we're going to have Kira during the day for a fortnight. Finola's given notice at the nursery. Dec's parents are going to have her for two weeks too, then Finola and Declan will take her on holiday before she begins school. Those nurseries cost a fortune, you know.'

'So I hear,' Ursula said, too cross and out of sorts about Steph to attend as she usually would. They chatted for a while longer and then said their goodbyes. Ursula went inside and opened a bottle of red wine she kept in her room for emergencies. Armed with a restorative glass, she returned to the balcony to try and pick out the stars above the lights of the island, while she calmed down. But *damn* Stephan. What a prick.

When she resolutely banished him from her mind, her thoughts only circled back to Colleen's account of the state of her marriage compared to Finola's version. Thoughtfully, she picked up the phone once again and dialled her father's number. She deliberately hadn't mentioned this possibility to Colleen, to avoid the response that she knew would follow: 'Did you have a reason for wanting to talk to him? I can tell him all your news.'

'Ursula,' Stanley boomed as soon as her call connected. 'I'm at Gerry's, trying to do something with his latest impulse purchase: a motorbike. And there's not enough room in this garage of his to swing a cat.'

Ursula was warmed and calmed to hear his rich, soothing, friendly voice and Uncle Gerry saying something in the background. 'I just talked to Mum,' she began. 'I want to say sorry you were bothered by bloody Stephan writing to you, and I hope he doesn't turn up.'

Stanley laughed. 'I hope he does. I'll give him such a flea in his ear that I doubt the laddo will visit us again.'

She laughed, too. 'Jeez, I despair of him.' Experimentally, she added, 'I think he's upset Mum a bit – unless it's having Kira for a couple of weeks that she's tense about.'

There was a noticeable hesitation, then Stanley said heartily, 'It'll be one of those, won't it? Don't worry your head. I'm sure she'll be fine.'

'Really?' Ursula let scepticism creep into her voice. 'How is she really, Dad?'

Another pause. 'She's trying,' he answered. Then he laughed. 'I mean *we're* trying to make a go of things, not that she's trying my patience.'

'That's good to hear,' Ursula said softly, wishing his hearty assurances rang truer. 'And what about you, Dad?'

'I'm fine, fine, darlin'. But I've got to get on with this bike for Gerry, OK? We have the petrol tank off.'

'OK. Bye, Dad,' Ursula answered. But when she'd put the phone away, she sat watching the city lights, wondering exactly *how* tricky her parents' tricky moments were going to turn out to be. Should she call Finola? Or would her reliable big sister feel she was getting enough of the parents without Ursula breaking into her Saturday evening to talk about them?

After consideration, she texted her instead. *Spoke to Mum and Dad tonight. Can see why you're bothered but they seem to be trying. Xx*

When her phone rang ten minutes later, just when she was thinking of getting herself another glass of wine, she assumed it would be Finola but was surprised to see the call was from Alfio. Her mind instantly changed tracks and her pulse picked up. '*Pronto*,' she said, trying to be all Italian.

'*Ciao*,' he answered. 'I'm with Rocco at a bar. His girl-friend Maria is with him. She has been learning English and her teacher criticises her accent. She would like to get some practise with you, if you feel you could join us for a drink.'

It was the first time he'd suggested anything like it since that Friday evening when they'd teased each other, and he'd dropped kisses on her cheeks – kisses he hadn't repeated. 'You explained that I'm Irish? My accent isn't much like the king's, you know.' But her heart gave a brisk skip at the idea of a drink in a bar, with all the cheery Saturday evening background noises she could hear over the phone. And Alfio.

177

He laughed. 'Irish, British, American, Australian – any native English speaker will help, she says. I'll come and collect you, if you'd rather not walk alone.'

As alone was how she had been taking any evening walks, she waved this away. 'Just tell me the name of the bar and the street. You're in Ortigia, are you?' And when he gave her the information she needed, she suggested, 'Get me a big bottle of cold Moretti and I'll see you in fifteen minutes.'

She combed her hair and ran the mascara wand over her lashes. Then she examined her reflection and decided the shorts she'd worn all day wouldn't do, even if they were her favourite sassy blue ones, so she changed rapidly into a summer dress. After grabbing her bag, she jogged downstairs, exchanging smiles with two female guests as she passed them puffing up the marble staircase, then burst out of the main entrance. Taking the most direct route, she passed a couple of busy cafés and then strode through the arch onto the upper road, turned left and followed her phone map to Via della Maestranza. When she came within sight of the bar he'd mentioned, she saw Alfio rise from a seat at a small square table to attract her attention by waving a bottle of beer.

She grinned as she arrived and swiped it from his hand. 'Is that for me? Good man.' She renewed her acquaintance with Rocco, and was introduced to his very beautiful companion, Maria, who had turquoise talons for nails and make-up that looked as if it had taken an hour to apply, making Ursula glad she'd changed into a pretty dress.

Alfio lounged in his chair, and gave her a smile. She took a pull on her chilled beer to hide how the smile made her spine tingle. Then she smiled at Maria. 'So, you're learning English?'

Maria rolled her eyes. 'I speak some, since school. But my office—' She paused to summon up the words. 'It is wanted that my English improves.'

Ursula gave her a sympathetic smile. 'Well, it's a lot better than my Italian already.'

Alfio agreed, with a roll of his eyes, then gave Ursula wink to show he was kidding.

For the next hour, Maria tried her English, asking Ursula about where she lived and why she was in Sicily, with pauses for Alfio to translate for Rocco's benefit, as his English was on a par with Ursula's Italian. It was fun and, about midnight, several rounds of drinks down, Ursula embarked upon teaching them Irishisms.

'Isn't your ma a dote?' she asked Alfio. 'That means your mother's one of the sweetest people. She never gives out to anyone – she never complains, in other words. And she's definitely not a fierce eejit – that's a big idiot. And *never* acts the maggot.'

'Acts the what?' Alfio paused with his beer bottle halfway to his mouth.

His astonishment was so comical that Ursula spluttered into laughter and could hardly get out the translation to 'acts the fool'.

He made his dark eyes wide with mock dismay. 'I have to learn another form of English to talk to you? Better you learn Italian.'

Maria, who'd been listening to Ursula in total non-comprehension got Alfio's riposte and laughed. '*Sì, sì.*' Then it was Ursula's turn to be put through her language paces, at the end of which she felt she knew enough Italian for now and tried to distract them with tales of leprechauns and crocks of gold.

'That sounds like a crock of shit,' Alfio observed, in a

demonstration of how idiomatic his own English could be, making everybody laugh.

Soon after, the party broke up. Ursula would need to rise at six and Alfio was usually up and about at the same time, helping her or dealing with whatever else cropped up. She, at least, could go back to bed at lunchtime on this occasion, as Fabio was going to visit his daughter in the middle of the island so there would be no need for her to try and avoid falling asleep over painted lemons. They trailed back to Residenza dei Tringali, the streets emptier than Ursula had ever seen them. She admired carved stone and ornate plasterwork on buildings they passed, feeling gently buzzed by the beer she'd consumed.

The flights of stairs up to the attic rooms seemed especially steep and long, and Ursula made a show of dragging herself up by the bannisters, until Alfio took her hand and towed her. 'That makes the stairs much easier,' she told him approvingly, her pulse pattering at his touch. She let her hand hold his just a little tighter, enjoying the feeling of connection between them. It was the first time they'd openly prolonged a physical touch, though his arm or leg had brushed against her several times this evening.

Outside their rooms, when he turned to say goodnight, she found he hadn't let go of her hand.

In fact, Ursula realised, he'd taken her other hand, too. And his gaze was on her mouth. Heat slithered into her belly. *Oh, wow* . . . Her heart rate picked up and suddenly she wasn't tired at all. The mood on the landing altered from jokey to charged, with that special, tingly kind of awareness that told her he was feeling the same. In response to the intent expression in his eyes, her libido jumped awake with a loud, *What have I been missing? Why have you ignored me for so long?*

This man, *this* man, was not threatening. He'd only had one teeny-weeny bout of moodiness when she first met him. This man was kind to babies and gave up his summer to help his mother and sister. This man was as single as Ursula. And this man was hot, in a slouchy T-shirt that rippled over his chest and shorts so fitted that they encouraged her to notice his body.

'You are OK?' he murmured. 'Suddenly you are quiet. You are thinking?'

She tried to access her rusty flirty skills. 'Yes, I was thinking that one Irishism I didn't teach you is "a ride". You can refer to someone as "a ride".' *OK, that might be a bit too direct, even after three beers . . .* Her breath tripped up at her own daring.

His dark gaze roamed slowly up to her eyes and the flare of interest she read there proved that direct was fine with him. 'Is that as sexual as it sounds?'

Huskily, she laughed. 'It is.' When he waited her out, she added, 'If I were to say, "Alfio, you're a ride," it would mean I found you attractive enough to go to bed with.'

His smile smouldered. 'So, if I say, "Ursula, you are a ride" . . . ?'

'The same,' she whispered. From somewhere below them came the sound of voices on the stairs, but no one would come this far, as Alfio and Ursula occupied the only attic rooms. 'But many women would find it unromantic and crass. It's not . . . sensual.' She felt the heat of him across the inch that separated them as he hovered so close that their bodies almost touched.

His eyes glittered beneath half-closed lids. 'If a woman said it to me, and I wanted the woman, I would like it

181

very much.' His mouth was close to hers now, his hands scorching around hers in the heated night. He seemed to be waiting, breathing as rapidly as she was.

Ursula heard her voice quaver. 'Alfio . . .' She had to swallow before she could get the next words out, and they emerged breathy and tremulous. 'You're a ride.'

Chapter Twelve

Gently, he closed the last fraction of space between them and touched his lips to hers. He didn't grab her or crush her to him, but tasted her with tenderness, stroking with his tongue, brushing with his lips.

Ursula closed her eyes and felt the velvet glide of desire slide down her spine. He kissed the corners of her mouth and the softness of her cheek, and then the sensitive, tingly places in the crook of her neck. Between kisses, he murmured, 'Should we say goodnight? Or would you like to come into my room? Or would you prefer yours?' His hot breath shivered across her skin.

Her eyes opened to slits to meet his hungry gaze. 'I don't think we should say goodnight,' she said decidedly.

His mouth brushed hers once more and she could hear a smile in his voice. 'I agree. I think we should talk.'

In surprise, she drew back to study him. Talk? That's where they were heading?

'But not here,' he added, as noisy laughter from guests heading for their rooms floated to them from the main stairwell.

'My room, then.' Ursula dipped in her pocket for her key and opened her door. Only the light shimmering through her open curtains illuminated the room. When Alfio closed the door and his arms slid around her, she pressed close, shuddering as his hardness pressed back.

He kissed her, but then paused. 'I want to know you feel secure,' he murmured. 'We have been drinking. I do not want you to regret.'

Warmth kindled inside her as she turned within his arms. 'You're a good man.'

Even in the dimness, she caught his smile. 'I hope that if we go further, it will be very good. If you want more?'

Ursula wondered if there was anything sexier than a man who refused to take anything for granted. She ran her fingers up the backs of his bare arms and then travelled on until her hands rested on his shoulders. 'You'll be the first since Stephan,' she whispered, wanting him to know, in case it made him feel weird.

He kissed the tip of her nose. 'There must be reasons that you have not been to bed with anyone in all that time. Two years?'

'Nearer three,' she amended. A sigh escaped her, and she kissed his jawline, feeling fine stubble rough beneath her lips. 'It meant trusting someone.' When she'd brought Alfio into her room, she hadn't envisaged talking about what was going on so much as just *doing* it. Now he'd brought it up though, it was a good idea to pause for thought. She paused. She thought. Then she said, 'I trust you.'

His arms tightened. But apparently, he hadn't finished with the discussion. 'One or both of us might leave Ortigia at the end of the summer.'

'Yeah.' She clasped her hands around his neck, getting

comfortable as it seemed he wasn't rushing into this with wild abandon. 'But adults frequently make love without promises or strings.'

Did he still hesitate? 'You can trust me with your body, Ursula,' he said softly. 'And I need no strings or promises from you. After all, I cannot provide you with any, either.'

'Then we're grand,' she murmured, and tilted her head to lick his neck, savouring the taste of his heated skin.

With a groan, he pulled her harder against him and cupped her behind, intercepting her mouth and kissing her until they were both breathing like trains and Ursula's knees were shaking. Breaking away, she glanced across the room. 'My bed's only three-quarter size.'

His mouth traced a path down her neck to her shoulder and he pulled the strap of her top aside so he could nuzzle the top of her breast. 'I'm jealous, because mine is single.' He withdrew to smile down at her. 'You want . . . ?'

'I do,' she breathed, swamped by a sense of rightness. Alfio was no stranger she'd happened on in a nightclub, but someone she'd come to know over the past six weeks, who'd shown himself trustworthy in every interaction. He hadn't used being invited into her room as a green light to rip her clothes off and pant all over her. He'd encouraged her to think about what was going on, even to question whether she'd drunk too much. She let out another sigh, this time one of exaggerated exasperation. 'Oh, but wait . . .'

He froze, his hand pausing in the act of stroking her breast.

'I don't have condoms,' she whispered.

He relaxed. 'I have some in my room.' With a last kiss, he slipped out through the door, leaving it ajar.

Ursula used the time he was absent to open the door to

185

the balcony, letting the breeze suck the open curtains out into the night because, up here in the top of the building, nobody could see them except the moon and stars.

Then he was back, quietly closing the door. She reached for him and drew him towards the bed.

The time for thinking was over.

It was a hot night with a hot man. And she was ready.

Alfio helped her slide his T-shirt off, murmuring his pleasure as she ran her palms over his lean chest, tentatively at first, then sinking closer to rub up against him. Slowly, he eased her dress down to her waist, then fumbled open the catch of her bra. His hand trembled as he cupped her breasts and dipped his head to them. 'You are beautiful.'

Heat exploded inside her at the slow sliding of his mouth and hands. Then her dress was slipping the rest of the way off her, the sheets cool on her naked back as he lowered her to the bed. A rustle, as he rid himself of the rest of his own clothing, and then his skin was skimming over hers. There was little soft about his body, and she ran her hands over the planes of his back and chest, and then he turned over so he was beneath her and she could set the pace, exploring him, resting her cheek against his chest while she watched her hand move on him and listened to the unsteady beat of his heart.

Then he turned his attention to learning her body, slow and searching, discovering, testing, joyful and excited. It was the most exquisitely tender lovemaking Ursula had ever known, building and building.

She thought she'd erupt like Mount Etna.

Finally, when her skin was damp with sweat and it felt as if every nerve ending was exploding, he grabbed the condom and lifted her over him. She settled astride as he looked up at her with a smile in his voice. 'So . . . the ride, yes?'

She laughed, rubbing against his hardness and sucking in her breath. 'And nothing ever felt so right.' And in minutes she hit a climax that spun her so high she felt she'd never stop falling.

In the morning, Alfio's body felt heavy as he showered. He closed his eyes as he shampooed his hair, remembering Ursula's fit, lithe body, and the dainty medallion-like tattoo at the top of one buttock. That small, beautifully executed decoration had aroused him, probably because it was normally hidden.

He'd been privileged to see the Ursula that not everybody would see. The abandoned Ursula with her head thrown back and her eyes closed or her mouth upon him as she slowly drew him to the edge of control. A luscious mouth at the most ordinary of times, but when she did that to him . . .

He switched the shower to cold before getting out, to keep everything professional. Last night had been amazing, *amazing*, AMAZING, once he'd satisfied himself that she hadn't drunk too much and wanted him as much as he wanted her. And he had wanted her. It had taken every atom of self-control to take the first time so slowly and gently. It wasn't that he was usually an inconsiderate animal but, knowing about her trust issues, he had taken as much care of her as he possibly could. In return, she'd been so sensual and responsive that it had blown his mind.

There had just been one moment when his conscience had been uncomfortable.

He knew about her father and his mother, and she didn't.

187

He *knew* she didn't.

What did intimacy etiquette say about that? Was it morally wrong not to tell her? He'd thought hard for several moments, but Agata didn't want Ursula to know, and Stanley must want the same as he could pick up the phone any time and tell his daughter. The Agata-Stanley relationship was over and was never going to affect anything that happened between Alfio and Ursula.

He'd decided the situation could safely be left in the past.

He dried and dressed quickly. His damp hair hung in ringlets beside his eyes, and he flicked it into place then ran softly down the several flights of stairs and across the lobby under the chandeliers that had hung there since his grandfather had owned Residenza dei Tringali. They were so familiar that he barely noticed them as he called, '*Buongiorno*,' to Nino and headed for the kitchen.

There, he found Ursula bathed in morning light, filling a tray with clean crockery to ferry into the breakfast room. Her sleeveless shirt was a cobalt blue that made her eyes more brilliant than ever, her plain black skirt respectable but arousing both at once. She glanced up as he entered the room and her lips curved into a slow smile.

After a rapid glance around to make certain no one lurked nearby, Alfio linked her fingers to urge her away from her task and into one of the cool alcoves off the main kitchen in case his mother or sister bustled out of the apartment. After dropping several kisses on her face, he murmured, 'OK, this morning?'

The faintest blush tinged her cheeks. 'I'm great this morning, if a little short on sleep. And you?' She nuzzled his neck, which shot a dagger of lust to his groin.

'*Benissimo*.' He inhaled her shower-fresh scent and

touched his lips to her satin skin. 'No regrets?' He was pretty sure of her answer before she gave it.

'None.' She slipped her arms about him. 'I forgot how it could be, with no agenda or subtext or undercurrents. You're so straightforward.'

He drew back to look into her face. Her words provided a startling insight into her marriage. Even *sex* had involved agendas and undercurrents? The most beautiful and pleasurable of things manipulated? Stephan must be . . . what was that thing she'd said? A fierce eejit. Alfio wasn't surprised that this idiotic man was making excuses to contact her. He'd probably woken up to what he'd lost.

He voiced none of this, though. Instead, he kissed her gently. 'Do you need my help with breakfast?' When she shook her head as she dimpled at him, he let her go, and went back into the lobby and then into the office behind the reception desk, catching a glimpse of Nino helping a guest out of the front door with luggage.

Settling into an old green leather chair that looked like a cross between office furniture and a studded armchair, he woke up the computer and began to run through the emails that had come in since Nanda had checked yesterday evening. Insurance . . . cancellation . . . booking enquiry . . . new terms and conditions from one of the accommodation wholesalers that placed guests with them.

He opened an email from an organisation called Minton Mafflin with his cursor hovering over 'delete' in the expectation of it being unsolicited advertising. But then he paused.

The email was addressed to his mother, Nanda and himself.

189

Allow me to introduce myself. I'm Russell Haug of Minton Mafflin, hotel acquisition managers. I have been tasked by a major global hotel chain to identify a boutique hotel in Ortigia that might sit comfortably alongside their other, similar properties in historic quarters. These 'historic' hotels accommodate discerning clients on the chain's escorted tours.

Frozen to the green leather seat, Alfio read on. Research and incognito visits had recognised Residenza dei Tringali as a contender. Might the Tringali family be receptive to learning more, initially via a video conference? Russell Haug worked out of the New York office.

Incognito visits? People they'd considered hotel guests had actually been assessing Residenza dei Tringali and reporting to an acquisitions agent? It was hard to take in.

He read the email twice more, then pulled himself together sufficiently to print off copies to present to Nanda and Agata. Then he paused and read it one more time. It was too early for figures to be mentioned, but this approach had the potential to change all their lives – if they wanted that. Agata could take things more easily. Nanda would have space to decide what to do with her future.

It felt unreal. His heartbeat stepped up as freedom from Residenza dei Tringali beckoned.

It was too late to prevent him from leaving Barcelona, but if he'd never left Barcelona, he'd never have discovered the flaw in his relationship with Hettie and he'd never have had last night with Ursula.

That thought steadied him to an unexpected degree. Barcelona was the past. He'd supported his family, and he'd experienced a magnetic pull to a woman who hadn't disappointed him. And now Russell Haug's email had opened up the possibility of a new future.

He left the office and hurried across the lobby, smiling automatically at guests at the check-out machines. In the kitchen, he found Ursula stacking dirty crockery and cutlery in the dishwasher. Her top buttoned down the front and, despite the burning need to talk to his family about the out-of-the-blue email, his thoughts strayed to undoing them one by one . . .

When she flashed him a smile that managed to be both sunny and sultry, he forgot his errand long enough to swerve across the kitchen to intercept her. He dropped a hand to her waist. 'We could go for a walk, after dinner. I'll show you a nice bar in the city.'

Her eyes dropped to his mouth. 'Sounds great.' Quickly, briefly, her lips brushed his, then she swung away to continue with her duties.

Alfio turned to let himself into the apartment. Nanda, Agata and Marilù were all up and dressed. Agata had a couple of small pastries on her plate – and could do with more, in his opinion. Nanda was feeding her daughter some kind of baby mush. Marilù, dressed in the thinnest pink cotton playsuit in deference to the summer heat, shook a noisy toy and banged it on her highchair tray as she ate. She grinned when she saw Alfio and brandished the red, blue and yellow toy, wrinkling her nose so he could see her new teeth. Her curls were thicker now. It was as if everything about her was growing, trying to make up for the time she hadn't been getting full value out of her food. 'Ba! Ba!'

'She's found her voice for things other than crying now,' he observed, chucking her under her – rather messy – chin. '*Buongiorno, bella bambina.*'

'Ba,' Marilù repeated, giving the toy a harder bash.

Nanda waited patiently to regain Marilù's attention, smiling at her daughter's antics. Again, Alfio thought fleetingly of Hettie. If she found it a 'sacrifice' to commit to a proper relationship, she would have needed trauma counselling if she ever had to dedicate herself to a child. He stooped and gave his sister a rare hug. 'Your daughter is lucky to have you as a mamma.' Then, seeing Agata's gaze on him, he turned to kiss her cheek. 'And we are lucky to have you as ours.'

While the two women stared at him in astonishment at this sudden sentimentality, he turned briskly to the printouts in his hand. 'We have a message that we need to discuss.'

Agata and Nanda each took a sheet of paper and read, almost immediately assuming matching expressions of shock. Only Marilù was unaffected, saying, 'Mm, mm, mm,' as she ate her food.

Alfio waited, watching closely for their reactions. Outside, someone came to the courtyard door and rang the bell, presumably a delivery person, as he heard Ursula's voice calling gaily, '*Buongiorno*.' A clock ticked on the mantel. Paper rustled as Agata turned her page over to see if anything was printed on the other side.

Marilù gave an imperious, 'Ba!' and banged her toy, prompting Nanda to resume the progress of the feeding spoon.

Agata stirred. 'This is a shock,' she said. Her eyes scanned the lines again, and she massaged her forehead as if trying to encourage her brain to work.

Alfio pulled a up chair. 'I'm stunned, too. We need time to think, but even if we take up the invitation of a video conference, there would be no obligation to take things further.'

Nanda wiped Marilù's mouth, causing a squeal of outrage from the baby at such an imposition. 'You'd like to have the video call, Alfio?' Her tone was neutral, but the look she turned on him was searching.

He shrugged. 'It's not my nature to make a decision without all available information.' He grinned. 'Except when I rushed back here to help my family without checking if they wanted my help. That was emotional, but this is business, and if neither of you want to hear what this Russell Haug wants to say, then I won't try and persuade you.'

'Of course.' Nanda switched her gaze to Marilù, who'd just bashed herself in the face with her toy and was frowning blackly at it. While she stroked the pink spot that had appeared on the tiny forehead, Nanda looked pensive, as if wondering what her daughter would want – Residenza dei Tringali there for her own generation? That would almost certainly mean both their lives dictated by the inflexibilities of a hotel. He and Nanda had been brought up right here in the apartment of course, but Agata and Domenico had run the hotel together, and there had been grandparents willing to take the children to play in the park or on the rocky foreshore. For Nanda and Agata to manage both the hotel and childcare between just the two of them would be exhausting. Marilù was better and the delights of walking and climbing were not far away in her little life.

Or would Marilù prefer a mother with plenty of time to give her and forget the hotel?

'They're well informed,' Agata observed, interrupting his ruminations. 'They've addressed each of us by name. I suppose our names, as directors, are on the *registro delle imprese*. All businesses are registered there.'

Absently, Alfio agreed. What would his mother do without the hotel? It had been her life since she married Domenico nearly four decades ago. It wasn't as if Stanley Quinn was going to be around to make her a new life.

'This concerns you two much more than me,' he ventured. 'You're the ones who run the place, so you should make the decision.'

Agata removed her glasses and put down the sheet of paper. 'We will decide together,' she said firmly. 'That is how it has always been at Residenza dei Tringali.'

'If you wish,' said Alfio diplomatically. But he knew that he was going to go with exactly what his mother and sister wanted.

That evening, Nanda cooked. They'd fallen into the routine of taking turns, and all eating together in the kitchen while Marilù went to sleep in the apartment.

After dinner, Alfio cleared up while Ursula drifted upstairs to her room. He made sure fifteen minutes elapsed before he excused himself and followed her to the attic, insulated from the ground floor apartment by several sturdy storeys of the old building. Neither had mentioned their plans to go out together, but the pleasant prospect had drifted into his mind throughout the day, even when he and Nanda had been poring over their computers, looking for clues as to which global concern might be interested in adding Residenza dei Tringali to its hotel chain.

Ursula opened her door as soon as he tapped, a bag already slung across her body and her eyes sparkling. Her top left her shoulders bare and he dropped several kisses on her warm, naked skin while she locked her room. Soon, they were downstairs, letting themselves out of the hotel's main entrance and turning right towards the bridges. He took her hand, though it did nothing to keep one cool in a Sicilian summer.

Ursula turned immediately to the news that had been the main topic of conversation at dinner. 'Has the idea of someone buying the hotel really come out of nowhere?' Dusk had turned the sky to apricot this evening, shading the boats of the marina and canal in sepia tones.

He blew out a breath. 'Completely. None of us knows what to think. I would like to hear more but Nanda and Mamma have yet to decide. There is more than just money to think about. It is Nanda's future life. Mamma's health. The inheritance of Marilù's generation.' He gave a short laugh as they turned the corner and the bowed bridges came into view, one new and one old. A small motorboat drew a creamy wake on the calm water, making the colourful rowing boats nod against their moorings. 'I suspect it will come down to what Nanda wants, as Mamma must retire sometime, and I'm only concerned financially.'

They passed Ponte Santa Maria and turned between the stone parapets of Ponte Umbertino, which spanned the canal between *la città* and Ortigia with its five arches. From the far pavement they could see over towards the other marina that was approached from *la città*.

Instead of crossing the entire bridge, Alfio diverted right onto a footbridge. On the other side, they passed an imposing, curved, cream-coloured building and entered a much less imposing car park.

'And what about you?' Ursula asked, strolling by his side. 'Wouldn't you like to sell and get pots of money?'

'*Pots* of money? Like a leprechaun?' he joked. They remained on quay edged with chain between what looked like concrete bells before turning left up a side street. 'You expect that is what I want?'

She shrugged. 'Plenty of people in your shoes would be hoping for a big payout. Even if you have some income from the hotel, it's not your career.'

They passed a slightly down-at-heel boatyard and took a footpath past a café, where elderly men smoked and argued beneath tall palm trees.

'I came here this summer because I was worried for my family—' he gave her hand a squeeze '—not understanding that Mamma had gained such an excellent helper. Most important to me is that they get what they want.'

'That's a great attitude,' Ursula said approvingly, as they turned right past a scruffy little basin of small boats, where the mooring fees could not be high. The marina could be glimpsed through more palm trees. 'Where are we heading?'

'There. Porto Piccolo.' He pointed at the marina.

'Really? I've tried to get into that other marina but it's not as easy as it looks on the map. I decided it was all *privato*.'

He laughed. 'It is not hard to access. One of my old favourite bars occupies a cellar near the waterfront.' He turned sharp right, up two steps, through a gap in the wall and then they were inside the seawall, with apartments on their other side.

'That's a cheat,' she objected, glancing back the way they'd come. 'You knew a secret entrance.'

'It is not very secret. Everybody local knows it.' It wasn't as swanky as having the entrée via the marina gates, but it was fine if you were on foot.

'If the hotel was sold, would Nanda and Agata stay here?' she asked, slowing at the end of the seawall where the pontoons began, to gaze at the hundreds of small boats, a much greater number than at the marina outside the hotel.

A chill slithered into his stomach. 'I would guess yes, but they have not gone so far in our discussions yet. It is possible that they would move away.' Although he'd left Siracusa as a young man, a big piece of his heart remained here. 'I suppose I have always taken for granted that I am the wanderer and when I came home everything would be the same.' He'd felt like a time traveller, sometimes, coming from the fast-paced life of a comms office in a global concern where he grew and flourished to the same building where his family had always lived.

Residenza dei Tringali wasn't the only thing that held his loving family together, but without it, where would his mother, sister and niece go? He looked up at a pink apartment block. 'Nanda lived there when she was with her husband.' Would she live in such a place again if the hotel sold? What about his mother?

Ursula, perhaps perceiving the uneasiness of his thoughts, changed the subject. 'So, this big marina is Porto Piccolo and the small marina outside Residenza dei Tringali is Porto Grande? Small is called big and big is called small? I think someone got their plans mixed up.'

He laughed and slipped an arm around her waist. 'We Sicilians, we do things our own way.'

It was almost dark by the time he rediscovered his old haunt at the far end of the marina, past the diving centre and a trattoria. Judging by the sound of laughter and voices floating off the sea, people were still swimming from the breakwater as Alfio steered Ursula left, down worn stone steps to an open door beneath a sign reading 'Bar del Porto'. The cellar they walked into was long and narrow with a low ceiling and a wooden bar down one side.

'How about a bottle of chilled rosé?' Ursula suggested and moved purposefully towards the bar. He didn't insist on paying. Ursula was as independent as Hettie had been in that direction and had meticulously gone fifty-fifty on expenses when they'd been out together. Ursula probably didn't see any reason to vary that just because they'd slept together.

'Sounds good.' Alfio watched the young guy behind the bar swerve quickly around another colleague, so he'd be the one to serve Ursula, showing a lot of interest in her body art. Between his basic English and Ursula's very basic Italian, it was a short conversation, mainly consisting of, '*Bella*,' on the side of the server and Ursula waiting patiently to pay. Alfio reached around Ursula to pick up the bottle and glasses and they secured a corner table.

Although Bar del Porto had once been one of his favourite places, tonight Alfio knew no one. It was not really a surprise, but it gave him a flash of the future.

He might one day turn up at Residenza dei Tringali and not know anyone.

There would be strangers at reception. The hotel interior would be gutted – these global concerns could get permission for things small hoteliers could never hope for. The lofty stairwell with the marble stairs might be butchered to make room for a bank of metal-box lifts and the family apartment become extra guest accommodation. The gold lettering that spelled out Residenza dei Tringali above the main entrance would be replaced with some neon sign of corporate identity. Russell Haug from Minton Mafflin had said the hotel was wanted for passengers on escorted tours. With them shuttled in and out every couple of days there would be no room for the really travelly folk that raved about his family's hotel on TripAdvisor; nor the arty types who came for the Ortigia Film Festival; or even the history buffs who wanted to spend weeks exploring. Instead, the Greek Theatre, the Jewish Quarter, the Temple of Apollo and the cave that Michelangelo had named the Ear of Dionysius would be crammed into a one-day tour.

It would be better never to return to Residenza dei Tringali than witness that. His heart twisted in his chest.

Realising that he'd drunk almost an entire glass of wine in silence, he shook himself out of his mood and touched Ursula's arm. 'Sorry. I am distracted.' Noting that she'd been studying a row of old blue and white plates on the wall, he enquired politely, 'How do you progress at Fabio Ceramiche?'

Her face lit up as she turned to him. 'Fabio has placed more of my stuff in a shop in Ortigia. It's from the same range as the plates I gave to Agata, with the lemons. Now, I've moved on to grapes and a different tattoo-inspired border. I'm not quick at the border yet – it's quite intricate and it must be even.' Her gorgeous eyes glowed at him through the light from candles on tables and in sconces on the walls. 'Fabio's even talking about opening his own shop in part of the studio. Isn't that amazing?'

Her obvious excitement tugged his heart. 'I did not know this. Does Mamma?'

She laughed, her eyes crinkling at the corners. 'Fabio only mentioned it this afternoon and you guys are taken up with the approach about the hotel.'

He picked her hand from the table and kissed it. 'I have been a bad date, thinking about my concerns. Tell me about this shop.' He listened as she described the interior of the studio, drawing the shape on the table with her fingertip, then marking how much space would be converted into a sales area, where there was already a door that was presently kept locked. 'And he would sell only your work?' It sounded as if Ursula was definitely considering a longer stay in Sicily.

Her fair eyebrows tried to escape up into her hair. 'When he's such an amazing artist? No, he will sell his own work and invite a few others to sell through him, too. He would like to position the shop as somewhere where you can get both contemporary work and new twists on old themes.'

'Like your tattoo pieces?' He ran his finger over a vine of leaves on her upper arm, feeling satisfaction when he thought he detected a shiver from her in response.

'Exactly. And I have an idea for motifs that combine two aspects of Sicily, as well. For example—' she began drawing on the tabletop with her fingertip again '—you know the statue of Alpheus chasing Aretusa, and the way their bodies waver like the water? I'm working on a design where the pomelia flower takes the same shape. The gorgeous white flower takes the place of the head and the stem and leaves kinda ripple. And Fabio knows a local artist who will create bespoke pieces, so is interested in her, too.'

'Bespoke?' He tried to remember if he'd ever heard the word.

She tilted her head as she selected another way to explain. 'Say that you wanted a special present for a special birthday. Maybe when Agata is sixty—'

'She is sixty,' he put in. 'Last birthday.'

She paused to stare. 'Go 'way. Wow. I hope I look as good at that age. OK, just pretend that she hasn't had her birthday yet and you want a special present. You go to this artist, maybe with some pictures of Agata's favourite things, and she'll create a design to commemorate the occasion. For Agata it might be . . .' Her eyes became

200

unfocused as she thought. 'Residenza dei Tringali in the centre, I suppose, then something that relates to you, Nanda, Marilù and your dad dotted around the edges along with her favourite flower and something in her favourite colour, with a border weaving in and out and a big number 60 at the top and maybe Agata's initials.'

His attention was caught now as he envisaged such a thing. 'You could charge more for those than for other designs?'

'Of course. You'd have to spend time with the client and then return to them with ideas. It could take four times as long as creating something for a range you've already designed.' She reached for the wine bottle and topped up their glasses. Then a shadow crossed her face. 'But my news isn't all good. I called Mum last night and apparently Stephan has written to her and Dad and says he might visit them when he has business in Dublin.'

He glanced at her in surprise. 'See them? Have they remained so friendly?'

The corners of her lovely mouth turned down. 'Not at all. He'd be turning up at their house uninvited.' A smile flickered. 'If he does, though, Dad says he'll send him off with a flea in his ear.'

Alfio had heard the expression but pretended to be confused, just to make her smile again. 'A what in his ear?'

She did smile, though it was fleeting. 'A flea. I have no idea where that saying comes from. He'll tell him to get lost. To leave.' Then, as if hitting on the perfect phrase. 'To piss off.'

He stroked her fingers where they lay in his hand. 'Why does Stephan wish to see them? Do you know?'

Ursula snorted. 'He's claiming that I have a piece of his

jewellery, a ring that once belonged to his grandfather. I *don't* have it. Everything that I have here fits in two suitcases and my hand baggage. He's a moron.'

'He sounds it.' He hesitated. 'He does not know your address here?'

Even by candlelight, he detected her blush. 'He doesn't even know I'm in Sicily, so you don't need to worry that he'll turn up at Residenza dei Tringali causing a ruckus.'

He slid a comforting arm about her. 'That is not my worry – only that he would upset you, or make you feel insecure.' They might have only slept together once, but Alfio felt protective of her. This Stephan was part of a big trauma in Ursula's past.

The conversation moved on to more agreeable subjects than hostile exes and, as the wine bottle emptied, last night caught up with them.

They climbed back up the bar's stone steps to Porto Piccolo, and then admired the lights on the water as they strolled with their arms loosely around each other's waists. They were almost silent as they took the bridge back over the canal, the concrete monument between the two bridges empty but for deserted benches and the two-metre-high statue of Archimedes holding what looked like a small satellite dish, but was meant to be a mirror. Alfio thought about summoning the story of the 'burning mirrors' with which Archimedes was supposed to have set fire to enemy boats, but he was too tired and, right now, Ursula seemed more interested in getting home than local history.

Finally, they reached the foyer of Residenza dei Tringali. Although reception wasn't open, Alfio paused when he saw two middle-aged women hovering at the desk as if they needed help, and was drawn into a conversation about the lack of lifts at the old hotel. 'We were not given permission from the authorities,' he said truthfully, without adding that nobody had tried to change that since his father's time and his suspicion that if a big enough concern came along, the necessary permission would be granted. 'Our hotel is old – Ortigia is an old city, of course. It is possible to request a ground-floor room in the future.'

The women were British and not athletic-looking. One said, 'It's the suitcases really. They were a pain to get up to our room and when we check out on Tuesday, they'll be a pain to carry down.'

'You did not request assistance when you checked in?' He frowned as he moved towards the self-checking machine close to reception. 'We can easily add it to your check-out.' He shot an apologetic glance Ursula's way and she winked and carried on up the stairs alone. Stifling a regret at missing out on goodnight kisses, he showed the women how to input a surname and room number to access the booking details and select a time for a porter – Nino or himself – to transport luggage.

'Thank you, lovie,' said one of the women, giving his arm a motherly pat. 'We do like everything else at this hotel.'

They said goodnight and then the stairs seemed to suck the last of the strength from his legs as he climbed the long flights, thinking wearily that if Residenza dei Tringali remained in the family then perhaps it was time to begin a new fight with officialdom over the question of lifts. As he climbed, he tried to imagine what space would have to be sacrificed to house lift shafts and whether there might be grants available. On the final flight, the bare wooden ones between the guest accommodation and the attic, he trod softly, so as not to disturb Ursula if she'd fallen straight into bed.

When he gained the landing, however, he saw with a dart of pleasure that her door stood open. He hovered in the doorway, and she looked up from a backpack she had open on the bed. 'Fancy a nightcap on the balcony?' she asked, withdrawing a green bottle with a cream label and a red top. 'I bought some Jameson's from duty free and haven't opened it yet. I can introduce you to the delights of Irish whiskey.'

Tiredness ebbing, he entered the small room that was full of her things, of the scent and feel of her, and closed the door behind him. 'I have drunk Scotch whisky. This is different?'

'Of course.' Most of the many pockets of the backpack were zipped, but she opened the end pocket and slipped out a neat metal cylinder. 'I brought this with me, too. It's pewter, and a birthday present from my sister Sorcha to remind me that I'm Irish.' On the outside of the cylinder was engraved, *Essential travel items*. He sank down facing her on the edge of her bed as she unfastened the screw cap and removed it to show him the glint of glass inside before gently slipping out two cut-glass tumblers. 'Irish crystal. Look how they sparkle when I pour the whiskey in.'

He held both glasses while she tipped the bottle to half-fill them with the amber liquid. He held them up to let the light shine through the decorative glass. 'They're almost as beautiful as you,' he said, before dipping his head to kiss her.

Despite their tiredness, it was a while before any whiskey was drunk. When they finally got their nightcap, they were squashed together on the bed rather than on the balcony, but neither of them complained.

Chapter Thirteen

Alone in the kitchen next morning, Ursula could hardly keep her eyes open. Then Alfio slipped in through the door from the hall and relieved her of a stack of crockery. Depositing it on a nearby countertop, he pulled her against him, his voice husky with sleep. He was shower-fresh, and she breathed him in, leaning into his firm body. 'I'm short of sleep again.'

'Me, too. But it was worth the sacrifice.' He tilted her head up so that he could brush his lips over hers.

Then she heard Agata's voice, talking to Nanda but nearing the apartment door, and eased away. Whatever she and Alfio were doing, it was too new and ephemeral to share with others. They'd said 'no promises and no strings'. Her mind was more than half made up to remain in Siracusa after the summer, but his immediate future was uncertain. *If* he decided to stay too, she wouldn't be upset . . . but she had no intention of pressuring him.

Breathlessly, she swept up the crockery again and as the door to the family apartment opened, Alfio said, as if they were mid-conversation, 'From today, we are full for several days, because of the film festival. Then there are a couple of vacancies later, coming up to July 20th.'

'That's great,' she answered, like any friendly colleague, and swung into her morning duties.

Over the next few days, Ursula discovered that the hotel had a different vibe during the film festival. The guests who arrived to fill every room were not just film buffs but directors and actors, entrants for the prestigious competitions for fiction or documentaries, sponsors, officials of cultural organisations, course attendees or those just trying to meet the right people.

Conversations overheard on the stairs or in the lobby were less about historical landmarks and beaches and more about backers and showings. Breakfast seemed endless, not just because the hotel was at capacity but because guests seemed to expect the breakfast room to remain open indefinitely while they held impromptu meetings around the tables, during which they expected constant top-ups of coffee or juice. Alfio and Nanda shared the load with Ursula, Agata now feeling equal to minding Marilù if she didn't need picking up, and for once extending Ursula's hours wasn't an issue as Fabio had already told Ursula he wasn't opening the studio from Thursday to Sunday. His daughter and family were coming to stay to enjoy the first few days of the festival.

It was a pleasant change for Ursula not to have every moment spoken for. On Sunday afternoon, she even found time to laze on her balcony, until Alfio leaned out of his window to say, 'I am going to take a siesta. Can I take it in your bed?'

She exploded with laughter, almost dropping her bottle of water through the railings and into the courtyard, which might have startled Agata and Nanda if they were in the apartment. After opening the door to her room and letting him steer her backwards towards the crisp cool sheets she murmured, 'Is this what people do during siesta? Or is the first rule of siesta that you don't talk about siesta?'

He slipped his hands beneath her T-shirt and stroked her back. 'The only rule.' Then slowly, he pulled her top over her head, switching positions so that he could sit on the edge of the bed and draw her to stand between his legs, which brought her breasts conveniently level with his mouth.

She let her head drop back. 'Mm. I'm a fan of siesta already.'

Later, as the sun moved to the front of the hotel and the breeze that stole in on them cooled their skin, he settled her against his naked body and told her that the first decision about the hotel's future had been made. 'Mamma and Nanda agree that we should accept the invitation to video conference with Minton Mafflin. To reject the approach would be crazy when we do not know exactly what it is we are rejecting. The date is set for one week from tomorrow.'

She stroked his chest to watch his nipples harden. 'You might have exciting times ahead.' Though she spoke lightly, her heart slowed. Surely, if Residenza dei Tringali were sold, he'd be gone.

From somewhere close by, her phone rang. She leaned out of the bed to burrow for it in her discarded clothes. 'It's Zia,' she informed Alfio. 'Good job it's not a FaceTime call, as I have a naked man in my bed.' Then, into the phone, 'Hey, Zia. How are ya?'

'I'm getting excited about your visit.' Her friend's voice bubbled over the airwaves as Ursula resettled herself comfortably against Alfio's chest. 'Lucia, Durante and Piero are looking forward to seeing you too. Lucia wants to know how your ceramic work's going.'

'Pretty good,' Ursula said, deliberately vague as she had a couple of examples of her work ready to take as presents and didn't want to spoil the surprise.

Zia moved on a subject, 'Are you still getting on OK with the Tringali family?'

Aware that Alfio could hear every word, Ursula grinned. 'Ah, they're not bad. The son is growing on me.'

'Good,' answered Zia. 'Because you didn't sound sold on him at first.'

Alfio pulled a face of mock outrage.

'He's OK now I see more of him.' Ursula tried not to gurgle with laughter.

Alfio, looking appeased, pushed down the sheet so Ursula could see as much of him as she could possibly want.

'Is he single?' Zia demanded.

'As far as I know.' Ursula raised a questioning eyebrow. Alfio nodded.

'Hot?' was Zia's next question.

Alfio nodded vigorously.

Ursula let her voice drop confidingly. 'Oh, yes. A big mop of curls, you know, and flashing Latin eyes. Kinda lean and hungry.'

'Ooh,' breathed Zia. 'Got a photo?'

Ursula laughed aloud. 'I don't. He'd think it odd if I started taking pix of him, now, wouldn't he?' But she turned the phone as if to use it as a camera. Alfio's eyes widened and he dropped a hand to protect his modesty.

Blithely unaware of their silent fooling about, Zia was still talking. 'Are you going to ask him out? It might do you good.'

Alfio nodded again.

'I'll think about it and tell you when I see you on the 22nd,' Ursula promised, having every intention of spilling the beans about her dalliance with Alfio when it was just Zia and her.

They chatted for another few minutes, Zia wishing that Ursula had found a position nearer to their home in Umbria and Ursula saying, 'But it has all worked out very nicely for me in Sicily,' while Alfio quietly demonstrated one of the things that was working out nicely, and her eyes drifted closed.

After the call, Ursula and Alfio crammed together into her modest shower, then went out for a late afternoon stroll to buy gelato, hurrying to eat the indulgent ice creams before they melted. Sitting quietly together on a bench, not quite touching, they watched the comings and goings of the boats, the white hulls of which were turning pink as the sun slid towards the sea. It was a gentle, comfortable interlude.

Ursula was just thinking about returning to the hotel to cook dinner, it being her turn, when Alfio's phone rang. He glanced at the readout, his expression one of obvious surprise. 'It's one of my old bosses.' He answered the call. 'Inigo. Are you well, my friend?' then switched to Spanish, which Ursula thought was cool. It wasn't surprising, when he'd lived in Spain for several years, but somehow, she'd never thought of him speaking more than Italian and English. It made her feel a proper dunce with languages, but also meant she didn't have to slip off anywhere to give him privacy.

It was a short conversation. Alfio alternated between frowning or raising his eyebrows into his hair, until he slipped back into Italian to say a brief, '*Sì. Ciao-ciao,*

Inigo.' He turned to her, the sea breeze flipping his curls from his forehead. 'Inigo is coming to Palermo in the west of Sicily soon on a holiday tour. He has asked if we can meet.' He pulled a face. 'He is not a fan of video conferencing and has not hired a car for such a short visit, so I have agreed to drive over. It is to be the 21st, after the film festival and before I take you to the airport at Catania on the 22nd.'

'I can take the train if you want,' she offered. 'He might want to talk to you about a job.'

'He leaves on the 21st.' Alfio slung his arm about her. 'And I want to have lunch with you on the way to Catania. I am due a treat after the madness of festival week.'

Ursula didn't argue further and, indeed, after that gentle Sunday afternoon, found that festival week just got crazier.

On Monday, after more protracted breakfasts, leaving the shopping to Alfio, Ursula hurried up to Fabio Ceramiche to find Fabio much relaxed by seeing his daughter, son-in-law and two granddaughters. Ursula turned to her latest design, the flowers that somehow took on the appearance of the swimming shapes of Alpheus and Aretusa, bordered by a Celtic band of interlocked triangles. Fabio seemed pleased, if his, 'Humph. OK. I fire them,' was what she should judge by.

On Tuesday evening, Alfio and Agata babysat Marilù as Nanda had asked Ursula to go with her to Piazza San Giuseppe to see a short film in French. It lasted only forty-five minutes, so Ursula barely bothered trying to reactivate her schoolgirl French, but just enjoyed being outdoors as dusk fell and watching passionate characters on a huge temporary screen.

Much more her thing was the couple of glasses of wine in a nearby bar afterwards, sitting out beneath the stars.

'You're more relaxed about leaving Marilù than last time we went out together,' she told Nanda.

Nanda propped her elbows comfortably on the circular white marble tabletop. She looked positively dreamy. 'Marilù is well, Mamma is a little better, and Alfio is a good uncle.'

'Aw, you make him sound so sweet,' said Ursula, wrinkling her nose. Then, steering the subject elsewhere as she remembered that last night Alfio had been more 'fast and furious' than 'sweet': 'Do you not think your mother's fully recovered?'

Firmly, Nanda shook her head. 'Perhaps you think so because you did not know her before. She still lacks energy and is not completely happy, I think.' She looked pensive. Then she brightened. 'Dessert with another glass of wine?'

'Fantastic,' agreed Ursula, having discovered a taste for almond granita served with a puffy dough, which went amazingly with her favourite wine, Solnia. It was almost midnight by the time they strolled back to Residenza dei Tringali.

The film festival period was so tiring that Ursula would be longing for her week relaxing with Zia . . . if not for the fact that being with Zia meant missing a week with Alfio.

The following evening, as the festival was drawing to a close, Alfio took Ursula to an Italian film that, even with English subtitles for tourists, she found hard going. 'What is it about?' she whispered to Alfio, after thirty minutes.

'It is about the sadness of angels,' he whispered back.

She put her lips very close to his ear. 'I've seen no angels. How do you know?'

His turn to put his lips very close to her, his breath fanning the side of her face. 'Because that is the title.

211

Otherwise . . . ?' He gave an exaggerated shrug that would have made Ursula laugh if she wasn't conscious of others in the audience glued to the screen.

The moment the showing was over, they snuck back to the hotel and up to Ursula's room. They had just one more day, then Alfio would meet his old boss in Palermo on Friday and Ursula would set off for Umbria on Saturday.

Just as the first time, Alfio was tender and slow in his lovemaking. When Ursula tried to encourage him to up the pace, he murmured, 'Patience, *amore*. I have to get my fill of you before you leave to visit your friend.' By the time he had had his fill of her, Ursula was an exhausted, quivering wreck.

'No dinner,' she gasped, flopping onto her side. 'I'm going to sleep till morning.' She did, in fact, sleep for half an hour, until Alfio bit her neck and pronounced her salty, which sent her to wake up in the shower. As she dried herself, watching him take her place in the cubicle and the water sluice over his skin to form rivulets in his dark body hair, she felt herself to be not just satisfied, but truly happy for the first time in ages.

They made their way downstairs together, not even bothering to stagger their arrival for once. They even linked fingers as they swung right at the foot of the stairs and passed through the short hall to the kitchen. Maybe it was because they were both relaxed by their afternoon activities, but neither was speaking as they pushed opened the door.

And that was probably why they caught Agata in a man's arms in the middle of the kitchen, being thoroughly kissed. By their feet stood a navy blue, well-stuffed suitcase.

Ursula and Alfio halted.

Ursula had the oddest feeling, as if her eyes had deceived

her for a second, or she'd seen something in a dream and for an instant believed it to be real. That head, that brindle hair, the set of the shoulders . . .

Either she or Alfio must have made a noise because the man broke the kiss and glanced up.

And there was no escaping the truth. Ursula gasped. 'Dad!' The room gave such a giant spin that she had to put out an arm to catch hold of the doorframe and steady herself.

'Ah. Ursula,' Stanley said feebly. 'I—I thought you were out.'

'What are *you* doing here?' Alfio hissed.

Slowly, Ursula turned to gaze at his lean, handsome face, shocked that the question wasn't, 'What are you doing?' or 'Who are you?' She watched him blink, then shoot her a sidelong glance. His lips compressed. *What?* In a daze, she looked back at her father and Agata. They hadn't entirely broken free, but each rested a hand on the other's waist as if it was comfortable and familiar.

Ursula swung back to Alfio, her astonishment and shock sliding sickeningly towards a feeling of pieces falling into place. 'What's going on?'

He licked his lips and stared at Stanley accusingly. 'I do not think it is me you should be asking.'

'Oh? Really?' She took in the way he wouldn't hold her gaze and read discomfort in the set of his mouth. 'Because it seems to me that you know all about it.'

He turned to face her with a sudden, jerky motion. He said nothing, but the dark brown eyes that had been laughing and loving all afternoon, were guarded.

And guilty.

Chapter Fourteen

Stanley was the first to unfreeze. He let his arms fall away from Agata and turned awkwardly to face his daughter. 'Ursula, darlin'. I owe you an explanation.'

Ursula gazed at the man she'd loved and trusted all her life, the one she could never remember letting her down, and had to lick her lips before forcing out words. 'I should say you do.'

From the open door to the apartment came the sound of Marilù crying and Nanda answering in a comforting croon.

Stanley edged towards the door to the courtyard. 'Maybe just me and you, eh, Urs?'

But Ursula, her pulse resounding through her body, didn't budge. 'I'm getting the feeling that this concerns us all.'

Agata glanced at Stanley and nodded. Soon, the four of them were positioned at the expansive island counter, Ursula and Alfio on one side and Stanley and Agata on the other.

Stanley clasped his hands on the surface. His white and

red golf shirt had gone limp around the collar in the heat. He began in a low, reasonable voice – the same tone, Ursula remembered from childhood disasters, such as the death of a hamster or the Disneyland holiday that had to be cancelled when Ursula's grandfather became ill. The gentle voice of doom.

He began. 'Agata and I knew each other when we were teenagers on those exchange visits that Uncle Gerry mentioned, organised by the church. We liked each other – a lot – but, though we wrote, Ireland and Sicily seemed very far apart, and we married other people.'

Woodenly, Ursula interposed, 'It never occurred to me that you went on those trips. Probably I assumed you'd have mentioned it when Gerry suggested I come here.' She looked around the large kitchen, where she'd worked every day since her arrival in May and felt odd to think that her dad was here in it. 'So, you wrote to Agata after you were married to Mum?'

'Just as pen pals, you might say,' Stanley hurried to assure her. 'Barely that. Just a letter in with a birthday or Christmas card.'

Ursula had no memory of Italian-looking greetings cards or Sicilian postmarks. 'Bet Mum didn't know.'

His gaze dropped. Awkwardly, he admitted, 'I used Gerry's address.'

'Auntie Josie turned a blind eye?' Ursula tried to imagine Josie conniving at illicit correspondence.

Stanley flushed. 'Gerry's work address.'

Slowly, she nodded. 'For, like . . . forty years?' Astonishment tightened her voice, and she was aware of Alfio, beside her but not close, moving restlessly, as if he was bothered by this news, too. She didn't look at him. Her disappointment and disillusionment were like giant dragons that had joined the gathering and pushed their way between them.

'Pretty much,' Stanley admitted. 'But platonic. Always platonic.'

Agata said nothing, but her eyes pleaded with Ursula. Ursula looked away, focusing on her father's red, twitchy, uncomfortable face.

Alfio shot in a question. 'Did Papà know about this long correspondence, Mamma?'

Her chin tilted. 'He knew I wrote to an old friend.'

'I am surprised I did not know,' returned Alfio.

Agata looked uncomfortable. Maybe she hadn't been any more open with her children than Stanley had been.

As if to cover up her lack of reply, Stanley hurried on. 'When Colleen told me to leave last summer, I accepted that I'd failed at my marriage. But I was relieved. There had been a lot of arguments – as you know, Ursula.' He paused, as if expecting Ursula to murmur something sympathetic. When she merely waited, he continued, rubbing his hands together like a fly. 'I emailed to tell Agata. We began to talk on the phone and on FaceTime. I visited last summer.' After a hesitation he added in a low tone, 'We became more than friends.'

It was Agata's turn to blush, but she didn't drop her gaze. In other circumstances, Ursula might have found it adorable, the picture she presented as embarrassed but refusing to hide her feelings.

Her attention flicked back to her father, who'd hidden so much from her. 'Then Mum wanted you back,' she said flatly.

'Yes.' The word emerged from Stanley as little more than a sigh. 'It was a hard decision, right enough, but I put the family first.'

216

Alfio made a scornful noise. 'And you let my mother down. You promised her a life together and then changed your mind.'

And that was when Ursula turned to look at Alfio again, at the mouth that only an hour ago had been making love to her most intimate places; at the hands that had made free with her body. It was as if she was seeing him for the first time, like that morning he'd turned up in the kitchen – this very room – unannounced and hostile. A stranger.

'I did,' Stanley said. 'I hated doing it.'

Agata spoke up. 'But I *understood*. I too have children and a grandchild. In his place, I would have made the choice to try again with the marriage. It hurt me, but I understood.'

Alfio was staring back at Ursula now, as if trying to judge her thoughts.

Ursula didn't think the anger she was feeling would be hard to read.

She forced herself to face her father squarely once again. 'And why in the world did Uncle Gerry suggest I come here?'

Stanley's eyebrows jumped up his forehead. 'That's the devil of it. I couldn't believe it, when you came back from visiting him and told me what he'd said. I got on to him as soon as I could to find out what he was playing at. He insisted it was a solution that worked for us all. I'd been upset at leaving Agata in the lurch. Things weren't going very well for you, and you wanted to travel to Italy. You know your Uncle Gerry,' he added with a trace of bitterness. 'Speak first and think later. I called Agata and asked if I should put a stop to it.'

For the first time since she'd found the couple in a

clinch, Ursula addressed Agata directly. 'Why in hell would you want me here?'

Agata blinked rapidly, as if fighting back tears. 'I didn't know you, but under different circumstances we would have been like family. Stanley said you needed a fresh start and coming here would help you. And it would certainly help me. I felt very unwell.' She smiled tremulously. 'Ursula, you have been wonderful these last months. You have made my recovery possible. And . . . I care for you.'

Ursula didn't attempt a response. She felt like a reporter, gathering facts and creating bullet points. It would be later that she'd work it into a cohesive story and decipher subtext. 'And Nanda knows about you two?' she went on rigidly.

'Yes,' Agata whispered.

Tentatively, Stanley began, 'Darlin', I can see you're shocked—'

She cut across him. 'So why are you here now, Dad? Where's Mum? Are you cheating, or does she know where you are?'

He paled, his face drawing into deep lines. 'I tried, Ursula – *we* tried – but the relationship was past saving after all. Maybe if we'd kept up with the counselling . . . but there you are. We didn't. She accused me of having another woman once too often and I broke down and told her I had given up another woman for her and was beginning to think it a big mistake.'

Agata made a soft sound of distress.

He paused to take her hand, before turning back to Ursula. 'I told her about Agata, and that it had honestly been platonic until Colleen and I split up. After that confession, there was no point pretending, not for your mother's sake or the family's.'

'And how is she? Will she be OK?' Ursula stomach pitched as he imagined her mother alone and bawling in that big house.

'Finola went to her.' Relief flickered in Stanley's eyes.

'While you ran away to your girlfriend? Lucky Finola.' Before Stanley could do more than recoil with shock at her bitterness, Ursula ploughed on. 'What about Caden and Sorcha? Do they know?'

'We told Finola, Sorcha and Caden together.' Stanley's voice was tight with strain.

Ursula imagined none of her siblings had been totally shocked that their parents' volatile marriage had foundered again, but the break-up itself wasn't what was prompting the queasy, cold feeling in her stomach. 'But you decided that the best way to let *me* know would be for me to find you snogging Agata?'

'How were we to guess you'd walk in just then?' Stanley objected defensively.

Ursula leaned towards him, making sure she'd collected his gaze before she spoke. 'I *work in this kitchen*, as you very well know. It was obvious that I *might* walk in. Did you not think of me at all?'

Stanley flinched. Then he took a long breath. 'I'm sorry. You're right. I saw Agata and kinda . . . lost my head. Your mother and I agreed that I would tell you in person, just as she and I had told your brother and sisters in person. It seemed best.'

'Best for who?' Suddenly, Ursula was on her feet, her stool screeching unheeded behind her across the floor. 'I'm off out. I need to think.' Her legs felt as if she was breaking them in for a stranger as she crossed unsteadily to the double doors and stepped out into the courtyard, in shadow at this time of day. Camocat sat atop the wall and fixed her green eyes on Ursula, the purveyor of scraps and water.

From the kitchen, Ursula heard Alfio burst into in a stream of low, rapid Italian.

Then Stanley was behind Ursula, laying a detaining hand on her arm, his voice urgent. 'I would not have started anything with Agata last year if I hadn't truly believed my marriage was over.'

Ursula turned to stare at his dear, creased, concerned face, feeling tears welling for the first time that this kind man, her hero, had such enormous feet of clay. She thought of all the times her mother had insisted that Stanley possessed a roving eye and Stanley had been vehement that it was all in Colleen's jealous imagination. Yet Stanley had been corresponding with Agata for forty years. Forty years! Dully, she said, 'Even suppose that's true, have you thought what position this puts me in? That I'm living with Agata, Mum's replacement? That I've become friends with her and her family?' *And I'm sleeping with her son,* she added in thoughts that immediately shied away from the subject. She'd have to deal with Alfio later. Not yet.

Looking stricken, her father did the nervous hand-rubbing thing again. It was getting on Ursula's nerves. 'Darlin'', don't be thinking you'll have to leave Ortigia—'

And Ursula exploded. 'How the hell do you think me staying would make Mum feel? And if I did stay, how will it be when she starts asking me about you and your doings? What will you expect of me, eh, Dad? To describe your days with your new love? Or to fend off my mother on your behalf?' Dimly, she was aware of Camocat darting off the top of the wall and disappearing. Evidently, shouting was not a new phenomenon in her life.

220

Silence.

Bitterly, she added, 'You won't trust me not to tell her things. She won't trust me unless I do. Trust's important. If you don't have trust, you don't have a thing.' Spinning on her heel, she stalked out of the gates and into Via Duca degli Abruzzi, turning blindly left and then right and crossing the busy road to where the bridges dreamed in the sun. She reached a patch of grass on the quayside between the bridges before her legs gave way, and she flopped down in the scant shade of palm trees and banana plants. A woman selling tickets for the tuk-tuks that carried tourists around Ortigia looked at her curiously and she realised that her small oasis was little more than a traffic island, surrounded by bikes and scooters, with people trying to park cars nearby.

So what? Her legs didn't want to carry her further.

She lay on her back, looking up through the fleshy leaves of banana plants at a cloudless sky softening to lavender, ready for dusk to steal in. She tried to will her heartbeat to slow so that the blood would cease rushing in her ears, but her emotions roiled like a nest of snakes, snarled up and impossible to control.

Outrage.

Disappointment.

Shock.

Disillusion.

And *hurt*. She hurt. She ached inside.

She must call her mother. She couldn't say to herself, 'Ah, well. It's up to the parents, really, isn't it? Best if I keep out of it.' Like it or not, she was neck-deep in this mess.

Without bothering to sit up, though the coarse grass prickled through her top, she dragged her phone from the pocket of her shorts and dialled. When the call connected, she said baldly, 'I've just seen Dad.'

'I've been waiting for you to ring, love.' Colleen's voice wobbled.

'I don't know what to say. How are you finding things?' Behind her, two cars got into a honking match in the parking area, and she covered her free ear to hear her mother.

'OK.' Colleen sniffed. 'In the circumstances.' A sigh broke and became a sob. 'I'll say the same to you as I said to your sisters and your brother. It's time to face facts. Me and your dad are just not going to work.' Her final few words trembled; sorrow was too heavy a weight for them to bear.

Ursula had to swallow a lump. 'But for pity's sake, you know why Gerry suggested I come here? Like, in Dad's place? Aren't you mad as hell?'

Colleen's laugh was bitter. 'For the first two days, I could have killed your father. And your uncle Gerry – I'm still not talking to him. All I could think about was Stanley with *her* and you with her . . . But I've calmed down. It was me who asked him to leave before, and without that he probably would never have gone to see her.'

Ursula examined this thought and found she agreed, but that now the point was moot. 'Do you want me to come home?' Mentally, she began to rehearse telling Zia and changing her flights.

Colleen's voice broke. 'Before, I would have said yes. It would be a great stepping stone to the moral high ground, wouldn't it? "I had to get Ursula away from that evil woman's house." Then I thought how happy you've been in Sicily and that you're getting on so well with Fabio, with him opening a shop to sell your gear and all. You shouldn't suffer for our problems, and you'll have your dad near, won't you?'

Spotting this as a corner for her to be backed into, exactly as she'd tried to tell her father only ten minutes earlier, Ursula said flatly, 'I have no idea if I'll be staying here, Mum. No idea at all.'

Colleen's caring mother side came through. 'You're going to visit Zia any day now, aren't you? You go and enjoy that. Finola's here if I need a shoulder to weep on.' There was a note of wry humour in that comment, but Ursula's conscience pinched her. Finola fulfilling the dutiful daughter role all over again. Sometimes you'd think Colleen only had one child, not four.

When the call was finally over, Ursula remained prone as the busy life of Ortigia went on around her. After allowing herself time to gather her thoughts, she dialled Finola's number then listened to the ring tone, reflecting how poor Finola ended up looking after everyone. At least she had her husband Declan, one of the good guys. It would have only needed Finola to have been lumbered with a lazy-arse partner for her to be run into the ground. And here was Ursula pitying herself on her gorgeous new situation, living the life of Riley, surrounded by historic buildings, yachts and motor cruisers.

'I'm sorry. You've copped the lot again,' were her first words to the eldest of her siblings. Disregarding Colleen's instructions, she demanded, 'Do you want me to come home?'

Finola answered wearily. 'You're off to Zia's this weekend, aren't you? Mum was saying.'

'I can change it if you want me home. You know Dad's turned up here? And why?' Ursula let her eyes close. The sun was low and laying sunrays on her, as if needing a hand down towards the sea as it ended its day.

223

'Hang on,' Finola said. 'Sorcha's just arrived, so I'll put you on speaker.'

For a few moments Finola's end of things consisted of a quick explanation to Sorcha and Sorcha's voice demanding, 'Why should she come home? What the feck could she do to change anything?'

Ursula almost smiled at her little sister's bluntness. But when the three sisters had talked for ages, Ursula and Finola concluded that Sorcha had a point. There really was nothing to be done and no sides to be taken and though Ursula was in a tricky spot, her scurrying back to Ireland wouldn't miraculously mend their parents' marriage.

'How did Caden take the news?' Ursula asked.

Sorcha answered, 'Oddly, he's taken it quite hard. I thought maybe it was just the childcare for baby Eoin he was worried about, but he seems genuinely disappointed. How about you? How did Dad break it to you?'

'Not with words,' Ursula said wryly. 'I walked in and found him sucking the face off Agata. I nearly shit a brick.' Alfio had been at her side, then. She was glad he hadn't come after her, but he was hovering at the top of her mind. She wondered what he'd said to his mother. Whether he'd had a go at her dad – another tricky situation for her if he had, but she wouldn't blame him.

As if reading her mind, Finola put in, 'Odd for you, being with Dad's girlfriend all this time. And you didn't know a thing?'

Ursula's sigh felt as if it sucked all the air out of her chest. 'Very odd, and no, not a thing. Do you think I would have kept you in the dark, if I'd had any idea?'

Finola gave a short laugh. 'I don't suppose so. But you've been quite friendly with her . . .'

224

The sentence tailed off, unfinished, and Ursula replied hollowly, 'Seems as if I didn't know her at all, though.'

When that call was finally over, she called Caden who, as Finola and Sorcha had suggested, was winded by the whole situation. 'I can't believe it of Dad,' he mumbled. 'I always thought there was nothing in it when Mum went on at him about other women.'

'He insists it was platonic till Mum kicked him out last year.' Ursula didn't exactly stick up for Stanley but felt she ought to point this fact out . . . presuming it was a fact. 'I hope this shit doesn't divide the family. I don't think Mum or Dad would want that. We weathered it last time.'

'Suppose,' Caden agreed noncommittally, and Ursula pictured him hunching his shoulders as he did when he wasn't convinced. He went on, 'Bree says she could see it coming a mile off and thinks Mum and Dad will be better apart. Dad's arrived in your area, presumably.'

She snorted. 'How come you all knew Dad was coming to tell me and not one of you let on?'

'Because that's what Mum and Dad wanted,' he said reasonably. 'One of them to tell you face to face.'

Something in his voice alerted her to an angle she hadn't properly considered, in all the shitty mess that today had turned out to be. 'Like, because Ursula is so fragile that she couldn't receive the news alone?' she demanded in outrage.

'A bit, I suppose,' he answered frankly. 'Mum and Dad went across to the UK to tell you last time, didn't they?'

It was true. She hadn't even questioned that. Sorcha, Finola and Cade had been told in person, so it seemed reasonable that they come and tell Ursula, too. Even though the others lived in Swords, and she'd lived a flight away, it hadn't felt like Ursula getting special treatment in case she needed extra support.

Bollocks. She was officially a weak reed in the eyes of her family. 'There was no feckin' need,' she said defensively. 'No need for Dad to come here – oh, except to be with his secret girlfriend. Agata accepted me substituting for Dad because, apparently, everybody agreed that I needed a fresh start. I wish people would discuss my needs with me!'

'You'd had such a heap of shit at once, with Stephan and then your job and flat,' Caden began. 'And if you were with Agata, she'd alert Dad if anything bad happened to you.'

'*Alert Dad?*' she half-bellowed. 'I coped with the shit; I don't need babysitting.'

But Caden, apparently, was in a direct mood. 'There was that one time, Urs. You took pills.'

'*That was—*' She took a long breath, remembering the dark day when, with no Zia to turn to because she was out of the country, she'd gone to bits. 'Sorry, Cade. I'm not mad at you.'

'Good,' he said mournfully. 'I should go help with Eoin while Bree cooks.'

By now, Ursula had almost no life in her phone battery anyway. After saying goodbye and sitting up to watch a couple of small motorboats lining themselves up to putter through the arches of Ponte Umbertino, she finally climbed to her feet and headed back to the hotel, going in via the front entrance. Although she flung a glance at the reception desk and the door to the area of the hotel not open to guests, she saw no member of the Tringali family or, for that matter, of hers.

Quietly, she slipped up the stairs, which seemed to have

doubled in number since she'd danced up them alongside Alfio this afternoon, eager for his delicious lovemaking. Treading especially quietly on the attic landing, she let herself into her room and locked the door. After plugging in her phone, she paused when she heard someone moving around in the next room. *Alfio*. Her heart twanged.

Angrily, she pulled out her backpack where the bottle of Jameson's was stored. The crystal glasses had been washed and put back in their pewter cylinder after she and Alfio had used them. She pulled out the top one and laid the cylinder on the bed rather than bother screwing the lid back on. She filled her tumbler almost to the brim and grabbed a packet of grissini, the Italian breadsticks she kept up here for snacks. Her appetite had deserted her, but she'd missed dinner and was going to need something to soak up the whiskey.

Opening the balcony door with a clatter designed to be heard, she took her glass out onto the balcony and flopped down onto the small iron chair. Almost immediately, Alfio's window rasped up.

She turned her head to regard him, noting the crease between his eyebrows, the vulnerable set to his lips. 'You are OK?' he asked softly.

It was for all the world as if he was worried about her feelings, she thought savagely. She ignored his socially acceptable conversation opener. 'You knew,' she stated flatly.

Slowly, maybe resignedly, Alfio swung both his legs over the sill and took up station, his bare feet dangling in the air as he faced her. It was a tacit acceptance of a new distance between them that he didn't ask to come to her. 'What I knew is this: for some time, Mamma was happy because there was someone in her life. He was Irish. She told me his name and that they had known each other when they were young. He was to come here to spend this summer to help after her operation and she hoped it would lead to something permanent. Later, she was unhappy and disappointed that he had let her down. I was angry with him.'

'It didn't occur to me that when you said you didn't like my father, you really didn't like my father,' she commented. 'So, you knew who I was when you arrived here?' She took a gulp of whiskey, welcoming the burn in her throat.

He tilted his head. 'Not on the first day. Then when I realised you had the same surname, I talked to Mamma. I was not pleased.'

'I wondered why you were so snitty with me. I remember hoping you wouldn't stay long.' Thoughtfully, she bit the head off a breadstick and crunched. When she'd chewed and swallowed, she asked, 'Why didn't you or one of your family tell me the truth?'

He hunched his shoulders. 'Mamma didn't want us to. After two bad summer seasons she felt the hotel needed to be careful with its financial resources and the arrangement with you suited her well. Her spirits were low. And, perhaps, like Stephan liked having a link to you, she liked having a link to your father. Also, as I found out later from Nanda, she took it seriously when your father said being here would help you.'

'Poor little Ursula,' she said ironically, swigging whiskey and feeling it burn her throat again, this time along with a mixer of unshed tears. 'Let's give her a nice little job to pay for her keep so she can spend her afternoons painting pretty pots.' Earlier she'd been unable to untangle and direct her emotions, but now she realised the outrage, disappointment, disillusion and shock was directed at Alfio, not just her dad. It was there for Nanda and Agata, too, of course, but towards them it was a kind of second-tier anger – which only told her that she'd begun to care about Alfio too much. 'You can't trust a fucking soul,' she told herself aloud, and drank a large mouthful. That's what made her eyes water, she told herself. It wasn't the tears refusing to be held back.

Alfio absorbed her comment in silence.

Her voice cracked. 'You came into my bed, knowing all these things, and knowing that I *didn't* know them.'

His head drooped. 'I realised. But I felt I must follow Mamma's wishes, and I thought it would never affect us. Their relationship was over, I thought.'

'You had no right to keep it from me,' she said brutally, surging to her feet. She faced him, placing a hand over her heart as if it pained her physically. 'You, your family and my dad have all lied, or at least not told the truth. Kept secrets. Patronised me by deciding what was good for me.'

'Ursula,' he said softly, his eyes pleading with her as much as his words. 'Nobody wanted to hurt you. It wasn't like that—'

'It was exactly like that,' she snapped and turned to the door back to her room. 'I can't trust someone who keeps the truth from me. Enjoy your business meeting tomorrow.'

He tried again. 'I'll cancel—'

'Don't bother. Tomorrow will be too soon for me to want to talk.' She half-ran into the sanctuary of her room and slammed the balcony door, twisting the latch that locked it. Her palms were hot and sweaty with anger, but ice had formed around her heart.

The need to flop down on her bed seemed to remove

229

the bones from her legs. The pewter cylinder Sorcha had bought her was in the way and she snatched it up and threw it aside, letting it tumble end-over-end across the bed. With no lid, the contents came flying out but, luckily, the second crystal glass only rolled harmlessly onto the sheet.

But something smaller flipped out of the cylinder and spun into the air. It somersaulted twice, then fell onto the floor and rolled.

Ursula swooped down to retrieve it. And then halted, horror and dismay rising up to choke her.

Gingerly, slowly, she picked up the item, holding it between finger and thumb. She groaned aloud when she saw the thick gold band, the old-fashioned setting and ugly purple diamond.

Although she'd worn herself out before bed, Ursula lay sleepless. It was hours since she'd found Stephan's grandpa's ring and though she'd need to get up soon, her brain wouldn't stop whirring.

She switched on the bedside lamp and picked up the chunky, worn ring from where she'd left it on the bedside. The last time she remembered seeing it, it had been in Stephan's old watch box with other small valuables. Its thick, hallmarked gold band supported a cushion-like purple stone and looked like something John Travolta might have worn in *Pulp Fiction*. Stephan had rarely worn it, claiming the claws that held the stone were worn and the ring would be ruined if they failed, though, truthfully, he plain hadn't liked it, and she hadn't blamed him.

So, what now?

She must return Steph's property to him, though she didn't know his current address, other than that it was

230

presumably in Brighton. She knew the solicitor who'd acted for him in the divorce, but who told a solicitor, 'Ah, look, I have something that's not mine?' She could send the ring to her ex-mother-in-law Claudia or even Charlotte and Drew, but she could imagine their reactions only too well. *Oh, really? You just 'found' it, did you? Funny you should, once you knew Stephan was looking for it.* The thought of their scepticism made her skin crawl. The ring might look cheap, but it wasn't, and even if it had been glass and tin, its worth was in its memories of a grandfather Stephan had loved.

One fact kept cartwheeling through her mind as bright and impossible to ignore as a Catherine wheel: the only way the ring could have got into Ursula's things was if Stephan had put it there.

It had been cunning of him to select an item she might not use immediately but, it being a present from Sorcha, would never throw away. While she was elsewhere in their house gathering up the shreds of her life to pack into boxes and bags, it would have been simple for him to sidle into the bedroom and secrete it. He'd been like a hacker, but instead of stashing spyware in her computer, he'd inserted into her possessions a reason to harass her, to infiltrate her life. Who *thought* like that?

For a split second, it crossed her mind to throw Grandpa's ring away or give it to charity. The counsellor Ursula had seen after having her stomach pumped had suggested she had an emotionally impulsive nature, but disposing of something that didn't belong to her would be a disgraceful carry-on. And Steph, the complicated man she'd once loved, would be gambling on her seeing things that way.

She put down the ring, switched off the light and turned

over in bed, naked in the hot night but for a sheet across her legs. In the echo chamber of her mind, she heard Stephan. *Why did you have to go to that club? How could you not look after your own drink? You're not eighteen anymore, Ursula. That bloke could have touched you anywhere.* Stephan wasn't the kind who liked other men to even look at his wife.

As if her ex-husband was there in the room, she said into the darkness, 'Anything but blame the real culprit, the person who spiked my drink, eh?' Stephan had refused to even read the research she'd amassed, which said roofying could be a random act, a power-versus-vulnerability thing often perpetrated by some guy who was generally unsuccessful with women.

The episode had shown her the real Steph.

Would what she did with the ring show the real Ursula?

Chapter Fifteen

Dressed in the now unfamiliar office clothes he'd put on to meet his old boss, Inigo, Alfio tugged at his collar and shifted in the seat of the little purple Fiat that Nanda had let him borrow. He'd agreed to a late-morning meeting because Inigo had to catch the hydrofoil to Malta in the early afternoon on the next leg of his holiday tour. That had meant leaving the hotel at a ridiculous hour and he didn't know why he was keeping the appointment at all, when Stanley Quinn had turned up only yesterday like a cat amongst previously peaceful pigeons.

And one of those pigeons had begun looking at Alfio as if he was in league with the cat.

Last night, after Ursula had been colder than he would have guessed possible, he'd lain awake, listening to her moving around her room. This morning, he'd had to rise even earlier than she usually did, and he'd heard nothing when he'd listened at her door, so had left her sleeping.

The early morning traffic between Siracusa and Catania was crazy. The satnav instructed Alfio that there were severe delays on the A19, which crossed the island east-to-west, and his fastest route was to drive the whole damned way around the coast, adding an hour to the journey time he'd hoped for – though at least the edges of Sicily were flatter than the middle.

His foot wavered on the accelerator pedal. Should he call Inigo and cancel? The guy was his boss no longer.

But Ursula's words were painfully fresh in his mind. *Tomorrow will be too soon for me to want to talk.* Had he stayed at Residenza dei Tringali, watching her bustle through the breakfast routine and take out scraps to the stray cat she'd befriended, he wouldn't have been able to stop himself from trying to change her mind and, on reflection, that was not the way to regain her trust. And Ursula was a woman with trust issues.

It was difficult to concentrate on the road when all he kept seeing were her enormous, shocked blue eyes, burning with hurt disbelief as she realised how many people, including Alfio himself, had been keeping a secret that struck at the very heart of her family.

Damn Stanley Quinn, he thought darkly. The congestion on the road approaching Catania allowed him plenty of time to think about the evening before, when Agata had told Alfio in no uncertain terms that she had no intention of sending Stanley away.

Nanda, just settling down to relax after putting Marilù to bed, had been stunned when she realised her mother's missing boyfriend had apparently left his wife and was standing before them, wearing an expression of apprehension along with his travel-crumpled clothes, while Agata gently indicated to her children that Stanley would be moving into her room.

And Stanley had given Agata a warm, intimate smile.

Nanda's gaze had met Alfio's, her eyes full of questions. *Are you comfortable with this? Aren't you shocked?*

He'd glanced at Stanley again. Part of him wanted to biff him on the nose for all the upset he'd caused but the look he was giving Agata was filled with love, and Agata was gazing at him in exactly the same way. He'd thought of Ursula, who'd slipped away into the evening before he'd realised that she was going, alone and hurting, and wished she was here, giving him soppy looks like that. He'd said to Nanda in Italian, 'I think it's Mamma's decision.'

Agata looked like Agata again. Roses were back in her cheeks and the air of frailty had vanished. She seemed to have shed ten years from her age since her prince had kissed her in the kitchen. Alfio wasn't sure if a sixty-something man with brushy greying hair and a not-particularly-trim beard was the prince of fairy tales, but probably Agata saw the young man she'd first known rather than the middle-aged man he'd become. It would have been different if Papà had lived, but they'd lost him. Then, she'd lost Stanley. Now he was back.

Agata had lived without a partner to love for a long time and now she looked to be an unsettling and uncharacteristic mixture of dizzy and joyful.

He felt dizzy himself, but there was no joy in it. Just a deep, frightening feeling that something valuable was sliding away from him.

The traffic became lighter once he'd driven past the area around Catania airport. Ursula would be taking off from there at four-twenty tomorrow, bound for Umbria. By then, Alfio determined, he would have made time to talk to her properly, to *apologise* properly – had he apologised at all, last night, perched on his windowsill just like the stray cat sat on the courtyard wall? Or had he only justified?

He owed her an apology.

As soon as he began sleeping with Ursula, he should have told Agata he was going to tell her the truth. Surely Agata would have understood, if – as they'd supposed at the time – it was all over with Stanley, anyway?

He yearned to call Ursula. But not respecting that she didn't want to talk to him yet would probably mean – what was that odd expression? – a flea in his ear. It didn't sound fun.

The traffic sped up again and he settled into the long drive, grateful for his sunglasses and the car's air conditioning as the sun began to blaze on the asphalt.

The rest of the journey passed on autopilot. He met Inigo at his hotel. His old boss, looking more relaxed than Alfio felt, greeted him with evident pleasure and plied him with cappuccino and biscotti.

'How is your family, now?' Inigo asked genially, smoothing his thinning, greying hair. 'It was your mother who was ill, was it?'

'She is almost better, and my niece's surgery was successful.' Alfio smiled, enjoying the feeling of Spanish on his tongue again.

'Excellent.' Inigo's smile widened. After a few more minutes of polite conversation, he got down to business. 'Now, tell me your plans.'

Alfio had no plans, at least not past getting Ursula alone tomorrow, so he shrugged. 'Fluid. It is perhaps still a little early.'

Unexpectedly, Inigo said, 'I'm retiring.'

Alfio took a second to place his empty cup on the table, his mind slipping mechanically into work mode, when work had been a busy comms office, rather than the family hotel. 'Oh? You will be missed.' Inigo had responsibility for offices in a large swathe of Europe and Alfio's mind flew automatically to whether someone would be brought in from outside to replace him, or whether restructuring might redefine his role.

Inigo inclined his head at Alfio's compliment. 'I was very sorry that you left our company. If you're free to leave Sicily again now, would you consider stepping up?'

'Into your role, do you mean?' Shock rippled through Alfio. Inigo's was in a senior management role, part of the executive team. It brought a bigger salary and a greater number of benefits than Alfio's old position. A few months ago, he would have had trouble not leaping from his seat in jubilation.

Now, he tried to think clearly and pragmatically. 'That's an amazing offer,' he marvelled, wearing an appropriately amazed smile. 'I'd love to hear more, but I should explain first that my family has received an approach to buy our hotel. I may not be free immediately.'

Inigo waved that away. 'There is some flexibility. I don't mean to retire overnight. Let me tell you what we have in mind.'

The late morning meeting ran into lunch, until, eventually, a taxi containing Inigo's wife Franca and their luggage turned up to run Inigo down to the hydrofoil. He got up and shook Alfio's hand. 'I will be in touch after the rest of my holiday. I hope that the way through your family business will be clearer by then.'

Alfio's journey home was even worse than the journey there, and not just because he was flabbergasted by today's turn of events. The satnav allowed him to drive across the middle of the island but then traffic ground to a halt because of an accident ahead, just when he was in the section just before Enna, where there were really no sideroads to take. While impatient hands thumped on car horns, he sat quietly, reflecting on the magnificent job offer and knowing that he should be jumping at the opportunity.

But Ursula kept crowding into his mind. The stillness of her body as she'd gazed at him and known the truth.

Again, he fought with the temptation to call her. It would be better to wait to see her in person . . . if he ever got the car moving again. It was troublesome that she'd be leaving for Umbria tomorrow, but at least that meant he'd have the car journey to explain to her how sorry he was that he hadn't seen a better way to go about things until it was too late.

It was mid-evening when Alfio finally parked Nanda's car in the courtyard in approaching twilight. The stray cat was waiting on the wall but when he emerged from the car, it gave a start and slunk down the other side of the stonework, out of sight. Probably it had been hoping for Ursula.

The kitchen was empty and, thankful not to have to deal immediately with family and whatever dramas the day had brought, he passed through it and was soon on his way to the attics. He paused outside Ursula's room but heard no indication of movement inside. Entering his accommodation, he threw up the window to let out some of the day's stultifying heat and checked for light from her balcony door. Nothing. She must be out.

Avoiding him?

Talking things over with her dad?

He sighed, threw off his clothes, showered and dressed again, this time in shorts and a T-shirt, then plodded downstairs on heavy feet.

In the apartment, he found Nanda rocking Marilù to sleep, one eye on her laptop, open on the sofa beside her.

Suddenly, he thought a baby cuddle was exactly what he needed. He stretched out his arms. 'Let me rock her, then you can get on with whatever you're doing.'

'Thanks.' Carefully, Nanda passed the baby over. Marilù gave a whimper, checked out Alfio and smiled, her eyelids heavy. She smelled sweet and freshly bathed. He gazed down at her, at her puffy curls and perfect baby skin, and set up a slow rocking.

His sister pulled the laptop closer and spoke softly. 'Mamma's out with Stanley. I'm looking for apartments. It's a good time for me and Marilù to have our own place again.'

'You're not comfortable here, now?' He adjusted Marilù's light sleep suit, moving a fold of fabric away from her mouth. Her eyes flickered for a moment and then closed, as if that was the final iota of comfort she'd needed before letting sleep waft her away.

Nanda wrinkled her nose. 'Stanley seems a nice man and I've talked to him quite a lot today, but would you want to be sharing your daily life with him and Mamma?'

Decidedly, he shook his head. 'It must be awkward. But will you be comfortable on your own with Marilù?' The baby, as if responding to the sound of her name, clutched at his T-shirt. He studied her soft untroubled face. If he went back to Barcelona, he'd miss seeing her every day and watching her grow.

'I think I'm more in favour of selling the hotel, now.' Nanda glanced Alfio's way.

Her words took him aback. 'Really?'

She nodded. 'Mamma's already sixty. If things are going to work out for her with Stanley, then even more responsibility will fall on me, but I was leaning this way even before he turned up. I have Marilù to consider. I can't give her the kind of childhood I want to if I'm working twelve-hour days.'

Marilù stirred and he realised he'd forgotten to rock. 'Sh-sh-sh,' he soothed her, setting up the gentle rhythm once again.

Nanda adjusted the angle of her laptop. She'd let her hair down and was wearing a T-shirt and shorts, looking more like a tourist than a hotel manager. 'It depends on the offer, but I anticipate a good one. When a global chain comes knocking on our door unprompted, they're going to expect to have to tempt us.'

He remembered a conversation with Ursula. 'Will you stay in Ortigia?'

For an instant, she looked unsure. 'I have no reason to leave. But who knows in the future?' After a few moments she added diffidently, 'I wonder if Mamma would ever go to live in Ireland with Stanley.'

'She might, I suppose,' he said slowly. It would be odd to think of Agata anywhere else but Residenza dei Tringali. 'Is Ursula with Mamma and Stanley now?'

For a moment his sister stared at him uncomprehendingly. 'Of course,' she murmured. 'You don't know.'

'What?' At her grave expression, his stomach began to sink.

'Ursula has gone a day early to stay with her friend in Umbria.' She dropped her voice. 'She must be awfully upset. She's packed her suitcases and left them standing in her room. She's just taken hand luggage, I suppose. She left very early, after pushing a note under the apartment door to explain her change of plans. She must have changed her flights online and caught the train or called a taxi.'

Alfio, frozen, watched Nanda uncurl her legs, shift the laptop aside and rise to riffle through paperwork tucked behind the mantelpiece clock. She located the note and brought it over to him.

Alfio read:

I'm going to Zia's today instead of tomorrow. The breakfasts are all yours, Dad. Agata and Nanda will tell you what your job involves.

He turned the sheet over but there was no more. Marilù's breathing had deepened into a gentle *uhhhh-huhhhh*. Absently, he stroked her little back as he read the note again with the sensation that the tone was more final than the words.

Nanda resumed her seat, and after a last sigh over Ursula's departure, moved the conversation on. 'Was your meeting with your old boss important, by the way?'

Alfio interrupted hoarsely. 'And you're only just telling me?'

Nanda glanced from Alfio to the note still clenched in his hand, her eyebrows curled like question marks. 'About Ursula? Why would I tell you earlier? Nino came to the apartment to say the guests were waiting for breakfast and we found the note. What could you have done? You were on the other side of Sicily. We all ran around setting out the breakfast, with guests glaring at us as if we had been trying to cheat them of the food they'd paid for.'

She pushed her fingers through her hair. 'Mamma and Stanley are upset. They've tried to call, email and text Ursula, but without reply. Stanley thinks that because she's packed her suitcases she's not coming back. She'll just ask for her things to be sent on to . . . well, wherever she

241

goes, I suppose.' She sighed. 'It's sad. Mamma and I liked her a lot.' Then, curiously: 'Alfio? Are you OK? You look funny.'

His voice emerged as if fighting its way past a fist clamped around his throat. 'We've been seeing each other – Ursula and me. Last night, she was angry and sad that I'd known about Mamma and Stanley and not told her.'

'*Oh.*' Nanda's eyes widened. She stared at him, aghast. 'You didn't tell her when you were . . . That's *very* unfortunate.'

'But I promised Mamma,' he pointed out.

Her nose wrinkled in a sceptical expression. 'I suppose so. It's just . . . Ursula was so off men. If she'd let her fences down for you, I can see why she's upset. You were sleeping with her?'

He nodded.

She shook her head in sisterly reproach. '*Sleeping* with her and you kept the information to yourself. That must have felt like a betrayal. Oh, dear. I would have been disappointed in you, in her shoes. You're the first man she's trusted since her marriage ended, I suppose. No wonder she's gone away. What a breach of faith,' she added, as if Alfio wasn't getting the idea.

'Thanks for sharing those thoughts,' he answered testily. As Marilù was now sound asleep, he passed his little niece back to Nanda and went upstairs to try to call Ursula.

Eventually, after several fruitless attempts at connecting with her phone, he threw it down on his single bed. Had she blocked him, as she'd blocked Stephan and his family and friends?

Would he ever see her again? The thought that he might not felt like a punch to his heart.

He recalled Nanda speculating whether Agata might

move to Ireland. If so, visiting his mother could mean him coming into contact with the family Ursula had come from. For an icy moment he imagined seeing Ursula there, perhaps with some other man, one who hadn't thrown away her trust.

He picked up the phone again.

Chapter Sixteen

Ursula had been at Zia and Piero's home for two days. Il Rifugio, their rambling stone house, stood on a shelf of mountain, looking out over a fertile valley containing the vineyard run by the brother of Zia's handsome Italian husband Piero. The Apennine mountains ranged across the horizon like a herd of dinosaurs in their summer clothes of green and lilac. The late-July sun turned the grass around the property to gold. A row of cypress trees wound a path to Bella Vista, the property of Zia's great-aunt and uncle, Lucia and Durante, another stone building built into the mountainside. Like Il Rifugio, it had once been part of the vineyard.

Ursula was enjoying feeling cut off – not from nearby Montelibertà, as the main road down to it ran behind the other side of the two houses – but from the shitstorm that had broken around her in Sicily.

Nobody apart from the inhabitants of Il Rifugio and Bella Vista knew exactly where she was. She'd often talked to her family about Zia living just outside the town, but that description covered a big area. It would involve serious detective work to find her exact location. Both Zia and Lucia bore the surname of Costa, common in Italy, and if she'd ever mentioned the surnames of Piero or Durante, the chances of anyone remembering were slim.

As soon as she'd arrived, exhausted from a night without sleep and a storm of emotions, she'd turned on her phone long enough to post on the family WhatsApp group. *I'm fine. Just give me a week or two to get my head round things. X*

Hoping that would be enough to prevent them all running amok with 'Ursula's delicate' conversations, she'd turned her phone off again. Fabio thought she was on holiday anyway and she couldn't bear to think about everyone at Residenza dei Tringali. Especially not Alfio.

By arriving a day ahead of schedule, she could enjoy more of Montelibertà's annual festa, lazing away the day in Piazza Santa Lucia with food and wine while various musicians played on stage. Durante, who'd grown portlier since Ursula had seen him last summer, acted as a roadie for one of the jazz bands. Lucia's hair was almost all silver now. She'd always been as pressed and smart as Durante was crumpled and her white flowered dress didn't even wilt in the heat as she shared a table with Zia, Piero, and Ursula. Ursula smiled to see Piero constantly checking that Zia, halfway through her pregnancy now, was shaded by the parasol. Zia had an Italian dad and looked as Mediterranean as the rest of them. It was Ursula who was all blonde and freckly.

Ursula was aware from exchanged glances and the careful avoidance of the subject of her early appearance that everyone knew that there was something wrong, though she tried to pretend that she wasn't boiling with anger and hurt and applauded the musicians and laughed with her friends as if that was all that was on her mind.

On Sunday evening, they left the festa in favour of a cold dinner, which Lucia and Durante served on the terrace of Bella Vista, reminding Ursula of when she and Zia had arrived two summers ago to occupy one of the holiday cottages. Zia had met Piero, found her family, and here she was.

Ursula brought out the bowls she'd created for Lucia and Zia, the design with the grapes. It took Zia about two seconds to identify the border as borrowed from Ursula's body art. 'Awesome,' she breathed, tracing the pattern with a finger.

Lucia, who'd once owned a whole ceramics factory, bent over the piece critically, turning it to catch the light. 'Gorgeous, Ursula. Really professional and a nice fresh idea. I must meet this Fabio.'

Durante, who spoke a less polished English than his wife, looked over his glasses at her and pretended to scowl. 'Another man? I think no.'

Lucia laughed and patted his cheek. 'We could go to Sicily together to visit Ursula.'

Durante's scowl switched to his usual cherubic smile. 'OK.'

Ursula smiled, too. She didn't say that she didn't know if she'd ever go back to Sicily.

By Tuesday, the festa was over. Piero and his brother had a pre-existing engagement to travel to Maranello, to the north, on a three-day trip to take a tour of the Ferrari Formula One facility and the track at Fiorano. Piero winked at Ursula. 'I would apologise for my absence, but I know Zia wants you to herself.'

'Yes, lots of lovely time, just Ursula and me,' Zia agreed, getting up from her stool in the kitchen to escort her husband out to the car. Ursula didn't bother to join them, knowing that they wouldn't need a spectator for their goodbye kisses.

After Piero had gone, Ursula and Zia prepared a light lunch and carried it out onto the wonky old patio area outside the kitchen door, where grass and herbs grew between stones that had been laid two or three hundred years ago. The wooden table Piero had made in his workshop beside the house fitted one specific shady position. If moved elsewhere, it wobbled. Zia added wine to the table for Ursula and a jug of pink mocktail for herself.

She sat, settling her chair as well as she could on the old stones. 'Now we're alone,' she said, with the total lack of ceremony that only the oldest and best friends could get away with, 'you can tell me what's the matter.' She held a hand up before Ursula could speak. 'And don't give me any of your bullshit. You have that haunted look, so spill. Is it Stephan?'

Ursula took bread and grated pecorino, a couple of black olives and some salami to arrange on her plate. 'No. Yes. Partly,' she answered, adding rucola, more to provide another colour on the plate than because she wanted it. She suddenly felt it would be good to get all the grey, unpleasant stuff out of her heart and hear what her oldest and best friend had to say about it. 'I'll update you on the Stephan stuff first, as you already know about him searching for his precious ring like someone out of *The Hobbit*, and me telling everybody crossly that I didn't have it. Well . . . I did have it.'

Zia froze in the act of pouring pink liquid into her glass, lips parting in disbelief. 'You *did* have it?'

Ursula recapped the find, sipping her wine, also pink and gleaming prettily in the summer light. 'He must have slipped it into that pewter case when I was packing. While

247

I went through cupboards and wardrobes for my stuff, he paced from room to room like an angry bull, doing everything but paw the ground.'

Zia finished pouring her drink, shaking her head. 'And he's waited nearly two years to start trying to get it back? Why? Oh.' She lifted her glass and pointed it at Ursula as she came up with the answer to her own question. 'You left Brighton! He stopped getting news of you from friends and found the tattoo parlour closed. Probably checked your apartment, too. Thinking he was losing track of you, he put the ring he'd planted to work.' She grimaced. 'Devious. He always wanted to know where you were when you were a couple.'

A small shock tingled through Ursula. 'Isn't that kind of normal? You know where Piero's just gone, and who with.'

Zia nodded, slicing into a dark red tomato. 'I take your point. But Stephan always went a step further. Back in Brighton, I can't count how many times I heard him slip in a question if you'd been somewhere without him. Like, "Have X and Y finished redecorating their lounge? What's it like?" Or, if you'd been out for dinner without him, what had you eaten, as if he needed to check that the menu tallied with your answer.'

Ursula nibbled an olive. 'Go 'way. He was just making conversation.'

Zia tucked into her lunch, no doubt feeding her baby bump. Between bites, she said, 'If it was, it was possessive conversation. His insecurities showing.'

Ursula considered, adding a tomato to her own plate and cutting it up. She scooped up pecorino with the bread. 'You never brought this up before.'

Zia shrugged. 'You don't go poking your nose into other

248

folks' marriages, do you? If it was OK with you, then it was fine by me. But don't you remember rolling your eyes and saying, "Steph, you've always got to know the ins and outs of a duck's arse"?'

'Now you've reminded me,' Ursula admitted. 'And that wasn't even after I was roofied, was it?'

'He just got a whole lot worse then,' Zia said gently.

They ate on quietly. Ursula tried to enjoy the good, wholesome food. Her appetite wasn't at lunch with her, but she didn't want to end up looking like some old scarecrow, so she forced it down. 'Zia,' she asked carefully. 'Do I come across as useless?'

Zia's dark brows rose. 'Not in the least. Why?'

Ursula gave up on her meal and out poured the story of her dad and Agata. She tried to be composed but soon tears were slipping down her cheeks. 'And everyone in the family kept it from me till Dad turned up to tell me in person, and they all acted as if I needed careful handling in difficult situations,' she finished on a sniff. 'Caden even thinks one of the reasons Agata let me take Dad's place was so she could contact him if I wasn't coping. None of them seem to accept that what happened when my marriage ended was a one-time thing. They're just waiting for me to mess up again.'

Zia pulled her chair around so she could pat Ursula's arm, her eyes wide with shock. 'Your dad and mum have split up for good? That must be hard.'

'It's certainly not very nice.' Ursula grabbed a paper napkin from the table and blew her nose. 'But I know they have their own lives to live and that I was lucky to have parents together all through my childhood. You weren't so fortunate.'

Zia shook her head. 'I would have been gutted if Gran

and Pap had split up, though. What a difficult chain of events. And it was a bit crazy of your uncle Gerry to suggest you went to Sicily.'

'He's mad,' Ursula agreed, after easing her throat with several sips of wine. 'He's always involved Dad in things. It was nothing to get home and find Uncle Gerry's car in bits on our lawn or him deciding that the perfect time to ask Dad for financial advice was lunchtime on Mother's Day, when the whole family was sitting down for the celebration meal.'

'Oh, Ursula,' Zia commiserated. 'I'm sure your family only acts this way because they love you. I can see why it upsets and frustrates you, though.'

The sun was high in its path across the sky towards the mountains and Ursula poured herself a glass of water, deciding that if she drank any more wine, she'd start a migraine on top of everything else. 'You know, I once saw a movie. A black comedy, where a woman lived a complete fantasy manufactured by her husband and parents to "keep her sane".' She made air quotes. 'Then the woman somehow saw outside the mirage and found her daughter wasn't working away on a cruise liner but was a crack addict in a squat. Her son wasn't bravely gathering intel for the military abroad but was incarcerated for mugging old ladies.'

'That sounds far-fetched.' Zia held her glass against her face to cool her skin. 'What happened when the woman found out?'

'She shot herself,' Ursula pronounced with macabre satisfaction. 'But *I won't do that*. I may have had teenage anxiety attacks, but now I'm thirty-two years of age. And I never took enough pills to . . . you know. End me.'

Zia eased her baby bump into a more comfortable

position. 'It's the first time you've admitted having controlled that,' she pointed out quietly. 'In fact, you denied it vociferously and said that your head had just got all messy, so you didn't really know what you were doing.'

Ursula cast her mind back to that horrible time and tried to explain truthfully. 'The "it was a cry for help" explanation is so infuriating. My head *was* messy, and my heart was in bits. Acceptance hadn't yet come. I was outraged, but helpless because Stephan had locked me out of my house as if I wasn't an equal partner in a twenty-first-century marriage. The pills were born of frustration as much as hopelessness.'

Birdsong drifted from the cypress trees, and insects buzzed. The heat seemed to press on the landscape. Not letting her off the hook, Zia asked, 'So, did you take the pills to get Stephan's attention? Or make him reconsider ending the marriage?'

'Neither,' Ursula answered shortly. 'Maybe I was punishing him for not supporting me. Making him sorry. When you make someone helpless, they look for a way to take back control.'

'Are you going to send back his grandpa's ring?' Zia probed gently.

'I don't know.' Ursula closed her eyes. 'He must have it back. He knew I'd think that way when he stowed it in my things, I expect. I'm still brooding on it.' She gave a deep groan. 'Finding the ring has scoured my insides out. I know, I know,' she added, holding up her hands as if in surrender, though Zia hadn't said a word. 'Either I'm tough enough to face things or I'm not. Well, I *am*. I'm fine. I can deal with Stephan. I can deal with Dad. Just . . . not yet. Let's talk about something else.'

'OK. What about this Alfio guy?' Zia said obligingly.

Ursula groaned still louder. 'Alfio? He's a ride,' she said tiredly. 'Literally. We were sleeping together.'

Zia grinned. 'I thought the way you talked about him that there was something going on there.'

'*Was* is right,' Ursula said with emphasis. 'If we'd both been staying in Sicily, and Dad hadn't turned up, I think we might have progressed things. But he *knew* about Dad and his mum. I'm just stunned about that. Gutted, to be truthful. I'd just begun to trust him—' The words dried her throat like sand.

'Oh, Ursula.' Zia leaned in so she could slide both arms around her friend. 'I'm so sorry it hurts. I suppose he was between a rock and a hard place.'

Indignantly, Ursula pushed Zia's arms away. 'Fuck off with yourself! You mean you see his point of view?'

'Can't you?' Zia looked confused – and overheated. It was too hot for hugs.

Ursula glared at her. 'Not really.'

'But, Ursula,' Zia said gently. 'We all keep the whole truth from someone, sometime. Whether it's torn loyalties or just something we'd rather the other person didn't know.'

Fleetingly, Ursula thought of the way she'd decided not to tell Alfio about taking pills after her marriage ended so hurtfully. The realisation softened her tone. 'Anyway, I couldn't think straight with him in the next room, with this puppy-dog eyes and hot bod. I had to get away.'

Zia looked as if she might want to know more about the puppy-dog eyes and hot bod, but contented herself with: 'Are you going back eventually?'

Ursula paused to look out over the rows of vines laid out like enormous green ropes, and wished her life was so orderly. 'Another thing I don't know. He might be gone soon, anyway, once he gets another job. He had a meeting with an old colleague on Friday, so it's obviously on his mind. And someone's after the hotel. Might be best if he left,' she said, pretending it didn't roast her guts to admit it. 'I could live nearer Fabio. His place is right the other side of the city, not even on the island of Ortigia where Residenza dei Tringali is. I'd probably never see any of the Tringali family.'

Zia quirked one eyebrow. 'Do you mean "best" if Alfio left? Or "easier"? Easier for Ursula Quinn.'

'Nothing is easy for Ursula Quinn,' Ursula said morosely.

Zia began to cover the food before it become an insect festival. 'You have bad feelings towards Nanda and Agata, too? You really seemed to like them.'

'But none of them told me about Dad. They all lied by omission,' Ursula pointed out.

Zia put down a bowl to stroke Ursula's hair. 'You know, you're not the woman in that black comedy, Urs. You didn't shoot yourself, so you'll have to deal with the situation. What are you going to do if your dad and Agata get married? I've a sneaking suspicion that Agata, Nanda and Alfio will all go to the wedding. Will you refuse to attend, to avoid them?'

Ursula gazed at her, trying to absorb this vision of the future. 'Do you think Dad will actually divorce? He's a Catholic.'

'You did,' Zia pointed out sensibly.

'But he's the kind of Catholic who goes to church.' Ursula began to help with the detritus of lunch. 'Can we talk about something nice, now? Like when you're going to ask me to be your baby's godmother?'

Zia assumed an expression of mock horror. 'You? A divorced woman? I'm really not sure about *that*.'

For the first time since fleeing Sicily, Ursula's laughter wasn't forced. 'Let's go down into Montelibertà to poke around the ceramics shops. Perhaps I can spot the difference between Sicilian and Umbrian, like Lucia and Fabio can.'

And it would be a good way to shelve the difficult questions for now.

Chapter Seventeen

Alfio felt as though he were made from lead from his forehead to the soles of his feet. His chest and stomach felt filled with the stuff, too, yet he'd had to drag himself through a weekend without Ursula.

She had answered neither message nor call.

Late on the Friday she'd left, Stanley had received a short text to say that she was fine, and there had been no other contact with anyone at Residenza dei Tringali. Nanda and Agata looked troubled whenever her name came up, and Stanley's eyes turned bleak. Alfio was afraid his were the same.

Stanley. To his surprise, Alfio was discovering a liking for him. Increasingly, he was seeing a man whose marriage hadn't worked out rather than just a selfish *bastardo*. Stanley had been clumsy in his torn loyalties – half his heart wanting to be with Agata but the other pulling him back to his position in the Quinn family – but his heart was in his eyes whenever he looked at Agata.

Maybe Alfio's softening stemmed from Stanley's likeness to Ursula, not in his colouring or features but the underlying kindness and self-deprecating humour. Stanley had even found it in himself to be amused by his daughter's sarcastic note handing her duties over to him. He'd sat down with a sheet of paper to list every last detail of what Ursula had done, so that, as he said, 'I don't fall down on the job and get the sack.'

Underneath, Alfio was certain Stanley was desperately worried that his middle daughter would never forgive him.

'What should I have done?' Alfio had heard him ask Agata. 'Skype her with the news while I was still with her mother? Demand Ursula come home, so we could speak in person? Would she have been any less angry with me?'

Alfio had stepped into the conversation. 'She is angry with us all. I am not certain of the right things we should have done, but we did the wrong thing.'

Stanley had rubbed his bearded chin. 'So, we should have told her about Agata? That would have meant her keeping secrets from her mum. That doesn't seem right, now.'

Alfio had seen his point. Nanda and Agata had been silent. Only Marilù had been unconcerned, banging a poor hapless doll on the floor. If Stanley was correct that they couldn't have told Ursula, and Ursula and Nanda were correct that he shouldn't have slept with Ursula without telling her, Alfio's only way of being in the right would have been not to sleep with Ursula. And how *could* that be right? Because something that special couldn't be wrong.

On Tuesday, Alfio's old director Ximena called him from Barcelona. 'Inigo told me about your meeting, so I thought perhaps we could go through it,' she said, without wasting time on social niceties. 'What are your thoughts about what he put to you?'

Alfio was in the office behind the reception desk at

Residenza dei Tringali. He removed his mind from Ursula and tried to focus on the rest of his life. 'I'm flattered that not only did Inigo break his holiday to see me, but now you've taken time out of your busy schedule,' he said mechanically. 'I think Inigo might have explained that my family has just received an approach regarding our hotel. That is where my attention has been for the last few days.' It wasn't even a half-truth. Like Nanda, Agata had agreed to talk to Russell Haug at Minton Mafflin about the prospect of selling Residenza dei Tringali. She was thinking of a new phase to her life, footloose and hotel-free with Stanley.

Alfio had always thought they should listen to the details of the offer but was now finding it hard to concentrate on anything other than Ursula's absence.

Ximena gave an impatient tut and began to talk him through the benefits that would come with taking Inigo's job. 'I'd like to think we might have you back in Barcelona by October,' she ended.

It could make Alfio's life incredibly easy – a job falling into his lap, much more senior to the one he'd left in May. 'You have given me a lot to consider,' he said, because that seemed a safe answer when he'd been too distracted to devote much thought to the meeting with Inigo, which had faded in importance once he'd got home and found Ursula gone. 'The whole situation has taken me by surprise. I thought I had left the organisation.'

Ximena sounded pleased, probably assuming him to be stunned by his good fortune. 'You are well thought of, Alfio. You have a facility for easing the interaction between languages and cultures. We were sorry to see you leave.' Delicately, she hesitated. 'Is there any reason for you not to return to Barcelona?'

Alfio realised she was asking about Hettie. Someone must have mentioned to her that the relationship had ended around the time he'd resigned. Hettie was still in Barcelona so far as he knew, but it was an immense city. There was room for them both. 'No,' he said, because to say, *My heart is sore and part of me wants to stay here forever in case Ursula comes back,* would be pathetic, and not at all pragmatic. He tried to force himself to give the offer the attention it undoubtedly deserved. 'On Wednesday, we have a video meeting about the possible purchase of our hotel. May I return to you after that?'

'Of course,' Ximena said, though she sounded as if she'd have liked Alfio to give her a firm answer here and now. 'I'll wait to hear from you soon.'

The Wednesday meeting was scheduled for nine a.m. in New York, which was three p.m. in Sicily. For Alfio, the morning dragged more than his heavy heart. Ursula had been in touch with nobody, not even Stanley. To pass the morning, Alfio helped Stanley with the breakfasts and explained Ursula's system with the laundry delivery. Then he drifted into the apartment.

'Ba!' Marilù greeted him with a waved biscuit, which was crumbling in a wet, sticky little hand.

'*Buongiorno,*' he replied solemnly.

Nanda snorted a laugh. 'Now she's able to enjoy her food, she eats like a little horse.' She edged Marilù further onto her yellow playmat, to encourage the slobbery biscuit away from the rug. Then she glanced at her brother beneath her lashes. 'When will you decide whether to take the new job in Barcelona?'

'It's hard to say,' he hedged. 'Let's hear from the American acquisitions agent first.'

Agata came out from her bedroom – or their bedroom,

258

now, as she was sharing it with Stanley – bright in a summer dress. 'The job sounds like a fantastic opportunity, whatever the agents say.' She gave Alfio a smile, but it looked an effort. 'I'm just sorry it's not closer to home. But—' Her shoulders lifted and fell in a fatalistic shrug.

He gave her a sudden hug. 'Will you stay in Siracusa, Mamma, if the hotel is sold?'

She glanced at the door that stood open to the kitchen, where the clattering of crockery signalled that Stanley was filling the dishwasher. 'I think so – with trips to see Stanley's family.' A faint blush edged her cheekbones. 'He'll go alone in a few weeks to begin the legal things.'

Alfio paused, surprised to hear plans had gone so far. 'He and his wife are divorcing?'

Agata blew out her cheeks. 'If that's what he wants. But to live together would be better than us marrying, I think, and straightforward when it comes to what will belong to my children and what to his.'

Marilù began to cry and Agata swooped her up. It was the first time Alfio had seen her do that since her hyster-ectomy. It was as if the moment Stanley had arrived, her recovery had sped up by a factor of ten. She rocked the infant on her hip, skilfully keeping hold of the little hand that still clutched the biscuit. 'He's used to seeing his family frequently. He's feeling cut off.' She looked sad on Stanley's behalf.

'Living away from where you've lived for a long time is exciting, but always has to be balanced against family ties.' Alfio reached for a paper towel and mopped up the worst of Marilù's mess, and, as if they'd planned it, Nanda substituted the biscuit for a drink, a swap that Marilù accepted.

His mother faced him. 'You mustn't worry about going

259

back to Barcelona. I'll be fine. You rushed back to help me this summer and I love you for it, but soon you'll be free to tread your own path again.'

Over her shoulder, he saw Nanda watch him with an interested expression. Only she was aware of his tie to Ursula, and he knew she'd leave it to him whether he ever shared details of the brief love affair with Agata or Stanley. His sister smiled at him suddenly, wistfully. 'Have the best life you can, Alfio. You never know when fate will surprise you with a change you can't control.' She took her little girl from Agata's arms and gazed into the tiny face.

He nodded, knowing she was talking about the way her husband had absented himself from her life. 'I'm glad I came back. I wouldn't have missed this summer. But you, Nanda, are you still in favour of selling the hotel?'

She sighed, sadness dulling her pretty features as she toyed with the wiggly tails of hair growing around Marilù's neck. 'I love the hotel. It has been my life. But I don't want to manage it alone.'

Agata patted her daughter's arm. 'You're a single parent. You and Alfio were almost grown-up when Papà died. Throwing myself into the work of Residenza dei Tringali helped me get through the worst of the grief but it's different for you. Your child is tiny. You must enjoy her.' She turned to Alfio. 'The hotel is a hard taskmaster. In the past few years, Nanda and I have done everything we can to automate check-in and check-out, but as you know, some mornings we hear nothing but the reception bell.'

As if it had been listening in, the bell gave an imperious ring, because it was Nino's day off. Alfio managed a laugh as he headed through the door to answer its summons, only pausing to say, 'If we sell the hotel, it could be months or years until it goes through.'

Mother and daughter nodded in unison and Agata said, 'Of course.'

He went off, surprised how far down the road to acceptance his mother and sister seemed to have gone in their decision making over Residenza dei Tringali. Each had devoted their lives to the hotel for so long, yet now personal circumstances were making them accept as inevitable a change they would once have resisted with their last breaths.

Still, appetites were small at lunch, that day. Even if selling the hotel was turning out to be the best option, the coming video conference was the first step to cutting ties with four generations of their family and removing the name Tringali from above the door.

As three p.m. approached, the family members arranged themselves around Alfio's laptop at the dining room table. Marilù was obligingly taking her afternoon nap. Stanley was minding the reception desk. He had better Italian than Ursula, making Alfio wonder whether he'd taken lessons ready to move to Sicily.

Stifling any nervous energy, Alfio watched Nanda go through the 'join meeting' procedure. Then suddenly they were facing a screen split in three boxes, *Russell Haug, CEO*, written under the face in one box, *Lena Amsey, CFO* and *Helmut Grohe, COO*, beneath the others. Agata sat with her children either side of her as Russell Haug, a florid, bulky man in his forties, beamed.

'Well, hello. Welcome to the meeting,' he greeted them in a pleasant American accent. He requested permission to record the conversation and Helmut arranged it when they agreed.

Lena and Helmut introduced themselves – Helmut mentioning that he'd been born in Europe but moved to

261

America as a child – then Russell retook the lead. 'As you know from our agents, Minton Mafflin, we're looking for just such a property as yours.' He went on to explain how Minton Mafflin worked with clients, identifying potential acquisitions and hand-holding concerned parties through the process. The word 'quality' cropped up in every sentence – quality clients and quality business and Residenza dei Tringali being viewed as very much a quality business.

Lena took over to talk about the global reach of the hotel chain that was their client, and its financial viability as a public company.

Helmut moved in with a presentation about the increasing popularity of escorted tours and the logistical challenges of tour companies maintaining robust and reliable partnerships with appropriate hotels. 'There are many calls upon room availability, especially select destinations and small countries like Sicily.'

Russell grinned. 'We do realise the Sicily is a region of Italy, but as it's surrounded by water, we treat it as a small country in destination terms. Ortigia is the cherry on Sicily's cake, individual and with a rich history. It's highly desirable for our client to have a modest-sized property under its control.'

The Tringali family had so far mainly listened to these strangers talking to them from the screen, but now Alfio broke in. 'What structural changes to the hotel do you envisage?'

Russell answered. 'Great question, but we'd need feet on the ground to determine that.'

Alfio gave a polite smile and pushed back against this non-answer. 'Your feasibility study must have given you some indication.'

Helmut took the conversational ball. 'We anticipate some updating and adapting.'

'Lifts?' Alfio queried. 'Larger dining accommodation and kitchen?'

'Those things currently have query marks alongside them,' Helmut replied. He was a smaller man than Russell, with a very straight parting in his hair.

Agata stepped in, very upright and composed. 'We are happy to hear your offer,' she said quietly.

'Well, now.' Russell looked almost taken aback at such a blunt gambit. 'We would need to put a document together.'

Agata wasn't to be brushed aside. 'And that document will contain a bottom line. What do you think it will say?'

'We would expect it to be healthy.' Lena smiled encouragingly from above the text that reminded them she was the chief financial officer. 'For today, we're hoping for your agreement to the next step, which would be myself and another representative from Minton Mafflin basing ourselves with you for a few days. We'd like to survey the building and start a conversation about the existing finances of the hotel.'

Nanda spoke up for the first time. 'But you are proposing a different business model from the one we operate. How will our accounts influence your decision?'

Lena nodded, as if acknowledging Nanda's question as a good one. 'We'd focus mainly on financial encumbrances and debts.'

Alfio made an impatient movement. 'All of which information is available from *registro delle imprese*, surely?'

'The barest of facts, yes,' Lena allowed. 'But we must do our due diligence.'

Alfio studied the trio, wondering how much they might

eventually offer for Residenza dei Tringali. Abruptly, he said, 'Thank you for your time today.' He turned to his sister and mother. 'Shall we discuss this request and return to Mr Haug and his company in due course?' He spoke in English, so the Americans could understand him.

Nanda lifted one finger to indicate that she wasn't quite ready. 'Ms Amsey, I should mention that it might be difficult for you to "base yourselves" here during the summer. With guests able to book online and our reputation and TripAdvisor rating, even cancellations are taken quickly.'

Lena's eyebrows lifted slightly. 'Thank you for managing my expectations on that point, Ms Tringali. We would expect to pay the going rate, of course.'

'Of course,' said Agata, with a shrug. 'But if the rooms are full, the rooms are full.'

Plainly not wishing barriers to be erected over a point of logistics, Russell broke in. 'Maybe we can find a window via email. Would it be too much to ask for some indication in the next few days as to if and when we can conduct a survey? Or maybe we can have another meeting if you have more questions.'

It was agreed.

After the laptop was closed, as if just to click 'end meeting' wasn't enough, the three Tringalis sat quietly at the dining table. 'It's an enormous decision,' Nanda murmured.

Agata stretched and sighed. 'I'm sure we'd all leave with regrets. But we must be clear-sighted about our options. Running the hotel is hard work and we have no realistic way of continuing for much longer.' With a fatalistic sigh, she rose and headed off in the direction of reception, presumably to tell Stanley that the meeting was over, so he no longer had to politely avoid the apartment.

Alfio looked at Nanda. She said, 'Mamma's right. We have to be practical and pragmatic.'

He nodded, but the heaviness that had invaded him in the six days since Ursula had gone was only emphasised by the meeting. To have a credible offer for the hotel on the horizon and find his family open to it should have been a relief.

But nothing seemed to give him much pleasure at the moment, and even if his life was about to take him away from Sicily once more, he wished Agata and Nanda seemed more delighted with what they'd heard today.

Chapter Eighteen

Ursula stood at Zia's kitchen window, staring out over the half-wild land that immediately surrounded the house and at puffs of grey cloud gathering above the distant mountains. 'Looks like a storm coming.'

Zia glanced up from chopping vegetables. 'I love summer storms. If it comes, we can sit at the window and drink gin while we watch it crash about the valley.' Zia didn't have to say that she'd be drinking alcohol-free gin.

'Cosy picture,' said Ursula, trying to sound interested.

Evidently, Zia saw through the shell Ursula was trying to wear, as she put down her knife and came up beside her, staring out at the gathering clouds herself. 'Unhappy?'

Ursula slipped her arm around Zia's expanding waist. It was odd to think of her dearest friend becoming a mother. Soon, she'd have a baby in her arms. It made Ursula think about Marilù with a pang. And Nanda and Agata . . . and Alfio. 'I'm unsettled more than unhappy,' she said, choosing the most positive reply she could summon. 'I'm thinking about changing my flight and going home to see that Mum's OK. It feels wrong not to see her. Especially with Dad being in Sicily.'

'Are you going back to Sicily eventually?' Zia pressed.

Ursula sighed and shrugged. 'To be decided.'

The moment passed, the storm passed, the next couple of days passed. Ursula lazed about, sharing meals with Zia, Lucia and Durante, and meeting up with Zia's half-siblings Riccardo, Caterina and Laura, when Ursula got a teeny bit tipsy on Orvieto Classico. She renewed her acquaintanceship with Fiorello and Roberto, Zia's grandparents, and even Zia's father, Gerardo, who hadn't always been the most fatherly of men, but did try.

Piero returned from Maranello on Thursday with a present for the expected baby, a teddy bear wearing a Ferrari shirt and cap, which made Zia laugh and hug both him and the teddy.

Early on Friday, the week almost at an end, Ursula decided it was time to turn on her phone.

Lying on her bed with the shutters closed against the morning sun, she watched the missed call notifications mount up. Only one person had left a voice message – Finola. 'Don't worry,' was all she said. Ursula listened to it again, taking comfort from her big sis's confident, brisk voice and hearing the love that lay behind it. *Don't worry.* It wasn't bad advice and she'd kind of been following it, given that she'd been resolutely ignoring the outside world for a week.

She scrolled through a host of WhatsApp and text messages from her siblings, each on the theme of 'look after yourself', which she also felt she'd had covered.

There was one message from her father: *I'm sorry you feel hurt and left out. I thought I was doing the right thing by flying out to tell you the news about Mum and me face to face. I may have handled the whole situation badly, but it was from the best intentions, trying to fit my life around what was best for the whole family. Love you, darling. Xxx*

Ursula reread it, hearing her father's voice in her head. With the perspective allowed by the passage of a week, she was able to see a glimmer of where he was coming from. She wasn't ready to talk yet, though. There was still thinking to do.

Agata's message said, simply: *I would love you to come back and enjoy the rest of the summer with us.* Maybe Stanley wasn't very good at the breakfasts.

Nanda had sent: *Hope you will return. Marilù misses you, and so do I. So do we all. Xx*

Ursula swallowed a lump in her throat, wishing that her time in Sicily had never blown up in her face and she felt none of the torn loyalties and hurt feelings that she did feel.

Was she as delicate as her family members hinted, as she seemed unable to cope with what had happened? Unable to see the situation as others plainly wanted her to see it?

Fabio's message read: *What day back? Need to produce.* She laughed, but her heart ached at the thought of giving up the opportunity she had with him and never returning to the studio to create the rest of her *Il Tatuaggio* range and see it selling in shops.

Her mother's message was next. *I hope you're having a grand time at Zia's. Don't worry about me. Xxx* Ursula felt a huge surge of guilt. She should have switched on her phone to check on her mother. Mainly, Ursula had been worrying about Ursula.

Alfio's message she left till last. In her call log, the figure next to missed calls from him stood at twenty-seven. Twenty-seven missed calls? Wow. She didn't return them, but, heart thudding, opened the only text message. *I am sorry if things between us have ended, and badly. This summer began in a bad way for me too, but the chance to know you was worth all that difficulty. I hope we meet again. I am sorry you feel betrayed. I did not do it to hurt you, but to protect others. Alfio.*

She rolled herself up to sit on the edge of her bed, rereading the message. No kisses, just *Alfio*, as if he'd hoped reading his name would bring his image cannoning into her mind's eye, his lean body, the intelligent face that always seemed slightly at odds with his wild curls, his tight arse in tight shorts . . . She swallowed. And sighed.

But she didn't feel the way was clear for her to return to Sicily. There were things she had to do before she could even consider it.

An hour later, she found Zia and Piero drinking cappuccino outside, holding hands and watching the sun paint the grapevines a vibrant green as it rose in the sky. It was already hot, but summer in Italy frequently meant heat twenty-four hours a day. She pulled up a chair beside Zia, sending Piero an apologetic smile for butting in. 'I've cancelled my flight back to Sicily. I'll get the train to Rome and fly to Dublin to see Mum instead.'

Zia looked at her carefully. Then she nodded. 'I'll take you to the train station.'

Piero said, 'What would you like to do today? It's your last day with us for a while.'

'Aren't you going to be busy in your workshop?' Ursula asked. Piero created beautiful and fanciful structures of

269

wood, such as gazebos and fairy-tale playhouses for the gardens of very lucky children.

'I can play hooky,' he said lazily. 'We could drive to Perugia and take the MiniMetrò into the old city to listen to the street musicians and eat gelato.'

Ursula felt tears prick the backs of her eyes at his kindness. To cover it up, she joked, 'Now I see why my bestie married you.'

It was a lovely day. Lucia and Durante went with them, though they were more interested in shady cafés than trekking along the cobbled streets and the spectacular views of the surrounding countryside from the enormous city walls. It was a day filled with the laughter and gentle chatter of friends. Nobody pressed Ursula for answers to questions such as what she was going to do with the rest of her life. They just let her be.

Later, back at Il Rifugio, Zia came into Ursula's room to watch her pack – not that it was a long job, with just one big backpack. Tomorrow would see an early start. Fabro-Ficulle railway station was only a ten-minute drive away, but then two hours on the train, a shuttle to the airport and the usual check-in hoopla stood between herself and a two-thirty p.m. flight from Rome Ciampino.

Zia flopped backwards on Ursula's bed and inelegantly flapped her striped maternity dress to fan herself. She stared at the ceiling, her baby bump pronounced from this angle. 'Do you remember how miserable I was when I thought things wouldn't work out with Piero?'

Ursula didn't need her degree to work out where this conversation was headed. 'Yep,' she answered briefly, rolling up clean T-shirts to thrust into the bottom of her backpack.

Zia sighed. 'I nearly made a big mistake. I nearly missed

out on all this happy.' She waved her arms in big circles to encompass the building they were in, and herself.

'It was Piero who came after you, as I recall. He turned up in Brighton with a plan and an obstinate expression.' Ursula cast her a glance.

'That's right.' Zia sounded sad. 'I did nothing. I'd given up, which meant I nearly threw him away. I'm trying to hint that you're on the verge of throwing Alfio away.'

Ursula had to blink before she could see the shorts she was about to pack. She hoped she could borrow a pair of jeans from Sorcha when she got home, or she'd bloody freeze. Ireland would be fifteen degrees cooler than Italy. 'He's probably left Sicily now, anyway. And if he hasn't? I'm not ready. I'm not you, Zia. I'm delicate, remember?'

In three seconds, Zia had rolled up and was beside her, hauling her into her arms. 'You're one of the best people in the world,' she said fiercely. 'Just stop putting yourself down and . . . stop acting like a victim.'

Horrified, Ursula froze. Very slowly, she turned her gaze on her friend. '*Acting like a victim?*'

Zia looked stricken. 'I'm not sure that that came out right.'

Ursula glared. 'How was it meant to come out?'

'Like, you have to fight, Ursula,' Zia pleaded. 'Fight for yourself. That guy who roofied you set off a chain of events. He made Stephan act badly, which made you question yourself, sort of lose your footing in the world and lose faith in your own judgement. You need to somehow find the real, strong, decisive you again, the one from before the trauma. Don't let that bastard take away the real you.'

Weakly, Ursula pulled away, sinking down onto the dressing table stool. 'You're saying I reacted in a weak way?'

271

'No.' Zia knelt and slid her arms around her friend again. 'You were hurt and frightened by the way the guy who spiked your drink took power away from you. I just wonder if there are ways you could take it back again.'

'Like what?' Ursula asked drearily, feeling that familiar sensation of life pressing down on her.

Zia hesitated. 'Maybe when everything went badly in Sicily you could have stayed to face it? And instead of merely saying to your family, "Don't treat me with kid gloves," you could find a way to *show* them how strong you are. You really are, Urs. The fight is still there, inside you.'

Ursula closed her eyes and leaned her head on her friend's shoulder and put her arms around her, being careful to give Zia's pregnant tummy enough space. 'Maybe you're right that I ran away. But I don't know how to show how strong I am.'

Zia cuddled her. 'I think you'll find a way.'

Chapter Nineteen

The number forty-one bus from the airport dropped Ursula at the Pavilions shopping centre in the middle of Swords. From there, it was a ten-minute trek to the family home where she'd spent the first eighteen years of her life, and many Christmases and family gatherings ever after. The square, brick house looked just the same: neat and well kept.

Ursula slid her backpack from her shoulders and felt inside the security pocket for her door key. Her fingers came up against Stephan's grandpa's ring, but she thrust that back down into a corner. Something else to be dealt with, but her mum got priority over that. As she'd already called from Italy to say she was on her way, she let herself in with a quick shout. 'Hello. I'm here.' She hoped her voice didn't sound as tired as she felt.

Colleen appeared from the sitting room, posting her reading glasses onto the top of her head to leave both arms free to hug with. 'Hello, my darlin'. You're a sight for sore eyes.'

'How are you?' Ursula drew back to regard her mother

273

keenly, noting the pallor and the lines of strain around her blue eyes.

Colleen looked away. 'Ah, I'll be all right. Have you eaten? I have a stew on the stove, bubbling while it waits for you.'

Ursula followed her mum's back view into the kitchen, thinking that Colleen must have lost twelve pounds since Ursula was here over three months ago. The bum of her jeans was baggy, and her grey jumper hung in folds like a Roman blind. 'Stew sounds great. Smells even better.'

Ursula helped herself to a big cardigan her mother often left on the hooks in the hall, ready for if she just wanted to step out to the shops. She'd been right. Swords was not as warm as Sicily or Umbria.

In the kitchen, she took out two bowls and spoons to set on the table. Colleen filled both bowls with mouth-watering stew while Ursula added the salt and pepper pots to the centre of the table. Ursula did justice to the meal, and Colleen ate something, which was good, as Ursula suspected she wouldn't have, had she been alone.

Pushing her empty bowl away, Ursula cupped her chin in her hands and propped her elbows on the table. It was covered by a clean cloth, orange seersucker that showed off the white porcelain bowls to advantage. 'How are you really, Mum? Was it all a giant shock?'

Colleen seemed to age ten years before Ursula's eyes. 'Not really.' She sank back in her chair. 'Your dad would say that I was up to my old tricks, accusing him of stuff he hadn't done. But things hadn't been right between us since he came back. The only thing that made sense to me was that he was thinking of someone else.'

Ursula's chest hollowed, as if her heart had literally gone out to her mother. 'I'm sorry,' she murmured.

Colleen wiped an eye. 'If he'd really wanted to come back to me, he'd have been chasing me round the bedroom after ten months apart, now, wouldn't he? And he didn't.'

It wasn't an image Ursula really wanted in her head. 'Right.' She nodded, as if this wasn't embarrassing at all.

Colleen rose to put on the kettle to make tea. 'Have you ever been in love with the wrong person? Your good sense tells you to do this, but your stupid heart tells you something different?'

Ursula's thought flew back to Alfio. 'I try and keep a tight rein on head and heart,' she said lightly. 'But I'm not entirely sure what you're getting at.'

Back to the room, Colleen sounded defeated. 'I'm saying that I'm still in love with your father, but I don't want to be. I keep telling myself not to be. But my heart just is.' She stirred the mugs of tea and brought them over, sitting down again and gazing into the tiny island of froth spinning in hers. In a low voice, she added, 'Ah, I'm putting a gloss on things. It's easy to get into habits, in a marriage. The habit of being together and thinking of the other person as your property, not realising that the love has changed. I do still love him; I will always love him some, but I'll be all right, when I get used to things.'

Ursula leaned in close and slid her arms about her. 'I'm sure you will.'

'Yeah.' Her mother heaved a massive sigh. 'If I'd been able to be different with your dad, maybe . . . But, there. You can't force another person to comply with your wishes. I'm coming to terms with the situation.' Then, when Ursula was about to laud her mother for such a pragmatic attitude, Colleen's brow darkened. 'The law says he's allowed to change his mind about his marriage vows, after all.'

Discomfort wriggled in Ursula's belly. Trying not to

sound judgy, she queried, 'On that basis, would you say that I ought to have stayed with Steph? When I couldn't get into my own house, should I have said, "OK, then. You keep everything we own, and I'll find a nice dry ditch somewhere in the hopes you might get in a better mood one day"?' She gentled her tone. 'We all have our rights. We can't be cornered or manipulated, or guilted into staying because our spouse wishes things were different.'

Colleen gripped her mug grimly. 'You make me sound so awful. But you're right. I was manipulative, sometimes.'

Ursula sat up. 'I was talking about how Steph treated me.'

'Oh.' Colleen gave a wavering laugh. 'Oh, dear. I thought you meant me. I must have heard my Auntie Bridie say, "Well, if the cap fits, you should wear it, my girl!"'

'Auntie Bridie sounds an old bitch,' Ursula replied vehemently.

Hands trembling, Colleen lifted her mug to her lips and sipped before she answered. 'She was. She left me craving love, but I don't want to blame her. I spent decades trying to force Dad to constantly reassure me, and it drove him away. That's on me.' Her lip quivered. 'I don't know how I fancy being single, though.'

'Sometimes, it's easier.' Ursula thought about how she'd let Alfio into her heart and other parts of her body and how much it had hurt when she felt he'd been there under false pretences.

Colleen turned wide eyes on her. 'But isn't it awful lonely? I was lonely last year, here in this house by myself. I felt like some little old hedgehog, when all the other hedgehogs had left the burrow. It seemed as if your dad was the one I could get back.'

'I think of it more as "independent" than lonely,' Ursula

volunteered, not reminding her that the reason Stanley had left the 'burrow' was because Colleen had told him to. 'I like doing exactly as I want. Can you imagine how my week with Zia and Piero would have gone if I'd still been married to Steph? Him wanting to know what Zia and I were talking about all the time, and what made us laugh, and going all quiet if he felt he wasn't getting enough of my time?' She knew she was channelling Zia's comments about her marriage as she said this, but now it had been pointed out to her she could see the truth of it. 'Aren't there some things you'd like to do that Dad was never keen on?'

Colleen thought for several moments and then brightened. 'I wanted a cottage by the sea. He said the winters would be too wild, facing the Irish Sea, and that I'd soon regret moving somewhere smaller when I couldn't host all the huge family dinners.'

Ursula snorted. 'I would take avoiding the dinners as a plus. It always looked like a ton of work.'

'And I have the car to myself, now,' Colleen went on musingly. 'I could still look after little Kira after school in September, couldn't I? And baby Eoin, when the time comes.' Tears flooded her eyes, but she managed a smile through them. 'And I'll never have to worry again whether Stanley's cheating. He is. It's over.' She made a chopping motion with her hand.

Heart doing that leaving-her-chest thing again, Ursula gave her another hug. 'You never know, Mum. One day you might find someone else too.'

Colleen grimaced. 'Ah, no. I'm going to try this freedom thing for a while. Let's look at coastal cottages on my laptop and eat chocolate.'

Ursula had only one improvement on this scheme to

offer. 'With a glass of wine.' She'd known her mother too long and too well to think that she'd successfully counselled her out of a lifetime's emotional habit, but it would be great to think positively, even if just for an hour. They could sip chardonnay and play a home-grown version of *Fantasy Homes by the Sea*, pretending neither of them was thinking of Stanley far away in Sicily, happy with his new love while Colleen struggled to get over the blow of her worst fear coming to pass.

By the time midnight struck, Ursula was yawning until her eyes watered, the wine bottle was empty, and Colleen had bookmarked four small houses in Portmarnock and had only had one little weep. They went upstairs, still discussing the terrible cost of property at the coast.

Ursula managed to message Zia to say she'd arrived OK, and then she cleaned her teeth, snuggled under the duvet on the bed in her old room and plummeted into sleep.

Next day, Sunday, she woke early, roused by the noise of the traffic outside. She had an internal alarm clock now, from getting up to put out the breakfasts at Residenza dei Tringali and Sicily was, of course, an hour ahead of Ireland.

A trip up the landing to the bathroom allowed her to hear Colleen gently snoring so she dressed rapidly, yanked on the big cardigan she'd appropriated last night and set off at a jog through the early morning – about half as hot as a Sicilian morning – until she arrived panting at Finola's house.

Declan opened the door, looking casual in a sweatshirt and bedhead hair. 'Ursula,' he said with a grin. 'We heard from Colleen that you were coming. You're bright and early.' He kissed her cheek, and then bawled in the general direction of the interior of the house, 'Fin, Ursula's here.' Then, to her: 'Just go in. She's fighting Kira over whether she can have chocolate sauce with her muesli. We're going out later, but I'm going to have a kickabout with the lads in the park for an hour first.' He jogged the five steps to the car as if to demonstrate his athleticism.

'Come in, Ursula,' called Finola from the depths of the house.

Ursula followed the sound of her sister's voice to the small kitchen. The house was a modest semi. Finola was always on at Declan to agree to the ground floor being made open-plan and Dec was always resisting, saying she'd hate it because she wouldn't be able to hear the telly when he made too much noise washing up. The rooms were small, though. Three stools were crowded at the bijou breakfast bar facing the wall, of which Finola and Kira were occupying two.

Her sister jumped up to hug her. 'Why on earth are you freezing your bum off in shorts? It can't be warmer than sixteen out there.'

'Sixteen what?' asked Kira, looking mystified.

'Degrees Celsius. It's a measurement of how warm the weather is,' Finola said, in automatic mother mode.

Ursula explained. 'I came straight from Zia's, and it's about thirty-five in Umbria. Maybe I'll have to go down to the Pavilions later and grab some jeans.' She didn't mention her intention to borrow jeans from Sorcha as Finola was a good two sizes bigger and would probably grumble about how unfair it was that her sisters were so thin.

'Breakfast?' Finola offered.

'Thanks. Muesli with chocolate sauce would be grand,' she answered, straight-faced.

Kira went off into a peal of giggles. 'Yes, yes, yes, Mum! See, Auntie Ursula has it, too.'

Finola grinned good-naturedly. 'Just this once, then, Kira, for a very special treat. And I'll let you have the TV on while you eat it. Auntie Ursula and I will go into the lounge to talk for a bit.'

Five minutes later they were alone, and Finola whispered, 'How's Mum?'

'Patchy,' Ursula said, tucking into her breakfast. 'Muesli and chocolate sauce isn't half bad, you know. But I've only seen Mum for a few hours. How are you finding her, generally?'

'Two steps forward and one back.' Finola scrubbed at her face. Like Dec, she didn't look to have done anything to her hair this morning and it stuck flat to her head on one side. 'Kira's really missing Dad. She can't understand. She expects him to be back in that little house in Malahide he lived in last time they split up, not a flight away. How is he?'

Ursula turned her attention to her breakfast. 'I didn't see that much of him,' she admitted. 'Not before I left for Zia's. My trip to hers was already planned, and I was in shock so I just . . . went.'

Finola's gaze softened. 'Ah. Are you coping?'

Ursula paused, her spoon halfway to her mouth. Zia was right. She must show her family her strength. How could she complain about them treating her with kid gloves if she earned it? 'I'm fine,' she asserted calmly. 'I just needed to see Mum to get a proper handle on whether she can really stomach me being in Sicily, or whether it's too much like taking sides. And I've got something else to sort out too,' she added. Then, on a big breath, 'In Brighton. I need to see Steph.'

Finola froze, her eyes rounding. 'Really? You need to see he's still an arse?' The bite in her voice showed exactly what she thought of Ursula's ex-husband.

Ursula almost choked on her muesli. 'I think that's exactly what I need.' She munched for a moment, gave Finola a précis of the finding-of-the-ring story, then said, 'I thought that I needed to give it back to him, and I do. But more than that, I think I need to say a few things to him. The psychologists would probably say I need closure. I need to get it off my chest, anyway.'

Finola cocked her head, regarding her contemplatively. 'Only if you're sure you're—'

'If you say "strong enough",' Ursula broke in calmly, 'I'm going to throw this chocolatey muesli all over your sofa and carpet.'

Her sister halted, mouth half-open. Then she closed it with a snap and mimed zipping it shut.

Ursula scraped up the last of the chocolatey mess, and the sisters grinned at each other, before Ursula moved on to the subject of Colleen's expressed yearning for a house at the beach.

'Jeez, has she looked at the prices? She'd be better renting, because Dad's got to have his half out of their home,' Finola commented with her customary pragmatism. They discussed their parents until Declan returned from his kick-about and found nobody was ready to go out, so made everybody a second breakfast of hot chocolate and toast.

'Can we go out for lunch?' Kira emerged from the kitchen to ask, an hour later. The sound of kids' TV floated after her from the other room.

'We could, you know,' Ursula declared. 'Let's call Mum, Sorcha and Cade and see who's available.'

They agreed to meet at a pub where Sorcha knew the

management and could coax them to open a side room for a big Quinn family lunch. Only Stanley would be missing from the gathering.

Ursula texted Sorcha: *Please bring me a pair of your jeans to borrow. My legs are bloody freezing.*

The lunch was great. They made sure to seat Colleen in the middle of the table so that she'd be central to every conversation, with Kira on one side of her and baby Eoin on the other. If Caden was still disappointed in his dad, he covered it up for his mum's benefit, playing peeping games with Eoin to make the baby laugh, which made Colleen laugh, too.

Sorcha spirited Ursula off to the ladies' and supplied her with jeans and a fleece – both purple, Sorcha's favourite colour. Studying the effect it had on her blue eyes, Ursula thought she might wear more purple herself.

As nobody had been in a hurry to leave the pub, it was nearly four when Ursula and Colleen walked home together – Ursula grateful for her jeans and fleece as the estuary wind treated them to its chilly embrace.

'What do you want to do this evening?' Ursula linked arms with her mum and could feel how much weight Colleen had lost.

'Drink tea and watch TV,' Colleen answered promptly.

'So, you won't mind me going out for a bit?' Ursula asked. 'I'm out of the way of TV and fancy a walk.'

Colleen didn't mind, so, a few hours later, Ursula left the house again and walked quickly to her uncle's house, following the well-remembered route past the park. Auntie Josie answered the door to her. 'Ursula! I didn't know you were home. You come on in, now.'

Ursula followed her. 'I'm just here for a bit. I want to talk to Uncle Gerry, really.'

Josie sighed. 'Your dad's phoned him. You're upset. I don't blame you.' She paused in the hall, where Gerry had begun scraping off the flowered wallpaper but had yet to finish. 'He's in the lounge. I'll pop round to see a friend for an hour. You go on in.' And Josie, who perhaps had learned to avoid being dragged into messy situations by her scamp of a husband, grabbed a jacket and slipped away through the front door.

Ursula entered the lounge and found her uncle playing Sudoku on his iPad. He looked up with an apprehensive expression. 'I heard your voice,' he said, by way of greeting.

Ursula flopped down in another chair, looking round at the room, the archway that led through into the dining room because Gerry had decided he wanted the house open-plan and set about the wall with a sledgehammer, and only later called a builder to check on the necessity to put in a beam. It was just one example of his impetuous nature, so different from her dad's.

'So.' She directed a level stare at him. 'You set me up to stay with Dad's secret girlfriend.'

Gerry dropped his gaze. 'I didn't think of it like that. It was more like . . .' He rolled his eyes to gaze at the ceiling, as if he'd written an answer there earlier. 'Like I was helping everyone. Stan was worried about Agata, Agata needed help and you'd lost your job and flat and all. It seemed meant.'

'Dad told me that you thought that way,' she acknowledged.

He grimaced. 'And he told me that you didn't agree.'

'I didn't. I don't.' They sat together for a minute, listening to cars passing outside and a group of lads laughing on the pavement. 'You didn't warn me what I was getting into,' she said at last, although she knew what his defence would be before he made it.

'You wouldn't have gone, if I'd told you who Agata was. You've had a grand time, haven't you?' He looked injured.

Tiredly she closed her eyes, feeling a bittersweet smile tugging up one corner of her mouth. 'I suppose I have.' There was still pain at the reason for her leaving, but, until the final days, she'd loved living in her attic room with the balcony. Agata. Nanda. Marilù. Fabio. And Alfio . . . Her heart turned over. *Alfio.*

It would be a warm evening in Ortigia because the summer sun would have been baking the golden buildings all day. Had all signs of the film festival been eradicated, yet? Was Residenza dei Tringali still busy filling up its coffers after a couple of lean years? Was her dad still with Agata? Was anyone feeding Camocat? Or, abandoned by Ursula, had she found a different courtyard to haunt in hopes of kitchen scraps?

How was Alfio? Did he miss her? Was he still in Ortigia sitting on his window ledge in the evenings to look out over the city? She hadn't answered his message or returned his calls. The thought made her feel guilty, but she needed to wait until she found some kind of peace within herself before she could make peace with him. She resolved just to acknowledge his text, at least.

Slowly, she rose. 'See you another time, Uncle Gerry.'

'That'll be grand.' He beamed, probably in relief that she hadn't turned into a screaming banshee over his inter-ference in her life.

Arriving home fifteen minutes later, she settled down to watch a quiz show with her mum, Colleen wrapped up in saying the answers at least as fast as the contestants.

During the ad break, Ursula turned to her. 'Will you be OK if I go off soon?'

284

Colleen pursed her lips. 'Back to Sicily?'

'Not yet. To Brighton, to give Stephan his bloody ring back and make sure he knows that what's past is past.' But now her mother had brought up the thorny issue, she might as well get the conversation underway. 'What if I want to go back to Sicily after that? Would it hurt your feelings?'

Pain flashed across her mother's face. But slowly, she squared her shoulders. 'It's your decision, Ursula. I'm just sorry you got stuck in the middle of everything.'

It wasn't exactly approval or encouragement, but it was probably the fairest Colleen could manage to be and Ursula appreciated the effort it must have taken not to hint that Ursula should stay away. She rose and gave her mum a big hug. 'Thanks for realising about the stuck-in-the-middle thing. I absolutely don't want you to think I'd be taking sides. If I went, it would be for the ceramics.'

'Right. Of course.' Colleen smiled, though it was close to a grimace. At least she didn't ask Ursula if she was sure she'd cope, which was progress.

Chapter Twenty

Ursula flew from Dublin to Gatwick on the early plane. It was the 7th of August, so they flew in bright sunlight; and she'd waited for Tuesday because Monday morning flights were always busy.

She'd bought her own jeans and hoodie – both black, because she'd been feeling serious when she'd shopped. Then she'd jazzed them up with a bubble-gum-pink T-shirt and let Sorcha plait a pink string through the long side of her hair, which still looked good even now she'd slept on it.

The Gatwick Express train took less than half an hour to whizz its way to Brighton, and soon she was passing under the dusty glass curved roof of the station. Outside, she gazed down Queens Road, familiar yet unfamiliar, struck immediately by the cries of the seagulls, loud and complaining compared to the polite 'eep' of the swallows in Ortigia. Buses that looked too big for the narrow road grumbled up the hill, a couple of buskers played beneath – would you look at that? – a big expanse of blue sky. The English summer day wasn't the overwhelming heat

286

of Sicily, but she could take off the hoodie and tie it to her backpack.

Further down Queens Road, close to the seafront, a room awaited her in a small hotel her family had used when visiting her. She'd booked two nights, to give her time to think and the privacy to communicate with people in a way that she'd felt unable to with her mum around.

She'd finally contacted Alfio, a short, polite text to apologise for not replying earlier, stating that she was fine and staying with her mum for a while. An equally polite reply had asked no questions but thanked her for letting him know. The text had concluded: *Hope you are enjoying.* No kiss, but then she hadn't sent him one.

It was too early to check in but the family who ran the tall double-fronted hotel was happy to stow her backpack in a luggage room. Lightened of the load, she set out to soak up the quirky streets of Brighton. They'd so suited her when she'd ended up here as a newly minted adult, leaving Swords and her volatile but loving parents behind. Well, volatile mother, mainly, she had to admit, having witnessed Colleen's moods passing through all seasons in the past days. Sunny smiles switching to cloudy frowns and thunderous resentment inside the space of an hour. It was exhausting, but she remembered the rocky weeks after her own marriage finally ended, when the reality of seismic change had smashed her in the heart several times a day.

One thing that was better in Brighton than Ortigia was the quality of the graffiti, she thought as she wandered into the London Road area. In Ortigia all she'd seen was a few scrawled slogans, yet it seemed everyone who felt like defacing a Brighton building was a budding Banksy, prepared to spend untold hours on gorgeous flowing script and images utilising clever perspective. That's what came of the city having an art school, maybe, though she'd never taken up the spray can or air gun herself.

Her footsteps took her on towards St James's Street and the tattoo parlour where she'd worked for years with Lou and the rest of the crew. Gone was the black and red colour scheme, she found. The unit had been converted into a hair salon in trendy greys with loads of chrome. She took a picture and sent it to Sorcha who returned: *Insipid. Don't get your hair cut there.*

The tang of salt in the air making her hungry, she headed towards the seafront to grab a lunch of chips on the Palace Pier, on guard against opportunistic seagulls who might swipe her meal from her hands. Enjoying the piping hot, salty, vinegary treat, she soaked up the racket of the funfair and the shouts of children and the quieter rattle of the sea breaking against the pebbly beach. Couples walked hand in hand or pushed buggies containing babies. She remembered being one of the hand-holding couples but was glad now that she and Stephan had never graduated to parenthood.

Briefly, she pictured herself with a baby, an infant with dark curly hair and dark eyes.

She shook her head to clear the vision. She was just picturing Marilù, anyway.

The sea glittered so brightly it was hard to look at. On the beach, kids in wetsuits fell over in the waves and teen girls showed off their bikinis, though the straps must have been kept up with goose bumps in the keen sea breeze.

She tried to let her muscles go soft and exist in the moment, a relaxation technique she'd read about, but it was hard to prevent her mind from straying to the tasks ahead of her.

Finally, when her chips were gone and she'd drained

her bottle of water, she vacated her bench and returned to the hotel to be checked in by a late teen who was probably one of the Brighton students who didn't always go home for the holidays. She'd been one herself.

Her room was on the first floor, facing across the busy road and with no balcony. She eased off her canvas shoes and dropped onto the bed. Before she contacted Stephan, she wanted to talk to her dad.

The phone rang four times and then his dear, familiar voice boomed a delighted, 'Ursula! Darlin'! How are ya?'

A lump leapt to her throat. 'I'm fine, Dad. You?'

'Grand,' he answered, his voice bursting with joy. 'Agata and Nanda are here, and little Marilù, but Alfio's taken himself back to Barcelona. Are you still in Swords? How is everyone?' He sounded both eager and wistful. 'I've been in touch with them, of course. And I'll be going back to sort out a few things, soon.'

Alfio had left? A numbness stole over her, making it difficult to work her lips or concentrate on what Stanley had said next. She had to gather herself to reply. 'Fine, they're all good. Everyone told me you're in contact. I stayed with Mum for a while but I'm in Brighton, now.' Mechanically, she told him why she felt she must see Stephan again so that she could move on.

As soon as she could insert it into the conversation, she said casually, 'So, Alfio's gone back to Barcelona? That means you can have his room?'

'He got an offer of the job senior to the one he had before, and with the family having the opportunity to sell their hotel, it's all working out,' Stan returned. Then, awkwardly, 'Erm . . . I'm staying in Agata's room.'

Ursula had had few doubts about that and felt mean now for obliging him to say it. To protect herself from the horror of imagining Alfio with his old girlfriend back in Spain, sending her melting looks from his intense brown eyes and curling naked with her between the sheets, she babbled the first sentences that came into her head. 'It's crazy how cheap it is to travel between Dublin and Brighton, if you book ahead. The whole trip by plane and train was less than forty euros.'

Her dad paused. 'Hang on.' A muffled sound of footsteps and then a door closing. When his voice came again, it was very gentle. 'Is it money stopping you from coming back to Sicily, Ursula? I'll send you the fare, if you want to come. Agata and Nanda would be thrilled because they're very fond of you. We all miss you. Your room's just as you left it. I'm up to speed with breakfasts so you could have more time off for your work on ceramics. Don't give up your dream because I upset you, darlin'.'

Ursula had to swallow a gigantic lump in her throat. 'I'm fine for money, Dad, thanks. I'm still thinking, though Fabio keeps texting me, "Must create! Must produce!"' What was meant to be a laugh gurgled in her throat like a sob and she half-wailed, 'Daddy, I don't know what to do.' She sounded like a kid, the time of her life when he'd been the person who'd always been reliable.

'Then come back and be happy working with Fabio,' Stanley coaxed, his voice tight with emotion. 'Everybody wants you to be happy. You can stay at Residenza dei Tringali, even if it's just till you get something else sorted out.'

'Or the hotel's sold,' she choked, rocked by the yearning to be back in Ortigia, back in Fabio's studio, but now knowing what she yearned for even more wouldn't be there. She drew in a slow breath. 'Thanks for worrying about money, Dad, but I have plenty of savings.' Another steadying breath. 'I'll probably return in a couple of days, then, if you're sure it will be OK.' She didn't mention Alfio again. He wouldn't be there, so it wouldn't matter to him.

The sound of the door opening at Stanley's end of the conversation was loud this time, and his shout still louder. 'Agata! Ursula's coming back soon.'

The cries that greeted his pronouncement were indistinct, but without a doubt sounded glad.

Her heart warming at an important decision seemingly being made, Ursula laughed shakily. 'I'll see you all then. I'm looking forward to it.' It was nearly true. The adjustment to Alfio not being there would be enormous but the remainder of her life in Sicily was still waiting for her.

After ending the call, she lay for a long time staring at the plaster mouldings on the hotel ceiling, listening to the traffic of Queens Road passing below her window, trying to absorb the fact that Alfio had already left. So *soon*. The news had caught her like a punch in the stomach. She'd known he'd be leaving sometime but was shocked at the speed it had happened. Only seventeen days had passed since she'd left . . . and he was gone.

She thought of Zia's protest that Alfio must have found himself between a rock and a hard place, but Ursula had refused to listen and acted ungenerously by cutting off his opportunity to talk her round. If she hadn't, would Alfio have disappeared off to Barcelona so soon?

By slipping away like a thief in the night, had she brought some of her current sadness on herself? Numbly, she confronted the notion that she might have.

Suddenly, violently, she wished her dad hadn't returned to Agata. The end of her parents' marriage had always been a possibility, but she'd never expected to be collateral damage.

If Stanley had stuck his marriage a few months longer, she and Alfio could have had the rest of the summer together, happy and horny. There would have been a lot more carefree nights in her three-quarter-sized bed, waking up squashed against his hot flesh – hot in both senses – with the breeze blowing through the open balcony doors.

If Agata and her dad stayed together, there was every chance that she and Alfio would meet again in completely different circumstances. Did anybody even know they'd been lovers? People might think of them as kind of family, with her dad the partner of Alfio's mum. How completely shit. Her lust for him had been anything but familial.

She shifted restlessly on the bed. Had she expected too much of him?

Was she now incapable of trusting a man? *Bloody* Stephan. He and the drink spiker had messed with her head and her heart and given her a past that she'd allowed to play too large a part in her present.

She sighed. It was time to confront that past and make what sense of it she could.

It was after four-thirty p.m., Stephan should be at work – if he still worked for the council. He might have become a pole dancer or an astronaut, for all she knew or cared. She unblocked his number to enable him to reply to her, and then began a text.

I am visiting Brighton, she typed. *Wish to meet this evening to return your grandpa's ring.*

While she waited, she thought about returning to Siracusa, picturing what her life would look like there, now Alfio was in Spain. It was time to pull on her big-girl panties – or big-girl thong – and focus on working with Fab to see if they could achieve something worthwhile.

The determination made her feel lighter, despite the regrets circling like a host of black clouds above her head.

Her phone buzzed and her heart kicked up. She read Stephan's reply: *Big surprise! Yeah, can make tonight. Where you staying?*

Ursula curled her lip. Did he think she was a complete eejit with all that pass-agg crap about 'Big surprise'. Was he expecting her to be apologetic about her having the ring when he'd bloody planted it on her?

She began a reply: *Let's meet . . .* Then she deleted, electing to show Stephan he wasn't in charge. *I'll meet you at the old lift in Madeira Drive, 7pm.* The lift and its pagoda-shaped roof had been a distinctive part of the landscape since Victorian times, and had recently been restored to life, linking Madeira Drive to Marine Parade above.

He returned: *That's a bit weird. Just say where you're staying, and I'll be there.* A thoughtful emoji, as if she was being confusing.

Crossly, she repeated, *I'll be at the old lift in Madeira Drive, 7pm.*

This time, he sent a laughing emoji. *Like a spy movie?*

Prickles of irritation made her feel as if her hair was standing on end. She would *not* let him cajole her into saying where she was staying, even if he could probably guess it was the same hotel her family had used. Swiftly, she tapped: *OK. Don't worry. I'll post it to your mum and tell her where I found it.* Ha. Without doubt, he'd want to avoid the interrogation that Claudia would subject him to, of which 'How on earth did it get in with Ursula's whiskey glasses?' would be just the first question.

He shot back. *Is it me, or is this getting silly?*

Victorious that she was annoying him as much as the ring saga had annoyed her, she smirked as she typed her reply. *Deadly serious.*

Long silence.

Ursula fidgeted, too antsy to watch TV. It was fine trying to be the one in control but what if Stephan simply refused to budge? She couldn't confront him about their joint past satisfactorily through Claudia. She snatched up her phone and called Zia.

'Hey!' As always, Zia sounded delighted to hear from her.

Ursula didn't bother with niceties. 'I don't think I'm good at brinksmanship.' She sketched in the details of her mission and how awaiting Stephan's reply was making her feel queasy and sweaty.

'You're doing great,' Zia reassured her stoutly. 'Any moment now he's going to remember how formidable you can be and cave in. Bet he's grinding his teeth.'

'Hang on, hang on, just got a text.' Ursula fumbled to switch screens. She read the message, then crowed, 'Yes! He says, "Fine. See you there."'

'Ha.' Zia sounded equally jubilant. 'See how strong you are? You kept your nerve, and he lost his.' Laughing, she added, 'OK, as you're such a great role model, you can be my baby's godmother.'

'You know I was always going to be, right?' Ursula laughed back, enjoying the feeling of relief, feeling almost as strong as Zia said she was. 'I'll be glad to have this meeting behind me, though.' After promising to update Zia later, she rang off, then texted: *OK* to Stephan.

Buoyed by her success, she used the time she had in hand to book her flight from Gatwick to Catania and messaged Stanley to tell him. On reflection, it seemed good

294

manners to text Agata and Nanda, too, as they owned the hotel. All of them responded with pleasure.

No point telling Alfio, though. He might own a quarter of the hotel, but he'd obviously returned to his role as sleeping partner. Not *her* sleeping partner.

At fifteen minutes to seven, she dropped Grandpa's ring in her pocket and set out towards Madeira Drive. An entire flock of Brighton seagulls had taken up residence in her stomach at the thought of seeing Stephan again. As she walked along the broad drive, which was closed to most vehicles so filled with walkers and cyclists, she calmed her nerves by thinking about her new-life-version-two that she intended to make for herself in Sicily, concentrating on the positives such as sun and work she loved. New-life-version-two was only a couple of days away – once she'd put the past behind her for good.

When she reached the lift, she checked out the drive in both directions, but saw no sign of Stephan. She took a seat on a nearby bench, watching people walking their dogs or pedalling along with children on bikes. The breeze scooted in from the sea and tossed her hair around. Gulls wheeled above the pebble beach. The small track for the Volk's Electric Railway stood empty, as it was too late for a train to come whirring and tooting along from the direction of the aquarium, towards Brighton Marina, carrying passengers in its open carriages to Halfway or Black Rock Stations.

At five minutes past seven, she rose and continued along Madeira Drive, frustrated and angry. If she had binoculars, she'd probably be able to detect Stephan somewhere in the vicinity, ambling along, deliberately messing her around, but she was damned if she'd wait on his pleasure.

Ten minutes after she'd begun striding towards the concrete edifice of Brighton Marina, her phone rang.

'Yes?' she answered, carelessly.

Stephan sounded breathless. 'I'm at the old lift. Where are you?'

'I was there on time. You were a no-show, so I left.' She continued walking.

'Aw, come on, Ursula, I left my phone on charge and had to run back for it.' Stephan sounded taken aback. 'I didn't mean to be late. I'm here now.'

She drew out a hesitation, as if checking whether she still had time for the meeting. 'OK. I've just passed Halfway Station. I'll hang on here and you can catch me up.' She heard him say something, as if to object, but she ended the call and dropped down on a nearby bench, facing the yellow kiosk that seemed too small to be awarded the grand name of 'station', with a chain-link fence and beach behind it. While she waited, she concentrated on appearing the picture of relaxed unconcern and inner strength. She'd let Stephan wind her up way too many times in the past.

Finally, he hurried up to her, panting. He looked older, she thought, rising not out of courtesy but because she didn't want him to tower over her. Lines bracketed the corners of his eyes, and his hair blew straight up from his furrowed forehead, making him look a bit like Gordon Ramsay. Against her expectations, he smiled and said, 'Hi, how are *you*? It's great to see you, Ursula.' His eyes glowed and, for an instant, it was as if the Steph she'd once known had shown up, the one who'd loved her.

She kept her smile small, stepping back in case he had some idea of swooping in for a hug, or even a kiss, and waved him to the bench. 'I need to talk to you about a few things.'

His smile faded at such chilly reception, but he dropped down beside her. 'Thanks for bringing back my ring. Are you in Brighton for long?'

As she had no wish to fall into the trap of letting him control the conversation, she bulldozed ahead. 'I want to tell you how badly I feel you acted and how much I didn't deserve it.' Calmly, she met his hazel gaze.

He did a great job of looking stunned. 'That's what you're here for?'

'It's one of the reasons I didn't just send the ring to you.' She hadn't rehearsed her speech, but now let it flow from the gash in her wounded heart. 'When I was the victim of drug assault, you turned against me.' As he opened his mouth, she spoke louder, to cut off whatever he meant to say. 'Without a shred of proof, you leapt to the conclusion that I'd cheated on you. And then you punished me for it. Even once we were aware that I'd been roofied, you made it about you and not me. When you finally ended things after our farcical reunion, you were particularly unpleasant.' Each word felt like a helium balloon appearing in her hands, making her feel lighter and lighter until it was as if she could float off, away from Stephan and away from Brighton, her old life and its unhappiness.

For once, Stephan seemed lost for words. He looked knocked off kilter by her calm litany of the ways in which he'd wronged her. All the right phrases flowed from her lips, and he could only sit and listen.

Finally, she reached into her pocket and brought out the circle of gold with the purple diamond that glinted in the evening sun. 'OK, I've said what I came to say. Here's your grandpa's ring, the one you planted in my things, knowing I'd find it sooner or later and would have to let you have it back. Another way of harassing me, I guess, giving you the excuse to manipulate others into calling me. Oh, and, by the way, don't bother to visit my parents if you go to Dublin. The house is to be sold.'

She held out the ring. Dumbly, he extended his palm to receive it still without a breath of argument, let alone the explosion she'd half-feared. Crisply, she ended, 'I don't expect to hear from you again, either directly or indirectly.' She bounced to her feet as if the swelling breeze was ready to lift her up by those helium balloons.

Fiddling with the ring, he said dully, 'It wasn't like that.'

Surprised, Ursula paused. 'What wasn't? You didn't react unforgivably to the drug assault? I distinctly remember you locking me out of the house.'

He gave a mighty sniff, as if on the brink of tears. 'I didn't put the ring in your things to harass you.'

Ursula stared, wrong-footed by his doleful delivery and the absence of his usual bluster and anger. Anger was how Stephan processed emotion, right? She'd steeled herself to face it.

But her ex-husband was looking shattered. 'I have a different perspective on every point you've made. I'd like to tell you, if you'll listen.'

Slowly, wary that this was just the start of some Stephan games, Ursula sat back down on the bench. 'You have excuses?'

The incoming tide was rattling the shingle on the beach. People continued to pass on foot or on wheels, but in smaller numbers now. Wearily, Stephan rubbed his hand over his eyes. 'You've shocked me – I won't lie. Part of me has always known I was victim-blaming. It seemed like you'd got drunk and thrown our fantastic marriage in the toilet.' He held up a hand as she opened her mouth to snap out a retort. 'I know – no proof. I understand that now, and how I hurt you. But I was heartbroken. I'd trusted you, loved you, and you'd let me down. I *thought* you'd let me down,' he amended hurriedly.

He gave another unattractive sniff. 'Then, when it became clear your drink had been tampered with, I was angry all over again, including angry with myself for misjudging you but . . . I find it hard to acknowledge when I'm wrong. I somehow made it about you getting in that situation, rather than me reacting like a prick. I—I couldn't seem to find my way back from that position. It was horrible,' he added, reflectively. 'I didn't know how to handle the mess I'd made.'

Ursula sank back on the bench, all the triumph melting out of her bones. 'You could have been angry with the perpetrator. Maybe even apologised to me.'

The gaze he turned on her was full of misery. 'We didn't know who the perpetrator was.'

'So that made it OK for you to take everything out on me?' Ursula could barely form the words, washed over by the echoes of that old pain.

'I'm just telling you my perspective, not justifying it.' Hunching into his collar, Stephan went on. 'Men don't get sympathy in certain situations. We're supposed to be strong.' He gave her a twisted smile. 'Do you know that many men feel they're not allowed to grieve over miscarriage or still birth, because it's all about the woman? Our situation was a bit like that. You never said, "If I was roofied, then I get that it's horrible for you, too. You must be tormented over what happened to your wife." Or, "Maybe I should have taken more care with my drink." You said a lot about being punished when you'd done nothing wrong, but it never crossed your mind that I felt

299

the same. I'd done no more than sit at home watching footie while my wife went out with her friends, and then some stranger exploded my happiness. I answered the door, and he cheerfully dumped you unconscious in my arms and said, "Sorry, mate. I found her like this". How do you think that *felt?*'

'Jeez,' Ursula breathed, reliving the scene through Stephan's eyes. It was true that she'd seen herself and her marriage as the victims of the person who'd roofied her but now, for the first time, she allowed the thought to trickle in that Stephan might be a victim, too.

His lovely marriage had suffered a trauma, just like hers.

People grieving a bereavement frequently exploded in unreasoning anger, so why shouldn't losing trust in his wife affect him the same way?

But . . . no. For fuck's sake, he was shifting the blame *again*. He'd done this all the time, altering his position by increments until he'd manoeuvred himself onto the high ground and left her feeling responsible. This time, she pushed back. 'But you shouldn't have expressed your grief by condemning me,' she said with steely emphasis. 'Even now, you're seeking to censure me with that comment about me taking care with my drink. You already know that I didn't buy either of the two rounds we had at that club, so can have no control over what happened before my drinks reached me.'

His jaw flexed. Instead of addressing her comment, he shifted his stance yet again. 'How would you feel if you'd thought I'd cheated on you?'

She gave herself a moment to consider that honestly. 'It would have been a shock,' she admitted. 'But as we'd been together for years and you'd never given me a reason to believe you'd cheat, I would have needed proof.' Maybe it was because she spoke with quiet conviction, but he seemed to have no reply to that.

They sat in silence for several minutes. Ursula watched a family pass, looking smart and freshly washed. Probably they were going to a restaurant at the marina for an early dinner before the parents took the kids home to bed.

Stephan waited until they were out of earshot. 'I didn't leave the ring in your things to harass you,' he repeated eventually. 'It was like . . .' He furrowed his forehead again, looking more like Gordon Ramsay than ever. 'It created a connection. A thin connection, but it was there, waiting for if I needed it – like when I realised you'd left Brighton. I never stopped loving you,' he added simply.

Ursula let out a squeak of outrage, but before she could remind him *again* that he'd locked her out of their frigging house, he dropped his head into his hands, his voice emerging muffled, hard to distinguish as the evening breeze rose. 'Ursula, when you took those pills, I was absolutely gutted. It was my fault. I'd let my anger get the better of me and *you tried to end your life*. I hated myself. But, contrary to what you read in novels, hating yourself doesn't necessarily make you behave better. It can make you act like a naughty child who's smashed something valuable and hides in the cobwebby space under the bed, too scared to own up to his mistake, looking for someone else he can make look guilty so he can feel better.'

Ursula gazed at his hunched figure, almost at a loss, feeling as if she was genuinely seeing this man for the first time, though he was the one who'd shared her life for years. He was finally trying to admit fault, yet, being Stephan, he was incapable of doing it in a genuine, open-hearted way. First, he'd tried to manipulate her into taking a share of the blame, and now he was hiding behind theatrics. The word 'sorry' was still conspicuous by its absence.

Still, as she watched his attempt to display grief without anger, some of the bitterness she'd harboured towards him faded. 'I can see you as that kid hiding under the bed. Your mum and dad always bigged you up and treated you like the sun shone out of your backside, so it shouldn't be a shock that you can't own up to mistakes.'

His laugh emerged in an ugly snort between his fingers. 'I'm not sure whether that's meant to make me feel better, but it doesn't.' He wiped his eyes with his sleeve and blew out a big breath as he sat up straight. 'We can't try again, can we?'

Though she heard desolation in his voice, Ursula was quick to say, 'No. I'm sorry.'

'I'm sorry, too,' he said, finally using the word. 'Sorry that the whole roofying shit ever happened to us, not just because it must have been horrible for you, but because it destroyed us. It's amazing how easily it happened, really. But I suppose that's mainly on me.'

She didn't think 'suppose' or 'mainly' were required in that sentence, and noted he was sorry bad things had happened rather than it being a heartfelt apology, but, tiredly, she tried to be the bigger person. 'It's too late for regrets, but thank you for finally listening to me, and I'm glad I heard your end of things. I'm going now, Steph.'

Despondently, he nodded. 'Where did you go after Brighton?'

'Ireland,' she said, because it wasn't a lie, but wasn't the answer he was looking for. She wanted to draw a line under Brighton and did *not* want to tell Steph about Sicily and have him turn up, pretending he was in the area on holiday. She'd remind her family again about being careful on social media, and finally, *finally* let her once-great-but-ended-badly marriage stop affecting her.

'Going back into the city?' he asked, as they both rose from the bench, stiffly, as if battered by the flying accusations.

After a hesitation, she answered, 'Yes. Shall we walk back together?' There was little point in pretending a meeting in the other direction. Stephan could follow her back to her hotel for all the good it would do him. The day after tomorrow, she'd be out of the UK and had no idea if she'd ever return.

They walked in step, but separately, beside the Volk's railway tracks, past the old lift and nearly to the pier, where the lights from the funfair spun and sparkled though it wasn't yet dark. To make polite conversation, she told him her old boss, Lou, had gone to live in Spain. He told her about a promotion at work.

'Someone else in your life?' he asked eventually, kicking a pebble.

'Loads of people,' she agreed breezily, deliberately misunderstanding.

He halted, hands in pockets and shoulders hunched. 'I still love you, Ursula.'

A shiver of distaste rippled through her, and she headed him off firmly. 'I hope you find someone else to love soon.'

Half-heartedly, as if he was having trouble accepting the inevitable, he persisted. 'Dinner, for old times' sake?'

She glanced out to sea, where white tops were forming on the waves and riding to the shore. 'I had chips on the pier.'

'Meal of kings and queens,' he said quietly, because that had been one of their jokes, when they'd been together.

Absently, Ursula nodded. As they'd trailed back along

Madeira Drive, past the ornate metal arches that supported Marine Parade above, her subconscious must have been working because now something slithered to the forefront of her mind. 'Steph,' she said slowly, 'did you really want our marriage to work out?'

His mouth dropped open. 'Isn't that what I've been saying?'

She turned her gaze to him. 'So, would you say that your lack of trust in me caused you to destroy a relationship you wanted?'

Dumbly, he gazed at her. Then, jerkily, he nodded.

She sighed, having to look away from the pain in his eyes, but thinking that her mum had done much the same to her relationship with Ursula's dad, which had played its part in him keeping his old flame a secret for forty years . . . until that flame turned once again to fire.

Did she want her life to mirror theirs? Letting herself be so hard, wary, and unforgiving that she couldn't work with someone to make a relationship a success? It wasn't a nice image of the future.

They reached the pier and she prepared to turn towards Queens Road. 'Part as friends?' he said suddenly.

'Yes, let's,' she agreed, and allowed him to squeeze her hand. Did she feel differently, having heard his confession? Yes. But mainly, she was feeling glad it was over, and so *strong* to have confronted him, and said all the things she'd failed to say about the end of their marriage and assured herself, just one last time, that it had been he who'd acted badly.

When she'd finally left him behind, wrung out and glad to regain the safety of her hotel room, she returned his number to the blocked list.

A strong woman knew how to protect herself.

Chapter Twenty-One

When Alfio had flown back to Barcelona, he'd been shocked that Ximena herself met him at the airport, looking cool and chic in a stylish skirt and blouse, her jewellery understated and gold. Though he didn't know her well, their past relationship having been local comms office manager to a senior director – his boss's boss – they were well enough acquainted to smile and shake hands.

In Spanish, she said, 'Welcome back, Alfio. You're booked into the Grand Hotel Central.'

'*Gracias.*' He hoped he hadn't looked too stunned to be accommodated at a hotel that was usually above his touch.

Ximena rattled her car keys. 'We can talk as I drive you there.'

Ah. Meeting him herself now made sense. It must be the only time she had available for him.

However, Ximena talked about anything but work as she navigated the congestion around the airport and then whizzed him into the city. 'Tonight, I would like you to be the dinner guest of myself and my husband. Inigo and his wife Franca will join us. OK?'

'Of course,' he murmured, feeling as if he'd landed in a parallel universe.

She swerved the car into a faster lane. 'Is there anyone you'd like to invite?'

'No, thank you.' He shoved Ursula ruthlessly from his mind.

'You will be able to walk to our apartment from your hotel,' she went on. 'It is maybe ten minutes.'

He murmured renewed thanks. Good job he'd brought a smart jacket, though he hadn't really anticipated anyone trying to woo him quite so obviously. After Ximena had dropped him off and he'd checked in, however, he gazed around the spacious, modern room he'd been allocated and accepted that wooing it must genuinely be.

That evening saw him giving his name to the doorman at Ximena's towering apartment block promptly at eight, clutching champagne and flowers he'd bought in the afternoon. Upstairs in a spacious apartment furnished in cream, he found it was Inigo admitting him, and greeting him like a valued friend. Inigo's wife Franca rose from a sofa to welcome him, too.

Ximena bustled out from behind the chic island unit that divided kitchen from living space, indicating a man in a pale pink shirt. 'Alfio, this is my husband, Esteban.'

With the increasing sensation of being out of his league, Alfio shook hands with the man who he knew to be a respected fund manager.

'Welcome to our home,' murmured Esteban, with a practised smile, while, over his shoulder, Alfio admired the cityscape through the apartment's panoramic glass wall.

Ximena and Esteban had cooked a delicious meal between them, and soon everyone was seated around a

306

glass-topped table lit with pink candles that almost exactly matched Esteban's shirt.

The dinner table conversion was initially about trips abroad. Inigo managed to make it a segue into what a boon it was to personally accrue air miles on business travel, as if saying to Alfio, *If you step up from local management to leadership, this is what you'll get.*

Although the new role would still be based in Barcelona, it would cover a patch of Europe from Portugal to Croatia and France to the Mediterranean Sea, centred not just in comms but comms policy; the creation of not just internal but external messages; strategy; and employing the best people.

Appealing was too small a word, Alfio thought, as he listened. *Fantastic. Amazing. Astonishing. Career-making. A big step up.*

That night, he tried to sleep in his six-foot bed at the Grand Central Hotel, head swimming with the glimpse of the lifestyle that had been outlined to him. He had no doubt that long hours and a truckload of stress and responsibility came with the role that seemed to be on offer but . . . wow.

In the morning, after a shower that came at him from ten jets situated around the tiled enclosure and drying himself on a towel almost as big as the bed, he jogged down to a dining room that made the breakfast room at Residenza dei Tringali look tiny. A glass wall looked out over a square with a tiled fountain and waitstaff glided around as if wearing cotton wool on the soles of their shoes.

He chose a table. As he settled down to check his inbox while he waited to be noticed by a server, he found an email from Nanda. The subject line was a single exclamation mark.

He opened the message and read: *The Minton Mafflin and hotel chain staff have been here only two days and have told us to expect an offer for the hotel. They have asked whether the family would prefer that the top-line offer be made via video conference or email.*

Heart trotting hard, he gazed fixedly at his screen. The hotel chain must want Residenza dei Tringali, as in really *want*. Without hesitation, he messaged back. *I think an email would be better but what do you and Mamma think?*

Nanda must have been in front of the computer as she came back in seconds. *We think the same. I will tell them.*

Then his concentration was broken as he realised someone waited at his elbow. He glanced up, expecting to see a black-suited server ready to take his order for cappuccino and pastries. But what he saw was a blonde woman wearing a tentative smile.

For a moment he had trouble believing his eyes. 'Hettie?' he said stupidly.

She smiled more broadly. 'I still have you on the app that finds your friends and saw you were back in Barcelona. I was intrigued. I couldn't resist calling in before my first class to try and see you.'

Remembering his manners, he rose, indicating the free seat at the table. 'Would you like to join me for breakfast?'

The smile burst into life. 'That would be awesome.' She plopped down so fast he thought she might have dented the chair. Her eyes sparkled. 'What are you doing here? Fancy hotel, or what?' She gazed around approvingly, while a waiter took their order and glided back in moments with a glass stand full of pastries, cappuccino for him and Americano for her.

He outlined the approach from his old employer, still

experiencing that sense of unreality that such an opportunity had dropped from the skies.

'Fantastic,' she breathed. 'I can't believe you're coming back.'

They chatted over breakfast, somewhat like old times, though they'd never managed such five-star grandeur.

Then Hettie's cheeks flushed a cute pink beneath her freckles. 'Alfio, at the risk of repeating what I said weeks ago, I know I made a big mistake in letting you go. I acted like a frightened kid, rather than an adult.' Her blue eyes were cloudy with regret, but also tinged with hope. 'I could hardly sleep last night once I knew you were in Barca. I know you felt I'd let you down. I *did* let you down. But I've had plenty of time to grow up, and I want to start seeing you again. I really do, Alfio.' She leaned in and posed prettily, letting him see that her smile was as beautiful as ever and so was her hair, her make-up, and her body, while she took one of his hands, her skin soft against his.

Into his mind's eye floated a different pair of blue eyes. A funkier blonde hairstyle. A willowier body. And body art.

And disappointment.

Ursula was out of his life. He'd called and called, without success, and finally sent an apologetic, olive-branch text. After several days, she'd replied, a stiff little message saying she was fine.

So that was that.

He tried to focus his attention on the woman before him, instead. 'Let's see whether I'm formally offered the job. Nothing's certain.'

Later, after Hettie had rushed off to the language school where she worked, a taxi arrived for Alfio. Apparently, he was not expected to take the train to the business park in the suburbs. Meetings were to begin at eleven in Inigo's corner office, two storeys higher than where Alfio's old desk had stood. If Alfio took the job, it would be his office.

Ximena hosted, sitting before huge windows affording a view of trees in landscaped grounds, and told him that his abrupt leaving had thrown out a succession plan that had been a year in the making. 'That is how long we have known of Inigo's retirement plans,' she said, with a cool look at Inigo, who was obviously inconveniencing her by leaving. 'We had been about to approach you when you handed in your resignation.' The slightly admonishing expression moved on to Alfio before she softened it with a smile and a shrug. 'You had family reasons, so what could we say? It was a roll of our dice for Inigo to ask to see you while he was in Sicily, or we would have had to begin recruiting.'

Inigo pulled a face. 'Which would have meant a longer time until I could retire.' He winked conspiratorially at Alfio.

Ximena ignored the light-hearted comment. 'One thing I should mention, Alfio, is that the new role carries a six-month notice period so it would be hard for you to leave as swiftly as you did before, should your family need you again.'

Alfio thought of Agata and her Stanley – who had hurled his summer into disarray. 'My mother's situation is much improved, and so is that of my sister and niece. Thank God it ended well.'

Ximena inclined her head, apparently finding her god aligned with his, and proceeded to outline a blockbuster offer – big increase in salary, bonuses and a car allowance

– that almost made his eyes water. Along with what he could only assume would be a healthy offer from Minton Mafflin, he would improve his previous Barcelona standard of living immeasurably. He'd never been poor, but with the change in fortunes, many people would consider him rich.

He'd loved living and working in Barcelona before and could even have his old girlfriend back, from what she'd said this morning. It was like a dream – and not of the nightmare variety, like the one that had started the entire chain of events leading him back to Sicily. 'I'd be a fool to turn down such an offer,' he said.

Ximena smiled with satisfaction. 'I'll have draft terms of contract sent over to you to read over. I'm out of the office tomorrow, but shall we meet again the day after, Thursday, to discuss?'

Everyone shook hands and Ximena left for her next meeting. Inigo had arranged lunch to be delivered, and he and Alfio discussed the specifics of the succession of Alfio into Inigo's role.

Later, Alfio took the train back into Barcelona centre, feeling a need to be the old Alfio who had been without access to the company's taxi account. Back in the city, rather than return to his hotel and be at loose ends, he stopped at a café on the paving of Plaça de Catalunya and ordered *cerveza grande*, which would in Italian be *birra media*, and roughly equivalent to an English pint of beer.

He rang Agata, knowing that she'd listen to the account of the whirlwind that was happening to him and respond with calm good sense. 'Are you happy?' was her first question. Followed swiftly by: 'Do you want this job? Do you want to live in Spain again?'

'It's an accolade to be offered such a fantastic opportunity,' he said cautiously. 'And I love Spain.'

She said, 'Hmm. I asked you simple questions, but you returned evasive answers.'

He replied with exactly what came into his head. 'Life isn't simple. How about you, Mamma? If we sell the hotel, will you retire? Or find another role somewhere?'

'Retire,' she said, surprising him with such a prompt and decided response. 'In fact, if we don't sell the hotel I shall retire. I've discussed this with Nanda.'

He gazed around at people at other tables, looking normal and grounded in their individual worlds, while he felt the life he'd known shifting around him. 'Then the decision to sell the hotel is made, without the need for much more discussion,' he said eventually. 'Nanda can't run it on her own and employing a manager would never be the same, or work as well.'

'To sell suits us all,' she acknowledged, with threads of sadness in her voice. 'I believe Stanley and I will make our main home in Siracusa. It's hard for him to be separated from his family but he can fly home often, and Ursula will be here.'

His beer glass slipped through his fingers and onto the table, rattling before coming to rest on its base. 'Ursula's back in Ortigia?' An image of her laughing up at him from her bed in her attic room blasted into his mind, leaving him suddenly sweaty.

'Soon, I think.' Her voice became muffled as she said something. Then the line cleared again. 'Yes. Stanley says Thursday. I haven't talked to her myself, but he seems to think she'll return to her room here until she finds somewhere else. She's talked of living near Fabio's studio in the centre.'

They ended the call soon after. With a weight dragging at his heart, he drained his beer and ordered another, and from then tried to drink his regrets away along with the rest of the afternoon and evening, watching the afternoon light turn the water in the twin fountains into a shower of diamonds, and then the sky turn lilac and gold as the sun posted itself down behind the grand old buildings that surrounded the square.

He was tipsy by the time he paid his bill and trekked unsteadily back to his hotel, but at least that made it hard to think. It was a relief from regrets and memories.

Morning came sooner than Alfio's body seemed to be expecting. He hadn't set an alarm, as he wasn't due back at the office today, but was shocked to see it was almost ten when he surfaced. It felt peculiar after getting up early all summer to deal with duties at Residenza dei Tringali.

His hangover slithered over him like a greasy shroud. Two bottles of water from the minibar helped with the dehydration, especially when consumed sitting on the floor of the capacious shower while lukewarm water played down on him. When finally dried and dressed, he ordered espresso to be sent to his room, lacking appetite for pastries or anything sweet. He drank the strong coffee, staring out over the cityscape of rooftops and skyscrapers, enlivened by the occasional church spire. His mind wandered to another, smaller cityscape, and evenings looking out over Ortigia from Ursula's balcony and then smooching her off into bed, to kiss the leaves and flowers that decorated her body as he slid himself inside her.

With a convulsive movement, he snatched up his phone and key card and decided to be a tourist for once. He wouldn't think about Ursula.

Though he headed for one of his favourite areas, the port, with countless rows of boats and cruise ships, ornate buildings and lovely restaurants, the day dragged.

His local friends were all at work and his solitary state gave him too much time to think. When he received an email with the headline *Terms of Contract*, he wished Ximena had been available today so he could have been distracted by discussing it.

Finally, he contacted a one-time colleague called Damijan, who'd come to Spain from Poland and was reliably single. Damijan, it turned out, had an arrangement to visit a sports bar that evening with friends and insisted that Alfio join them.

For the second night, he drank too much – but not enough to bring on another hangover, this time.

In the morning, he breakfasted in the sumptuous restaurant before returning to his room to change into office clothes for the meeting with Ximena.

At the last minute, when he was preparing to leave to formally accept his elevated role, he knew a moment's panic, a feeling of turning his back on something wonderful and cutting himself off from possibilities. He snatched up his phone and tapped on *Ursula* in his contacts.

Greeted by voicemail, he sent a text. *Can we talk? It is important.*

But it didn't matter how many times he looked at his phone in the taxi that took him to the office, or even in the lift up to Ximena's office. There was no reply.

He gazed dumbly at the blank screen, feeling as if happiness had escaped him.

Then he went to embrace his future.

Chapter Twenty-Two

Ursula had just about talked herself to a standstill, lying on her hotel bed in Brighton after her meeting with Steph on Tuesday evening. She'd dissected her life with her mother, both her sisters, her brother, and, of course, Zia. Nobody really dissented from her view that her showdown with Stephan constituted progress in her personal journey.

Her successful confrontation had been cleansing and liberating. It had enabled her to want to learn to trust again. In fact, she *refused* to live the remainder of her life trusting no one. People were imperfect and you had to accept that or live your life alone. That was her journey of the heart.

An echo of a conversation she'd had in Swords with her mother had kept sounding in her mind. Colleen had said, *I let a good man get away by always being suspicious.* Those suspicions hadn't been without foundation, as Stanley had carried a torch for Agata for decades and reignited their relationship when opportunity knocked, but Ursula understood that her parents' marriage had been helped along the road to failure by her mother's insecurities. A pang seared through her. *Alfio*. His fantastic new job meant he'd 'got away', just as surely as Ursula had run away . . . from him, because of her inability to see that he'd had his own perspective and other claims on his loyalty.

Now it was Wednesday, time to embark on her physical journey that would carry her back to Ortigia. She had an aisle seat, her backpack was stuffed under the seat in front, and the little boy next to her was trying to draw her into conversation. He looked about six years old and wanted to show her a game on his iPad.

The mother rolled her eyes. 'Troy, not everyone wants to watch you play *Way of the Turtle*. Sorry,' she added to Ursula, with an apologetic smile.

'I don't mind,' she said. 'I have a niece just a little younger than Troy and I'll bet she'll be mad at me if I don't learn the game.'

Troy, who wore cute glasses on his snub nose, gave his mother a triumphant look and began to show Ursula how to earn shells to enhance abilities.

'Hang on while I put my phone on airplane mode,' she said, as the cabin crew member made the usual safety announcements. 'OK, now. How does it go?'

Ursula took turns on the game with Troy and the busy, noisy plane took off almost unnoticed. Troy's mum, who looked to be in her mid-twenties and gave her name as Nancijane, which Ursula thought was gorgeous and unusual, watched for a while, then gently drifted off into a nap.

Troy's chatter was the perfect distraction for Ursula, whose thoughts were apt to stray to Ortigia and how she was going to adapt to seeing her dad with Agata, when she'd spent most of her life till now seeing him with her mum. It would be an adjustment, that was for sure.

And so would the attic room next to hers being empty. Her heart began a long, slow descent towards her toes at the thought.

'No, you're getting that all wrong,' Troy chided her in exasperation, taking his iPad back and jarring her back to the present. 'Look, I'll show you again.'

Ursula applied herself more thoroughly, charmed by the sweet little boy who showed her a gap where a tooth used to be whenever he smiled.

Nancijane woke with a jolt when the meal trolley rattled up, staffed by two female cabin crew. 'I didn't mean to sleep,' she told Ursula apologetically. 'Panini, Troy?'

Ursula ordered the same and when the food arrived, Troy had to put away his iPad to pull down his tray table, over which he scattered copious crumbs. He acquainted Nancijane with the astounding fact that Ursula had never played *Way of the Turtle* before while Ursula took out her phone, ready to watch a movie she'd downloaded, sipping her coffee and tucking into toasted bread filled with chicken and melted cheese. When, after a few minutes, her seat began to shake, she glanced up, expecting to see the seatbelt sign illuminated and hear a public announcement about turbulence.

But she realised that it was only their row of seats shaking at the same instant that Troy gasped, 'Something's wrong with my mum.'

Ursula swung her head around to see Nancijane jerking spasmodically, and her eyes rolling back in her head. Troy was gaping at his mother, shock and horror written all over his freckly, snub-nosed face.

'Jeez. Is she choking?' Ursula demanded in alarm. Discarding her half-eaten panini, she swept everything off her tray, uncaring that her coffee spilled on the carpet, and urged the frightened little boy out of the middle seat. 'Here, sweetie, let me see if I can make her cough it up.'

Three hard bangs on the back was what Ursula had been told you administered to someone choking, but Nancijane's spasms continued, and no food flew from her mouth. A repetition brought the same lack of result.

Troy began to cry.

Panic rising, Ursula grabbed the tearful boy by the hand and urged him up the aisle in the direction of the nearest member of cabin crew. Breathlessly, she said, 'The lady in the window seat is having a seizure, I think. She's this little boy's mother.' She didn't want to say much more, with Troy, wet-eyed and terrified beside her, but the cabin crew proved that they were much more than the airborne waiters and waitresses people often seemed to think them.

The female crew member grabbed an oxygen bottle and hurried down the aisle. A nearby passenger who said he was a GP arrived on the scene to assist while a male crew member who introduced himself as Roberto took charge of Ursula and Troy, ushering them into free seats a few rows away.

'Is Mummy OK?' Tory sniffed, clinging to Ursula as if he'd known and trusted her for years.

'I don't think she's too well,' Ursula replied honestly. 'The best thing we can do is sit quietly and let the doctor help her.'

Roberto smiled reassuringly. 'And I'll sit with you, too, OK?' He smiled at Ursula. 'I understand you're not of the same party so if you'd rather be seated separately—'

'I'll stick with Troy,' Ursula told him firmly, unable to imagine prising Troy's little hand off hers, let alone abandoning him in a scary situation. She gave Troy what she hoped was a reassuring smile. 'After all, you taught me to play *Way of the Turtle*, so it's only fair, isn't it?'

Mutely, Troy nodded, clinging on to Ursula's fingers harder than ever. Minutes passed like hours before another crew member arrived, dark bun immaculate despite the emergency. She gave Troy a wide smile. 'Your mum's awake. But the doctor thinks she should be quiet for a few minutes, if you don't mind staying here in these new seats with Roberto.'

'And Ursula,' Troy whispered, all the fun and happiness knocked out of him by seeing his mum so ill.

Ursula felt the panic in the grip the little boy had on her and said cheerily, 'I'm not going anywhere, Troy. Don't worry.'

And not long after that came the news that the captain and crew had made the decision that a passenger suffering a medical emergency should be taken to hospital, so the flight was rerouting to Marseille, in the south of France.

Troy burst into fresh tears.

Ursula and a smiling Roberto tried to reassure him, but he refused to be cheered by requests to show Ursula what other games there were on the iPad, when a crew member brought it over to them, along with the rest of their possessions.

'I just want Mummy,' he whimpered.

The crew member widened her eyes at Ursula as if to telegraph that seeing poor Nancijane ill might be more frightening than being kept from her. Ursula cuddled Troy, hoping she wouldn't get arrested as it was a public place and Roberto was taking duty of care on behalf of the airline, and talked and talked to him through what seemed like hours but actually was about twenty minutes before they touched down in Marseille.

Once down, passengers were asked to wait in their seats while Nancijane was attended by paramedics who boarded the aircraft and took her off, lying on a gurney and wearing an oxygen mask. Roberto ushered Troy in their wake and Ursula grabbed their things, then stuck with the little boy, who would not give up her hand in favour of Roberto's. Soon they were in a room inside the terminal, Nancijane and Troy were given into the care of an airline representative. Troy let go of Ursula long enough to throw his arms around Nancijane, who was looking drowsy and disorientated.

'The hospital is expecting the patient,' the airline representative said, a Frenchwoman with excellent English. 'The little boy will go with his mother.' She smiled at Ursula in the obvious expectation of her rejoining her flight.

Troy must have sensed her meaning as he held out a grasping hand. 'I want Ursula,' he choked.

Nancijane pulled her oxygen mask down. 'I'm not sure, Troy . . .' But the eyes she turned on Ursula were worried and vulnerable.

With one look at Troy's panicked face, Ursula said, 'I can come along, if you want.' She agreed that the plane could take off without her, because of schedules and crew hours and other stuff she barely bothered listening to. 'I don't have any hold baggage,' she murmured. 'Just my backpack here.'

Roberto was all professionalism. 'We have your details. We'll be in touch with you, and you'll be able to reclaim your hotel bill.'

The Frenchwoman chimed in, 'The nearest hotel is a Holiday Inn Express.'

'Fine.' Ursula tried to be determinedly cheerful to distract the white-faced boy. Troy was silent now, and glassy-eyed. 'We're all going to have a ride in an ambulance,' she told him, trying to make it sound like fun.

Tearfully, he nodded, barely looking at Roberto when he said goodbye, but still clinging to Ursula as they followed the wheeled stretcher and climbed in the back of the ambulance. She contrived a lot of bright chatter about there being seats with seatbelts, casting glances at Nancijane still on oxygen on the bed. She hoped someone at the hospital would contact Nancijane's next of kin.

It wasn't until they'd been rumbling along for several minutes that Ursula wanted her phone, realising that she needed to tell her dad that she'd been delayed. It wasn't in the pocket of her jeans, as she'd expected, and searching every pocket of her backpack twice proved fruitless, too. Oh, *crap*.

Resisting the urge to drop her head and howl, she remembered it being in her hand when Nancijane had taken ill and imagined it tumbling to the floor with everything else on her meal tray. It had probably ended up beneath a seat and the crew member who'd restored their things to them had understandably missed it.

She'd report it to the airline, but she had little expectation of being reunited with it soon, if ever. At least her laptop was safe in her backpack, so she stopped worrying about things she couldn't change and concentrated on hanging on to Troy and following Nancijane into the depths of the hospital, providing what details she had to staff members and explaining her lack of relationship to Nancijane and Troy, but, falling back on her translate app when necessary, declaring her intention to remain with the party until Troy's dad turned up. Nancijane had managed to provide the necessary contact details.

Then she bought bottles of drink and snacks and tried to reassure and entertain a small, frightened, tired boy.

It was a huge relief when, in the middle of what felt

like an endless evening, a blond, beefy man was shown in. Troy jumped up and cried, 'Daddy! Mummy's ill.' He flung his arms around his father's neck and burst into noisy tears, the sobs seeming to come right from his little heart.

Luckily, Troy's dad had brought with him his mother, Troy's gran, to look after the boy. 'Thank you, thank you so much,' the man gabbled about twenty times to Ursula, his eyes full of tears.

Ursula didn't even get his name before the family hurried off to be reunited with Nancijane. 'Bye, Troy,' Ursula called after them.

Troy, sniffling in his dad's arms, looked back and gave her a wave.

Then they were gone.

Ursula stared after them down the now empty corridor, feeling decidedly surplus to requirements. She got a taxi to the Holiday Inn Express, and was thankful to be able to secure a room. The man on reception spoke wonderful English. Ursula could have kissed him when she told him her story and he said he would contact the local representative of the airline to explain the missing phone and that Ursula needed a flight to resume her journey.

Soon, he was handing the call over to Ursula so she could give the representative the details of what she needed and agree to be contacted care of the hotel or via email. She gave her email address about ten times, just to make sure.

Then she went to the hotel refectory and drank two glasses of wine and ate a big slice of the most gorgeous chocolate cake she'd ever tasted.

At last, in her room, she threw off her clothes and showered before falling onto the bed to fire up her laptop

322

and hook up with the hotel Wi-Fi. The iMessage app allowed her to text Stanley, explaining that she was perfectly fine but had taken a detour to the south of France and would arrive the next day.

That was when she saw the text from Alfio. *Can we talk? It is important.* It had been sent that morning, probably after she'd put her phone on flight mode.

On a little tingle of anticipation, she responded. *I'd like that but I've lost my phone so I'm not sure how, except by laptop text or email.* ☺ Briefly, she sketched the medical emergency and that she was overnighting in France, before returning to Sicily.

His reply was prompt but vague. *I am sorry to hear of your troubles but glad you are OK. Keep safe and we will talk soon. There is an old phone at Residenza dei Tringali. I will ask Mamma to give it to you.*

Disappointed by his casual reply after his 'it is important' message and her warm response, she comforted herself that at least a borrowed phone would enable her to set up with a temporary SIM card until she was reunited with her own phone or had bought another.

She slipped between the cool bed sheets and read until she fell asleep.

Chapter Twenty-Three

On Thursday, finally outside the butter-yellow *stazione* after what seemed like a slow, hot train journey, Ursula hefted her backpack onto her shoulders and shoved her hair from her eyes, giving herself a moment to acclimatise to the stifling heat of an August afternoon in Siracusa. It felt like being wrapped in hot, wet sheets, and then expected to breathe.

The familiar sweet scent of oleander wafted over her as she glanced at the nearby station café, thinking longingly of a nice cold Moretti beer. But, really, she just wanted to finish her journey, exhausted by the events of the past few days.

Troy's dad – who had turned out to be called Nathan – had tracked her down at Marseilles airport before her afternoon flight. It was the first time she'd ever heard herself being called to a phone over the PA.

Nathan had sounded out of breath. 'I've been ringing round the hotels, but they won't give out information, and then I thought about the airline. I just want to say thanks very much for looking out for my Troy. I hardly talked to you last night because I was off my head with worry, but Nancijane's much better today, and they think she can fly home tomorrow. She's got to see our doctor because she hasn't had a seizure since she was a kid. I'm just so, so, *so* grateful to you for staying with Troy, and sorry it messed up your trip.'

'Don't worry about that,' said Ursula. 'Just give my best to Nancijane and say I'm glad she's going to be OK. And thank Troy for teaching me the turtle game.'

Nathan had laughed ruefully. 'That bleedin' game. His mum and me, we're sick of it.'

Ursula thought that if Troy hadn't got to know her via the game, he might not have been so willing to accept her escort while Nancijane received medical aid, but she just laughed back and said her goodbyes.

If she'd left Brighton with any apprehension about returning, her uncomfortable diversion had made the prospect of her dad, Agata, Nanda and Marilù expecting her for dinner comforting. She'd be able to relax. Their dinner conversation would satisfy her hunger for news of Alfio, because they'd no doubt be full of his swanky new job.

It was a slog from the station to the hotel, a solid half-hour in view of the heat and the Friday afternoon traffic that swarmed with scooters dodging between larger vehicles. Each road that needed to be crossed felt as welcoming as a crocodile-infested river. The longer side of her hair clung damply to her cheek, making her think that if she was to stay in Sicily, she either needed to grow it out so she could put it up, or cut it. Maybe she'd go short and spiky again. She hadn't done that for a couple of years.

It seemed ages before she was trudging over Ponte Santa Lucia, where there was no shade from the late afternoon sun and small boats bobbed lazily in the canal either side, exactly as they'd been when she left in a taxi three weeks ago. Then, she'd viewed them under the lights on the bridge, with the statue of Archimedes seeming to watch her hurt and angry departure. Now she was feeling positive and much more like the Ursula who'd existed before some bastard had spiked her drink and turned her world upside down.

'Forward,' she murmured to herself, dodging an electric scooter on the pavement, and resisting giving him a sideswipe with her backpack as he whizzed by. She zigzagged her way to the back entrance of the hotel, passing Nanda's Fiat in the courtyard, its purple paintwork dusty, as usual.

Then she caught sight of Camocat on the wall, regarding her through basilisk eyes. 'Well, hello,' Ursula murmured, and crept nearer, expecting the street cat to vanish with a whisk of her tail, as she had so many times before when Ursula had tried to invade her space. Today, though, she remained atop the bricks, her tail curled neatly around her feet. Ursula put out a tentative hand and stroked the soft, patchwork-of-colours fur on Camocat's head. 'I'm back,' she whispered.

Camocat gave a single, near-silent miaow before she finally turned and jumped down the other side of the wall. Maybe it was cat-speak for 'good to see you'.

Oddly comforted by as near a welcome as Camocat had ever offered, Ursula turned to the double doors to the kitchen and strolled in as if she'd never been away.

Agata was standing at the central island, slicing tomatoes, while Stanley, at the hob, stirred something that smelled deliciously of herbs. 'How are ya?' Ursula asked, trying to shuck off her backpack but finding the straps sticking to her sweaty arms.

'Ursula!' Stanley roared, dropping his stirring spoon, and throwing wide his arms. 'Come here, my darlin' girl.'

'Ah, *ciao, buonasera,* Ursula,' Agata chimed in, sounding just as pleased as Stanley to see her.

Then Nanda appeared, beaming. 'Ursula, you are back. Welcome.'

Ursula found herself trapped between a dad-hug and her backpack, her eyes stinging with unexpected tears, not just for the warmth of the greetings from these lovely people, but because there was no Alfio, the Tringali whose absence wrenched her heart. Finally ridding herself of the weight of the backpack, she hugged Stanley, then Agata and Nanda, letting the tears be those of joy and not regret. 'It's great to be back,' she choked. 'Really great. Thanks for letting me come.'

Agata gave her arm a little shake. 'No, do not thank us. It is our joy.'

Then Marilù shouted crossly from within the apartment and a laughing Nanda hurried back to swoop her up and bring her into the reunion. To her delight, Marilù grinned at Ursula and held out her arms as if the few weeks since they'd seen each other hadn't elapsed.

'Hello, sweetie,' Ursula crooned, accepting the youngster into her embrace. 'My, you've grown. And look at all your lovely curls.'

'Ba, ba,' Marilù answered, making a grab for one of Ursula's earrings.

Ursula slotted back into the Tringali family unit as if she'd never been away. It was alien to see Stanley as part of it and there were probably storms ahead, when Colleen had bad days and got onto Ursula about it, but she couldn't help noticing that her dad never stopped beaming, particularly at Agata. In recent years she'd considered the lines on his face simply a manifestation of age, but now she understood that they'd been lines of unhappiness.

Over a delicious meal of herby chicken with potatoes and salad, she told them all about her eight days with Zia and Piero. When she moved on to her time in Swords, she faltered. Was there etiquette around restructured families? Subjects it was politic to avoid?

Agata made it easy on her. 'Do not hesitate to speak of your mother in front of me,' she said gently. 'I do not ask questions and you will want to talk to your papa in private, but she is your mother. Naturally, you love her and will speak of her.'

Gratefully, Ursula caught Stanley up on family news, aware of Agata and Nanda listening with interest, an early sign of the blending of families to come, perhaps. Next, she covered her meeting with Stephan with a brief statement that they'd talked, she'd put the past in the past, and she, at least, had gained closure.

'And what about all your news?' she asked, looking at the other three, on edge and waiting to hear Alfio's name crop up.

Nanda's eyes sparkled. 'We have had *very* good news about the hotel today. Very good. I am so happy.'

Agata beamed. 'Me, too. *Very* happy.'

'A good offer, then.' Ursula didn't expect them to talk money with her, but looking round the smiles and shining eyes, their joy was obvious.

'A very, *very* good offer,' Nanda confirmed. 'Better than I'd ever dreamed might be possible.'

Ursula put down her fork to lift her wine glass. 'Then here's to us all, to our futures and to happiness.' After they clinked glasses and drank, she returned to her dinner, saying casually, 'And Alfio has a fantastic job, too. I'm made up for him.'

'He, too, received a wonderful, wonderful offer,' Agata agreed, addressing herself to her meal.

Nanda added. 'More travel around Europe, more money, more everything.'

Stanley pushed the basket of breadsticks closer to Ursula. 'Who'd turn down a job like that?'

'No one,' Ursula declared with forced enthusiasm. 'So great that he has such a wonderful opportunity. He was only ever here for the summer, wasn't he? He came back to help, but you look so well, Agata, I'm sure he felt comfortable going off to lead his own life again.'

'I am better.' Agata sent Stanley a coy look. 'Better in my heart and my health.'

Stanley glanced at Ursula anxiously, as if hoping she wouldn't be upset on Colleen's behalf, but Ursula reminded herself that, eventually, her mum might be happier out of the marriage, too, now she was no longer trying to hold on to a relationship that simply wasn't working. Her talk of her marriage being a 'habit', had convinced Ursula of that. It might be at snail's pace, but Colleen would move on. She was beginning to already, as she was to view a little house at Portmarnock soon.

After dinner and a glass of grappa to round off after a strong-but-sweet tiramisu, Agata and Nanda cleared away, leaving Stanley and Ursula free to wander out into the evening for private conversation. Stanley wiped his brow inelegantly with the tail of his lightweight shirt. 'How about we sit out on that little bit between the bridges? It's usually quiet and you get a bit of breeze down the canal.'

'The Archimedes monument?' Ursula didn't ask how he'd come to know where to catch the breeze, thinking it might be somewhere he and Agata went together. The evening was cooler than the afternoon had been, but still in the mid-twenties Celsius. The air stirred more at the canal than in the streets, though, and they found a vacant bench behind the statue.

Stanley pointed at it and joked, 'That fellow's eaves-dropping.'

Ursula smiled. 'Archimedes was a scientist. He'd probably rather do maths in his head than listen to the likes of us.'

The smile faded from her father's face, and he gazed into her eyes. 'Are we OK, darlin', you and me?'

He looked so troubled that Ursula linked his arm. 'Sure, Dad. I guess there will be rocky moments ahead with you and Mum splitting up, but we'll get through them. I'm sorry I flounced off to Zia's instead of having a grown-up conversation with you.'

He patted her hand where it lay on his forearm. 'You felt tricked. I saw afterwards that I should have said I was coming over to talk to you and told you the truth, rather than turning up at Agata's with a sheepish look and "by the way, she's my new girlfriend".' He heaved a huge sigh. 'I've always tried to put my family first, even if sometimes I've failed. I love you all so much. I loved Colleen too, but I was always the one to keep the peace and shield you kids from the tension in our relationship. When she asked me to leave, before – I hope you won't mind me telling you – the relief was incredible. When she wanted to try again, I tried to believe she'd been changed by the counselling, but she still tried to make me responsible for her happiness.'

330

He paused to scratch his beard and sigh. 'No, that's not the whole picture. The truth is that I'd fallen properly in love with Agata, so I felt incredibly guilty, aware of the way I'd hidden Agata's friendship for all those years. Your mum must have always sensed me holding back a tiny piece of my heart.' He gave her another of those apologetic glances, as if acknowledging that hearing that her father loved someone other than her mother was probably hard for Ursula. 'Agata seems to love me as I am. I don't feel as if I need to fit into her expectations of me. I'll always be fond of your mother, but this is different.'

They lapsed into silence. Nearby, small boats shifted languidly at their moorings as rumbling traffic passed them on the bridges either side. Somewhere, a group of men burst into laughter, hooting and catcalling at each other. It sounded as if they were having fun. Ursula admitted, 'If you hadn't tried again with Mum, I'd never have come to work at Residenza dei Tringali myself.'

Stanley turned to her with a wistful smile, his bristly hair damp at the hairline. 'You'd have come to Siracusa to visit me, I hope. I had planned to be here this summer, don't forget.'

'True. But I wouldn't have this chance of working long-term with Fabio. I would have gone on that other ceramics course in Salerno instead, and then maybe back to the UK.'

The lights from the bridge gleamed in Stanley's troubled eyes. 'Do you wish that had happened?'

'No,' she said frankly, thinking of those weeks with Alfio, weeks that seemed increasingly distant now. The ending had been painful, but if you found joy, its ending always brought grief. It would take a time before she could catch sight of a tall, lean man with curls that blew into

331

his face and not feel her heart lurch; it was going to be hard when their paths crossed again, as they must; but she could not regret their time together. 'I'm going to have a shot at settling here. I'll get an apartment, so I'll be out of the way when the hotel's sold.' She licked her lips. 'Will you be trying to get a divorce, Dad?'

Stanley shrugged. 'I haven't talked to your mother about it or gone through the pluses and minuses with a lawyer, but Agata and I aren't going to get married anyway. It makes a lot of sense to live together, for financial reasons.'

Ursula mulled this over. 'So Agata's family doesn't think you're gold digging, when she gets her dosh from the hotel you mean? I can see that.'

'That would be a good reason.' Stanley unlinked their arms and slipped his around her shoulders instead. 'You won't be embarrassed by your old man living in sin nearby?'

Ursula let her head fall on his shoulder and laughed. '"Living in sin"? Where did you dig that phrase up from?' Then she sobered. 'Dad, I want you to be happy. If you can't be happy with Mum, then that's tough on the family . . . but it's a fact, and we all love you.'

He squeezed her fiercely. 'I love you and want you to be happy too, darlin'. I'm crossing my fingers that you will be.'

They sat on for a while, talking softly about the family in Swords and that Stanley and Agata were to move out of the apartment so Nanda and Marilù could have it. 'Nanda's a dear girl,' he said, in his deep, Irish rumble. 'She was all set to do the moving out, but Agata says it will be easier for Nanda to be with the hotel, at least for now. And Agata had lived there with Domenico, her husband, you know, so we want our own home.'

'That's grand,' Ursula said absently, thinking about Alfio growing up in those very same rooms and wondering if part of the reason he'd jumped at the job in Barcelona so quickly was that he didn't want to see another man with his mother.

Finally, she stretched, ready to move. 'Shall we wander back? Maybe I can borrow your phone to talk to the folks at home? Tomorrow I'll have to sort out whether mine was handed in at the airline and if I can get it back.'

Stanley rose, holding out his hand to pull her up. 'Agata has an old one for you. I got you a temporary SIM today, with a few euros on it. You'll have your contacts on your laptop, I expect? Then you're good to go while you sort out something more permanent.'

'Thanks.' Ursula squeezed his hand before she let it go. 'You're the best, Dad.'

'I know,' he joked. Then he hesitated, sobering. 'Before we go, darlin', I'm wondering about Stephan, because you didn't go into much detail about your meeting. As your dad, I need to know you're OK.'

She considered how much she wanted to say, gazing at the pretty lights of Ortigia, some on the land and others on the boats, their reflections dancing with the ripples on the sea. 'There's not much more to say, really. I've accepted that his marriage was buggered up by what happened just as much as mine. He was in mourning for it and anger was his way of processing and expressing his pain. Though I can see his manipulative ways more clearly, I'm also beginning to see him as more of a victim than I did.'

'Well, I don't.' Then Stanley halted and rubbed his chin through his beard. 'Grudgingly, I see that a bit,' he temporised at last. 'Irrational behaviour is prompted by something. Not necessarily something logical, or easily

333

understood, but something. He just behaved so horribly, and you were so hurt, I don't want to feel sympathy for him.'

'No,' Ursula acknowledged. 'And I suspect that he finally accepted some blame hoping that we could try again. But he did tell me he was horrified and felt guilty when I . . . y'know, the pills.' She heard Stanley suck in air as if in pain at the memory. 'I believe him about that. But there's no way back. I'm only going forward from now on.'

'Good girl.' He dropped a kiss on her hair and then said in fatherly bluntness, 'Sheesh, you need a shower.'

She laughed, giving him a friendly push. 'Go 'way. Women don't sweat. Only men do.'

Still gently teasing each other, they strolled back beside the sea to Residenza dei Tringali, so Ursula could claim the phone from Agata and go up to her room, the one with the balcony that was just waiting for her, up above the old city.

Chapter Twenty-Four

Ursula did sluice off the travelling grime, back in the bijou shower room in the attic where the memory of Alfio squeezing in with her to 'help' brought tears to her eyes. Thinking that crying was just for things you couldn't find the words to express, she washed and then dried her hair, too, as if she was about to go on date.

She wasn't, but she'd decided that the first thing she was going to do with her borrowed phone was text Alfio, and she wanted to be presentable in case he suggested FaceTiming. The thought made her heart flutter, though she knew his wanting to talk must only be to put their ending on a nicer footing. She wanted that, too. It would be soothing to untangle the end to their relationship and part as friends. He'd chosen a life in Spain, and she'd chosen one in Sicily, but, like her, he'd probably realised that if their parents were together, their paths must surely cross.

Her suitcases stood in the centre of the room where she'd left them, and she opened one to pull out a cotton dress to slide over her naked body before taking her laptop

335

and phone out on the balcony. The phone warming in her hand, she switched it on and transferred a few numbers from the contacts on her laptop – all the family . . . and Alfio.

She wiped a damp palm on her dress and licked her lips as she clicked on his name and began to type. *Thanks for getting Agata to lend me a phone. Dad got me a temp SIM and this is the number. Your family is buzzing about your new job. Congratulations! It sounds fantastic.* She paused, gazing over the rooftops at the swallows that squeaked like bats as they cleared the twilight sky of insects. *I'm free to talk when you're ready,* she tapped in conclusion. Then she pressed send and had to swallow a lump at a vision of Alfio, in the depths of his new life in Barcelona – perhaps with Hettie back at his side? – glancing at the message and thinking that he'd maybe ring tomorrow. Or at the weekend. Or even—

Beside her, the window of the other attic room flew up and Alfio slid onto the windowsill. 'I'm ready to talk now,' he said.

'Holy shit.' Ursula clutched her suddenly galloping heart, as she took in the half-smile on his lean face. 'Where the hell did you come from?'

There was enough light left to let her see his grin. 'From Barcelona. Some conversations should be held face to face.' Then, as she'd once worried about him doing before she knew that he'd never be creepy with a woman, he leaned out over the metre of thin air that separated his window from her balcony, grasped the rail, took a stride and scrambled over the ironwork to stand beside her.

Then he swung a backpack off his shoulders, which she hadn't even noticed in the shock of him appearing like a

336

genie but from a window, not a lamp. 'How are you?' he asked, as he undid the zip, attempting the remains of her Swords accent so that it emerged, 'How ayya?'

Uncertainly, she laughed. 'Shocked. Wondering if I'm dreaming. Heart thundering.'

He nodded, as if this was no more than expected. Then he produced from his bag wine glasses and a chilled bottle of Solnia, her favourite wine. Passing those into her keeping, he delved again, and – with exaggerated care – withdrew a plate of pastries. '*Dolci*,' he said, as if he'd said, 'Abracadabra' and produced dessert by magic.

'Wow.' Completely at sea, she scrabbled to make sense of the crazy situation. 'Have you come to Sicily to pack up your things?'

In answer, he said, 'I want to tell you about my new job.' He slid the plate onto her lap so he could take the wine and the glasses and pour, before pressing one glass in her hand. '*Salute*.' He raised his glass.

'*Salute*.' Ursula had to tiptoe her feet to prevent the heavy plate from slipping from her lap and smashing – and brace her spirits to prevent her heavy heart from following right after. Brightly, she added, 'Let's hear all about the new job, then. You must be excited.'

Alfio settled on the floor of the balcony beside her chair, his back against the wall. He took one of the pastries and urged her to do the same. 'I tried to remember your favourites.'

'Thank you.' She took a *cannolo*. 'I thought you guys only ate this kind of thing for breakfast.'

He shrugged. 'You like them.' He took a stuffed, fried pastry called an iris. It was gone in two bites, and then he took a cornetto, the thing that wasn't a croissant and wasn't a brioche but was something in between. 'Mm,' he said, as he wolfed that down, too.

'You seem hungry. Is that because you weren't at dinner?' Ursula's appetite had deserted her, but she nibbled the *cannolo* and gave her own little 'Mm' of appreciation that she felt was only good manners.

Alfio lifted his hands in a vague gesture. 'I think Mamma has kept some dinner for me.'

Ursula sipped her wine, wondering that rather than having the kiss-off conversation she'd expected, they were eating pastries and drinking wine as if she'd never told him, bitterly, how much he'd let her down, throwing in the entire you-can-never-trust-a-man malarkey. She had laid at Alfio's door all her hurt at no one telling her about Agata and her dad. The problem had been that none of them had told her the truth, but him not telling her hurt the most. 'When do you begin your new job?' she asked, hoping her voice didn't sound too husky.

'Almost immediately. I am looking forward to it.' He glanced up at her from his seat on the floor and his voice changed, becoming soft, the tone she remembered from when he'd murmured to her in bed. 'The plate is for you, too, Ursula. It is something I hope you will like.'

'Really?' Startled, she glanced down at the heavy ceramic plate. 'Very nice.' Then she looked more closely. Now a few of the pastries were gone, she could see the border, a narrow, interlinked pattern she recognised. Involuntarily, she glanced at where the same Celtic pattern encircled her wrist. Next to the border but still on the plate's broad rim, a selection of items had been painted. Slowly, she put down her wine glass to look closer.

Paintbrushes.

She pushed pastries aside to inspect flowers and leaves,

which she also recognised, this time from her forearm. She turned the plate in her hands.

A tiny, but cunningly painted image of Residenza dei Tringali.

A house exactly like the family home in Swords.

A tiny outline in the shape of Ireland and one of Ortigia.

A heart.

Another heart.

Her hands began to tremble, feeling Alfio's gaze like a ray of the Sicilian sun.

'Fabio's work is wonderful,' he said softly. 'But he makes a big fuss about putting on the kiln for a rush order.'

A laugh caught in her throat. 'It's expensive to run the kiln.'

Between the pastries in the centre of the plate, she could see what looked like writing. Alfio scooped up the remaining sweets and, heart taking on a queer rhythm, she bent her head to read the letters set in a semicircle.

I love you, Ursula Quinn.

She turned the plate to read the opposite arc. *Ti amo, Ursula Quinn.*

Heart beating so hard that her vision shook, she lifted her gaze to Alfio's.

Gently, he took the plate and placed it on the floor, then rose, drawing her with him. He kissed each of her hands. 'I love you, Ursula Quinn. I am sorry I made love to you without telling you everything, but I love you – and that is absolute truth.'

Hot tears gushed into her eyes. 'You were in a difficult position,' she murmured, feeling a welling of disbelief and joy. *Alfio loved her.*

A lopsided smile flickered on his lips. 'I could never be sorry about the lovemaking itself, even if you would never speak to me again. But I should have told my mother you needed to know the truth. She is angry with me that I let it get between us.'

Maybe it was the idea of Agata being angry with Alfio, but Ursula suddenly felt guilty. 'Zia felt I should have shown more understanding of your torn loyalties. She asked if I'd never hidden anything from anyone and I realised that I'd hidden something from you.' Haltingly, she told him about the overdose she'd taken when in the pits of despair about Stephan. It felt important now that he know all of her, good and bad.

His dark eyes grew huge with horror as he gazed at her. 'Oh, Ursula, *cara*. Why would you hide this from me?'

She sighed. 'I wanted you to think I was strong. But maybe admitting weakness is a strength unto itself.'

Slowly, he folded her into his arms, his skin hot against hers. 'Even the strongest of us have moments when we do not know how to cope.'

'I'm sorry I left Ortigia in a huff,' she whispered, one of her hot tears tipping out of the corner of her eyes. When she saw him frown in obvious lack of understanding, she amended, 'I left in a bad temper with you. We should have talked.' It was delicious to feel him close once again.

'We can talk now?' His gaze was dark and fixed on her. 'I want to tell you about my new job.'

Her joy subsided. Oh. That. He'd just taken a fabulous job in Barcelona, hours away from Sicily where she'd planned a new life of her own. One of them was going to have to compromise and by his opening words, she guessed he was hoping it would be her. She supposed she could begin again in Spain. They had artisan ceramics there, too, and she'd be able to learn the Spanish style. But the idea of her being the one to alter her dream to suit him, before she'd even had a chance to say 'I love you' back, gave her a heavy feeling. 'Yes,' she sighed, staring past him at the open window to his room and the muslin curtain fluttering in the breeze. 'You'd better tell me.'

'It is here,' he said.

Her gaze returned to his face in a rush. 'No, it's in Barcelona.'

He smiled and brushed a kiss across her lips. 'No, it's in Ortigia. It's in Residenza dei Tringali. When it came to the realities of selling this place, our birthright – your father told that phrase to me – something inside me hurt. When I came back to Siracusa at the end of May it was because I had a very strong feeling that my father wanted me to. I dreamed it, in fact. But this time the feeling has come all from me. I want to work here, in this building, with my family. So, I proposed it to Nanda. Mamma will retire and Nanda and I will manage the hotel together. Nanda is very happy. With two of us, she will have plenty of time for Marilù, and Mamma will help a little.'

'Was that the offer she talked about tonight?' Ursula gasped. 'An offer from you? I thought it was from the hotel chain.'

His laugh was low. 'I have to confess that I, Nanda, Mamma and your papa have been keeping things from you again, but I hope that this time you will not mind. I arrived last night and came to agreement with Nanda this morning. I asked everybody not to tell you I was here until I could talk to you alone.'

The joy wanted to bubble up inside her again, but she had another question first. 'But you don't want to be a hotelier, do you? It was one of the first things you told me.'

'First, I needed to go out in the world and do other

things,' he admitted. 'But being back here this summer, it felt right. We have turned the offer down from the hotel chain, without hearing the numbers. Even if you tell me that you do not want me, or love me, it is what I am going to do.'

And, finally, Ursula let herself feel joy. Sinking against him so that their bodies touched all the way up, she spoke against his mouth. 'I want you. I've been sad without you. I want and love you very much.'

Then she was swept harder against him, and he was speaking between kisses. 'We can travel together to Ireland or England whenever you want to.'

She gasped, tipping back her head and closing her eyes, her skin setting on fire as he blazed kisses down her throat and his hands stroked her body. 'Ireland definitely. England . . . not so much.'

Then Alfio halted, drawing back so he could stare into her face, making her worry for an instant that he'd thought of a problem. But he was breathing heavily. 'Ursula. You have no clothes beneath your dress.'

She gurgled a laugh, fresh heat sweeping into her cheeks. 'I got out of the shower and threw on the dress to come out here. I didn't bother with undies.'

A noise came from deep in his throat, even more appreciative than when he'd been eating the pastries that now lay ignored on the floor at their feet. 'I like it.' He began to inch up the fabric, so the hem slipped up her thighs.

Her breath stopped in her chest. 'Inside?' she whispered.

'That sounds *fantastico*.' A smile rang in his voice.

'I mean *indoors*,' she clarified, stifling a giggle. '*Al chiuso*.'

'That too.' He began to smooch her backwards through the open door, inching her dress higher and higher.

And as they sank down in each other's arms, he murmured, 'We must get a bigger bed.'

'And air con.' She pulled at his T-shirt.

He helped her ease it off, then paused to smile down at her, his thumbs stroking the dips above her collarbones. 'Where shall we put these things? An apartment, perhaps? Or a villa overlooking the sea?'

Her heart felt as if it sprang from her chest and catapulted back again.

He must have read shock on her face because he said swiftly, 'Perhaps I go too fast. You would like your own apartment. I can have one too, and each can have a large bed.'

Her heartbeat started up again, and she sank her fingers in his hair and pulled his head down for a kiss. 'The villa overlooking the sea sounds awesome.' She sighed happily. 'One with a balcony large enough to share.'

With their future settled, they got down to the important stuff.

Epilogue

Ursula's heart was beating a rapid *chud-chudda-chud-chud* beneath her new dress, bought especially for this evening. It was October, now, and they'd had storms recently, cooling the air.

She glanced at Fabio. It was the first time she'd seen him in trousers rather than shorts and he'd had a haircut and trimmed his grizzled beard for the opening of Siracusa's newest ceramics shop – Fabio e Ursula Ceramiche. 'We're ready too early. No one will be here until about eight.' She ran her eyes over the bottles of prosecco in coolers and the tray of polished glass flutes that awaited their guests.

Fabio shrugged. 'We will start.' With unhurried movements, he opened the nearest chilled bottle and let the contents froth into two glasses, holding one out to her. '*Salute*, partner.'

She raised the glass to the grizzled older man. '*Salute*, Fabio. Thanks for all your amazing teaching and mentorship—'

344

He held up a hand. 'Drink,' he instructed economically. 'I need no thanks. We work together.' With a large, work-manlike hand, he indicated the shelves of hand-painted goods in glowing colours, items both functional and ornamental, the fruits of both of their labours over the past couple of months. They'd catch only the tail end of the tourist season this year, but planned to spend the winter creating stock, and Fabio was also to tutor Ursula on throwing pots as well as painting them. Otherwise, he'd given up teaching and was now back to the life of a ceramic artist. Ursula understood why the death of his wife had made him lose his way for a few years but was glad that he was creating again. He was a real artisan.

She took a gulp of the prosecco, enjoying the delicious tickle on her tongue. 'It's amazing how quickly everything has happened. It's only about six months since I arrived in Sicily. I thought I'd never progress past studying other artists in your books of traditional designs – and my own book, when the Tringali family bought me one.' That seemed a long time ago, when they'd bestowed the gift on her to thank her for her help.

Fabio grunted, smiling with his eyes. 'Very expensive.' He sipped from his glass and smacked his lips.

She stated. 'Expensive? The book? It was just second-hand.'

He shook his head. 'Quite rare. Alfio, he pay two hundred euro.'

'*Two hundred euros?*' Bubbles went up her nose and she gasped.

'He asks for nice gift. A big thank you. I find for him.' Fabio pronounced this with satisfaction, as if he'd been storing the information up to bring out at just the right moment to stun her.

345

'Jeez. I'd probably never have accepted it if I'd known.' She thought of how she'd packed it in a suitcase and left it behind, when she hadn't known if she'd ever return to Ortigia.

Then suddenly she spotted Alfio at the door, gazing through the glass with the smile that made his eyes gleam and set her pulse racing. Abandoning her drink on the nearest surface, she hurried to let him in, unsurprised that he hadn't waited until the official start time of the opening party. '*Cara*,' he murmured, kissing a spot beside her mouth.

'Is it true you paid two hundred euro for that book on ceramics your family gave me?' she demanded.

Alfio shot Fabio a look of reproof. 'I don't remember.'

'You do,' she hissed accusingly.

He poured himself a glass of prosecco and offered her a toast. 'To Fabio e Ursula Ceramiche on the opening of their wonderful studio and shop.'

Fabio rumbled, '*Grazie*,' and lifted his glass in return, so that Ursula had little choice but fall in with the etiquette, though she rolled her eyes at Alfio at the same time.

He winked, clearly enjoying her indignation and quite unrepentant. Then people began to arrive, and he quietly assumed the role of server, making sure everyone got prosecco or water or fruit juice as Fabio and Ursula greeted their guests – initially by Ursula, as Fabio remained two steps behind her, rumbling, 'Welcome. *Benvenuto*,' or '*benvenuta*' if the new arrival was female.

First came Agata, Stanley and Nanda, having left Marilù in the capable hands of a babysitter for the evening, kissing Ursula's cheeks, although she'd left Residenza dei Tringali only an hour or two before. 'Hi,' Ursula cried, kissing them all back. 'You look smart, Dad.'

346

Stanley smoothed down his new shirt. 'I'm getting the Italian look, aren't I?'

With them had travelled Sorcha, with her hair plaited crown-like around her head, making Ursula resolve to one day have a go at creating one of the heads of the Queen of Greece, so popular on the island as part of the history of Siracusa – when Fabio had taught her to model in clay, which would come after throwing pots on a wheel.

'It's so amazing you've all come over from Ireland,' Ursula exclaimed, casting her arms around her little sister. 'And you look *bella, bella.*'

'So does this.' Sorcha looked around the shop in awe. 'I don't have to ask which pieces are yours, because of the tatts.'

But Ursula couldn't reply because Finola, Declan and Kira had just arrived in a hire car that they parked in Piazza Brancaccio, Finola keeping a firm hold on Kira's hand.

Next came Caden and Bree, who'd been happy to leave baby Eoin to share Marilù's babysitter in Nanda's apartment. 'Not bad, sis,' observed Caden, eyebrows raised at the delicately painted designs on jugs and plates arranged around the shelves.

All of Ursula's family except Colleen had come over for the opening and were guests of Residenza dei Tringali. Friends of Fabio or the Tringali family and those Ursula had got to know in the piazza streamed in to help drink the prosecco. Ursula found herself buttonholed by Finola. 'Mum will come to see you, you know. It's a bit early and a bit raw and she and a friend are going on a cruise, so she needs to save up.'

'I know.' Ursula smiled, though her eyes prickled, picturing her mum sitting home alone in Swords – though she was almost ready to move to Portmarnock. 'I FaceTimed with her this afternoon. We both cried a bit, but she's moving on with her life, which is good.'

Finola gave her another hug. 'Maybe me and Dec will bring her later, and stay just outside the city, you know? So that she won't have her nose rubbed in things. Let her move on at her own pace.'

Ursula nodded. The family had begun to get used to the new situation, but still occasionally explained the facts to each other, as if it helped to establish the ground rules out loud. Luckily, Agata was easy to like, so none of Stanley's children had caused issues with her.

'There's Lia, Fabio's daughter,' Ursula said, as a new family pushed their way in. 'She's a nice woman with kids a bit older than Kira. Let me introduce you.'

Although she and Fabio had agreed that they'd each say a few words of welcome in their own language, she found, when the time came, that it didn't take long to say, 'Thank you all for coming, especially my family from Ireland who've travelled a long way. This studio and shop are a dream come true for me, and is all down to Fabio,' which Alfio translated swiftly into Italian for those who didn't speak English, and Fabio said something in Italian, though it seemed to take fewer words. The party steamed along in a ripple of chatter and laughter, with everyone touring the shelves to admire the skilfully hand-painted ceramics and having explained to them the difference between artisan ware and the cheap mass-produced fridge magnets for sale on the tourist trail, also classed as 'ceramics'.

To add to the celebration, Ursula produced plates for her family, each bordered by her own tattoo designs. Stanley and Agata's was decorated with joined hands (no rings) to represent the future, a misty young couple to represent how they met in the past and, borrowing on the plate Alfio had asked Fabio to create for her, outlines of Ireland and Sicily. Sorcha's bore a secondary, interior border of whorls and plaits of hair, and the Instagram and TikTok logos, which Ursula had risked borrowing without permission, as she didn't intend to sell the design commercially. Caden had been more difficult, because he was just such an ordinary, sweet man, so Ursula had used a pattern of joined hands of a man, woman and baby to represent him, Bree and Eoin, and a pattern of golf clubs and balls, because it was about the only thing that he'd ever showed interest in outside of his family and work. Each gift was met by exclamations of awe and pleasure, passed carefully from person to person to admire.

Then she turned to Alfio, who was watching the present-giving, a half-empty prosecco glass in his hand, and produced the final plate. 'And this is for you, Alfio, to go with the one you asked Fabio to make for me, though it's never a good match when created by two different artists.'

Eyes darkening with pleasure, Alfio dumped the prosecco so he could take the plate. 'But, twice as valuable to me,' he murmured, taking it carefully. 'Like us. Two different people but we make a wonderful pair.' Within the border she'd painted Residenza dei Tringali, silhouettes of his family group, including his dad. 'And this is the Claddagh,' she explained, pointing to the emblem of two hands around a heart and a crown. 'In Ireland it's the symbol of love, loyalty and friendship.' She lowered her voice. 'It's the nearest Irish symbol I could find to "trust".'

Wordlessly, Alfio pulled her in for a proper kiss, which everyone discreetly pretended not to see as it was so obviously a moment for Ursula and Alfio alone – apart from

Kira, who hissed, 'They're *kissing*,' with all the outrage of someone who was now at school and knew that kissing was yucky.

Fabio cleared his throat and presented Lia with a plate he'd made himself, so she wouldn't be left out. Ursula hadn't seen it up close but knew it to include allusions to his late wife, Lia's mother. Lia was tearfully pleased and hugged her father.

As guests fell back into gentle chatter, Sorcha bossily gathered up all the precious plates and made amazing arrangements to photograph. 'It'll make great material for your social media channels.'

Fabio frowned in confusion, so Alfio explained in Italian. 'Nothing to do with me,' Fab declared firmly.

Ursula grinned. 'I'll be creating the social media channels, don't worry.'

Sorcha gasped, aghast. 'What? You mean you're ready to open and you don't have a platform already?' She swiped Ursula's phone and began opening accounts for 'Fabio e Ursula Ceramiche', screenshotting passwords and usernames as she went along, shaking her head at her sister's lack of media preparation, although taking time to whisper, 'No one expects you to have pics of yourself on there, if you don't want.'

Ursula shrugged, much less worried about having her image on social media than she once had been. With Alfio at her side, she felt secure enough these days to do almost anything.

Finally, the party wound down.

Finola and family were the first to leave, Kira almost asleep on Dec's shoulder. Alfio and Stanley now both owned cars, and somehow everyone was squashed in to be ferried back to the hotel.

There, parents took their kids to bed. Sorcha faded away discreetly after whispering to Ursula, 'I'm going back to that restaurant near the Fonte Aretusa where the waiter with the wicked grin accosts tourists and hands out menus. He tells me that I'm "*bella*".'

'As I told you myself,' Ursula declared in sisterly pride.

Finally, Alfio and Ursula climbed hand in hand up the familiar marble stairs that formed the backbone of Residenza dei Tringali, up all three floors and then to the attic rooms, which they still shared. Alfio had put a new lock on the door at the top of the stairs, just in case of wandering guests. They'd moved Ursula's wardrobe and drawers into Alfio's old room, but still hadn't been able to squeeze a proper double bed into hers. It gave them a kind of bedroom and dressing room arrangement, though, and they utilised the landing for overspill possessions.

'Too many stairs,' Alfio complained, slipping his arm around her waist. He'd had plans drawn up to add two guest lifts to the hotel in what had previously been a ventilation shaft, as he'd been advised that suitable ventilation could be provided in alternative ways, but bureaucracy moved so slowly he had no idea when they'd gain permission. The surveyors from the hotel chain that had wanted to buy Residenza dei Tringali had been confident they'd had a quiet go-ahead, though, so he intended to bulldoze up that avenue, if necessary.

Ursula laughed, leaning her head tiredly against his shoulder. 'The stairs keep us fit.'

It was just about warm enough to sit out on the balcony, which now sported a two-seater padded bench. Alfio kicked off his shoes and brought out his laptop. He snuggled her against his side. 'It's time we looked for somewhere larger to live.'

Ursula planted an apologetic kiss on his neck. 'I know. I've been so busy—'

'Which is why I have made a start.' He turned his head so her next kiss landed on his lips. Then, together, beneath the stars and above the rooftops, he showed her the details of five villas he'd identified as being close enough for Ursula to get to work, him to get to Residenza dei Tringali and which also overlooked the sea. 'None are in Ortigia, of course. There are mainly apartments, here. But this villa across the bridge has a big, big balcony. And this white one has several balconies – one outside each bedroom, another leading from the upstairs lounge.'

'It's amazing to think we can live somewhere like this.' Ursula scrolled back and forth between images of flat-roofed dwellings in almond white, butter yellow or rose pink, almost in tears of happiness.

'We can,' he said. 'We could live somewhere bigger, if we wished to stretch ourselves.'

'These are just great.' Ursula hugged him tightly. 'Can we view them all?'

'Of course, we can. I will make calls tomorrow.' He closed the laptop and placed it carefully aside so he could take her in his arms for a series of leisurely, hot, arousing kisses.

'Mm-mm-*mm*,' Ursula groaned, slipping her fingers in between the buttons of his shirt. 'The breeze is a little chill, now. Bed?'

He laughed, deep in his throat, and kissed her again, but he didn't move. 'There is one other thing.'

When he hesitated, she drew back to peep into his face. 'What?'

'Would it bring back bad memories if I was to wish to give you a ring?' He sounded uncertain, watching her eyes carefully. 'Not a hidden ring with a hidden message that I am trying to bind you to me. A ring to tell you how much I love you. *Ti amo moltissimo*. Or am I moving too fast?'

Shock ricocheted through Ursula, but the happy, fizzing kind, rather than something chilling and unpleasant. Understanding that he was referencing Stephan's grandpa's ring being used to maintain unwanted contact, she was swift to offer reassurance. 'I'm very happy to move fast, with you. A ring would be a wonderful symbol of our love.' She lifted her hand so she could thread her fingers through his springy hair.

He smiled. 'Not my grandfather's ring, but one he gave to my grandmother, when I was a boy. I remember him bringing it home in his pocket. He said, "It's just to say I love you." I still remember how they looked at each other, with so much love in their eyes.' Then he withdrew from his pocket a pretty golden band that widened into an intricate pattern.

'Oh,' Ursula breathed. 'Alfio. That is so beautiful. Won't Agata mind?'

'It was never hers,' he assured her. 'Nanna's jewellery went mainly to my sister, and I got Nonno's watch and a couple of other things. I asked for this ring, though, because I remembered day Nonno gave it just out of love, not for a birthday or at Christmas.'

'I adore it.' Ursula thought she'd never been on the brink of happy tears so many times in one day before. She had to sniff and use her dress to wipe her eyes. 'I love it, Alfio, like I love you.'

He held the ring so that it twinkled in the lights from the old city. 'It will not make you sad?'

'No.' She looked into his eyes. 'Because this is yours

353

and comes with such a loving story.' She sniffed and laughed. 'I just don't know which finger to wear it on, because in Ireland to wear it on my left hand would suggest an engagement, but here in Sicily it's the other way.'

'Perfect,' he said, sliding it onto the ring finger of her left hand, where it fit beautifully, warming quickly at contact with her skin. 'Because I hope there will be other rings for you in our near future. Then, whichever country we are in, we will be covered.'

Her eyebrows lifted. 'Did you just propose?'

He gathered her into his lap. 'I pre-proposed. We will do things our own way, yes? Tomorrow, I will book appointments to see all those houses and later we will decide.'

Ursula slipped off his lap and urged him to his feet, feeling his hands in hers, strong and warm. 'Alfio Tringali,' she murmured. 'I hope your nanna's ring isn't easily embarrassed . . . because I'm about to show you how much I love you.'

Loved

An Italian Island Summer?

Then why not try one of Sue's
other sizzling summer reads
or cosy Christmas stories?

The perfect way to escape
the everyday.

Grab your sun hat, a cool glass of wine, and escape with these gloriously uplifting summer reads . . .

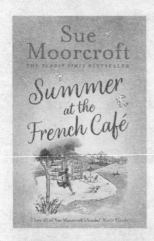

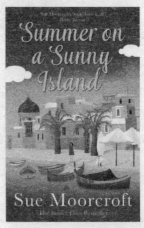

Dive into the summer holiday
that you'll never want to end . . .

Curl up with these
feel-good festive romances . . .

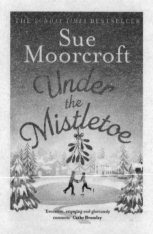

More heartwarming stories of love, friendship and Christmas magic!